Family is all that matters to these proud
and passionate kings of the desert, so
discovering they're fathers means
claiming their children at any cost...

THE

Desert

LORD'S LOVE-CHILD

Three intensely emotional stories
from favourite authors

OLIVIA GATES
KATE HEWITT
MEREDITH WEBBER

The Sheikh Collection
4 exciting volumes!

Available in January 2012

Available in February 2012

Available in March 2012

Available in April 2012

THE

Desert
LORD'S LOVE-CHILD

OLIVIA
GATES

KATE
HEWITT

MEREDITH
WEBBER

MILLS &
BOON

Mills & Boon, an imprint of Harlequin (UK) Limited, Eton House, 18-24 Paradise Road, Richmond, Surrey TW9 1SR

THE DESERT LORD'S LOVE-CHILD
© Harlequin Enterprises II B.V./S.à.r.l. 2012

The Desert Lord's Baby © Olivia Gates 2008
The Sheikh's Love-Child © Harlequin Books SA 2009
The Sheikh Surgeon's Baby © Meredith Webber 2008

ISBN: 978 0 263 89625 1

010-0212

Harlequin (UK) policy is to use papers that are natural, renewable and recyclable products and made from wood grown in sustainable forests. The logging and manufacturing processes conform to the legal environmental regulations of the country of origin.

Printed and bound in Spain
by Blackprint CPI, Barcelona

The Desert Lord's Baby

OLIVIA GATES

Olivia Gates has always pursued many passions. But the time came when she had to set up a "passion priority", to give her top one her all, and writing won. Hands down. She is most fulfilled when she is creating worlds and conflicts for her characters and then exploring and untangling them bit by bit, sharing her protagonists' every heartache and hope and heart-pounding doubt until she leads them to their indisputably earned and glorious happy ending. When she's not writing she is a doctor, a wife to her own alpha male and a mother to one brilliant girl and one demanding angora cat.

Please visit Olivia at http://www.oliviagates.com.

To an incredible lady, my editor
Natashya Wilson, for her belief in me, her
constant encouragement and spot-on guidance.

And to wonderful Melissa Jeglinski for
opening up a fantastic new path for me.

Prologue

"Do you know what it felt like, being trapped for two days in those hellish negotiations, away from you?"

Farooq's voice swept over Carmen, dark and fathomless like the night sky she was staring into, the exotic accent turning it into a potent weapon, an irresistible spell.

She'd felt him the moment he'd entered the penthouse. The skyscraper. Long before that. Probably the moment he'd stepped out of the closed negotiations that had taken him away from her every day for the past six weeks. The nights had been all hers. All theirs. Madness and magic's.

She'd thought she'd braced herself, was ready for her first exposure to him after forty-eight hours of deprivation.

After she'd found out something that had changed her life forever.

She wasn't ready. His approach felt like that of a hurricane. Her teeth chattered with the convulsion of emotions ripping through her. How she *loved* him.

It had happened so fast, so totally. When she'd thought she stopped believing in love, wasn't even equipped to feel lust. Then, everything inside her had shuddered with the first sight of him, stumbled with the first hours in his company, crashed with the first night in his arms. She'd been hurtling deeper ever since.

She'd known that, when her time with him was up, she'd keep on plunging, hadn't cared what would happen then, had only been desperate to experience every minute afforded her of him.

Until today.

She gazed blindly through the floor-to-ceiling reinforced glass overlooking Manhattan, which sparkled beyond the sprawling darkness of Central Park. Each quiet step of now-bare feet on the luxurious carpet echoed inside her, along with the hiss of cashmere sliding off silk, then silk off living velvet steel, his masterpiece body slowly revealed, not in reflection, but in her memory, where his every nuance was etched in obsessive detail.

She still couldn't turn to him. The scalpel edge she'd been balancing on began to slice into her, cutting slow and deep.

This would be their last night.

She wanted to cram a lifetime into it. Tear open every second and fill it with him, with them. She wanted to consume him, *needed* all his contradictions, patience and arrogance, tenderness and ferocity, all devastating, all at once.

"Wahashteeni, ya ghalyah." His croon dipped into the bass reaches of her torment. Hearing him say he missed her, the endearment he favored—precious, treasured—hit a chord of blind yearning inside her. Her breasts heaved, her nipples hardened to points of agony. She couldn't bear the crush of cotton over her inflamed skin, the chafing emptiness inside her. Then he made it far worse. "I shouldn't have stayed away no matter what. Now I'm almost afraid to touch you, afraid that when I do, it will take us to the very edge of survival."

He was half a breath away now, and inside her a tornado tore everything apart. She gasped for air. It screeched down her lungs, riding a scent of intoxication, the musk of tension, virility and desire. Of him. A phantom touch moved her cascade of burgundy hair to one shoulder, exposing her neck. He leaned a fraction closer…and breathed. Inhaled her. Drew her whole into him.

Then his hands moved over her, hovering an inch away, creating a field of sensual friction. He brought his lips to her ear and his soft rumble hit her with the force of a clap of thunder. "I couldn't even call you, knew I'd lose every ground I'd won if I heard your voice, felt your desire. I would have dropped everything and come to you."

And she knew. She couldn't take even tonight with him. If she did, she'd stay. And in six more weeks, he'd know. He'd know she was pregnant.

And she couldn't let him know.

She'd promised him it was safe to make love without protection. And it hadn't been. He'd see her as a liar, a cheat. He'd be incensed. Or worse. Far worse.

He might have behaved magnificently with her, but she had no illusions about what she was to him. She was a diversion to let off steam during negotiations that taxed his soul and psyche. After that first night together, his offer had been clear. Be his lover during his three-month world tour to broker peace and relief. She was certain he intended to end their arrangement with all the largesse of the prince that he was, probably with an ultragenerous settlement. A settlement she would never have accepted.

But fate had given her something far more precious than anything he could have offered her, the ultimate gift…

She shuddered. She'd been so lost in misery, she'd left it too late to move away. Now he took her, wrapped her in his cabled arms, her back to his chest, her head in the curve of his neck as his towering body encompassed her, sending her reeling with wave after wave of such craving, she almost risked everything for one more taste of heaven in his arms. Almost.

She lurched out of his tightening embrace, tottering, trying to pretend it was a natural move, and croaked a distraction, "Did you manage to propose your relief projects without the Ashgoonian prime minister screaming that your monarchy has some nerve, criticizing his 'democracy's' internal affairs?"

It took him a moment to answer. A moment during which he tried to pull her back into his arms. A look of incomprehension stained his overpowering beauty when she evaded him again.

Then he seemed to dismiss her action as nothing to analyze, shrugged his Olympian shoulders. "He did better than that. He gave me unconditional access into Ashgoonian territory for a hundred-mile zone across the borders with Damhoor."

A surge of pleasure and pride in his extraordinary achievement, something the UN itself hadn't been able to manage, overtook her, momentarily suppressing her misery. "Oh, Farooq, that's incredible. You're going to save so many lives."

His sensuous lips twisted. "Let's not count our saved lives before they're saved, Carmen. In diplomacy I project only worst-case scenarios. But enough of that. I'm not Prince Aal Masood now. I'm the man who has untold pleasures in store for the woman who's his most magnificent gift for his life's best birthday."

His birthday. She'd found out only yesterday, and it had been during her shopping trip for supplies to make the man who had multitudes of everything a handmade gift that she'd collapsed, ended up in hospital and found out that what she'd thought impossible had happened. Farooq's baby was growing inside her.

He reached for her again. This time when she dodged him, his arms fell to his sides and bewilderment flashed over his sculpted face. Then comprehension dawned in the honeyed depths of his eyes.

He exhaled. "It's that time of month at last?"

He thought she was having her period? God, how ironic. She grabbed at the excuse, nodded.

He sighed again. "It has been longer than expected coming, hasn't it?" He didn't even know how long it had been. And why should he? He wasn't counting the moments with her, counting down to the moment their time together came to an end. A wicked gleam suddenly entered his hypnotic eyes. "It'll never stop stunning me, how delightfully wanton you are at times only to squirm with shyness at others." She looked away from his teasing. A finger under her chin dragged her aching gaze back to his. "I may be burning to possess you, *ya ghalyah,* but I'll take equal pleasure in comforting you. You look so tired, so pale." He took her arm, pulled her toward the gigantic, circular bed draped in midnight blue silk. "Are you in any pain? I'll summon my physicians."

She shook her head, faltered. "I'm just…cramping a bit."

His smile was all indulgence. "Then I'll give you a massage. And under my hands, rubbed down with my kingdom's magical oils, all your aches and discomforts will dissolve."

The images he provoked speared through her loins, his thoughtfulness through her head and heart. She lurched away. *"No."*

The rugged majesty of his face stiffened with confusion. He approached her again, his hands spreading in solicitude that became bafflement, then frustration when she jumped out of reach again.

He finally rasped, "What's wrong?"

She had to do it now. Before she weakened. Before she succumbed. She blurted it out. "I'm going back home."

He stared at her, all expression frozen on his face. At last he inhaled.

"Again I ask, what's wrong?" His voice was measured now, careful, as if he were talking to a frightened mare.

"Nothing's wrong. I just want to go back to L.A."

Puzzlement and watchfulness still hovered in his eyes as he persisted. "And the reason is?"

Her gaze wavered, her lungs closed. She hadn't thought for

a second that his response to her declaration would be anything beyond a sigh and a shrug, before he moved on to the next conquest. His unexpected probing cornered her, made her blurt out the first thing that came to her. "I thought I was free to go whenever I wanted."

Imperiousness, something she knew was innate in him but which he'd never subjected her to, blazed in his eyes. "You're not. Not without justification for your abrupt demand."

Floundering, she said, "It's a *decision*. And it's not abrupt. I've been meaning to tell you for some time."

Harshness crept into his eyes, into his voice when he drawled, "Oh, yes? Were your cries for more forty-eight hours ago part of telling me you wanted to cut our time together short?"

She turned away. She'd collapse where she stood if she tried to hold his gaze one more second. He didn't let her get far, his hands clamping her shoulders, his lips feathering along her neck.

"Enough of this, Carmen." His groan jolted more longing and misery through her. "Whatever *this* is. If you're angry with me for some—"

She jerked out of his hands, rasped, "I'm not."

His jaw muscles worked. "There must be something. You can't just want to leave. I won't let you—"

And she cried out, the shrillness of panic creeping into her voice. "I'm not *asking* you if I can leave, I'm *informing* you."

His face became implacable. "You're going nowhere until you tell me the truth. If you're in any trouble—"

"I'm *not*." God. She'd underestimated his sense of entitlement. She'd forgotten he was more than the man she loved with everything in her. He was a prince of unlimited power. He expected, and always got, his way. He'd probe and press until she broke down, gave him what he asked for. And she *couldn't*.

One way out flashed inside her mind. Desperate. Dangerous. She could think of nothing else.

Suppressing tremors of anguish and anxiety, she murmured, "Contrary to what you're used to in your native Judar where your word is law, this is a free country, your highness. A woman has the same rights as a man here to take her pleasure where she pleases, and change her mind when she pleases."

He flinched as if she'd slapped him. "And you've changed yours? When you can barely stand with wanting me?"

She felt the twitches of loss of control seizing her. God. She'd made her life's worst mistake coming back here, being so weak she'd needed to see him one last time. She should have just disappeared.

Feeling crazed with desperation, she taunted, "That is what you'd like to think, isn't it?"

He stared at her, his eyes deadening.

When he finally spoke, he sounded smooth, tranquil. "How about we drop the charade? I have nothing but games everywhere in my life. But in my bedroom I allow only sexual ones. You think the remaining six weeks should carry a more substantial price tag than sharing my bed and privileges? How remiss of me. I should have put an offer you can appreciate on the table. So if you have demands…" He suddenly yanked her to him, bent her over a potent arm, his other hand pressing her hips to his, his erection grinding against her long-molten core, the refined man she'd known receding fast. "*Make* them. I'll meet them, whatever they are."

Her heart crumpled.

Oh God. This had gotten uglier than anything she could have imagined. He thought she was bargaining with the unstoppable desire that had raged between them from the first glance. Though his repugnance was total, he seemed willing to pay anything for more of her.

She tore herself out of his arms. She had to end this. *Now.*

Only the ugliest lie would do.

Feeling the resignation of a death sentence settling over her, it flowed from her in a lifeless voice. "I thought I owed you the courtesy of not disappearing without saying goodbye. But it seems I should have spared myself the unpleasantness, should have known you'd react with the barbarism of your culture and the conceit of your inherited status. You may be good in bed, Farooq, but so are a hundred other men. I like variety, and I always leave when my lovers start to bore me. I thought it best to go before I was sick of you. I didn't want to spell it out, but it's clear I shouldn't have bothered with civility."

Before she collapsed at his feet in a weeping mess, she staggered around him, snatched up her handbag, images of a baby who looked like him fueling her march out of his bedroom, out of his world.

But the image that would remain imprinted on her retinas for the rest of her life was of his face. The face of the hostile stranger she'd managed to turn him into in mere minutes.

The hostile stranger she'd never see again.

One

"Bagha...bagha..."

Carmen paused in the middle of hanging the nursery's new curtains. She looked down at Mennah, listened to her chirping her latest "word," her heart in a state of expansion.

She'd gotten used to feeling her heart filling her whole chest, her whole being, since she'd given birth to her daughter.

She'd demanded Mennah the moment she'd come out of her womb, disregarding the doctor's grumbling that he had to close said womb first. He'd succumbed, though, had placed the smeared, nine-pound miracle on Carmen's bosom. And for long moments, as she'd first touched her baby, felt her precious weight, her flesh and heat and reality, Carmen had been afraid she wouldn't survive the explosion of emotions raging through her.

She'd searched for the right name long and hard. She'd found the perfect one, what this baby was, in her father's mother tongue. Mennah. Her gift from God.

Now her gift was latching chubby fingers onto her playpen's railings, hauling herself up to a standing position. She then tried to stand unsupported and landed on her diaper-padded bottom with a cry of chagrin-mixed glee, tearing a laugh from Carmen's depths.

"Oh, Mennah, darling, you're in such a hurry."

And she was. At only nine months, she'd been sitting unsupported for almost three, crawling for almost two and was now clearly on her way to overtaking another milestone.

Carmen slotted the last hook, climbed down the ladder and headed to the playpen. Her sunny angel grinned at her, good nature brimming from golden eyes, displaying her newly acquired set of teeth, her dimples flashing in the perfection of her cherubic face. A surge of emotions clogged Carmen's throat, rising to her eyes.

Could she have been so blessed?

Mennah held up her arms. Carmen obliged at once, bent and cradled the robust little body that was her reason for living. Mennah mashed her face into her mother's neck, and Carmen's arms convulsed around her. It was a good thing Mennah loved fierce hugs. Carmen bore down on the flare of love, rocked Mennah in her arms, one hand luxuriating in the raven silk of her locks. Hmm, the bald patch from before Mennah started rolling around was totally gone.

Suddenly Mennah pushed away, looked up expectantly. "Bagha bagha."

Carmen tickled her nose. "Yes, darling, you're trying to tell me something and your mommy is so dense she hasn't figured it out yet. But that's a new word. Give me a day and I'll figure it out. Say—could it be you're telling me you're hungry? It has been a couple of hours since you've eaten." Carmen started to undo her shirt only for Mennah to slap her hands on top of Carmen's, squealing, part playful, part admonishing. Carmen sighed. "No mommy-produced sustenance?"

Mennah giggled. Carmen sighed again. She'd been hoping

to prolong nursing. But this was another area where Mennah was in a hurry. She'd been refusing to nurse more and more ever since she'd been introduced to solid foods, decreasing Carmen's milk flow. This was the second day with no nursing at all. During that time Mennah had even given her grief about eating previously much-loved foods. And Carmen could guess why.

"I shouldn't have given you a taste of my filet mignon, darling. Seems you share more than your looks with your father. He, too, is a big panther who relishes red meat—"

Carmen stopped. Mennah was looking up at her with such absorption, as if she was memorizing everything her mother said.

Carmen had been indulging in the heartbreaking pleasure of constantly talking to her about her father. Maybe she should resist giving in to the urge. There was no way Mennah understood now, but maybe before Carmen realized, she would. And she didn't want to explain her father's absence for years. Not that she'd ever have enough time to come up with an adequate explanation.

Exhaling, shaking off a resurgence of the despondency that had suffocated her all through her pregnancy, she walked out of the nursery, headed to their open-plan, sunlit kitchen.

She secured Mennah in her high chair, dropped a kiss on top of her glossy head. "One bagha bagha coming up."

She placed plastic toys in front of Mennah, set the iPod to a slow rock collection and started preparing the dish that had converted her baby to gourmet cuisine. Amidst singing along with her favorite songs and Mennah's accompanying shrieks of enthusiasm, she stopped periodically to gather the toys with which Mennah gleefully tested gravity, giving them back to her so she'd restart her experiments over and over again.

She was finishing the mushroom sauce when she noticed it had been a couple of minutes since she'd fetched for Mennah, since her daughter's squeals had disharmonized with her singing.

She turned around and her heart overflowed with another gush of love. Mennah was out like a light on the high chair's tray.

She always did fall asleep without warning. But she couldn't have been hungry after all, if she could fall asleep among all those mouthwatering aromas.

Sighing, eyeing the meal that had to be served hot to be good, Carmen turned off the music, unbuckled Mennah from her seat then went to put her down in her crib.

The singing had stopped.

The crashing of Farooq's heart hadn't.

And it wasn't only his heart that manifested his upheaval. Every muscle in his body was clenched, every nerve discharging.

He'd been standing there for what felt like a day, listening to the sounds coming from inside. Wistful love songs accompanied by the gleeful noises of an infant. And the overpowering melody of a siren.

He'd willed himself over and over to ring the bell. Better still, to break down the door.

He'd just stood there, his ear almost to the door to catch every decibel of a slice of life of the tiny family that lived inside, his hands caressing the door as if it were them.

He felt as if he'd disintegrate with an emotion so fierce he had no name for it, no experience and no way to deal with it.

It had to be rage. An unknown level that made what he'd felt when Carmen had told him she was leaving pale in comparison. It dwarfed what he'd felt when he'd pursued her, bent on erasing the ugliness, the madness of that confrontation, on bringing back his Carmen and the perfection they'd shared, only for more betrayal to tear at him when he'd seen her getting into his cousin Tareq's car. It even eclipsed what he'd felt when he'd confronted Tareq and discovered why she'd really left.

His cousin and arch nemesis had confessed that he'd sent

Carmen to seduce Farooq, to get pregnant and create a scandal large enough to stop Farooq's rise to the succession. Tareq had snickered that their uncle's latest decree had thrown a sabot in the cogs of his treachery, turning a pregnancy into an asset, not a liability, forcing him to order Carmen to leave, going back to the drawing board to think of something else to eliminate Farooq from the running.

It had all made sense to Farooq then. From the moment he'd seen her to the moment she'd walked out on him.

Or he'd thought it had.

It had been only hours ago that he'd learned the full truth.

Another tidal wave of emotion crashed over him.

Ya Ullah—he'd never struggled for control, had never even contemplated its loss. He'd been born in control, of himself before others. His urges and desires were his to command, never the other way around. Then there was Carmen.

He'd lost control with his first sight of her, had lost his discretion while drowning in her pleasures, had almost lost his restraint upon her desertion.

Now he was a hairsbreadth from losing his reason.

And it was her doing yet again.

He leaned his forehead on the door, forced inhalations into his spastic lungs, order into his frenzied thoughts, willing the blinding seizure to pass.

It took minutes and the nosiness of two neighbors to bring him down. He regained at least enough control to settle a semblance of composure over the chaos, smothering it. Enough to make him reach a resolution.

He'd never let her affect him that deeply again. Ever.

He'd go in, take what he wanted. As he always did.

He straightened, set his teeth with great precision and almost drove his finger through her doorbell.

Carmen jerked up from watching Mennah sleep. The bell! Though it almost never rang, she'd been waiting for her super to come fix the short-circuit in the laundry room. He'd said within the next two days. *Four* days ago.

But it was the way the bell rang that had made her jump. It had almost…bellowed, for lack of a better description. Maybe it was about to give, too, and that sound was its dying throes?

Sighing, she checked Mennah's monitor and the wireless receiver clipped to her jeans' waist. On her way to the door, she smoothed her hands over her hair but gave up in midmotion with a huff. A disheveled greeter was what her super got for coming unannounced, catching a single mother with a dozen chores behind her and a shower still in her future.

Fixing a smile on her lips, intending her greeting to be thanks for his arrival if no thanks for his delay, she opened the door.

Her heart didn't stop immediately.

It went on with its rhythm for a moment, the kind that simulated hours, before it lost the blood it needed to keep on pumping. The blood now shooting to her head, pooling in her legs. Then it stopped.

And everything else hurtled, screeched, into consciousness.

Denial, dread, desperation.

She'd changed her career to work from home, had relocated to the other side of the continent, had still remained scared that he'd find her. But he hadn't, and eventually she'd believed he hadn't tried, or hadn't been able to.

But he *had* found her. Was on her doorstep. *Farooq.*

Filling her doorway. Blocking out existence.

She found herself slumped against the door, her fingers almost breaking off with the force with which they clutched it. Some instinct must have remained functioning, saving her from crashing to the ground. Some auxiliary power must be fueling her continued grip on consciousness.

"Save it."

That was all he said as he pushed past her, walking into her apartment as if he owned it. And his voice…

This wasn't the voice etched in her memory. The voice that

echoed in every moment's silence, haunting her, whispering seduction, rumbling arousal, roaring completion, always charged with emotion. *This* voice contained as much life as a voice simulation program.

God, what was he doing here?

No. She didn't care what he was doing here. She didn't care that her insides were crumbling under the avalanche of emotion the sight of him had triggered.

She had to get rid of him. *Fast.*

She had to regain control first, of her coherence, to think of something to say, of her volition, to be able to say it.

She leaned against the door she didn't remember closing, feeling as if the least tremor would shatter the tension keeping her upright. She watched his powerful strides take him into the formal living room, felt him shrinking it, converging all light on him like a spotlight in the dark.

And even through her shock and panic, everything inside her devoured each line of his juggernaut's body, even bigger and taller than she remembered, the sculpted suit worshipping it from the daunting breadth of shoulders, to the sparseness of waist and hips, to the formidable power of thighs and endless legs.

Memory was a sadistic master, lashing open festering wounds with images and sensations, of those shoulders dominating her, those hips thrusting her to a frenzy, those thighs and legs encompassing her in the aftermath of madness.

She tore her gaze and memories away, choking on longing. Then he turned, and everything in her piled up with the brunt of his beauty, the rawness of her still-burning love.

His heavy-lidded gaze documented her reaction before he raised both eyebrows, a movement rich in nonchalance and imperiousness. "Finished with your latest act, or shall I wait until you've delivered the full performance?"

It wasn't only his voice that was different. This wasn't the Farooq she remembered. This wasn't even the hostile stranger she'd walked out on. That man had been seething with harshness, with emotion. *This* man was even more forbidding, as he eyed her with the clinical coldness of a scientist dealing with inanimate matter.

His lips pursed as if he were assessing a defective product. He finally gave a slight shake of his awesome head, lips twisting on his unfavorable verdict. "As an unbiased viewer, I must tell you, your acting abilities are slipping. Exaggeration is not your friend."

Before she could even process his dispassionate comment, let alone find words to answer it, he relieved her of his focus, cast his gaze around her space.

She could see his connoisseur's mind adding up the worth of every square foot, every piece of furniture, brush stroke and decorative article and felt defensive. Though she'd made this place chic and cheery, it could well be derelict compared to the opulence he was used to. Which was a stupid thing to feel and think.

She had to make him leave. Now. Before Mennah woke up. Before he saw the childproofing she'd begun installing.

He finally returned those empty eyes to hers as he walked back toward her. She watched him cross the distance between them with the fatalism of someone about to be hit by a train.

"It cost a bundle, this place," he murmured. "I would have wondered how you afforded it. If I didn't already know."

She almost blurted out "What do you mean by that?"

She didn't. She couldn't locate her voice. Her heart had long invaded her throat. She could barely breathe enough to keep from passing out. And his indifference and disparagement were encasing her in frost, hurrying her descent. Everything was taking on a surreal tinge. She began to hope this was a scenario out of her Farooq-starved imagination.

Then he was within touching distance. And she had to prove to herself he was—or wasn't—really here.

She reached out a trembling hand, half expecting her fingertips to encounter a mirage. Instead they feathered over black-silk-covered flesh, the layered sensations of softness and steel, heat and hardness. Her fingers pressed into him, shudders engulfing her, like an electrocution victim unable to break the deadly circuit.

And she saw it, in his eyes. A response, blasting away the ice, mushrooming like a nuclear cloud before the wave of annihilation followed. Before he clamped onto her intruding hand.

A moan punched out of her as he squeezed awareness from her flesh and bones. Then, with scary precision, he removed her hand from his chest, let it drop like a soiled tissue.

With his eyes empty again, he half turned, raising his head as if sniffing for an oncoming storm.

"Hmm…filet mignon with mushroom sauce?" He turned his eyes to her. They weren't back to impassivity at all, the harshness she'd seen in them that night in his penthouse polluting the amber. "Expecting a guest? Or is it a sponsor?" She gaped at him. His voice dipped into an abrasive bass. "I hope you've had enough of the shocked routine and will contribute to what started as a monologue and is now bordering on a soliloquy."

Contribute. He wanted her to contribute. She had exactly four words to contribute. The sum total of what was left of her mind.

"Why are you here?"

Something feral flashed in the depths of his wolflike eyes. "So, you deem to end the mute show. If only to put on the dumb one."

Each word was a lash on her rawness. "Please…*stop.*"

He inclined his head, a predator at leisure, his prey cornered, with all the time in the world to torment it. "Stop what? Critiquing your below par performance? You have only yourself to blame for that. It seems you haven't been honing your craft of late."

"Please…I don't understand."

"More acts, Carmen? Don't you know the key to a successful acting career, especially an offstage one, is sticking with your strengths? My advice: never try the particular roles you just churned up for my benefit again. They neither suit nor work."

"For God's sake, stop talking in riddles. *Why are you here?*"

He raised an eyebrow. "Intent on dramatizing to the end, aren't you? Or are you just intent on testing the limits of my patience? The reason I'm here is self-evident."

She shook her head. "Not to me. So please, drop *your* act and just say what you came here to say, and then—*please*— leave me alone."

He seemed to expand like a thundercloud about to hurtle down destruction, a beam of the day's dying sun striking a solar flare of rage in the gold of his eyes.

"I once told you that I have my fill of games. I thought you had enough intelligence not to join the would-be manipulators who swarm around me. At least not to try the same trick twice. Evidently I've overestimated your IQ. This will be the last time I take part in one of *your* games, so savor it while you can. Try another at your peril." He inclined his head at her, sent her heart slamming in her chest. "You want me to pretend I don't know that you know why I'm here? *Zain.* Fine." He gave a pause laden with the irony of someone about to deliver something redundant, the disgust of being forced to play an offensive game of make-believe.

Then he drawled, smooth and sharp as a razor, "I am here for my daughter."

Two

Farooq's words shot through Carmen, pulverizing the framework holding her heart in place. Yet something kept her on her feet and conscious. Probably hope that she was hallucinating. "W-what did you say?"

He exhaled, the icy armor not back in place, the underlying volcano seething through the cracks. "Spare me further theatrics. You had my daughter. You *have* my daughter. I am here for her."

He knows about Mennah.

How could he know about her?

He somehow did, had said…said…

I am here for my daughter.

What did that mean? Here for her…how? It couldn't mean what it sounded like. It couldn't mean he…he…

He wanted to take Mennah away from her.

The ground softened. An abyss yawned beneath, pulled at her…

But no. *No.* Not even he could take a baby away from her mother. This wasn't Judar, where he was the law. This was America.

But how did he find out? Had he had her investigated, found out she'd had a baby, done the math and come to the conclusion Mennah might be his? Why would he want her even if he realized she was? He couldn't consider her anything but a disastrous mistake.

That first night he'd had no protection, and even in the inferno of arousal, he would have stopped if she hadn't assured him she was safe. She'd been certain she was. She'd had a dozen reports from as many specialists declaring her infertile.

He'd told her in blatant detail how he wanted to invade her, feel his flesh inside hers without barriers, to pour himself inside her. It had sent her up in flames in his arms…

Stop. *Stop.* She couldn't let those memories assault her now. He hadn't been risking repercussions, had believed her assurances. That was why she'd known his reaction would be violent if he found out about her pregnancy. He would have looked upon it as an ultimate breach of the trust he didn't give easily. Most important, she couldn't have projected how damaging it would be to him, a prince in line to the throne of one of the world's most conservative and richest oil states, to have an illegitimate child.

Suddenly her heart nearly fired out of her ribs.

Could he be here to make sure Mennah disappeared, so she'd never compromise his position?

Out of her mind with dread, she asked, "What makes you even think my daughter can be yours?"

His answering stare was long and pitiless, lava coursing beneath the dark, hard surface.

Then he dipped one hand inside his jacket, as if he were extracting a gun.

Next moment she wished he had pulled one out, had shot her straight through the heart with it.

He pulled out a photo instead. Of Mennah.

A photo of Mennah sitting in strange surroundings. Holding an unfamiliar toy. Wearing unknown clothes. Mennah was laughing at the camera, secure, pleased, knowing how to please.

Mennah was only like that around her.

In the few times she'd seen other people, she'd clung to Carmen, fearful, tearful. If someone had managed to get her alone...

Was she losing her mind? How could she be wondering that?

She'd *never* left Mennah alone, except when she was sound asleep in her crib, like now. She'd diverted her career to work from home so she could be with her daughter at all times.

How had he gotten his hands on Mennah?

"I—I've never left Mennah. When—how did you get the chance to—to—"

"I didn't." His voice slashed across her babbling. "This isn't a photo of your...of *my* daughter. This is a photo of my sister, Jala, at Mennah's age. Mennah is also my feminine replica at that age. That Mennah is mine is indisputable. So let's drop the hysterics and get to the point of all this."

"Wh-what is that?"

"That I'll never forgive you for keeping her from me."

Farooq's gaze clung to Carmen as she flinched as if at the lash of a whip, his fascination beyond his control.

But that was an improvement on what had happened when she'd opened her door with that smile ready on her lips. Everything had stilled then. Thought, heartbeats. Time itself had seemed to stop.

Then it had hit a screeching reverse, catapulting him to the moment he'd first laid eyes on her in that conference hall a year and a half ago.

As a tycoon and a prince, he had the world's most spectacular beauties flaunting their assets and practicing seduction for his benefit. His attention had to be worked for extensively, was held with utmost effort for periods never surpassing days.

Then *she'd* come forward, hesitant, prim, and his focus had been captured and his lust aroused, effortlessly. Absolutely. A surge of something he'd never entertained feeling—possessiveness—had followed.

He'd wanted to banish every male around, shield her from their eyes and thoughts. Not that she'd been inviting attention. No doubt as part of her plan to stand out.

Apart from her aloofness, she'd been smothered in a navy skirt suit from neck to mid-calf, when all the women around her had worn skirts riding up their thighs and blouses opened on deep cleavages.

Her closed expression and concealing clothes had made him more eager to tear through them. He'd seen himself stripping her of that guarded look, those offending coverings, arranging her on that conference table, spreading her for his pleasure and hers, her reserve melting as she begged for his pleasuring, writhed for his domination…

It must have been the response she'd counted on. That the mystique of her reticence in manner and dress would rouse the hunter lying dormant inside him. And it had worked. Spectacularly.

For the first time ever, he'd been fazed, couldn't account for his violent response. Unlike many men of his culture, he didn't prefer fair-skinned, light-eyed women, certainly never redheads.

But she'd approached him like a wary gazelle, her equal attraction and alarm blazing in those heaven-colored eyes, had put that supple hand in his and everything about her had become everything he craved. Her face and body had become the sum total of his fantasies, every feature and line the source of his hunger, the fuel for his pleasure.

He would have done anything to have her in his bed. And when by the end of the night he'd had her there, he couldn't let it end, had offered what he'd never offered any woman. Three months. In the private space he never let anyone breach. With every minute, he'd wanted her for longer. He'd even entertained forever.

Then she'd walked out.

Ever since, he'd been trying to wipe her taste from his mouth, the memory of her from his psyche, to reacquire a taste for other brands of beauty, build tolerance for another's touch.

After each dismal failure he'd damned her, damned his addiction more. And here he was, renewing his exposure.

She'd opened the door, and it had been as if everything he'd learned since she'd revealed her true face had been erased, and she was again the woman he'd run back to that night, intending to offer forever.

It had taken her spectacular reaction to seeing him to jog him out of his amnesic haze. To fire his memory of when she'd done the unprecedented. The unimaginable. Thrown his desire back in his face. Been the one to walk out.

He'd pretended interest in his surroundings to tear his senses away, only for everything about her new home to send his fury cresting, proof of her crimes against him.

Had this place been stripped of even a coat of paint, it would still cost a fortune, with its location in an elite building in an upmarket neighborhood of one of the most expensive cities in the world, New York. The fortune she'd made being Tareq's mole.

Tareq had planted her in his life at the perfect time. During his taxing world tour, as he'd fought for his goals on all fronts, amidst Tareq's escalating efforts to discredit him.

He'd thought her a godsend. Instead she'd been sent by a devil. A devil whose evil had backfired.

With Farooq's father dead—of a broken heart, Farooq was convinced, just a year after Farooq's mother had died from a long illness—Tareq had thought that, as the king's oldest nephew, he'd succeed Farooq's father as crown prince.

Tareq's own father had died of a heart attack when they were all quite young, leaving Tareq his only heir and the oldest of the royal cousins.

But, knowing that Tareq favored certain unkingly, depraved activities, their uncle the king had at first said he'd reserve the crown prince title for his own son. A son he could only have if he took a second wife. When he couldn't bring himself to take another wife, he'd then said he'd name his heir according to merit, not age, with the implication clear to all that he meant Farooq and would soon officially name him crown prince. Tareq had then launched into non-stop plotting to overrule the king's decree.

During Farooq's tour, Tareq had suddenly started talking as if he'd secured the succession, bragging that he'd be the first king who never married. Farooq guessed he'd said that to gain the support of the enemies of the royal house of Aal Masood by intimating that they would therefore get a turn to rule after him. He now realized that Tareq had also thought his plot with Carmen had been about to bear fruit, creating an illegitimate, half-western heir for Farooq and eliminating him from favor.

But Tareq's assertions had only given the king ammunition to overcome the reluctance of the members of the Tribune of Elders—the king's council—who had resisted bypassing Tareq for Farooq. With Tareq adding contempt for the Aal Masoods' future to his depravities, the king knew that all Farooq needed to do to drive the last nail in Tareq's coffin was to overcome his own reluctance to marry. Didn't he have a woman he'd consider marrying? his uncle had asked.

Farooq hadn't even hesitated. He had a woman. Carmen.

And his king had issued the decree. The heir who married and produced the first child would succeed to the throne.

And Tareq had ordered Carmen to leave the very next day.

During their confrontation, Tareq had thanked his lucky stars that Carmen hadn't conceived, casting aspersions on Farooq's virility and fertility. Sixteen hours ago, Farooq had realized she'd left because she *had* conceived, the child that would have snuffed her employer's dying hopes.

She couldn't have known what she'd lost when she'd run out on him. But he still didn't know why she hadn't stayed to use the child as a bargaining chip, had taken Tareq's offer instead. Even if she'd shown Farooq the face of a woman he could never marry, he'd been in addiction's merciless grip, would have given her light years beyond what she had now.

Had she thought he'd sate himself, wreak vengeance on her then discard her with nothing? Or did her subservience to Tareq mix greed with fear? Or even lust…?

His thoughts boiled in an uproar of revulsion.

Thinking of her in Tareq's filthy arms, succumbing to his sadism and perversions… Bile rose up to his throat.

But the sick image of her as his cousin's tool and whore, and her own words as she'd left him, clashed with everything radiating from her now….

No. He'd never believe anything he sensed about her again. He could still barely believe how totally he'd been taken in, how seamlessly she'd acted her part. It had been a virtuoso performance, the guilelessness, the spontaneity, the unbridled responses, the perpetual hunger, the total pleasure in him, in and out of bed.

But all that faking had borne something real. A daughter. And he'd missed so much. The miracle of her birth and every precious moment of the first nine months of her life.

And if it had been up to Carmen, he would have never found out about her. She would have grown up fatherless.

But among all Carmen's crimes, what most enraged him had been that *touch*.

She'd touched him as if to ascertain he was really there. And that touch had almost made him drag her to the floor, tear her out of her clothes and bury himself inside her.

Now he relished repaying her for shredding his control yet again, seeing her with her composure shattered.

Oh, yes. *That* was real. She must be frantic, thinking her cash cow had run dry. Now that Farooq had learned of Mennah's existence, Tareq would stop paying for her luxurious lifestyle.

Seething with colliding emotions, he inclined his head at her. "Nothing to say, I see. That's very wise of you."

She gulped. "H-how did you find out?"

He wouldn't have. Ever. If he'd stuck to his oath never to seek her out. But instead of fading away, her memory had burned hotter each day, and the need for closure had almost driven him mad.

It had taken months, even with the endless resources at his fingertips, to find her. His best people had finally gotten him the basics—an address, a resume…and a photograph. Of Carmen and a baby. A baby recognizable on sight as his.

That photograph now burned a rectangle its size over his heart, though he'd chosen to show Carmen Jala's photo instead, to cut things short. He'd expected her to contest his paternity.

Pursing his lips, he pushed past her. "I find out anything I want. Now, I'll see my daughter."

"No." She grabbed him, aborting his stride toward the hall leading to the bedrooms. Her touch, though frantic, still sent a bolt of arousal through him. He added his unwilling response to her transgressions, looked down at her hands in disgust, at her, at himself. She removed them, took a step backward. "She's sleeping."

"So? Fathers walk in on their sleeping daughters all the time. You've taken nine months of my daughter's life away from me. I'm not letting you take one more minute."

She jumped into his path again, her color dangerous, her chest heaving. "I'll let you see her only if—if you promise—"

He slashed his hand, cutting off her wobbling words. "Nobody *lets* me do anything, let alone you. I do what I see fit. **And everyone obeys.**"

He took another step and she threw herself at him, imprinting him with her lushness. His body roared even through the fury.

He gritted his teeth. "Get out of my way, Carmen. You're not coming between me and my flesh and blood again."

She clung, gasped, "I didn't—"

"You didn't?" He held her away with fingers that even now luxuriated in the feel of her resilient flesh, longed to run all over her. "What else do you call what you did?"

A sob rattled deep inside her, made him want to clamp his lips on hers, plunge inside her fragrant warmth, plunder her until he'd extracted it, and her perfidious soul with it. Instead he relinquished his hold on her, unhooked her frantic fingers from his flesh with utmost control, put her away. She stumbled back, ended up plastered to the hall entrance, her eyes, those luminous pieces of his kingdom's summer skies, welling with terrible emotions. Emotions he knew she didn't have.

His anger spiked. "What do you call keeping her a secret? Or trying to deny my paternity now?"

"Please, stop." She spread her arms over the entry when he moved, intending to brush her aside. "I did it because I know that, in your culture, illegitimacy remains your deepest entrenched stigma and that to a prince like you, having a lover bear you an illegitimate child would be an irreparable scandal..."

He looked down into her eyes. *Ya Ullah,* how could they be so guileless? So potent? How could lies be so undetectable?

"So you are an expert on my culture and my status?" he grated. "And you left, and left me in the dark that I'd fathered a daughter, to observe the demands of both?"

She nodded, shook her head, at a total loss. "Oh God, please..." She paused, then panted, "How could I have told you I was pregnant? When I told you it couldn't happen?"

He gave a shrug. "Just like any woman who gets pregnant after such protestations would have. That it just happened. I'm sure the statistical failure of contraceptive measures has come to the rescue of countless women in your position." Those ruby lips trembled on what he knew would be another ultra sincere-sounding protest. Before he closed them with his own, he plowed on, "And then I'm well aware of the facts of life, and if I'd wanted to be positive I didn't impregnate you, I would have handled protection myself, not left it up to you and your assurances of safety. But I didn't."

And how well he remembered why he hadn't.

That first night, by the end of their dinner, he'd been in agony. But he'd been willing, for the first time in his life, to wait for a woman. He'd wanted the perfection to continue, had wanted to give her time, give himself more of her, without the intimacies he'd been burning for. The unprecedented feelings of closeness and rapport, the sheer delight in everything about her had been incredible enough; he would have savored them without fulfillment of the carnal promise indefinitely. He'd resolved to end the night with a kiss and no more. Then she'd sabotaged his intentions, pulverized his expectations.

She'd offered herself with such a mixture of shyness, passion and resolve that he'd almost refused. She'd aroused in him what he'd never felt toward a female outside his family. Tenderness, protectiveness. She'd seemed in an agony of embarrassment at her demand, yet in the grips of a hunger she couldn't control. She'd tremulously told him she knew she'd be a one-night stand for him but she had to have it, would settle for any taste of him.

He'd had her in his quarters without realizing how, had too late remembered protection, had been loath to send for it. He'd told her he'd still pleasure her, and she could pleasure him, if she wanted. She'd clung to him, said she was safe, in every way.

He hadn't even questioned her honesty, his relief sweeping. He'd wanted her to be his first. The first woman he experienced to the fullness of intimacy, his flesh driving in hers, feeling the heat and moistness of her need for him, without barriers. The first woman he poured himself into. And all through the magical six weeks he'd done that, had each glorious time abandoned himself inside her in the throes of completion. And trust.

His lips twisted in disgust, at what even memories did to him. "I didn't," he repeated. "So whatever blame there is, I share it in equal measure. Not that the word *blame* applies anywhere in the conception of a child. Certainly not my child."

She crumpled against the entryway, as if from a blow, and hiccupped, "I—I had no way of knowing you could have felt this way. You didn't want me beyond those three months and I thought you couldn't possibly want the baby I accidentally got pregnant with…"

He growled a laugh. "Accidentally? Really? But no matter how or why you got pregnant, I don't care. I don't care how my daughter was conceived, I don't care who conceived her, not even if it's you. She's mine. And I want her."

Her reaction to that was spectacular.

Springing from the entryway, she advanced on him like a lioness ready to defend her cub to the death.

"No," she growled. There was no other way to describe it. She *growled*. "She's not yours. She's mine. *Mine*."

He frowned. This felt too real.

But no more real than what *he* felt. He, too, felt like baring his fangs in demand of the daughter who'd been kept from him. His body bunched with the elemental instinct, its fire spitting through eyes slitting on fury and challenge.

"You want to fight me for her?" he snarled. "Do I need to tell you that nobody wins in any kind of battle with me, that your chances of winning anything against me are below non-existent?"

The contortion of horror and desperation that crumpled her expression did something similar behind his breastbone.

Ya Ullah, how did she *do* that?

She sagged back against the door as if the knowledge of his unstoppable power sank inside her, draining her of hers.

At last she rasped, "Why are you doing this?"

Could defeat have a sound? If it did, this must be it.

"I told you. I want my daughter." He paused, unsure what he wanted to say or do anymore. Her essence was seeping through him, dissolving his resolve, rearranging his thoughts, rewriting her character in his mind again. He ground his teeth against the weakening. "And I will have her."

And the eyes that had been brimming with tears gushed.

He'd seen her tears before. When he'd drawn out her torment before he'd ended it, shattering her with releases so fierce she'd wept with them. Now, seeing new tears pouring from eyes so crimsoned he feared they might seep blood at any moment, he could no longer dispute her state.

Whatever the reason behind her anguish, it was real, profound. She was more terrified, more desperate now than if she believed he intended to end her life.

He stared at her, an overwhelming need rising, to soothe away the pain he'd caused her. He curled his fists against the urge.

"Please…understand…I o-only hid my pregnancy b-because I was s-scared you'd make me terminate it!"

Her words detonated inside him, the belief that it was all an act erased in the blast. All he heard was the accusation, all he believed was that *she'd* believed it.

"You thought I would ask you to kill an unborn child? *My* unborn child? And you think you know anything about my culture or me? And when she was born, what did you fear? That I'd bury her alive like my land's barbarians of old?"

"No." Her cry was engulfed by shearing sobs. She still talked through them. "All I thought was you—you might fear her existence, might think her a threat to your honor, your status… And I wasn't risking it. I would do anything—*anything*—to keep her from harm."

"And you thought I'd harm her? You saw me fighting to bring relief to millions of children and thought I'd harm my own?"

B'Ellahi, what was he saying? He was playing the part she'd shoved him into with all the oblivious fervor of the past. He was answering her as if he believed concern for her baby and true fear of his reactions had been the reasons behind her disappearance.

"*B'haggej'Jaheem*—by Hell, I thought you'd come up with better than that. Or maybe you didn't give it much thought since you were sure this confrontation would never come to pass."

She shook her head, sending her tears splashing everywhere. A few fell on his hands, felt as if they'd burned him to the bone.

"But why do you want her?" And if he'd thought she'd given defeat sound, she now gave desperation tone and texture. "Don't Judarians value only male sons? What is a daughter to a prince like you who surely wants only heirs?"

"So, first you dare to imply that I might have gotten rid of her for being born at all, and now that I'd discard her for being born female."

She spread her hands in a helpless gesture, a lost gesture, beseeching his understanding, his mercy.

He had neither to give. "Enough of that."

She again threw herself in his path, but was shaking so hard she couldn't even cling. "I didn't dream you'd want her... please..."

He looked down at her, struggling with the need to slake the accumulation of hunger in that body that had deprived him of finding pleasure elsewhere. He'd been unable to contemplate marrying another after she'd walked out on him, even as a damage-control measure when Tareq had rushed out and married the first woman to accept him. Instead, Farooq had decided to expose Tareq's ineligibility to rise to the succession once and for all, had asked his king, who couldn't go back on the marriage-criteria decree, to stall everyone until he furnished irrefutable proof of Tareq's perversions and crimes.

He was close to gaining that proof, but now he'd found Carmen and Mennah—and they were the fastest route to securing the succession. Not that he would let Tareq go unpunished. Or Carmen, either. But he wouldn't touch her. Not yet.

Putting her away was harder than anything he'd ever had to do. Then he strode through the entrance she'd been guarding, went deeper into the apartment, felt her stumbling behind him, her tremors buzzing through his flesh, her sobs constricting his lungs.

He ignored the feelings, stopped before the door that he just knew had his daughter on the other side. Then he turned.

"Show me my daughter, Carmen."

He had no idea why he asked her permission when he never asked anyone's, gave her that consideration when she'd shown him none. Worst of all, he had no idea why he'd done it so…gently.

That was for his daughter, he told himself. He didn't want to enter her room, her life, with anger polluting those first magical moments. Children picked up on moods, deciphered tension between adults. And he wasn't poisoning her mood or introducing fear and anxiety in her life for any reason, was even willing to make peace with her mother, if only around her, for her sake.

"Stop crying. I won't have my daughter see me for the first time with her mother weeping beside me. She'd forever link me with your pain."

"A-and she'd be right…you're destroying me."

He grimaced his distaste at her exaggeration. "Cut the melodrama, Carmen. Or are you willing to risk scarring her impressionable psyche just to paint me black in her mind?"

"No, no…I'd never…never…" She almost fell at his feet, forced him to take her full weight, his hands around her rib cage, so close to the breasts that were now shuddering with emotion, that had once shuddered in his palms, beneath his chest in ecstasy. She raised rabid eyes to his and wailed, "Don't take my daughter away…I'd die without her."

Three

Farooq stared down at Carmen for a stunned moment.

He had heard about the power of tears before, had had them shed for his benefit on countless occasions, by both women and men. The only power they'd held over him was that of testing the limits of his goodwill. But *her* tears…

Ya Ullah, hada mostaheel—it was impossible the way they affected him, the way her outburst had.

She thought he intended to take her baby away.

It was only in this moment that he realized he'd stormed in here not knowing *what* he intended.

He'd gotten the intel sixteen hours ago, had been on his fastest jet within an hour, had spent the time on the nonstop transcontinental, transatlantic haul seething with realizations and convictions. Some of the latter *had* been of how an exploitative mother didn't deserve to keep her child.

He now realized those thoughts had colored the way he'd stated his intention of having his daughter, making it sound as if he'd snatch her away from Carmen.

He believed that drastic action should be reserved for women who were a danger to their offspring. But, couldn't he equate a mother who used her daughter to maintain a luxurious lifestyle with an alcoholic or a drug addict?

Rage shot to another zenith as he looked down into her drenched eyes. Then, to his further fury, her anguish fractured his grip on his convictions.

As their eyes meshed, all he could think of was that this was no act. This wasn't someone afraid for her income. This was someone who feared something far worse than death.

Could it be true? She'd conceived Mennah for an ulterior motive, but she now loved her? And that much?

He *could* take her—*his*—daughter from her as easily as taking a toy from an infant. Considering what she'd done to him, he should at least entertain retribution. The thought only scorched him with mortification.

She had to be some sort of witch.

But then, all he'd meant when he'd declared she couldn't fight him was that she couldn't deny him his right to his daughter. She'd taken his words to their worst possible conclusion. That was in keeping with the fear she claimed had driven her to run away. So could he believe that had really been the reason she'd run?

Laa, b'Ellahi. He couldn't. He *knew* the truth.

Still, whatever her motives then, for some maddening reason, against a hundred insisting he shouldn't, he believed her fear now. Worse, he had no desire to see her so anguished. Though he had every right to hurt her, he didn't want to. Not this way.

Damning himself for a fool a thousand times for feeling he should kneel and beg her forgiveness for making her feel this way he rasped, "I won't take her away. Now stop crying."

Among the crashing in her head, the detonations tearing apart her chest, Carmen heard him say, "I won't take her away."

Suddenly there was silence. And darkness.

From a timeless void, sounds returned. Blood drumming in her ears to a sluggish rhythm. Another set of heartbeats booming there. Slow, steady, powerful. Coming from the living granite wall her ear was pressed against.

The rest of her senses coalesced. Smell, soaking in the scent of virility and vigor. Touch, transmitting the luxury of cashmere and silk and power. Orientation, placing her in his embrace, her head on his chest, her breasts molded against his upper abdomen, his arms around her back, her thighs. Then her sight focused on the fierceness drawing his winged eyebrows together, chiseling his features deeper, clouding the translucence of his golden eyes.

Such *intent*. He was carrying her to yet another session of delirium and ecstasy. The tension that had started to gather in her limbs melted into the enervation of expectation, her body readying itself for his onslaught, his possession…

But as each of his strides transmitted their effortless power to her bones, realization seeped through, until everything crashed back into her awareness.

This wasn't the past. He wasn't carrying her to his bed, or anywhere else where he'd ravish her with pleasure. This was now. In the oppressive present.

She might have imagined the words he'd said pledging he wouldn't take Mennah from her.

She convulsed in his arms from the resurrected dread. His scowl deepened, and his hold firmed as he shouldered open her bedroom door. "Be still. You passed out."

"Put me down. I'm all right now."

"I'll put you down on your bed. *B'Ellahi,* quit struggling."

She shook her head, crushing his lapels in spastic fingers. "You said you w-won't…?"

He didn't answer her amputated question, deposited her on her bed with utmost care, leaning over her with arms flanking her head. His eyes swept down her length as they'd always done, as if he were struggling with the decision about which part of her to ravish first.

When he had her quaking, he swept back up to her eyes, drawled, "I won't take Mennah away from you, Carmen. I'm not the monster you insist on painting me."

"I never thought you were a monster."

"No? The man you claim to think would have forced you to abort your baby, or would take her from you to banish her somewhere, make her live her life unknown and illegitimate so he'd secure his position? If this isn't a monster, what is?"

"I'm sorry, Farooq. So sorry." She clung to his forearms as he began to withdraw, desperate to make him understand. He extricated himself as if from slime. She shuddered. "I was so afraid…it was too huge, I couldn't afford a margin of error, could only consider worst-case scenarios. I was afraid you'd think I'd lied on purpose, meaning to compromise you. I didn't know you long enough to know how you'd react to perceived betrayals or threats. And then it wasn't about you, or me. It was about her. Everything is about her. She's everything to me. *Everything*."

Emotions she couldn't define blasted from his eyes, flaying her. It was a minute before he had mercy on her. He wrenched his gaze away, razing her single bed, her room, instead. She felt him wrestling his temper under control and began to realize the depth of his affront, his fury.

Everything he'd said was the opposite of what she'd imagined. It shriveled her to know she'd taken extreme actions that had hurt him on so many levels….

No. They had hurt him on only one level—where Mennah was concerned. He suffered anger that she'd hid the baby, offense that she'd dared fear him concerning any child, even one conceived without his will and knowledge. What *they'd* shared was not worth mentioning except to reference her exit act, which he'd made clear had been so pathetic he'd seen right through it.

Suddenly a gurgle tore through the silence. One of the sounds Carmen lived to hear. Mennah's. As if she was right between them.

Farooq stiffened, his eyes slamming back to hers for a moment of incomprehension. The sounds continued, the cooing and burbling with which Mennah entertained herself upon waking up. Astonishment invaded his eyes as they fell on the miniature receiver buckled on Carmen's waistband. Then he murmured, clearly not to her, his deepest baritone soft with amazement, "*Ya Ullah,* she's awake…"

He exploded to his feet and toward the nursery right next door. Strength flooded Carmen's limbs and she flew after him, catching his arm as his hand gripped the door handle.

"Let me go in first."

His gaze burned down on her for a moment, accentuated by Mennah's happy babblings emanating from the receiver and through the door. The feel of his muscles flexing in her grasp screamed down her nerves.

He turned away, a shake of his arm making her hands fall away like shedded leaves, making her believe he'd disregard her request.

He stared sightlessly at the door for one more moment then exhaled heavily. "*Zain.* Fine. Again I ask you to show me my daughter, Carmen. I hope you won't faint again to put it off."

Her body heat shot up another notch, this time not with awareness. "You think I was pretending?"

A growl rumbled from his gut, impatience made into sound. "Does it matter what I think?" Before she cried out a denial he ground on, "*Laaken Laa…*no, I don't think even you can pretend such a dead faint. Now quit stalling."

"Great," she grumbled. "To be exonerated from a con, only because you think my acting abilities aren't up to pulling it off. And I'm not stalling. You think I'd leave her alone for long even to thwart you? Now, can you move aside? I'll call you in when…"

He seemed to expand, blocking her way like a barricade. "I'm letting you walk in *ahead,* not *alone.* Don't test my patience anymore, Carmen."

"Or you'll do what?" she bristled.

He raised both eyebrows. "So, the falling-apart act is over and now comes...what? The hellcat one?"

She exhaled forcibly, letting out some of her tension. She couldn't walk into Mennah's nursery seething. "Who's wasting time now? Now move out of my way so I can go to my daughter. She's content to lie in her crib yammering to herself when she wakes up, but I never leave her alone for more than a few minutes."

He gave a theatrical gesture, inviting her to precede him.

She opened the door a crack.

"You make her sleep in the dark!"

The hiss lodged between her shoulder blades. She closed the door, glared up at him. "You have a problem with that?"

His scowl was spectacular. "You should leave a nightlight on. She'll get scared if she wakes up in pitch-black like that."

Her lips twisted. "And this is your expert opinion as an experienced dad?" Again the growl rumbled from in his gut, softer, no doubt because he feared Mennah might hear. She challenged him again. "Does she sound scared to you?"

His jaw muscles clenched in what she could only describe as grudging concession.

God, had he always looked that—that indescribable?

Struggling to bring yet another pang of response under control, she found herself saying, "My mother never made me sleep in the dark, and I developed a phobia of darkness. It took me years of agonizing self-conditioning to get over it."

Why was she explaining her actions as if she was defending her maternal ability? He could hear with his own ears that Mennah wasn't in the least disturbed to be awake in a dark room, had already conceded that, no matter how unwillingly.

And what was that strange expression that flared in the depths of those lion's eyes of his?

Slowly she started to reopen the door. He took the door

from her, closed it again. "This is the first time you've mentioned your mother."

She stared up at him, huffed a sarcastic breath. "And you're what? Surprised I had one?"

"Had?" he probed. "She's dead?"

She nodded, her throat closing all over again. "Cancer."

"When?"

"Just over ten years now. She died on my sixteenth birthday."

His eyes narrowed, the amber intensifying. "On the very day?"

She nodded, tears she hadn't shed then brimming.

What was he doing, interrogating her this way? What was *she* doing, pouring out information about herself? She'd never talked about her past with him. There was so much she'd never wanted to share with others, especially someone as blessed as he was.

Their time together had been consumed in conflagrations of mindless passion. When they had talked, it had been about their tastes, fantasies, beliefs. She'd assumed he'd run a background check on her, had a full report with her statistics somewhere in his security files, one he probably hadn't bothered to read. And why should he have? He surely didn't clutter his mind with the particulars of the steady parade of women who warmed his bed. And she'd already known of his background, since he was such an international figure.

She broke contact with those eyes that made her feel turned inside out for his inspection. "We'll go in now. But I'm warning you...when Mennah sees you, she may be upset, may even cry. She doesn't like strangers."

"I'm not a stranger."

He was so close he singed her cheek, the side of her neck with the heat of his vehemence, the intoxication of his breath. She shuddered, leaned on the door.

"You're still one to her..." The words petered out on her lips, in her mind, evaporated by the intensity in his gaze.

Mennah's yammering took on an excited edge. She must have sensed them even through the noise she was making. Carmen opened the door, turned up the dimmer, drenching the cheery room in soothing illumination. Mennah let out a squeal, started kicking her legs in welcoming delight as soon as she saw Carmen.

"Oh, darling, me, too." Hungry strides took her to Mennah, before she froze. Farooq had clamped her shoulder.

Suddenly Mennah's happy noises ceased, her smiles dissolving into a look of surprise. She'd seen Farooq towering behind Carmen.

Wide-eyed, she stuffed both hands in her mouth and stared at him, chewing on her chubby fingers. Carmen felt apprehension rising, thoughts streaking over how to stop what she knew would come. The wobbling chin, the down-turning lips, the whimpers and tears and the arms outstretched for her.

She wondered why she'd want to spare him that.

The answer formed alongside the question in her mind.

She'd misjudged him, deprived him of Mennah's first precious months of life. He should have been the second person who held her, whom she saw. She should have been secure in his presence from her first moment of life, should be squealing her pleasure at the sight of him now, too. If, after Mennah's delightful welcome to her, she whined and whimpered at Farooq, Carmen didn't know what she'd…

"Ya Ullah, ma ajmalhah."

Farooq's awed words jolted through her heart. *How beautiful she is.* Being fluent in Arabic had secured her the opportunity of organizing his conference, the reason she'd met him.

He went on, in a more ragged rasp, as if to himself, *"Ma arwa'ha, hadi'l mo'jezah as'sagheerah!"*

How marvelous she is, this little miracle.

And he had no idea just how miraculous Mennah was. The baby everyone had sworn Carmen would never be able to conceive. Now, after her hysterectomy, the only baby she'd ever conceive. Mennah was beyond a miracle. She was Carmen's every reason to go on living.

Overloaded with emotion, she felt him brushing past her, watched with breath gone and heart stampeding as he leaned down in leashed eagerness, reaching one powerful finger to brush Mennah's cheek, a sound of agonized enjoyment escaping him.

Transferring his gentleness to the hands still half-stuffed in Mennah's mouth, he whispered, *"Ana abooki, ya sagheerati."*

I'm your father, my little one. Delivered in a vocal caress that was delight soaked in wonder and pride and possessiveness and a dozen other emotions.

Carmen's heart splintered.

Oh God. Oh *God.* If she'd had the least doubt before, she no longer had it. He wanted Mennah. *Fiercely* wanted her.

And she'd once had a taste of how fiercely he could want...

Her eyes snapped to Mennah, dread of her reaction mounting, every muscle ready to snatch her up at the first whimper, to soothe her, ameliorate his disappointment, promise she'd soon get used to him. Not that she had any idea how Mennah would do that, when she had no idea how he intended to be in her life from now on, at best as a long-distance father...

Mennah's piercing squeal had her heart almost kicking her off her feet. She surged forward, but Mennah was...she was... She was smiling!

And not any smile, but a huge, dimpled one. Then she was eagerly rolling to a sitting position, holding up her arms, her chubby hands closing and opening, beckoning, demanding to be picked up. By Farooq!

Farooq whooped in elation, scooped her up. *"Erefteeni, ya zakeyah!"* He held her up, his large hands spanning her rib cage. "You're so clever you recognized me at once." He tickled her and she kicked her legs, screeching sharp sounds of pleasure, reaching out both hands to his face, her palms landing anywhere. He let her paw him, his chuckles escalating into guffaws.

Suddenly he took her to his chest, enfolded her, closed his eyes on a deep, long groan. Carmen's heart swelled so fast, so hard she felt it might burst. Next moment, it almost did.

Mennah mashed her face into his neck and went still. Closed her eyes, too. As if to savor her father's feel, inhale his scent, absorb his power and protection.

And Carmen's tears wouldn't be held back anymore.

She swung around, ran out, needing to get as far as possible before a storm of anguish like those that had overcome her all through her pregnancy overtook her.

She closed the door to the bathroom, slumped on it as sobs shredded through her.

To see them together, father and daughter, to know what she'd deprived them of, to know she hadn't had to run, to endure all the pain alone, that he would have been there for her, if only for the sake of the daughter she'd been carrying...

A knock at her back almost heaped her to the floor again.

"Mennah wants to see you now, Carmen."

Farooq's voice was...tender. It had to be the distortion of hearing it through the door... But no, it was tender for Mennah. *She* would never know anything soft or indulgent from him again.

She wiped both sleeves over her eyes, ran shaking fingers through her mess of tangles. Then she opened the door and stepped back into the hall. The sight that greeted her almost sent the dammed anguish flooding again.

Farooq had discarded his jacket, now stood with shirt half unbuttoned, raven mane mussed, glossy locks raining down his leonine forehead, with Mennah perched on his left hip, looking at her gleefully as if asking her to share this incredible find, this giant she'd already twisted around her little finger. He, too, was smiling hugely. She knew it wasn't at her. This was his pleasure at holding Mennah, his whimsy at his unbridled reaction to her.

"So this is what a bundle of joy is." He looked down on Mennah, giving her a playful squeeze. She squealed, buried her face into his chest, her fingers going for the hair. He winced, his lips spreading wider with her first pull. He carefully disentangled her fingers. "*Ma beyseer, ya kanzi es-'sagheer.* It doesn't work that way, my little treasure. Your father's hairs remain where they are. Let me give you something else to maul."

He dipped into his pocket, produced what Carmen assumed was a cell phone. It had probably been designed for him. He pushed a button, had it displaying a video of animals in the wild. Mennah grabbed it in eager hands, lost interest in the moving pictures in just seconds and decided to find out if it was chewable.

Carmen groaned. "Farooq, she'll ruin it."

He gave her an imperious glance. "What if she does?"

"Oh, no, you're not!"

"I'm not what?"

"You're not walking into her life and showering her with grossly overpriced stuff and letting her tear it apart. I'm not letting you turn her into a brat who thinks nothing has value."

Imperiousness gave way to scorn. "A harping mother already?"

"A responsible adult, you mean. Maybe you don't know what that is, having been born submerged in golden spoons, but I'm not letting you do that to my daughter."

"You're contesting my parenting methods? When I haven't had ten minutes to put them into practice? You think I'll indulge her into becoming a thoughtless, useless, destructive creature? Another assumption, Carmen?"

Mennah saved Carmen from withering under his barrage by performing her favorite trick. Testing gravity. The phone clattered on the hardwood floor.

Carmen swooped down to pick it up, looked at him accusingly.

He shrugged, secured Mennah on his hip as she tried to pluck out his buttons. "It's too sturdy to be damaged by anything Mennah can do. That's why I gave it to her."

She simmered. "That's not the point. Now she'll think it's okay to throw stuff that isn't her toys around."

Imperiousness rose further. "She won't. I'll see to it."

"*I'll* see to it. As long as you don't sabotage my efforts."

Their eyes locked, dueled. Carmen felt her heat rising, her breath shortening as she hauled all the height she could into her five-foot-seven frame in answer to his straightening from his relaxed pose for their confrontation, dwarfing her in size and aura.

Challenge suddenly drained from his eyes, intimidation flooding in its wake. "Who were you waiting for?"

She blinked at the abrupt change of subject. "The super. I have a short in the laundry room. He was supposed to come fix it."

One eyebrow rose. "You make filet mignon *au champignons* for him whenever he comes to install a lightbulb?"

"It's for Mennah."

His lips twisted on derision. "Of course. Because filet mignon is a staple of a nine month old's diet."

"I gave her a taste two days ago and she's refused to nurse ever since, so I thought if I gave her another taste, she might…"

The rest of her words backed up in her throat. At the word *nurse,* his gaze moved to her breasts. Breasts that immediately throbbed, their nipples conquering the thickness of her clothes, jutting their hunger. And that he could do this to her with a look, that he should see her helpless response…

His eyes dragged back to hers, pupils almost engulfing the gold in blackness. "So you were waiting for the super. Who didn't come." She jerked a nod. "Show me your problem."

"I'm sure it's just a short. I would have investigated it myself, but I was almost electrocuted once …"

"When was that?"

"I was twelve..." She groaned. "What's with the interrogation?"

"You have quite a lot of hang-ups."

"And you what?" She kept her tone sweet for Mennah. "Think someone who has a couple of phobias shouldn't be a mother?"

He smiled down at Mennah, drawled, "You said it, not me."

"You mean you do think it!"

"I *mean* you said it, not me." The words were sharp steel, the tone softest silk. Of course for Mennah, too. "I say exactly what I mean. You'd do well to remember that, Carmen."

She held her tongue as he haughtily gestured for her to lead the way. At the laundry room, he handed her Mennah. Then, without needing a ladder, he stretched up his six-foot-five frame, examined the bulb socket by the light coming from the corridor. In a few precise actions, with the screwdriver she kept handy on a tool shelf, he dismantled it, did something to the wires inside, put everything back together, screwed the bulb back in place then flicked the switch. The light burst on.

Mennah yelped. Carmen croaked, "I'm amazed."

His lips twisted. "That I know basic maintenance techniques?"

"Considering you have hordes of people waiting on your every blink, I'm wondering why you deemed to pick up the skills."

"I was taught every survival skill early on, then made myself fully self-sufficient. I can do anything anyone does for me better than them. I only abide others' services to save precious time for the more important things only I can do."

Okay. Whoa. "So you're Sheikh MacGyver, huh?"

He smiled. But not at her, at Mennah, held out his arms to her again. Mennah pitched forward, eagerly throwing herself at him.

Carmen berated herself for her stupid reaction. He'd said he wasn't taking Mennah from her, and she shouldn't feel jealous of Mennah's instantaneous and unrestrained delight in him. He was her father. He deserved the same love Carmen got from her.

His lazy drawl aborted her chaos. "About that filet mignon…"

She gulped down the silly tears. "What about it?"

"You say Mennah loved it, and it did smell delicious when I came in. It's a pity to let it go to waste."

"You want to *eat?*"

"I've been known to indulge in the practice."

"But it's already cold."

"You do have means to reheat it, don't you?"

"Reheating will overcook it, destroy its buttery softness…"

"Let me…" He dropped a kiss on Mennah's downy cheek as if compelled before going on, "Let *us* worry about that." Suddenly all ease evaporated, suspicion flaring in eyes that slammed back into hers. "Are you sure you're not waiting for someone?"

"Someone?" she jeered, seeing red. "You mean my 'sponsor'? One of many, no doubt. You think I entertain men in rotation, a few feet from my sleeping infant? Why don't you just call me a whore? C'mon, get it off your chest. I know how men of your culture view easy women and I *was* easy, with you. But I never let you 'sponsor' me. Oh wait, I did. I shared your 'privileges.' But surely you didn't think that was enough for me. You must have checked your collection of priceless cuff links to make sure I hadn't 'shared' more than your hundred-star existence. I trust you weren't too disappointed to find everything accounted for."

His eyes spat danger, sending a frisson of anxiety radiating through her limbs. "Such caustic wit and a rapier tongue. You hid them well."

"I didn't hide them. There was no reason for them to surface. You weren't a domineering brute back then."

The flames in his eyes leaped. "The domineering brute would have walked in here with bodyguards and diplomatic attachés, snatched his daughter and walked out over your weeping, begging body. *I* am still waiting for you to remember basic courtesy and invite me to share the meal you were preparing when I arrived."

And if it were possible to die of mortification, she would have keeled over.

Embarrassed, cornered and mad as hell about it, and at him, she mumbled sourly, "Okay. Fine. But if the meat is leathery and the sauce is congealed, I don't want to hear it."

He pursed his lips. "Eat in silence, you mean?"

She rolled her eyes. "As if."

He smiled then—a slow, hot smile, all for her this time, amused at her wisecrack.

She didn't know what held her up all the way to the kitchen.

Once there she shakily tried to take Mennah to put her in her high chair. He declined, did it himself as if he'd been doing it every day. Then, without being told, he placed Mennah's toys on her tray and she immediately began the game of throw and fetch.

After her bones solidified enough in her limbs, Carmen began the reheating procedure then turned around, only to be stabbed in the heart again by the poignant sight Farooq and Mennah made together, so alike, sharing such an elemental, almost tangible bond.

She located something resembling her voice. "You're taking to your father role spectacularly. And I've never seen her like this with anyone. Not that she's seen many people."

"She recognized me. As I did her. The bond is...elemental."

What she'd just thought. "Yes," she choked. "And I—I'm truly sorry for depriving you of-of..." She made a helpless gesture at them, her hand trembling. "This. But please believe I thought I was doing the best thing. For her."

He said nothing to that. Not out loud. His eyes said he believed nothing she said.

Oh, well. He wouldn't get over his anger that fast.

She inhaled before she blacked out. "I'll cooperate in any way so you'll be a part of her life, be with her whenever possible."

"I will be with her always." This wasn't a statement. This was a pledge. A decree.

"A-always? B-but you live halfway across the globe…"

His gaze hardened. "And so will she."

"But you said…"

"I said I won't take her from you, and I won't. You will both be with me. We will marry."

Four

Something was burning.

Was that her sanity going up in flames? Why else could she have imagined he'd said—said…

We will marry.

But she wasn't imagining him exploding from his relaxed pose by Mennah's high chair and…charging at her…

She blinked as he zoomed toward her, couldn't even brace herself, couldn't think, blink, breathe.

Next second he bypassed her. She whirled around in the draft of his movement, uncomprehending, watching as he yanked the pan off the stove, quickly poured its contents onto the serving plate she'd prepared before turning off the flames.

Then he looked at her, one eyebrow raised disapprovingly. "You seem bound on not feeding me this filet mignon."

Carmen stared at him. Had he really said *we will marry?*

But how? *Why?* He didn't want her. Or at least, he'd never wanted her for more than a passing diversion. He—he…

He was doing this for Mennah.

Comprehension materialized like a jagged rock inside her heart, expanding outward, tearing it apart.

She might have loved him at first glance, but she'd never entertained the fantasy of being his in any way but a fleeting one. That he should be offering the ultimate commitment, no matter the cause, and no matter that he wasn't actually offering, but decreeing it, was…was…

Her mind screeched to another halt.

Oblivious to the effect of the bomb he'd just dropped on her, Farooq bent to the serving plate then straightened, crowding her view, draining the spacious kitchen of light and oxygen. Or she might be about to pass out again…

"Your efforts weren't successful. I believe the dish is still edible. All it now needs is a hostess who deems to serve it."

She gulped, kept staring, frozen.

"Well?"

It was the way he said it. The condescension was too much. She smirked. "Didn't you brag about not needing people to serve you? Why don't you serve it yourself? Or are you handy only with macho stuff? Is serving food a lowly female chore?"

He stared at her as if she'd grown another head.

No wonder. He must be shocked that she could still talk. She knew *she* was. And more, that she could talk to him that way. No doubt people didn't dare sneeze in his presence.

Mennah squealed, demanding their attention. And again this incredible transformation came over his face. His very vibe changed to a soothing transmission as he turned to Mennah with a smile that tampered with Carmen's heart and brain function all over again.

"You heard that, *ya sagheerati?* Your mother thinks she can get away with anything as long as you're around." He turned eyes heavy with disturbing things on Carmen. "She forgets there will be times when you won't be."

The sheer danger of the sensuality infusing his words

kicked into Carmen's heart and loins. It made her melt. It made her mad. It made her reckless.

She tossed her head, straightened from her swooning position. "You really know nothing about me if you think I'd use Mennah as a shield—or as anything. And I need no shields against you."

"You don't?" His stare was all mock-serious interest, giving her more rope. "Are you certain about that?"

Oh God, what was she doing, provoking him this way? She knew she was no match for him, even in her own country. No one was a match for him, anywhere. He was just too powerful, as a diplomat, a tycoon and royalty. She was audaciously speaking her mind counting not on Mennah's presence but on his restraint, his basic benevolence. Both qualities she'd already strained to the limit.

But there was no stopping her now. After the upheaval of the last hour, her emotions were hurtling at the speed of her chaotic thoughts, without brakes.

"It's clear you have an ego of planetary proportions," she taunted. "You must have Atlas-level strength to be able to lug it around. And to think I once contributed to expanding it."

His gaze scraped down her body, making her feel he'd taken off every scrap of clothes, leaving her exposed, vulnerable. "You think your being the first and only woman to ever end a liaison with me contributed to my cosmic ego?"

Was that an edge of bitterness? Had her desertion meant something to him after all, on a personal level?

No. This intensity must be the outrage of a prince who expected people to prostrate themselves before him, who couldn't believe that, for whatever reason, she hadn't, just that once.

She shrugged, all artificial animation and contentiousness draining out of her. "Oh, I'm sure I caused a chink in it. One that could be detected with a microscope."

"We're talking galactic scope. Don't you mean a telescope?"

"Whatever." She exhaled, ran both hands through her hair. "I'm sure your ego is satisfied, now that you know why I did end it."

His eyes followed her movements, the way her shirt stretched over her breasts, spiking her arousal as he drawled, "Oh, I'm not satisfied. You'll have to work to that end. Hard. And long."

And it detonated in her every cell. The memory of every sensation, every tremor of the ecstasy he'd inundated her with, how hard and how long he'd done it, taking her the way she hadn't known she'd needed to be taken, giving her far beyond what she'd imagined she could be given or thought she could withstand.

Her legs wobbled, sending her groping for the counter's support. "If you feel that strongly when only your ego is involved, you take yourself way too seriously. You must try the occasional letdown, maybe even criticism. Very therapeutic."

In answer, he picked up the serving plate, prowled toward her like a panther measuring the moment he'd pounce, savoring the kill. He looked at Mennah. "Your mother is being very brave, Mennah. Or very foolish. Or she knows exactly what she's asking for."

"I'm only asking that you—that you—" The rest struck in her throat. He was nearing her as if he intended to collide into her.

"That I what? Take you up on your challenge?"

She leaned back. At the last moment he slowed, imprinting his body on hers as he reached around her with a hand holding the plate, the other joining it, imprisoning her with an arm on either side as he put the plate on the counter behind her. She once again felt something burning. Her skin this time. Her nerves.

He looked down into her shocked eyes, the gold of his turned to lava. "Wise of you to know when to stop."

Before she showed him just how unwise she was and answered with something inflammatory, he leaned harder into her, pressing his erection into her midriff.

Before she could process that he was aroused, berate

herself for the surge of elation that she affected him still, he pulled back, pulled up the high stool for her, his gaze steady on hers, telling her to sit down and shut up.

As if she could talk now, still feeling his potency digging into her, liquefying her insides. She sat. More like collapsed. Not to obey him or the voice of reason, but because she no longer had solid bones inside her limbs.

She watched with surreal fatalism as he served the filet. Until she noticed he'd taken two thirds himself.

"Relative body mass," he murmured at her glare. "But I'll feed Mennah from my share. Let's see what she can consume."

He sat down beside her, picked up a knife and fork and sampled a piece of the filet. His eyes rose to hers in surprise.

"It's even more delicious than it smells." Before she voiced the crack that catapulted to her tongue, he turned to Mennah. "And you, *ya kanzi,* are so clever you knew how good it is, how to ask for more." He cut a tiny piece over and over, mincing it. "Open up, here comes more..." He carefully forked it into Mennah's eager mouth.

Carmen tensed, ready to jump if Mennah choked, felt Farooq's echoing vigilance. Mennah gulped it down easily, asked for more in delighted shrieks. He chuckled, complied at once.

It didn't even occur to Carmen to eat as she watched father and daughter demolishing his portion. It wasn't until he turned enquiring eyes on her that she realized she was gaping at them.

At that moment Mennah repeated her sudden sleeping maneuver making him relieve her from his silent interrogation, his eyes captured by Mennah once again. And once again the tenderness there shocked Carmen. It was something that, despite his generous ways with her in the past, she hadn't suspected he was capable of.

"Does she always fall asleep that suddenly?"

Carmen could only nod. His lips melted with indulgence as he rose and removed Mennah from her chair, then, enfolding her, walked out of the kitchen. It took Carmen a minute to lurch after him. She caught up with him as he exited the nursery.

He closed the door, said without preamble, "You don't need to pack anything. Make a list of your needs and everything will be at the palace on our arrival in Judar. If you forget anything, order it and it will be brought to you within the hour. After you've settled in, I'll order major store managers to come to the palace with their catalogs for you to pick whatever you wish."

She stared at him. "What are you talking about?"

An edge hardened his rich, dark tone. "We're leaving right away. My jet should be ready for the return trip."

She felt the tethers of her sanity snapping one by one, groped for an anchor against his sweeping incursion. "Listen—"

He cut her off. "If you decide you feel nostalgic about your things, I'll send people to pack every shred you have here later."

"Now wait a minute. I'm going nowhere…."

"You are going exactly where I take you. To my kingdom."

She shook her head, groped for breath. "I—I can't travel…my passport isn't valid…."

"I don't need one to take you out of the country and into mine. My word is enough. Anyway, I'll arrange for one. It will be waiting for you when we arrive at my home."

"I'm not leaving *my* home."

"You are. In case you haven't grasped it yet, I'm having Mennah. Since you are her mother, this means having you, too."

His declaration felt like a slap. A stab.

A hurricane of emotions started churning inside her.

Even if he had wanted her for real, she would have been in turmoil. He wasn't just the man she loved—had *thought* she loved—he was a prince from another culture. She had no idea what being his wife entailed. But to have him state his intentions this way, as if she could have been anyone he'd endure now that he'd accidentally impregnated her, that she *was* just an unwanted accessory that came with the daughter he wanted so much…

Trying to hide her humiliation from his all-seeing eyes, she tried to scoff, "Phew, I hope this isn't how you make your peace proposals. Your region would be up in flames within the hour."

He gave her a serene look. "I save my cajoling powers for negotiations. This isn't one, Carmen. It's a decree. You had my child. You will be my wife."

The world began to tilt, overturn, nausea rising with his deepening coldness and clinical unconcern.

She somehow found her voice again, found something logical to say. "Okay, I appreciate the strength of your commitment to Mennah. But if you want to be her father, you can do that without going overboard. Parents share a child's upbringing without being married all the time, all over the world."

"I'd never be a long-distance father. My daughter will be brought up in my home, my land, exposed daily to my love and caring, taught her privileges and duties as a princess with her first steps and words. But for her best mental and psychological health, she also needs her mother constantly with her. By marrying you, that's what I'm providing for her."

Put that way, what he'd said was incontestable. But… "This can all happen without marriage. I don't want to live in Judar, but I would for Mennah. We can both always be there for her."

"And what would she be if you don't marry me? My love child? Do I even need to state that a marriage, to give her her legitimacy, her birthright, is beyond question?"

"But I…" The quicksand beneath her feet snatched at her. And she cried, "I don't want to get married ever again!"

Carmen's vehemence hit Farooq like a gut punch.

He'd been fighting the urge to close his eyes every time she spoke, to savor that voice that could bring a man to his knees begging to hear it moaning his name.

That was until she'd said…

"You've been married before?" he rasped.

Her face contorted before she looked away.

Something hideous sank its fangs into him. Jealousy? Why? When he'd long known everything they'd shared had been a sham?

He knew why. His instincts still insisted he'd been her first passionate involvement. How could they be so misled? Even after she'd claimed he'd been one in a hundred? How did they still insist *that* had been the lie, and what he'd felt when she'd abandoned herself in his arms had been the truth?

But her upheaval indicated true involvement. A husband who'd meant so much, his mere memory brought that much pain.

Another thought struck him with such violence he wanted to drive his fist through the wall. Had she been on the rebound when she'd accepted Tareq's mission? Had her seeming abandon been part of her efforts to forget the man she'd loved?

"When were you married?"

At his question, she kept her eyes averted until he thought she'd ignore him.

Then a whisper wavered from her. "I wasn't yet twenty. He was three years older. We met in college."

"Young love, eh?"

Her color rose at his sarcasm. "So I thought. Long before he divorced me three years later, I realized there was no such thing."

So *he'd* divorced *her.* And she was still hurt and humiliated that he had. But if she'd been twenty-three then, she'd met *him* two years afterward. Had she still been pining for her ex then?

But what man could have walked away from her? *He* wouldn't have been able to. Hell, he'd been willing to marry her. Granted, he would never have gone as far as marriage if it hadn't been what was best for Judar, but she'd been the only one he could have considered for such a permanent position in his life, the only one he'd wanted in his bed indefinitely.

"I swore I'd never marry again."

Emotions seethed at her tremulous declaration. "Don't you think it's extreme to swear off marriage after such a premature and short-lived one? You're still too young to make such a sweeping, final vow. You'll still be young ten years from now."

She shook her head. "It has nothing to do with age. I realized marriage isn't for me. I should have known from my parents' example that marriage is something that's bound to fail, no matter how rosily everything starts."

"Your parents' marriage fell apart, too?"

"Yeah." She leaned on the wall, let out a ragged breath. "Theirs lasted a whopping five years. Half of them in escalating misery. I was only four and I still remember their rows."

"So you have a couple of bad examples and you think the marriage institution is set up for failure?"

Her full lips twisted, making his tingle. But it was the assessing glance she gave him that made him see himself taking her against the wall. "Don't *you?* You're—what? Mid-thirties? And you're a sheikh from a culture that views marriage as *the* basis for life, urges youths to marry as early as possible and a prince who must have constant pressure to produce heirs. You must have a worse opinion of marriage than mine to have evaded it this long, to be proposing a marriage as a necessary evil to solve a problem. Uh…make that a potential catastrophe."

He gritted his teeth. "Marriage, like every other undertaking, is what you make of it. It's all about your expectations going in, your actions and reactions while undertaking it. But it's mainly hinged on the reasons you enter it."

"Oh, my reasons were classic. I thought I loved him. I thought he loved me. I was wrong."

"Then you were responsible for that failure, since you didn't know him or yourself well enough to make an informed decision. And then, love is the worst reason there is to enter a marriage."

"I can't agree more now. But I know *us* well enough to know that what you're proposing is even crazier, and your reasons are even worse. At least I married with the best of intentions."

"Those famous for leading to hell? Figures. But my reasons are the best possible reasons for me to marry at all. They don't focus on impossible ideals and fantasies of happily-ever-afters and are, therefore, solid. Our marriage won't be anything like the failure you set yourself up for when you made a wrong choice."

"And you think this isn't another one?"

Another argument surged to his lips, fizzled out.

What was he doing, trying to change her mind? This wasn't about her, neither was it about him. This was about Mennah. And Judar. What they wanted didn't feature into the equation.

"This *isn't* a choice. There isn't one," he said.

"There has to be!" she cried, her eyes that of a cornered cat. "And—and you're a prince. You can't marry a divorcee!"

"I can marry whomever I see fit. And you are my daughter's mother. This is the only reason I'm marrying you. What's more, I will declare that we are already married, have been from the beginning. Now we'll exchange vows."

"Ex-exchange vows? But—but we can't do that!"

"Yes, we can. It's called *az-zawaj al orfi,* a secret marriage that's still binding. All it requires are two consenting adults and private vows, recited then written in two papers, a copy for each of us, declaring our intention to be married. We'll date the papers on the day I first took you to my bed. Once in Judar, we'll present these papers to the *ma'zoon,* the cleric entrusted with the chore of marrying couples and we'll make ours a public marriage."

She stared at him openmouthed. At last she huffed in incredulity. "Wow, just like that and voilà, you'll make me your wife in retrospect. Must be so cool to have that loophole with which to rewrite history. Wonder how many times you've invoked that law to make your affairs legitimate."

"Never. And I couldn't have cared less if everyone knew I'd taken you out of wedlock. Everyone knows I accept offers from the women who mill around me, and that I make sure there are never repercussions. I didn't with you. Now it's fortunate I have this method of damage control to fall back on, to reconstruct your virtue and protect Mennah from speculation on the circumstances of her conception."

Her breathing quickened as he flayed her with his words until she was hyperventilating, her color so high she seemed to glow in the subdued light of her corridor.

At last she choked, "God, you're serious." Then a strangled sound escaped her as she whirled around and ran.

He stared after her, his body throbbing, his nostrils flaring on her lingering scent.

If he'd thought he'd wanted her in the past, that was nothing to what he felt now. It was as if knowing all the ecstasy they'd wrung from each other's bodies had blossomed into a little living miracle had turned his hunger into compulsion.

And then there was the way she was resisting him.

That was certainly the last response he'd expect from any woman to whom he deemed to offer marriage. And he'd only ever thought of offering it to Carmen. She'd thwarted him the first time he'd been about to offer it. Now that he had, she seemed to think throwing herself off a cliff was a preferable fate.

It baffled him. Enraged him. Intrigued him. Aroused him beyond reason. It wasn't ego to say he knew that any woman would be in ecstasy at the prospect of marrying him. As a tycoon and a prince, he assured a life of undreamed of luxuries. So what could be behind Carmen's reluctance and horror?

He entered her bedroom, found her facedown on her bed, her hair a shroud of silk garnet around her lushness, her body quaking with erratic shudders.

Was it upheaval over her ex? Was it fear of, or allegiance to Tareq? Was this another act? Or was it something else altogether?

No matter what her reasons were for being so averse, they were of no consequence. He didn't just want to pulverize her resistance, he *needed* to. It was like a red flag to an already enraged bull.

He came down beside her on the bed and she lurched, tried to scramble away from him. He caught her, turned her on her back, captured her hands, entwined their fingers then slowly stretched her arms up over her head. She struggled, arching up in her efforts to escape his grip. She only brought her luxurious breasts writhing against his chest. He barely stopped himself from tearing open his shirt, tearing her out of hers and settling his aching flesh on top of hers, rubbing against her until she begged for the ravaging of his hands and lips and teeth, until she screamed for the invasion of his manhood. That would come later.

But she was panting, whimpering, twisting in his hold, and his intentions to postpone his pleasure, her possession, dwindled with each wave of stimulation her movements elicited.

He had to stop her, before he gave in.

He moved over her, imprisoning her beneath him. She went still as if he'd knocked her out. Anxious that he might be suffocating her, he rose on both arms, removing his upper body from hers, found her eyes the color of his kingdom's twilight. She wasn't breathing.

Before he took her lips, forced his breath into her lungs, he grated, "Now repeat after me, Carmen. *Zao'wajtokah nafsi*—I give you myself in marriage."

She tossed her head on the bed, writhing again. He pressed harder between her splayed thighs, fighting not to reach down and take hold of her hips, tilt her, thrust at her as his body was roaring for him to do. Even without seeking her heat with his hardness, the pressure he exerted still wrenched dueling moans from their throats. "*Say* it, Carmen. *Zao'wajtokah nafsi*."

"God, Farooq…" she pleaded. "Be reasonable. You don't want to marry me. We can find another way…"

"There is no other way. Now say it, Carmen."

Her stricken eyes meshed with his, her flesh burning

beneath him, reminding him of all he'd once had with her, the overwhelming hunger, the affinity he hadn't been able to duplicate with anyone else. He knew that, if he wanted, he'd be buried inside her in seconds, would find her molten for him, knew she'd attain her first orgasm as soon as he thrust inside her. He could get her to promise anything when he was inside her. But he didn't want her consent that way. "Say it, Carmen. For Mennah."

At hearing Mennah's name issue from him like an invocation, she went still beneath him again.

Staring at him with eyes now the color of his kingdom's seas in a storm, she finally nodded her acquiescence, her defeat. *"Zao-zao'wajtokah nafsi…"*

Triumph roared in his system, her quavering words the most coveted conquest he'd ever made. *"Wa ana qabeltu zawajek."* He heard the elation in his voice, was unable to leash it in, saw her wincing at its harshness. "And I accept your marriage. *Alas'sadaq el mossammah bai'nanah*—on the terms we name between us. Again, Carmen, what are your demands? Make them."

"I just want Mennah."

"And you will always have her. What else do you want?"

"I don't want anything."

She was lying again. She had to be. She wanted luxuries and privileges, like any woman. That was why she'd been with him. Why she'd betrayed him. But she knew she'd get them by default being his wife, was pretending she cared nothing for them. A trick as old as woman.

She was also lying about something else. She wanted *him*. He could smell her arousal, feel the need for satisfaction tearing through her as it was tearing through him. He'd soon give it to her, give her everything she wanted. He'd have it all, too.

He'd give his daughter his love, her birthright. And he'd quench his lust for Carmen until he was sated. He'd relegate her to the role of Mennah's mother when he had no more use for her.

He might even divorce her if he wished. He didn't need her consent for that. He'd decide it, and it would be done.

But if his memories of what they'd had were anywhere near accurate, if the agony he was in at the moment was any indication, that wouldn't happen for a long time yet.

A very long time.

Five

"Will you need anything else, *ya Somow'el Ameerah?*"

Carmen squinted up at the thin, dark, bird-of-prey-like man who stood above her, body language loud with deference.

He'd called her *Somow'el Ameerah.* Again. She couldn't get her head around it. Wondered if she ever would.

It had been *Somow'el Ameer* Farooq this and *Somow'el Ameer* Farooq that since they'd set foot outside her building. All the way out of the country. It *had* taken his word—well, under a dozen words—to get her out of there. It had taken even less to make her *Somow'el Ameerah.* Highness of the princess. Her royal highness in Arabic. He'd waved his magic wand and made her a princess....

It had really happened. He'd stormed into her life, had uprooted her existence all over again.

He'd literally uprooted it this time. He'd snatched her from her home, from her country, from everything she knew, had soared with her to the unknown. And she had a feeling she'd never be back. Not for more than visits anyway. And since she had no one to visit anymore, she doubted she'd even be back at all…

Her lungs emptied as another breaker of anxiety slammed into her, pushing her under, the foreboding of stepping into the quicksand of Farooq's existence pulling at her, the forces synergizing, paralyzing her under their onslaught.

Oh God, what had she let herself in for?

She was on board his jet, on her way to Judar. There was no going back, no way out, now or ever…

"Ameerati?"

The concern in that word slowed down the spiral of agitation. The man with the hawk's face and eyes was doing it again. Probing her with solicitude, scanning her with an insight she'd bet could read her thoughts. She'd also bet he'd seen through Farooq's declaration that he'd reclaimed his wife and child, ending the misunderstanding that had led to their separation.

She remembered him well. He'd been there from the first time she'd seen Farooq, his shadow. Hashem. Farooq had told her to ask Hashem for anything in his absence. He was the only one Farooq trusted implicitly, in allegiance and ability, discretion and judgment.

Had he trusted him with the truth? Or had the shrewd man worked it out for himself? Or was everything obvious to everyone?

What did any of that matter? Hashem would take what he thought to his grave, would reinforce his prince's version of the truth with his last breath. No one else would dare even think but what Farooq had declared to be the truth.

"Ameerati—are you maybe suffering from air-sickness?"

Carmen winced at his gentleness. It made her realize how raw she was, how vulnerable she must seem to him. She shook her head.

His gaze was eloquent with his belief that she needed many things but couldn't bring herself to ask for any.

"Please, don't hesitate to ask me anything at all. *Maolai Walai'el Ahd* wants you to have all you need till he rejoins you."

Smart man. Being the über P.A. that he was, he knew the best way to make her succumb to his coddling was invoking his master's wishes, the master he'd called…

Maolai Walai'el Ahd.

Carmen started, the three words that had flowed on his tongue with such reverence erasing all she'd heard before and after them, blasting away what remained of her fugue, blaring in her mind.

Had she misheard? Was her Arabic translation center offline…?

She'd heard just fine. All her senses had been functioning to capacity since she'd set eyes on Farooq. In fact, she felt she was developing hypersensory powers. Everything was amplified, sharpened, heightening the impact of every stimulus, yanking responses from her that ranged from agitation to anguish.

Her translation center was fine, too. That was the sturdiest part in her brain. She understood what *Maolai Walai'el Ahd* meant all right. It was literally my lord successor of the Era. Aka, crown prince.

Farooq was the crown prince now?

But how? A year and a half ago, he'd been only second-in-line to the throne of Judar. What had happened to the first-in-line?

This information jogged another in her mind, igniting it with new relevance. The king of Judar was ill. From all reports there wasn't much optimism regarding his return to health. And if he died…

Farooq would soon become king of Judar.

And she'd graduate from plain Ms. Carmen McArthur to *somow'el Ameerah to Maolati'l Malekah* in no time flat.

Malekah. Queen. Yeah, sure.

The preposterousness of the whole thing burst out of her.

Hashem's dark eyes rounded at her outburst. Self-possessed as he was, she'd managed to shock him.

Yeah, him and her both. In fact, the cackles tearing out of her shocked her more than they could him.

"Ameerati?"

His bewilderment, the way he kept calling her "my princess," spiked the absurdity of it all. She spluttered under an attack of hysteria, felt her sides about to burst with its merciless pressure. "I'm s-sorry, Hashem, I'm j-just—just…"

It was no use. She was unable to stem the racking laughter, to muster breath enough to form a coherent sentence.

The man stood before her, watching her with heavy eyes that seemed to fathom her to her psyche's last spark, until she lay back in her seat, trembling with the passing of the fit as if in the aftermath of a seizure.

"God, you must think me a total flake," she wheezed.

"I think no such thing," he countered at once, his voice a soothing flow of empathy that jarred her.

God, she would have preferred anything to bristle at, to brace against. His kindness only knocked her support from beneath her, left her sinking. She hated it. She'd survived by counting on no one's goodwill, by doing without support of any kind. She had to keep it that way, now more than ever. Or she'd be destroyed.

"I apologize if my surprise gave you the impression that such an unfavorable opinion crossed my mind for a second, when the exact opposite is true. I fully realize how overwhelmed you must be. Everything has happened so fast, and *Maolai Walai'el Ahd* is formidable—and, when he has his sights on a goal, inexorable." This man *was* all-seeing. And they sure saw eye to eye in evaluating Farooq. "But he is also magnanimous and just. You have no reason to feel apprehensive, *ya Ameerati*. Everything will be fine."

Okay, here was where their concord ended. Even if she agreed the qualities mitigating Farooq's ruthlessness existed,

Hashem didn't know that Farooq no longer considered her entitled to his magnanimity, was dealing out his brand of justice by using Mennah to pressure her into giving up her freedom and choices. She was also not buying Hashem's prognosis for a second.

How could everything be fine? Ever again?

She could only pray it would one day grow tolerable.

To have Hashem's allegiance as an extension of his to Farooq, mixed in with his pity for her as a casualty of his master's inescapability, a man of such insight and importance in Farooq's life, might grow comforting. Right now she had to make him leave her to her turmoil.

She answered his original question. "Thank you, Hashem. I promise to avail myself of your services if I think of anything."

With a last probing look, he bowed and walked away, obviously loath to leave her in her state without offering service or solace.

Instead of relief, the moment he disappeared from her field of vision, chaos rushed in to fill the vacuum he'd left behind. Everything her eyes fell on contributed to her imbalance.

In both her personal and professional lives, she'd lived and worked where power brokers weaved their pacts, where billionaires flaunted their assets in an addiction to competition and for leverage in business. She'd been in the bowels of private citadels, of diplomatic and hospitality fortresses. She'd studied beauty and luxury, learned their secrets and power and how to utilize their nuances to enthrall the most jaded senses, smoothing her clients' path to winning their objectives through the goodwill engendered by perfectly designed and realized events.

This jet surpassed anything she'd ever experienced in taste and sheer, mind-numbing opulence. She'd had an idea it would be something unprecedented when she'd laid eyes on it. It was surely the first bronze-finished Boeing 737 she'd ever seen. Then she'd set foot on its plush carpeting and had plunged deeper into the surrealism of being with Farooq, being introduced as his wife and deluged in the veneration of a culture that revered its royals. All her knowledge of the best that money could buy had only sent her mind boggling in appreciation of every detail around her.

She gaped again at every article of genuine art, every flawless reproduction in design, everything spanning centuries and cultures, the classical meshing with the modern, the Western with the Middle Eastern, disparate forms of beauty melding with luxury and futuristic technology in a symphony of unlikely harmony.

She fingered her seat's armrest. A panel slid open, exposing a set of buttons. Hashem had said they gave her control over all amenities, from service to entertainment to climate control. She pushed one with a screen icon. Her head snapped to the left as an eighteenth-century mural disappeared with a smooth whir to reveal a screen of a size she hadn't known had been manufactured yet.

No need to experiment further. There'd only be more wonders, a refresher course as well as a first-time close-up of Farooq's affluence and power. And this was only his transportation…

She was staring down at her sweaty palms, fighting another wave of dizziness when her senses overloaded. She almost moaned at the force of the breach. Farooq.

She didn't want to raise her eyes. Didn't want to watch him approaching, obliterating her autonomy, shrinking the world into the parameters of his presence, his desires, his decrees.

She did, saw his eyes firing with satisfaction at her slumped pose. He closed in on her like a force of nature, two men from his extensive entourage trying to keep up with him, documenting his muttered orders. They'd disappeared by the time he reached her, a partition sliding behind them to isolate the dining area where he'd seated her before going to "arrange matters" from the rest of the jet.

He looked down at her with the same intensity as he had when he'd been on top of her, demanding she repeat his land's ancient marriage rite.

Her heart lurched like a captured bird in her chest.

Oh God, she'd really done it.

She'd really married him.

She'd lain beneath him, feeling him imprinting her, hard with an indiscriminate reaction to feeling a female body beneath him, had repeated the words that had bound her to him in a marriage without love or respect—or anything, really. A sham. A cold-blooded ruling on his part, a capitulation on hers.

It's all for Mennah. It's all for Mennah.

Maybe if she repeated the mantra enough she could endure this. The feeling of forever plummeting into an abyss.

She snatched her gaze away from his, fingered Mennah's baby monitor receiver, praying for her daughter to wake up so she could run to her and be spared another exposure to Farooq.

All she heard over the amazingly low drone of the jet's engines was the soothing Middle Eastern music through the surround sound system, and Mennah's soft breathing.

Mennah had awakened during their departure, had bubbled with excitement in response to Farooq's delight in her all through the trip in his limousine right up to the jet and through takeoff. She'd executed her sudden sleeping maneuver an hour ago, and he'd secured her car seat in one of the jet's bedroom suites.

"You haven't eaten."

At his rebuke, her eyes fell on the masculine, square-cut silver service set and cutlery, laid out before her on midnight-blue silk tablecloth, nestling among sparkling crystal and crisp white napkins. She'd picked something from the extensive menu Hashem had provided. It had been served with great fanfare under polished brass domes, placed to simmer over gentle flames. Hashem had raised the covers to show her the cookbook perfection below and the aromas of the haute cuisine creations had hit her salivary glands. Her stomach had fed on its emptiness, churned with revulsion against being catered to as if she was a beloved mistress when she was just a necessary evil, an abhorred hostage.

Corrosion surged again in her throat. "I'm not hungry."

His jaw hardened. "You haven't eaten in the last seven hours. Your stomach must be feeding on itself by now."

Gee. What was it with men suddenly being able to read her mind? Or was she just too predictable to live?

"You'll have to excuse my stomach if it isn't functioning to your calculated expectations. After all that's happened in said seven hours, all it feels now is the urge to heave out its nonexistent contents. Just imagine what it would do to existent ones."

"You're trying to tell me I make you nauseous?" Exasperation flashed across his face before morphing into derision. "Still playing games? Still challenging me to expose your proclamations for the feminine taunts that they are?"

She pressed a fist to her head in an attempt to mitigate the pressure building inside. "Just why do you want me to eat? I wouldn't miss a few pounds. If I ever manage to part with them."

His eyes changed hue, melted down her enervated body like his fingers once had, following a path of seduction, of destruction over her. "You *have* gained some weight."

She snorted. "Yeah, tell me about it."

"I will. In detail. When I'm in...possession of the full range of...particulars."

"Gee, thanks. Just what every woman wants to hear. An inventory of her expanding assets."

He leaned, ran a light touch down her left forearm to her ring finger, circled a nonexistent ring before sawing his finger between hers. "Expanding is an inaccurate word. Your assets have...appreciated." He pushed a button on her seat's armrest, swiveling it around, picked up her hand, tugged her out of her slouch, bringing her face level with his groin. "See for yourself how appreciated they are by inspecting *my* expanding assets."

A second before he had her performing a hands-on assessment, she snatched her hand from his as if he'd been forcing it into an open fire, darting a look around.

He encroached closer, coming between her legs, making her feel dwarfed, dominated. "Don't worry about accidental audience. We won't be disturbed for anything less than an impending crash. Do get on with your reconnaissance, put your mind to rest about the efficacy of your weapons."

She rolled her eyes, tried to resume breathing. "One more transparent double entendre and you win a food processor."

His lips spread on a grudging smile as his legs did the same to her knees. He leaned down, his arms braced on both sides of her head, one hand weaving into her hair, pinning her head to the seat, tilting her face upward as his descended. "Don't start a game you don't intend to play to the end."

She lurched as his breath lashed her lips, fresh and male and all him, the movement wrenching at her anchored hair, bringing tears stinging her eyes. His pupils flared, almost obliterating the irises, her name rumbling low in his chest. "Carmen..."

He was going to kiss her.

Every sensation of every time his heat and hunger had devoured her, deluged her with pleasure, drained her of will blossomed, a surround-memory replaying the glide of his flesh on hers, the taste of his tongue, of his vigor inciting her greed for more. Her heart stampeded, her lips, her nipples stung, every nerve discharged...

She couldn't sit there and pant for him to kiss her.

Her fingers landed on her armrest. The seat swiveled away, taking her out of his reach.

She felt him brooding down on her bent head for a breath-depleting moments, before he exhaled, moved away.

He lowered himself in the seat beside her, swiveling it to face hers. "More games, I see."

She huffed. "I didn't comment before because your accusation left me speechless. What games, for God's sake? The only act I ever pulled in my life was when I was out of my mind needing to get away before you found out I was pregnant. It was so transparent you must have laughed your head off every time you remembered it. I wouldn't know how to play games if I wanted to. If I did, don't you think I'd be in a better situation now?"

His eyebrows shot up. "What better situation is there? Every woman alive would kill to be in your place."

This time the laugh that tore from her hurt. "Every woman alive would kill to have her motives, her *anguish* ridiculed, her character reviled, her life railroaded?"

His gaze hardened, flared before something like amusement flooded its depths, softening the edges, putting out the fire. "Any more R words? Recounting how I routed you out, ran roughshod over you then through a bit of rough-and-tumble got you to reiterate the vows that have roped you to me, *ya rohi?*"

The endearment, *my soul,* speared her with its sarcasm. Its impossibility. The rest of his wickedness had a counteractive effect, tickling her. And she couldn't help it.

She made a face at him, stuck out her tongue. "Show off."

He threw his head back on a surprised guffaw, his face blazing with enjoyment, turning his beauty from breathtaking to heartbreaking. She found herself smiling back at him in yet another demonstration of unabashed idiocy.

And it was as if they were back to those magical times a year and a half ago, when everything between them had been rich in rapport—to use two more *R* words—when they just had to say anything and the other would understand, appreciate, the desire to please as strong as the desire to pleasure or be pleasured, the smiles flowing uncensored, unfettered.

But like any illusion, the moment of communion passed. The warmth kindling his face evaporated, the mirth drained to be replaced by the coldness that had turned him into the stranger she'd left a lifetime ago.

He finally drawled, "So you claim you're not playing games. What's this about being nauseous then? Are you going to go on a hunger strike in protest of my alleged crimes against you?"

"I *am* nauseous. If you were flying into the unknown to a strange land where you knew no one, wouldn't you be?"

His chin rose. "You know me. That's all you'll need."

She shook her head at the irony. "*Do* I know you, Farooq? In the biblical sense, you mean? Oops, wrong faith here."

He leveled his gaze on her, his eyes glinting with danger and a resurgence of reluctant humor. "You'd be surprised how alike all faiths are. And besides knowing me, thoroughly, in that sense, you know every other thing that counts."

"Really? So being the crown prince of Judar now is one of the things that don't count? I just discovered that—by accident."

His eyes narrowed. "And the discovery disappoints you?"

She sagged further in her seat. "It *staggers* me. Staggers me *more,* to be accurate. You're not just a prince, you're *the* prince. And to think I was going to pieces contemplating what being the wife of a Middle Eastern prince entailed. Now I'm scared witless at what is expected of the crown prince's wife. If I'm woefully unsuited for the first position, I'm disastrous for the second."

He looked away, presenting her with the magnificence of his slashed profile. He was silent for a long moment, looking lost in thought.

Then without looking back at her, he drawled in a distant, distracted tone, "You speak Arabic. It was why you were chosen. I never thought to ask if you did. You never spoke it, but when I thought of it later, I realized you understood when my men did, when I reverted to using it in extremes of passion."

She blinked. What was this jump in logic? And she was "chosen"? For what? But what had her heart shriveling was his indifference as he mentioned his reversion to Arabic during their intimacies. That had always sent her spiraling into mindlessness, knowing it was what had heralded his loss of control, his plunge with her into the depths of ecstasy.

When he didn't add anything more, continued staring at nothing, she had to say something. "I do speak Arabic. If you mean that's why I was chosen to organize your conference, it *was* what made me stand out, made me land such a huge opportunity. Though I'm better in the formal dialect than your colloquial Judarian—"

He cut across her aimless rambling. "You read and write it?"

Her heart dropped a beat at the sub-zero inflection in his voice. "Y-yes. Better than I speak it, actually. Pronunciation has always been a bit tricky. I'm okay I guess, but I could be better—"

He again cut her off. "Besides Arabic, you speak, read and write French, Italian, Spanish, German and Chinese?"

He'd finally read the file his security/intelligence machine must have compiled on her, had he?

She exhaled. "Yes, if not all with the same proficiency…"

"And apart from being an events planner, of which conferences of international scale were but one type of event you handle, you've worked as an interpreter, a hostess and a facilitator in the range of diplomatic functions and every other sort of multinational event. You've set up a cyberconsultancy service organizing such events, networking providers, coordinating themes, putting every detail together from the ground up from the comfort of your home."

Still unable to understand where this was leading she answered, "Yes, but how is that—"

He again aborted her query, still staring into space. "The wife of the crown prince of Judar has to be beside him in formal and informal meetings with dignitaries from around the globe. She must be acutely aware of the cultural protocols of every nation and faith, be versed in the art of etiquette and dialogue with everyone from servants to magnates, from emissaries to heads of states. She has to have an appreciation for all forms of art, an understanding of global historical landmarks, be up-to-date about contemporary world state and technologies. Mastery of seven languages which include Arabic would turn such a wife into an unprecedented find."

He looked at her then, held her stunned gaze, his giving nothing of his thoughts away. Then he drawled, "If I'd tailored a woman for the position of my wife, I wouldn't have come up with one more suited for it than you."

Six

Something frantic flapped inside Carmen's chest.

It felt too much like hope.

She pressed her palm over it, trying to stem its painful surge. Not that she knew from experience, but she'd heard that where it blossomed, hope defied logic, sprouted with a life of its own, blasted through barriers of caution and self-preservation.

It seemed to be doing so now. It kept saying, if he believed her experience and skills would be of use to him, maybe her life in Judar wouldn't be a prison of duty outside her role as Mennah's mother, and she'd find purpose and function there, in his life. And maybe—just maybe—one day they'd forge some sort of relationship, and their marriage wouldn't remain the lie he intended to propagate for Mennah's legitimacy and birthright...

"Now you heard what you're fishing for, what more reasons will you give for being 'staggered' that I'm now the crown prince?"

His disparagement hit her with the force of a landslide, smothering the chain reaction of optimism.

So he didn't believe she could be valuable to him in his new position? He'd been leading her on only to slap her down?

Shoved back into the pit of resignation, her hand shook as she raised it from her chest to her eyes, pressing the stinging away. "I already told you why I think this a huge mistake. But you've made up your mind about me and whatever I say, no matter if it's the truth, won't change it for you." She shot him what she hoped was a look of unconcern. "Why bother wasting more breath?"

His cynical pout was proof of her deductions. He still prodded, "Waste some more, just for me. Tell me your version of the 'truth.'"

"What do you care about my 'version' when you already know everything about me since the day I was born, Farooq? You're probably in possession of details I don't even remember or know."

"And how am I supposed to possess that omniscient knowledge of your life?"

"C'mon, Farooq. Your intelligence machine must provide you with a phonebook-thick dossier on everyone who comes within a hundred feet of you."

"That's true. But I don't have one on you."

He didn't? But he must have…*oh*. Oh. A sarcastic huff escaped her. "That's right. My life would fill two pages. Double spaced."

He clicked his tongue. "That's not a version of the truth, that's an outright lie, Carmen. The things I found out about you from talking to you, from *taking* you, would fill a book. I was wrong about the content of the book, but whatever the truth is, it'd still fill a book. But neither book would contain the most basic data about you, what you never divulged. And for some reason, it didn't matter and I didn't have you investigated." She knew the reason, all right. Because *she* hadn't mattered. "Then I did, but you'd erased your existence so well, I came up with only your professional portfolio, address—and a photo." His palm pressed over his heart, like hers had done minutes ago. Was that where the photo was? "Of you and Mennah."

Her eyes remained prisoner to the telling gesture, her own heart battering itself against her ribs, even when she wasn't sure what it told her.

It was his claim that he knew nothing about her that slowed her heartbeats. Could it be?

She *had* used methods learned in the circles where people erased their pasts or reinvented themselves for safety and second chances, first to cover up parts of her past to escape the heartache, then to remain hidden with Mennah forever. But she hadn't thought her cover-up tactics would be so effective that he wouldn't find out everything about her if he put his mind to it.

But then he probably hadn't; had only tried to find her, not find out *about* her. Trailing someone wasn't the same as researching them. Yes. That had to be it.

She sighed. "Well, what you came up with was enough. You found me, found out what I ran to hide. Anyway, I never tried to hide who I am from you, so you do know everything that counts."

"Really?" He mimicked her recent irony. "Beyond knowing what you can do, in your job, in bed…" The way he said that, in such menace-coated sensuality, made her snicker. He raised one eyebrow. "So glad you find me funny. Even when I'm not trying to be."

Her earlier outburst rippled to the surface, her facial muscles hurting under its renewed onslaught. "It *is* hilarious, hearing you refer to me as some sort of femme fatale."

"They don't come any more fatal, Carmen."

She looked around, looked back at him, pointed to herself

in open mockery. "You're talking about me? Boy, now *that's* a parallel universe version of the truth. A Bizzaro world one. Whom have you been talking to? Someone I turned down and he decided to paint me as a black widow? To justify his failure as he propagates tales of his lucky escape? One thing's for sure. You didn't get this from my ex. Apart from him, you're the only man who was in a position to comment on my so-called sexual powers, and you both certainly…"

Her voice trailed off. What was it with those attacks of truthfulness? Had she misplaced her discretion during the months she'd barely talked to another adult?

It was futile to kick herself over it now, anyway. She'd already said too much. The whole truth and nothing but.

Now his eyes were glinting with things that sent goose bumps cascading through her like a storm through a wheat field.

Before she could theorize what those things were, impassiveness blanked his gaze, neutralized his voice. "You're telling me I'm one of only two men in your life?"

His ego relished that, did it? So what? She was only expanding it from planetary to stellar proportions. Nothing mere mortals could tell the difference between.

"I *am* telling you that," she ground out. "And you know what, you're not only the second, you're the last."

He sat forward, coming closer like a tide that would overwhelm her if she didn't back away. "Of course I'm the last."

She didn't. "You are, because even if I wasn't off men after you and my ex, I'd never expose Mennah to a strange man."

He stilled, intensifying the menace in the calmness of his next words. "You're likening me to your ex-husband?"

She didn't care. "And it's blasphemy to liken your highness to anyone? Well, considering he's a mommy's—and daddy's—boy with loads of unearned wealth and power, the similarities are plenty. If this arouses your royal fury, it sure isn't worse than practically calling me a liar, a fraud and an all-round whore."

* * *

Farooq was lost for words for the first time. Ever.

Not because he found none to answer her insults with. What struck him mute was Carmen's allegation that he was the only man, besides the husband she'd married too early, she'd been intimate with. In effect, her only lover. The claim had flowed from her with the impetus of a statement of fact, had lodged into him with the force of an ax in the gut. Of the truth.

Could he believe it? She'd been Tareq's mole, but not his plaything? She hadn't been anybody else's? Her abandon in his arms had been just for him, as his had been just for her? Discounting the ex-husband she spoke of now without continuing emotional attachment, with disdain even, he'd been, no matter the reason, her first, and as she vowed, her last passionate involvement?

Everything in him insisted that was the truth. That she'd told him many truths today.

But she'd done so only up to a point. He could feel her hiding things. Major things. Her deal with Tareq, no doubt. And fool that he was, he didn't want to corner her into a confession.

He didn't want to hear it. Not anymore.

With each moment near her, he believed more and more that it hadn't been as sinister as he'd believed on her side, that she hadn't realized the scope of the damage she'd been sent to do. That maybe Tareq had even convinced her she'd be serving a greater good by toppling him from the succession.

If this was true, maybe Tareq had caught her at her lowest ebb, and she'd made an out-of-character decision. But once she'd succumbed to their affinity, to the pleasure they'd shared, seen him for what he was and Tareq's lies for what they were, she'd forgotten her mission. But she'd gotten pregnant and Tareq had changed the rules, and she'd panicked, feared retribution from all sides, feared for Mennah for real, had fled, hidden…

Or maybe he was looking for ways out for her because he was falling under her spell again.

And he was. Instead of the cold loathing he'd believed would be his only reaction to her, he was mesmerized by everything about her, reveling in her company, unable to get enough of her wit, her outspokenness and contentiousness and defiance, all so in contrast with the vulnerability she strove to hide. Then came her physical effect. She'd had him hard and aching within minutes of seeing her again. It was all he could do now not to drag her to the floor and just have her. Just *take* her again. And again.

He would have her. Would take her. Just not now.

He'd wait. For their wedding night.

As for the truth, whatever it was, there was nothing to be gained by ripping open festering wounds. It wasn't as if he needed to have this resolved. It was all pointless now that he'd won. Now that the throne of Judar was safe from falling into Tareq's hands. Now that she'd fallen into his. For as long as he deemed to hold her there.

And *now* he could turn to her taunt.

She dared imply he and her ex had unearned wealth and power in common? Was that how she viewed him? When she must know of the global enterprises he'd built from the ground up, multiplying his kingdom's wealth? After she'd seen for herself a six-week sample of his life as peacemaker and relief-bringer?

No. She'd meant it as the worst insult she could think of.

But even if she'd qualified it as retaliation, he'd make her pay for it. Make her beg. For the chance to atone. For the end of torment. For the pleasure he knew, just *knew,* beyond doubt, only he had ever brought her, could ever bring her.

His equilibrium regained, his mind ordered and made up once more, he challenged her, "So you take exception to my…assumptions. What others could I have when I know nothing about you beyond what your actions led me to believe?"

She seemed to shrink in her seat. "There isn't much to know. I was born to Ella and Aaron McArthur, a megawealthy businessman and his ex-P.A. second wife. Their marriage fell apart and I lived with my mother and her assortment of... strange men, until she died, then moved in with my father and his fourth wife till the day I turned eighteen. On acquiring my first boyfriend, whom I eventually married, a year later, my father, who hadn't checked to see if I was still alive since I moved out, popped back in my life all eagerness and blessings. Turned out the marriage was part of a coveted merger. When it turned out I wasn't the asset they all thought I would be, both the marriage and the merger were dissolved and my father moved to Japan with his fifth wife. When I was twenty-five, my mother's estate became mine—her accumulated alimony and divorce settlement from my father, plus what she got from her 'sponsors.' It was a bundle, the fortune you intimated I got from a 'sponsor' of my own. I bought the apartment, put the rest for Mennah in a trust fund, since I earn enough to support us both in comfort. See, I overestimated the complexity of my life. That's *one* page, triple-spaced."

Farooq stared at her, thoughts rearranging, long-entrenched ones being forced out, new questions rushing at him.

She'd been born then had been married into money. But she'd implied her father hadn't supported her after she'd moved out, that her ex-husband had divorced her without compensation. Was that why she'd accepted Tareq's mission? Had she gotten so used to the good life her mother and her "sponsors" followed by her father and her ex's wealthy family had provided that she couldn't bear to wait months till she claimed her inheritance?

That no longer felt like enough of a motive. Or a motive at all. Not with her disinterest in anything material while she'd been with him replaying in his mind, another manifestation that had the conviction, the texture of truth.

So it hadn't been about money after all? Had it been maybe

a reckless lashing out after all the major relationships in her life had failed or ended, throwing herself into something dangerous, maybe even self-destructive? She *could* have easily been throwing herself into an abyss when she'd thrown herself in his arms. She'd had no way of knowing he'd turn out to be a civilized or even sane human being, let alone the lavish lover he'd been with her. He could have been a monster who lived to collect slaves, or to abuse beauties and maim them before snuffing out their lives.

Suddenly he was incensed. Far more so than he'd ever been. At her for endangering herself that way. Whether her goal had been financial gain or temporary rebellion or oblivion.

His rage deflated as fast as it had mushroomed.

No. She might have been groping for the catharsis of a wild fling with a sheikh prince, or the fantasy of playing Mata Hari or securing a quick fortune or all combined. But she hadn't risked herself. She *had* known she'd be safe with him, would be cared for and catered to, pleasured and pampered. She'd known it, felt his nature and intentions with the first look into his eyes.

As he'd thought he'd felt her nature and intentions with the first look into hers?

But if what he'd seen was all she owned, and he could now find out the truth about her inheritance, if she still had to work, where had the money Tareq had said she'd cheated him for gone? Or had Tareq cheated *her* out of their agreed upon price?

Ya Ullah, was this how men went insane, revolving in unending loops of suspicion?

Kaffa. Enough. It didn't matter anymore, how it had been.

Suheeh? Really? If he told himself that enough times, would it register so he could finally let it go?

Another question blasted through, proving that letting go didn't seem possible. But then, it was a paramount question.

How had his people not found out all she'd just told him?

Before the question fully formed, the answer detonated in his mind. Tareq. His counterintelligence must have foiled Farooq's investigations, in fear he'd find her, find Mennah, the final card pulverizing Tareq's conspiracies to hang on to the succession.

B'Ellahi, how had he not seen this before?

Loathing for his cousin shot to a new zenith.

But anger and hatred aside, now that he knew what he had to counteract—what he might not need to counteract now that Tareq had no more reason to block his research into her past— it would be easy to check out her story. As she must know he would.

This meant one thing. She'd told him the truth.

His gaze clung to her averted profile. He no longer saw the seductress who'd breached his barriers, entrenched herself in his responses, his fantasies, his cravings, or the traitor who'd deprived him of his child, who'd almost let Judar's throne fall into the hands of a man guaranteed to topple it. He saw only the little girl who'd been exposed to her parents' damaging behavior, who grew up let down, neglected, used, maybe even abused, by everyone who should have cherished and protected her. He saw only a woman who'd suffered. A lot.

He gritted his teeth against a resurgence of fury, against all the people who'd blighted her life. Against the softening that assailed him toward her as he realized she'd been doing everything to protect her—*their* daughter, from all she'd suffered, living for Mennah, thinking only of her safety and happiness.

He might be starting to understand her motives, her psyche, but it made no difference. He couldn't forget, nor would he ever forgive what she'd done.

He exhaled, casting away the weakening, pushed a button. It was time to get back on track.

"Are we crashing?"

Farooq turned inquiring eyes on Carmen at her croak.

She gestured toward Hashem, who'd entered their compartment carrying what looked like a treasure chest right out of the times of genies and flying carpets. "You said that's the only time we'd be disturbed."

"This is a planned intrusion." He beckoned to Hashem who strode forward, his eyes scanning her, ascertaining her condition before casting a look of disapproval on the untouched food.

Farooq rose, extended a hand to her. She must have taken it, risen, walked. Either that or he had hypnotic and/or teleportation powers, too. Without knowing how, she found herself sitting on a plush couch in yet another compartment drenched in sourceless lights and deep earth tones, in the serenity of sumptuousness and seclusion.

Hashem placed everything on a two foot-high, six-foot-wide, square polished mahogany table in front of her and Farooq. He opened the chest, produced two boxes, one the size of a shoebox, the other half its size, both like the larger chest, handmade, ornamented in complex mosaic patterns of gold, silver and mother-of-pearl. Next he produced a variegated brown leather folder and small drawstring pouch. Everything was in perfect condition, but looked ancient, heavy with history and significance.

An urge rose, to run her hands over the textures and shapes, feel their mystique and power flowing through her fingertips. She settled for soaking in each detail. The folder and pouch embossed with intricate gold-leaf borders, Judar's royal crest at their center: an eagle depicted in painstaking detail, its wings arched up to enclose the kingdom's name written in the ornamental *muthanna* or "doubled" calligraphy with each half of the design a mirror image of the other in a tear-drop oval. The boxes' blend of repoussé, inlaid and engraved *zakhrafa* embellishments that married Arabian to Ottoman, Persian and Indian designs.

Hashem's deep murmur tore her gaze back to him. She couldn't believe how welcome his presence was. How she didn't want him to leave. She couldn't take more of Farooq undiluted.

Not that an army would make effective reinforcements. Not against Farooq. Or what she felt.

Sighing, she eyed Hashem in resignation as he bowed to them and retraced his steps out of the compartment.

Farooq opened the pouch, producing two brass keys that looked designed and forged in the Saladin era. He opened the small box, produced three stamps and an inkpad of the same design, before opening the folder and extracting two papyrus-like papers and two crimson satin ribbons. Then he reached into his suit pocket—opposite the one she assumed held the photo—and extracted a gold pen.

He extended it to her. "Let's see how well you write Arabic."

She gaped from the pen to the papers to his eyes. "You're giving me a written Arabic proficiency test?"

"I am interested to see your level, yes. But I'd hardly give you royal papers reserved for documenting state matters of the highest order to test your spelling and handwriting."

So all this stuff was as momentous as she'd sensed. Her heart wrenched to a higher gear. "So what do you want me to write?"

He pushed the pen into her flaccid hand. "I'll dictate to you."

"Yeah, you live to do that, dictate," she grumbled.

One side of his lips twitched. His eyes remained solemn. "Write, Carmen."

The depth of the command, the gravity, squeezed her dry of breath. She sat forward, tremors buzzing through her like a current, took in the papers in front of her, handmade, each one a unique blend of beige-tan with multicolored fibers off-setting its pearly, heavy silk finish.

She put down the pen, wiped her hand on her pants. His clamped onto it. She bit her lip on the jolt as his other hand delved inside his jacket again, produced a monogrammed hand-kerchief, placed it on the paper, put the pen back in her hand.

As soon as the tremors allowed her to firm her grip on it, he started dictating. She geared her brain to the right-to-left writing of the exotic letters that always felt more like drawing.

She'd written a whole sentence before it registered.

This was a verse from a sacred scripture invocation.

She raised her hand off the paper, her eyes to his. "What is this? An incantation to sign over my soul?"

His eyes smiled now, a smile drenched in that overriding sensuality that was as integral to him as his DNA. And in seriousness. "Essentially, yes. This is *az-zawaj al orfi* language. You are free to add to the basic pledges, if you're feeling creative, to express how eager you are—were—for our union."

"This is the paper the cleric will read?"

"Yes. And along with my copy, it will reside in the royal files, proof of Mennah's legitimacy."

"So it's an official document. And you want me to get creative." The teeth sprouting in her stomach sank into its walls. "Just give me the exact language. Better yet, paraphrase."

He pouted in mockery, continued dictating. She kept writing until he told her to sign her name. She did, raised her eyes. She'd only written two paragraphs. "That's it?"

He shrugged one massive shoulder. "It takes only so many words to pledge oneself unto eternity." He reached for the paper, ran his eyes over her efforts. "I'm impressed."

Without waiting for her reaction to his praise—an upsurge of irritation for wanting it, for being so pleased at having it— he turned to his own paper, started writing the words he'd dictated her. And she forgot everything as she watched those fingers that had once owned her flesh, moving in the certainty of expertise and grace, producing a *req'uh* script of such beauty and elegance, such effect, it did feel like a spell.

After he signed both documents, had her sign his, she rasped, "So not only a prince, a tycoon, a philanthropist, a diplomat and a handyman but a calligrapher, too."

"Yet another side-product of my unearned privileged existence." His eyes mocked her, documented her chagrin at being caught out at a pettiness, at the need to apologize for it, at her anger at that need and at him.

Not that he waited for her to come to a decision about which urge to obey. He let go of her eyes, pressed three stamps to the inkpad, marked the documents with each. Judar's royal insignia, the Aal Masood family crest and the date. The one he'd fixed to the day they'd first made lo—had sex.

She stared at the seals. The dark red ink became viscous as it dried, like congealing blood. She did feel she'd just signed a blood pact. A binding, unbreakable one.

He rolled up both documents, tied each with a ribbon, placed them in the larger box. "Those papers aren't considered legitimate without two witnesses. As soon as we land in Judar, Shehab and Kamal, my brothers, will add their seals and signatures to ours." He rose, extended a hand to her. "Now we'll check on Mennah."

Everything in Carmen squeezed. Fists, guts, lungs, heart.

Mennah. The reason he'd just taken her on.

The reason she'd just signed her life away.

Seven

A gentle nudge jogged Carmen out of the twilight between exhausted sleep and strung wakefulness.

It took her a second to realize they were touching down.

Her sandpaper-lined eyes scraped open. And there he was.

Farooq sprawled opposite her, an indulgent lion letting his overzealous cub crawl all over him. He was still watching her.

He scooped Mennah up with kisses and gentleness, rose, came to stand over her. They both looked down on her from what felt like ten feet, his face opaque, Mennah's ablaze with glee.

"Do you need a few minutes to wake up, or shall we go?"

She shook her head, sprang to her feet. Her sight darkened, disappeared. His arm came around her, would have released her the moment she steadied if not for Mennah. Their daughter threw an arm over Carmen's neck, bringing the three of them into an embrace.

Carmen went limp with the blow of longing at feeling him imprinting her in such tenderness, even if borrowed, at

Mennah mashing herself against them as if seeking their protection, their union. At the hopelessness of it all.

She lurched away before her eyes leaked, held out her arms for Mennah. Mennah reached back.

Farooq only walked on. "I'll carry her."

She scampered, kept up with him. "But she wants me now."

"Do you want your mother, *ya gummuri?*" he cooed to Mennah, who looked back on Carmen with dimples at full-blast, as if she thought her father was playing catch-me-if-you-can. Carmen gave him a glare from an angle Mennah wouldn't witness. His Mennah-smile remained on his lips but his eyes frosted over. "She will see her land for the first time, be seen in it in my arms, a princess held up by her father the crown prince for all to see."

Carmen's legs gnarled with the power of image he projected, the poignancy. She rasped, "Put that way, you go right ahead."

Not that he was awaiting her approval. His strides ate up a path to the exit, leaving it up to her to keep up or not.

She scrambled in his wake, looked at the multitime zone clock on the way out: 9 a.m. in New York, 5 p.m. here. It had been sixteen hours since she'd found Farooq standing on her doorstep.

Sixteen hours. They felt like sixteen days. Sixty. Far more. It felt as if her life before those hours had been someone else's, her memories sloughing off to be replaced by another reality that had unfolded with his reappearance.

Then she stepped outside and into another world.

And it was. Though her life had taken her all over the world, Judar felt...unprecedented, hyperreal. The azure of its spring skies was clearer, more vibrant, the reds and vermilions starting to infuse the horizon as the sun descended were richer in range and depth, its breeze, even in the airport where jet exhaust should have masked everything, felt crisper, more fragrant, its very ambiance permeated by the echoes of history, the lure of roots that tugged at her through her connection with Mennah, whose blood ran thick with this kingdom's legacy.

Mennah, who seemed to recognize the place, too.

Secure in her father's power and love, she looked around, eyes wide, face rapt as she inhaled deep, as if to breathe in the new place, fathom it, make it a part of her.

Carmen knew how she felt. With her first lungful of Judarian air, she felt she'd breathed in fate.

Then she heard his voice, the voice that had steered *her* fate since she'd first heard it, that seemed would steer it forever, permeated with intensity and elation.

"Ahlann beeki fi darek, ya sagheerati."

He was welcoming Mennah home. And only her.

Carmen groped for the railing of the stairway, feeling as if a wrecking ball had swung into her.

How stupid could she get? She wanted him to welcome her home, too? When it wasn't her home, only Mennah's? When the only reason he'd brought *her* here, where he didn't want her, was Mennah? How could he welcome her where she wasn't welcome?

She nearly gagged on the toxicity of her feelings of alienation. She *had* breathed in fate, could feel it all around her. Mennah's. She was just its vehicle. Her fate was not even a consideration here.

Farooq's arm came around her shoulder.

She couldn't bear him to act the supportive husband, lurched away, continued her descent, blurted out, "I thought you were taking us to Judar, not to some space colony on another planet."

A look of satisfaction chased away the watchfulness in his eyes as he glanced around. "The airport meets your approval?"

"Approval?" Her gaze swept the spread of structures extending as far as her vision reached into the horizon in all directions. "Try stupefaction. This place looks as if it covers all of Judar."

"What you see is the rest of Judar Global Central, Judar's latest and largest project, a Free Zone residential, commercial and manufacturing complex, the biggest and most advanced in the world. The airport is but part of this new community and is the world's largest passenger and cargo hub."

"Tell me about it. This is the first airport I've ever seen with…" She counted. "*Ten* parallel nonintersecting runways."

"It is built for the future, designed to handle all next-generation aircraft. The parallel runways allow up to eight aircrafts to land simultaneously, minimizing in-air queuing. Last year it handled twenty-six million passengers. This year we plan on exceeding the thirty million mark." He tickled Mennah, who was waving around, demanding his attention. "You want me to explain to you, too, *ya sagheerati?* You see those huge glass and steel buildings? Those are four passenger terminals, twelve hotels and I can't remember how many malls. It's lucky we have over two hundred thousand parking spaces, eh? And you see these signs? Each color leads to a transportation linking the airport to Durgham, Judar's capital and your new home, a high-speed freeway, the rail system and the metro."

He turned to Carmen, catching her elbow as her feet wobbled with her first step onto Judarian soil, on a red carpet, no less.

She averted her eyes to the black stretch limo parked at the end of the carpet as his entourage flitted in and out of her field of vision. "It's amazing how everything feels—I don't how to say this—steeped in the stuff of Arabian Nights fables. I don't know how, when everything is so modern, futuristic even. It must be those subtle cultural touches to the designs." She stopped because he did, shifted her feet on the ground, suppressed a shudder. "No, scratch that. It's the land itself."

He looked down at her, the declining sun infusing the gold of his irises with fire, or probably just revealing it. "You feel the land, don't you? It's calling to you. What is it saying?"

It's saying, run now, or you'll never leave. In life or death.

Before she confessed her thoughts out loud, a rumbling separated itself from the airport's background noise, rose to the pitch of approaching thunder.

Caught and held by his probing gaze, she felt no alarm. Probably because he transmitted none, and Mennah seemed to fear nothing in his arms. Carmen interpreted the din only when he released her from his focus, turned it toward the source.

Her reaction still lagged until he said, "Here they are."

It was the pleasure and affection in his voice that made her follow his gaze toward a helicopter the like of which she had never seen, a matte-black majestic alien lifeform.

In seconds it landed a few dozen feet from them in a storm of sound and wind, deafening her, sending her hair rioting, her loose clothes slapping against her flesh. Farooq and Mennah were all smiles as he pointed out the chopper to her, their hair flapping like raven wings. She heard Mennah's screeches of excitement only when the rotors winded down as both doors opened and two bronze colossi descended and started toward them.

Both Farooq's height, one maybe even taller, in body-molding casual chic, one in blacks, one in grays, they looked like the embodiment of the forces of darkness and twilight, modern-day gods descending from the heavens to rule the earth.

And she wasn't being fanciful here. Not by much. She bet they inspired such hyperbole in everyone. She'd bet everyone felt everything holding its breath, slowing down like in movies to emphasize the gravity of their approach.

As the sun slanted golden light and shadows on them, worshipping every sinew of their bodies, every slash of their faces and strand of their hair, it was clear they didn't possess only the same physical blessings and impact as Farooq, but like him they had power and the entitlement of an ancient birthright encoded in their genes. The same genes. Though they resembled him only vaguely, it was unmistakable that they were his blood.

And it was as unmistakable that they were both staring at her, giving her what felt like a total body and mind scan.

She found herself groping for Farooq, this time sagging into him when he contained her in the curve of his body.

As the two men came to a stop at arm's length, they had mercy, terminated their visual and spiritual incursion of only her and instead took in the image of the nuclear family they made.

Did they know how far from the truth this image was?

They had eyes only for Mennah now, who was looking back at them with fascination. And excitement.

A shard of mortification drove in her heart.

Had Mennah's agitation in the presence of strangers been *her* fault? Had she infected her daughter with her own fear, of losing her, transmitted her distrust of everything and everyone? Had she been influencing her into developing neuroses without knowing?

If she had, that was over now. With Farooq's appearance in her life, Mennah had learned fast that she had a defender for life, one with the power to wrestle the world to its knees.

Gray man looked at Farooq before his gaze was dragged back to Mennah. But it was enough. In that moment as obsidian eyes had melded with gold ones, she'd seen a lifetime of understanding, of unbreakable loyalty and unshakable love. Though she'd never had anything like that in her life, she recognized the connection, understood its significance. Even had Farooq not told her about this meeting, she'd have known. This had to be his brother.

Curious about him now she was certain of that, she examined him as he initiated interaction with Mennah, an approach of both eagerness and sensitivity, which the baby responded to wholeheartedly.

He was Farooq's height, with the same daunting proportions, but his face was more symmetrical, his hair a longer sweep down his collar, a rainfall of deepest black with strands kissed by indigo as if manifesting his electric aura, deepening the impact and darkness of his eyes. The eyes of a hypnotist.

He let out a harsh sigh, his rugged face becoming etched with tenderness and wonder as he flicked a finger down Mennah's velvet cheek. *"Ya Ullah, ma ajmalhah."*

Farooq exuded pride and pleasure as Mennah rewarded the ragged comment with a "squee" and a grab of the exploring finger. *"Naffs kalami bed'dubt lamma ra'ait'ha."*

My exact same words when I first saw her.

"Mafi shak, hadi bentak."

No doubt, this is your daughter.

Those words, spoken in a bass voice that was even deeper than Farooq's, brought her eyes to the man in black. She'd been avoiding looking at him. Of the three of them, he unsettled her most.

He was taller than Farooq, maybe by an inch or so, but that wasn't why he overwhelmed her. It was his face, his eyes, what radiated from him, similar to Farooq and the man in gray, but laced with more harshness and danger. The slashed angles and hewn planes of his face were more merciless, the night of his hair total, the trimmed beard deepening the impression of ruthlessness, echoing the desert and its raiders, his eyes that of a lone wolf, hard and unforgiving.

"W'hadi maratak?" he said without looking at her.

And this is your woman?

And she found herself saying, "If you're speaking Arabic to exclude me from this exchange, *I'll* be courteous and tell you it won't work and warn you not to say anything not meant for my ears. According to Farooq, my grasp of Arabic is 'impressive.'"

Four sets of eyes turned to her, three of them boring into her with reactions comparative to each man's character. Farooq's vacillated between that humor he kept losing control over and his intention to add this to her running tab. Gray's was the surprise of someone who couldn't believe he'd mistaken a tigress for a housecat, both amused and intrigued by his faux pas. Black's was unimpressed, his eyes telling her he was quick to judge and impossible to budge. No one got a second chance with him, and she was another false move away from eternal damnation.

But since she was already eyes-deep in it, what the hell.

She shrugged. "I see Farooq has no intention of introducing us. But you know who I am, and, while your identities seem to be need-to-know info he evidently thinks I don't need to know, they're not hard to work out. You must be Shehab and Kamal. And here I have to ask, is this what I should expect from now on?"

Farooq cocked an eyebrow at her. "What is 'this'?"

"This." She swept a gesture from him to Shehab and Kamal. "Are all Aal Masoods like this?"

"Like what?" he persisted.

"Larger-than-life? Description-defying? Will meeting you in your masses be like stumbling into a superhero convention?"

His lips tilted at the corners, his eyes crowding with a cacophony of emotions. She was surprised to feel amusement ruled them all. "Are you flirting with my brothers, Carmen?"

"I'm not even flirting with *you*. I'm stating facts. The three of you are the biggest proof of how grossly unfair life is. Giving you all that must have created severe deficiencies elsewhere. Your personal assets could be divided among three hundred men and they'd still be damn lucky devils."

Gray threw his head back, gave a hearty guffaw. "*B'Ellahi,* I've made up my mind. I like you already, Carmen." She looked at him, unable to hide her gratitude at finding one among the hulks surrounding her who wasn't impossible to reach. He extended a hand to her. Her hand rose automatically, trembled as his closed around it. His smile turned assessing at feeling the tremors arcing through her. He shook her hand slowly, the fathomless black of his eyes brimming with astuteness and good nature. "I'm Shehab. Second son. Kamal is our baby brother."

Said baby brother shot her an implacable look, not following his older brother's example and extending a hand of acceptance.

Gathering the rest of her courage, feeling Farooq's eyes burning the skin off the side of her face, she turned to Kamal. "I'm Carmen. And you don't look like anyone's baby brother."

Was that a hint of surprise in his eyes now? That someone dared breathe, let alone speak her mind, in his presence?

"With two years between me and my 'big' brother, I don't feel like such a baby." Was that a hint of relenting, too?

"So that's why you all look the same age." She cast her gaze between them, shook her head at the magnitude and range of virile beauty displayed before her. "I bet it's great to have siblings so like yourself, so close in age. I would have loved to have any siblings at all, any family—but there you go. I hope you realize how lucky you are to have each other."

The three men exchanged glances, betraying no reaction to her words. She felt it anyway. Surprise. At her words. At their reaction to them. And to her after hearing them.

When they turned their eyes back to her, it felt as if it was with new insight, more interest. She wasn't sure she liked the intensified focus she'd provoked.

She waved between them. "I didn't know you could do that."

"Do what?" Shehab asked, his eyes intent on her.

She wondered at how relative everything was. Seen alone, Shehab would be intimidating. Among his harsher brothers, he was the one who felt kinder, more approachable, the one she gravitated toward, counting on his leniency, his empathy.

She exhaled. "Stand around in the open like that, together."

"You mean Judar's heirs in one sniper's bull's-eye?" A definite shard of lethal humor glinted in the depths of Kamal's eyes. "Though we always take every precaution, it *has* been drilled into us from birth never to put all eggs in one basket, so to speak. Farooq failed to tell us why he made an exception this time."

Farooq shrugged, seemingly no longer concerned with the progress of her first meeting with his siblings, playing with Mennah. "I had to coordinate with you face-to-face. As for the rest, I told you everything there is to know."

Shehab huffed in mockery. "*Aih,* you sure did. I have a daughter," he reproduced Farooq's voice. "Be there when I arrive. I get married tomorrow."

"Tomorrow…?" Carmen choked on the word.

"You didn't get that telegram, eh?" Kamal sounded as if he relished knowing Farooq hadn't put her in the picture, either.

She shook her head, everything getting hazy, the juggernauts surrounding her cutting off air and light and reason. "I got nothing. He only mentioned you to explain your role as witnesses to our—to the-the *orfi* marriage and…and…"

Shehab and Kamal stared at her, no doubt feeling her about to snap with anxiety, then turned to Farooq, eyebrows raised.

Farooq ignored him, his eyes on her, hard with—what? Suspicion? Of what? Her reluctance, her outright panic? Well, surprise. "Do you have any reason for wanting to put off the ceremony?"

"I—I barely set foot here, I need more time…"

"You had sixteen months."

The endlessness of space around them turned into a vise, crushing her. She'd thought she'd have more time…

At that moment, Mennah lurched forward, throwing herself into Carmen's arms. As if she knew how much she needed her, to abort the spiral of agitation, to remind her of why she was doing this.

Shehab, it seemed, thought it time to end the confrontation. He held out his arms to Mennah, who pitched herself at him, as if continuing a game she'd devised of throwing herself around the circle of her new-formed family.

"*Ana amm.*" Shehab held her up, smiles wreathing his face as she wriggled and giggled, performing for her captive audience, pushing her enchantment factor to maximum. "I'm an uncle to this delightful treasure. It's amazing, humbling, and it puts everything in perspective. We're *uncles,* Kamal. Farooq, you're a *father. Ya Ullah,* do you realize what a miracle this is? It's all that matters." He turned on them, holding Mennah out. "She is."

Kamal held out a hand to Mennah, as if unsure whether he could touch her. She grabbed his hand, tried to use it as a chewing toy, before repeating her catch-me maneuver. He caught her, the large hands capable of crushing men trembling, shock and other fierce emotions detonating in his eyes. Pride, protection, possessiveness. He was Farooq's brother, all right.

After a few moments of surrendering to Mennah's pawing, he groaned, "Let's get those marriage papers signed and sealed."

Farooq's face was satisfaction itself at his unyielding brother's capitulation, at how Mennah had secured it without effort. He beckoned, and Hashem materialized carrying the chest.

Farooq took Mennah back from Kamal. Shehab reached for the chest, his eyes on Carmen, as if saying he was on her side. Kamal's eyes, clearing of the emotions Mennah had provoked in him said he'd be watching her, that one step out of line, even if forgiven by Farooq, would guarantee her a formidable enemy for life.

Well, one out of two—make that three—was better than zero.

Farooq pulled her back to him, looked down at her for a moment before he let her have Mennah. "Wait for me in the limo. I'll coordinate tomorrow's ceremony with Shehab and Kamal. Then I'll take you and Mennah home."

Home. They were going home. A home she couldn't even imagine. Farooq's home. Mennah's now. Would it be hers? Could it ever be?

The questions ricocheted inside her until she felt pulped.

She again tried to let the splendor rushing by distract her. It wasn't every day that she drove through a city that had materialized out of revolutionary architects' wildest dreams while retaining its ancient mystery through restored historical sites that blended into the whole, its rawness in preserved natural sights.

No use. She felt no pleasure at the amazing vistas they were sailing through. Thanks to Farooq. He sat at the end of the couch that ran the side of the limo beside Mennah, who was passed out in her car seat, worn-out by her uncles' delight and stimulation, by her newfound extroversion.

"I must know now what you want for your *mahr*."

She lurched. She'd thought he had nothing more to say to her.

He'd always have something to say to her. Something distressing. This time something she'd only heard about, never imagined could ever be applied to her. The *mahr*. The dowry. Paid to the bride in exchange for the right to enjoy marital relations.

She huffed. "Thank you, but I still don't want a sponsor, even a legalized one. A certain amount of 'sharing your privileges' is unavoidable since I'll live with you and Mennah, but that's as far as I'm going, so let's leave it at that."

Imperiousness fired his eyes, tempered by tinges of…what? Humor? Deliberation? Astonishment? She had no idea. "The *mahr* is an obligatory gift from groom to bride. It is your right."

"I can't get my head around the words "obligatory" and "gift" in the same sentence. To my mind they're mutually exclusive."

"Obligations govern relationships, and when observed at their beginnings, they ensure you aren't short-changed or victimized if anything goes wrong. You entered a relationship before observing only the dictates of romantic rubbish, and where did it lead you?"

"Out the other side without owing anyone anything. To freedom with dignity. I wouldn't have it any other way."

He leaned forward, scooped her up, brought her to rest half over him in one move, one of her legs pressing against his hardness. He kept her gaze tethered as he whispered, soft and inescapable, "Name your *mahr,* Carmen."

She lay against him, flayed by his warmth and breath, suffering a widespread neurological malfunction. "I can name anything? You once told me you'd meet any demands I made."

His hand weaved in her hair, his eyes intent on her lips. "Anything. As long as it isn't something unreasonable."

She tried to sit up, felt him expand at her wriggling. "Let's see, what *can* be unreasonable enough for you? How about your fleet of jets? And a hundred million dollar token?"

He ground her harder into his erection. "Done. And done."

This jolted her enough to break the body meld. "Whoa. *So* not done. I was joking. You know the concept, don't you?"

His eyes glowed like slits into an inferno. "I appreciate a slap and tickle as much as the next man, Carmen, but this is no joking matter. Your *mahr* is something only you can estimate, and it is something I'm honor-bound to give you."

She ran her hands through her hair, raised them. "Okay, okay. How about a blinding stone in an obscene size?"

"You will have my mother's betrothal jewelry and whatever you wish of Judar's royal jewels. This is your *shabkah,* not your *mahr.* Shall I consider my fleet and the sum you specified your choice?"

She shot up sitting straight. "You certainly shall not. What would I do with a fleet and a hundred million dollars?"

His pout was cynicism itself. "You want investment advice?"

"Listen, I'm not cut out to be a businesswoman or a shopper, so assets and money would be wasted on me." His eyebrows rose, spoke volumes. She cried, "Does this *mahr* have to be material?"

He threaded his fingers together. "As long as we're alive, yes. When we're ghosts you can have an immaterial one."

"Clever. You know what I mean. Can't it be something…moral?"

"Material things can be quantified. And they last."

"If you think so," she scoffed, "then I feel sorry for you."

"Says the woman who married for 'moral' considerations only to find out how lasting those were. And what would the 'something moral' you want to ask of me be? Love?"

The word, his ridicule as he threw it at her, skewered her. "We agreed that doesn't exist. Or if it does, it doesn't matter."

"Then what do you want?"

She took a deep breath, asked for something as impossible. "A clean slate."

Eight

In a life that had exposed him to betrayals, danger and conspiracies of world-shaking scope, few things ever took Farooq by complete surprise, by storm. If fact, only three things had.

They all involved Carmen.

The way he'd felt when he laid eyes on her. Her telling him she'd had enough of him and walking out. And now, her request.

A clean slate.

She was asking him to surrender his anger, to deny his memory, to erase his knowledge of her crimes. She wanted to start fresh. What for? A way back into his good opinion and goodwill? Into his emotions? Another shot at his faith? Everything she'd once made him lavish on her, and she'd squandered?

The worst part was how she understood him. How she always said or did the perfect thing at the perfect time to have the desired effect on him. His first reaction to her request had been to snatch her in his arms, singe her skin off with the violence of relief, the liberation of capitulation. He still wanted to let his new insight into her ordeals and her expo-nential effect on him wipe his memory, soothe away the lac-erations, drive him to hand her power over him again. He fought the temptation with all he had.

She wasn't here because this was a shiny new beginning and it was her choice to start over, but because he'd given her none. If it had been up to her, no matter her reasons, he would have never found her and Mennah, and Judar would be heading for destruction.

He must never forget that.

But she was flushed with the agitation of hope, while the dread of the little girl who'd grown accustomed to being turned down clouded the heavens of her eyes, made the red-rose petals of her lips tremble, and his convictions evaporated as they formed.

And that was why he couldn't relent.

She'd been destructive as his mistress. As his wife, the mother of his daughter, she'd be devastating. If he let her.

He braced against the pain as he ended this hope for some-thing he wanted as much as she seemed to…more. "Since temporal control to change the past isn't one of my powers, a clean slate is probably the one thing I can't grant you."

It was a good thing he'd given himself that pep talk. Oth-erwise he would have relented upon seeing her flame dim.

Which was what she probably wanted him to see.

Which he *did* see. That this was no act. That she was scared of her new life, wanted to make peace, wanted a chance. A second chance. And he'd just denied her that.

He bit back a retraction, a promise of all the chances she wanted, if only she'd promise never to lie to him again. Which proved her spell was turning into compulsion. She'd promise anything he wanted. Words were easy.

Or they were supposed to be. The ones with which he fought the thrill her seeming lack of avarice provoked had to be forced to his lips kicking and screaming.

"Since you won't name your *mahr,* I'll use my discretion. And you'll accept it. I'm not having this debate again."

Her flame went out.

Unable to bear the dejection coming off her in waves, he looked out of the window, pretended to ignore her again.

Tomorrow night he'd give her his undivided attention.

Approaching Farooq's palace was like one of those scenes in movies where the heroine nears a boundary that, once crossed, would plunge her into a fairy tale. Or a nightmare.

She was about to cross into one wrapped in the other.

Not that she cared right now. She'd asked for the impossible. He'd pointed that fact out. And she felt…gored.

She knew why she had. Asked. Why she did. Feel this way. Because he made her hope there was a chance it wasn't impossible. A chance to start over, be more than a stray lost in a world she had no place in, clutching a tattered shield of wisecracks and the inconsequence of her dignity.

"Is all this yours?"

The question surprised her. She hadn't intended to ask it.

His eyes turned back to her. "I have my own home, but even if I haven't been living here for the past three years to deal with all that my uncle can't deal with now, we would have come here first anyway. The royal palace is where all royals marry."

This kept getting better. "You mean this is *the* royal palace? And we'll live with the king? And his family?"

His expression filled with mockery. "I assure you your in-laws will not be a source of intrusion. The palatial complex stands on over one hundred hectares, with a three-mile stretch of beach, and its connected annexes boast three hundred twenty rooms and ninety-five suites. And that's not counting the central building housing the royal quarters and halls for royal functions. It will be like living in a hotel compound where you only see other residents with a previous appointment."

"Oh." She couldn't imagine living in the place he'd described, let alone having any role, any say in it. The moment she tried to fine-tune a picture of herself as the crown princess, or the queen overseeing it all, her mind screeched at the enormity of projections, groped for anything to wrench her focus away.

The sights unfolding before her came to the rescue.

Draped in the illumination of a breathtaking sunset, jutting from a peninsula hugged by crystalline waters, the palace crouched like the starship of some giant alien race among many satellites, nestled between expanses of lush landscaped gardens and pristine white beaches, a construction conjured by the highest order of magic, the collaboration of a thousand genies in the era when impossibilities were everyday occurrences, and transported intact through time. She found herself saying all that out loud.

He gave an amused nod. "The forces creating this place were those of hundreds of masters of their trades, from designers to builders to painters to engineers from around the world, who combined faithfulness to Judar's legacy of design and architecture with luxury and state-of-the-art technology. Who needs genies when the magic of imagination and skill can create this?"

"Who indeed."

That was the last thing said as the limo, which she'd long realized was part of a cavalcade, passed through gates ensconced between two towers flying the Judarian flag high above the thirty-foot fence, through street-wide paths lined by palm trees and flower beds and paved in cobblestones. They passed through one tier after another of more gates, courtyards and pavilions until they reached the central grounds of the palace and its extensions.

Everything bore the intricacies and distinctions of the cultures that had melted together to form Judar, the towers leaning toward the Byzantine, the gates toward the Indian, the pavilions the Persian, each twist of metal, each arrangement of stone, every arch and pillar and spire a testimony to one culture's influence or the other, and all ultimately Arabian.

She finally exhaled her admiration. "This place sure gives Buckingham palace and the Taj Mahal a run for their money."

"Since construction was completed five years ago and the royal family moved here from the old palace in Durgham, it has become a national symbol of similar importance, and in this last year has been rising in the ranks of the world's most coveted tourist attractions."

"Tourists are allowed inside?" That was a surprise. She knew how Middle Eastern monarchies guarded their privacy at all costs.

"In certain areas of the palace and its satellites, two days a week, yes. I recommended this to my uncle and he obliged me. Tourism has spiked by three hundred percent since the practice was implemented."

"Wow. That was a great thing to do, Farooq, to give as many people as possible a chance to experience the wonder of this place. To tourists it must feel like walking through an oriental fable."

His smile was tinged with cynicism. "I've heard this is the impression this new palace creates. It doesn't have much to do with reality but that's tourism for you, capitalizing on the notions held by strangers to the land, on the fantasies the culture projects."

Before she could analyze his words, wonder if any pertained to her, the limo stopped. And before she could blink, Farooq grabbed Mennah's car seat, exited the car, then handed her out, too.

And she set foot on the ground of what he'd called her new home.

She stumbled. He kept her up, then had her walking, saved her from looking like a clumsy idiot instead of a self-possessed princess in front of his subjects and employees. He had her caught up in his body, held up by his power, propelled by his will. Her pulse escalated until she feared her heart would either burst or implode. The majesty bombarding her oppressed her, its implications in her tiny life unthinkable. Her breath sheared through her lungs in a mini panic attack as they walked up the expansive steps of the stone palace, which soared four towering levels and echoed every hue of the desert, its roof system sprouting with a hundred domes covered in mosaic glass and gold finials.

"This place...it's amazing." That wasn't what she'd intended to say, but a strange excitement was taking over through her agitation. "I can almost see the grounds and terraces with the stairs leading down to the beach and marina lit with strings of lanterns and brass pillars bearing torches, live *ood* music playing between a blend of accents as head honchos from around the globe move from one world-shaping banquet to another."

She turned up entranced eyes, found him staring at her in the semidarkness, his eyes flaring like burning coals.

Then he exhaled. "Who better than you to see the potential of this place? Regretfully, with my uncle ill for so long, it has seen no such events in the five years it's been in existence. Our marriage will be the first festive occasion to take place here."

He fell silent as footmen dressed in ornate uniforms materialized to open the palace's twenty-foot, inlaid-in-gold-and-silver mahogany double doors. She looked back to catch its details, then turned to find more wonders to capture her eyes. The circular columned hall they were crossing had to be at least two hundred feet in diameter, with a soaring ceiling at least one hundred feet high, its center sprawling under a gigantic stained-glass dome.

Her gaze swam around the superbly lit space, got impressions of a sweeping floor plan extending on both sides of the hall, of pastels and neutrals, of Arabian/Moorish influences in decor and furnishing, modern ones in finish and feel on a floor spread with polished marble the color of the sand the palace lay on.

Suddenly Farooq said, "Had we had more time, I would have turned over the ceremony to you. Judging by the success you made of the conference you arranged for me, with this place and every power at your disposal, you would have turned it into an event that would have become the stuff of new fables."

His seeming belief in her abilities sent her heart soaring. The images he provoked shot it down, rent and bloodied. Images of the whirlwind of preparations for a life- and world-changing event, the reign of *her* imagination and skills when freed from constrictions of budget and possibilities, of escalating excitement, of jitters of responsibility, of pride of achievement. Of anticipation of ecstasy…

If-onlys cut off her breathing. She stumbled again.

Again he kept her upright, kept talking as if he hadn't crushed her with more futile dreams. "But with my uncle so frail, I wouldn't have gone all-out even if we had the time. It's for the best we didn't."

They entered an elevator that seemed to be an extension of the hall, seemed not to move at all before the doors opened again. Into the past. Into the heart of Arabian Nights.

He tugged her through a huge hall ringed with Arabian-style arches leading to the bowels of a palace within the palace.

The incense fumes rising from mosaic burners hanging from the ceiling hit her compromised balance. He supported her, his touch deepening the dreamscape quality of it all as they passed the central arch through pleated damask drapes woven in rich-earth Berber/Moroccan patterns into a passage lined by sculpted-rock columns. At the base of each, an antique brass lantern blazed, giving the columns' engravings the impact of incantations.

She stared ahead as they approached massive cedar double

doors worked in camel bone and silver that looked as if they'd been transported through millennia intact. They swung soundlessly open with a murmur and a touch from Farooq.

Whoa. Holy voice recognition and fingerprint sensors!

The feeling of stepping centuries both backward and forward in time intensified as they entered another hall with golden light radiating from henna sconces on warm sand-colored walls leading into gigantic living and dining areas interconnected by more arches. Many rooms lay hidden behind closed doors. The whole place, with its enormous proportions, its lavish yet tasteful decorations and furnishings with that incredible ethnic and ultramodern blend, redefined the laws of beauty and luxury.

He led her into one of the living areas. A spherical, intricately fenestrated brass lantern hanging from the ceiling with spectacular chains lit the space. The starry canopy it created showcased the Egyptian mosaic, hand-carved furniture and the plush Moroccan-style couches. It also cascaded over Farooq, adding an unearthly effect to his beauty.

Finding her eyes back on him, he said, "All the things you specified are here. If you need anything else, order it from Ameenah, your head lady-in-waiting. She's Hashem's wife. She'll also get you acquainted with the mechanisms running the place, privacy, security, Internet and entertainment, to mention a few. I'll give her a list of what needs to be done tomorrow. Tonight, relax, take a shower and have an early night. I want you well rested. Tomorrow is the biggest day of your life."

The last sentence rocked her. She turned her swaying into a bend to pick up a hand-woven silk brocade pillow, her tremors into interest over its intricate patterns.

"So these are my and Mennah's quarters?"

He gave her a steady look. "These are my quarters. Ours now. Our bedroom suite is through this passageway." He flicked a hand toward it before indicating the closed doors around them.

"Pick one of these rooms to be Mennah's, where your ladies-in-waiting can tend her when both of us are occupied."

"But I thought…" She couldn't continue, couldn't breathe. Just *couldn't*.

He gave her a serene look. "You thought…what?"

She fought to the surface at his prodding, rasped, "I—I thought I'd have separate quarters."

"And how did you come by that thought?"

Suddenly anger slammed into her. She grabbed at the strength it infused into her limbs, her voice. "I came by it because this isn't a real marriage."

He smiled. As mirthless a smile as those got. "Oh, this is a real marriage. I'd say it's far more real than any you've ever heard about. Notification of our belated marriage ceremony has made it to every embassy. During our flight I received the personal congratulations of every head of state on earth, and though it's on such short-notice, the confirmation of attendance of four major powers' presidents and a dozen kings and queens."

A stunned giggle escaped her. "That's what you call not going all-out? Oh, man…"

"All-out would have been having everyone here for ten days as the royal wedding proceedings unfold. Three days and nights of festivities ending in your henna night, and seven more of palace on national celebrations following the wedding. Having a ceremony after sunset with a banquet for two thousand or so, most of them the entourage of the dignitaries who can't afford not to pay their respects to my king and me in person, *is* keeping it beyond simple. Everyone understands the reasons for that, though, what with us being 'married' already with a child, and with King Zaher not in the best of health."

God. This was too huge. Could he be pulling her leg?

One look into his eyes told her he wasn't. It was probably bigger than her malfunctioning mind could fathom at the moment.

Which gave her hope. "So staying in your quarters is to keep up appearances, right?"

His expression dulled with boredom. "If it pleases you to think that, by all means, go ahead." The boredom evaporated as his pupils engulfed his irises like a black hole would the sun. "But I won't be keeping up appearances and it won't be for an audience's benefit that I'll take you, feast on you, ravish you every night."

Her heart almost fired from her rib cage. "But—but that isn't why we got married."

He inclined his head at her, goading, relishing shredding her nerves. "Why did we get married?"

"Spare me the rhetorical questions, Farooq," she quavered.

"*Zain.* I'll answer them for you. We married for Mennah. And pray tell how did she come into being? Isn't she the living, glorious proof of how much we enjoyed each other's bodies?"

A harsh sound tore open her shutting down lungs. "Sorry to disillusion you but enjoyment doesn't have much to do with conceiving."

"Granted." He moved toward her with the leisure of a cat that had all the time in the world to give his kill a nervous breakdown, putting her out of her misery not even on his mind. "But Mennah's conception *was* a product of absolute pleasure."

She backed away a step for each of his. "That was then."

"And this is now. You dare tell me you don't want me now?"

"I dare all right. Tell you I don't want…this. I don't know what *you* want."

"How can I possibly be more blatant about what I want?"

"You don't want *me.*"

His stare lengthened in the wake of her impassioned cry. Then he picked up her hand, dragged it to him, and this time, he pressed it to his erection. "How do you explain this then?"

She quaked in his hold, her depths gushing in response, unable to muster strength or coordination to snatch her hand away. Not wanting to. Wanting to cup him, map the hardness she wouldn't come close to encompassing, go down on her knees before him, expose him, feel him, taste him, worship him. Only him.

But for him, it wasn't and would never be only her.

The knowledge bled out of her. "You just want sex. Any good-looking woman would do."

"So I'm indiscriminately promiscuous *and* terminally shallow." Before she could define his reaction as mocking or insulted, he went on, his pupils fluctuating, giving his eyes the look of flickering flames. "But if sex with any 'good-looking woman' will do, and we both know I can take my pick of the best-looking who exist, why do I want it with you?"

"Why indeed." And that was a legitimate question. She had no solid theories why he had before, beyond the lure of her total eagerness for him and the why-not factor. Now, she could think of one reason. She said it out loud. "Maybe it's the novelty of a woman you can't have."

"Ah, a challenge to jog my jaded senses." He took the pillow she was holding like a shield, swung it with an effort-less flick to the sofa, reached out a hand to her hair, wound a thick lock over and over his fingers, then tugged. Gentle enough not to hurt her, inexorable enough to show her where he wanted her. Against him. He had her there, from breast to calves, his erection pressing into her hip, one leg between hers, rubbing, sawing, until all she wanted was to open them, beg him to end the torment, do all the things he'd threatened, all the things he'd promised. Then his whisper poured into her brain. "I already had you. I have you again. And I'll have you again. And again. And all the time."

She pushed against him, her breath burning, everything shaking out of control. "No. You won't."

He let her go, left her to stumble with the force of her un-opposed struggle, smiled at her. "Are you sure about this?"

"I won't let you have me. Not like this."

"Like what? In total hunger, giving you ecstasy?" His certainty, its truth, sent response surging like lava inside her. "Is this what you're objecting to? Too much satisfaction? Maybe you want something a bit…racier, riskier? Maybe some domination, a tinge of danger, of pain? I can oblige you. I probably will, after all this time. I'm not feeling anywhere near gentle. But then, I'm sure you won't want me to be."

She sank deeper in the mire of desire and desperation. "No, Farooq, I don't want this."

The translucency of his eyes fogged, his lips stretching to reveal teeth perfect but for too-sharp canines. "You want nothing more than this. You want nothing *but* this."

She couldn't deny his verdict. But she had to know. "What changed your mind? You were cold, angry…"

His lips remained frozen in that smile that filled her with dread and lust and anticipation. "I'm still cold and angry. It will probably make it all the more explosive."

She raised her hands, an attempt to dilute his convictions, stop her capitulation from being total. "If you think I'm riling you, if you think I can enjoy force…"

He barked a laugh. "Force? The only force I ever used was what I needed to unlock you from around my body."

"That was when there was only goodwill between us, not this—this malice. Don't make it change your mind about the marriage in name only you proposed."

He raised his eyebrows in mock bafflement. "Were we in the same scene back there in your apartment? When did I propose or even imply that 'in name' bit? We were tearing at each other within hours of meeting, and now that we're married, you think it a possibility to keep our hands off each other?"

"We only got married for Mennah." She tried again, desperate to hang on to her separateness, knowing that this time, if she surrendered, there'd be nothing left of her.

"That we married for Mennah, that I would have never married you if not for her, has nothing to do with the fact that I've been burning for sixteen months, needing to feel you underneath me, writhing and screaming your pleasure as I pound into you. No matter how we came to be married, we are. I'm your husband. And I *want* you. You will share my public life as my wife, and you will be my mistress again in private. And I will do everything to you, with you, for you. Everything, Carmen. And then more."

Her legs gave out. She went down like a demolished building, missed the sofa, ended up on the floor leaning on it. She looked up at him, fighting the urge to beg him, if not for the tenderness he'd lavished on her before, then for some assurance what he felt wasn't a cold lust that would consume her to ashes.

"I would have stayed and made you beg for everything you're pretending not to want, but I have to meet my uncle now. I won't be coming back, so you have our bed for yourself for the night. I won't see you again, as is our custom, until the ceremony."

He turned away, strode to the hall. At the connecting arch, he tossed over his shoulder.

"Get all the rest you can. You'll need it."

Nine

Carmen lay on her face on the massage-table, staring at her hands. Her skin had turned into reddish brown lace of extreme intricateness, a different design on each hand. It was as if she was turning into an alien species. A very pretty one, though.

"This is my best *mehndi* henna ever!" Ameenah exclaimed, marveling at her handiwork. She raised shining black eyes to Carmen, her smile displaying her lovely teeth and nature, deepening her dark beauty. "But then it's your input that turned it into a masterpiece. It is ingenious, how you designed those patterns made of *somow'el Ameer* Farooq's name in all the languages you know."

Yeah. She'd gone all-out, to borrow a word of his.

Ameenah rose from her kneeling position before her. "I so hope he'll decipher your homage without being told."

Carmen only smiled. *She* was hoping he wouldn't notice.

Writing his name all over her body was something she'd done for herself, on an unstoppable impulse, as if she'd feel closer to him this way, say all the things she couldn't and had never been able to say out loud, make all the confessions he had no use for.

She rose, put on her clothes, marveling at how she'd been able to strip almost naked in Ameenah's presence to get her henna done. Just like her husband, Ameenah made her, and Mennah, feel they'd known her forever, could depend on her. She already had in so many things during the day. Her wedding day.

After Farooq left her last night, she was too agitated to do anything, let alone sleep. But Ameenah breezed in, all smiles and welcome, bearing the list Farooq had given her to perform on Carmen in preparation for the wedding. And the wedding night.

After her first pensiveness and reluctance, Ameenah's cheerfulness and enthusiasm infected her, made everything feel so much better, even fun.

She threw herself into the spirit of things, surrendered to Ameenah's mastery of coddling as she carried out her crown prince's directives. With the help of Salmah and Hend, her daughters, she sorted through her things for Carmen, got her acquainted with the mind-boggling facilities in the palace. Then, while Carmen fed Mennah dinner and answered e-mails, they went out, returned with a rack of clothes from which to choose a wedding outfit.

She'd known this was coming. She should have been surprised at the range and lavishness of the outfits and nothing more.

She did more. She burst into tears. She, who'd never shed a tear even when her mother had died, who hadn't known what crying was until after she'd left Farooq. But she'd never thought she'd wear a wedding dress again, and for it to be something of this caliber, in which to marry Farooq…

The good part was the ladies were totally sympathetic. More, it seemed she won their hearts by displaying such human frailty, such emotional involvement. Ameenah let her know it was only fitting that Farooq married a woman who so deeply recognized the blessing of marrying him, who worshipped him as he deserved to be worshipped.

At the sight of the clothes, Mennah crawled at top speed, hurled herself among them, yelling in excitement at the feel of the rich layers of cloth, at the colors, no doubt recognizing the sheer decadence of each creation. She tried to chew and taste her favorites and, clever baby that she was, the one she chewed hardest was the one Carmen felt had been created for her.

An incredible burnt red-orange the exact color of her hair three-piece Pakistani/Indian/Arabian-design creation, it had a *jamawar* silk corset top with wide shoulder straps and a concealed zip closure at the back. It was scalloped on all edges, more elaborate at a décolleté that dipped just above her cleavage. It was heavily hand-embroidered with intricate floral designs of silver and gold thread and embellished in sequins, beads, pearls, crystals, semiprecious stones and appliqué in every shade of turquoise, azure and sky-blue, all the shades of her eyes. It had echoing armbands that rained gold beaded tassels, with matching chiffon veils attached that cascaded to her hands.

The skirt was a trailing *lehenga* of turquoise chiffon over shimmering azure silk taffeta lining, its embroidery and embellishments echoing the top's, in coral, ruby and garnet shades with scalloping at the hemline. The third piece was a veil *dupatta* in dual shading of coral/crystal-blue with scalloped, heavily embellished borders and vivid azure edging on the corners.

When Ameenah moved to the next item on the list, adjusting it to fit her, Carmen threw herself into the pleasure of handling such exquisiteness, letting her sewing skills loose. Among them they turned it into a custom-made creation in under an hour. The enjoyment lasted until it was time for the next item on the list.

Choosing the accessories.

From Farooq's mother's jewelry. And Judar's royal jewels.

Ameenah and half a dozen guards escorted Carmen to a gigantic vault deep underneath the palace. As she stepped inside, she knew how Ali Baba had felt on entering the cave of the forty thieves.

Beyond dazzled at the treasure she thought reason enough to have an invasion mounted on the palace, on Judar, she hesitantly chose a set matching her outfit's colors. She wouldn't have been able to choose based on anything else. It was a twenty-four-karat gold-lace Indian-style choker with a design undulating to a central pendant reaching below her collarbone, matching shoulder-length earrings, bracelet and anklet. All pieces were inlaid in aquamarines, sapphires and rubies, with eight-point star motifs with a diamond center, one karat each in the necklace and a ten-karat stone in the pendant.

She still wanted to be reassured that Farooq had been serious when he'd said she could wear them. Ameenah insisted she *owned* them.

And she panicked. "Who'd want to possess something that needs to be kept in a vault and guarded by an army round the clock?"

"Now you are the crown prince's wife," Ameenah said sagely. "Without a stitch of possessions, you're worth far more, would be ransomed for a hundred times the royal jewels' worth."

Carmen was stunned that she hadn't realized this before. "God, you're right. I'm still thinking as an ordinary person, thinking how vulnerable I'd be if people knew I possessed something of that value. But we're not ordinary anymore. Mennah and I have become two of the most coveted targets in the world."

"This is true of every member of the royal family," Ameenah soothed. "But it's a potential that has never come to pass. And it will never be a consideration for *somow'ek or somow'el Ameerah* Mennah. Beyond the invisible protection *Maolai Walai'el Ahd* will provide for you, no criminal or power in the world would touch a hair on your heads anyway. No one would risk his wrath. Or that of *somow'wohom,* Shehab and Kamal."

She conceded that, her alarm subsiding. No one would be stupid enough to piss off any of those all-for-one-and-one-for-all men at all, let alone that much.

On returning to Farooq's apartments, Carmen took a bath with Mennah in one of the magnificent bathrooms spread with marble and gold, then collapsed into a bed by Mennah's crib. She woke up eight hours later and Ameenah started the henna even as Carmen and Mennah had breakfast, to give it time to dry and stain.

Ameenah wasn't happy that the color wouldn't ripen to its deepest for the ceremony or even for the wedding night, but said, "There's tomorrow night, and the night after, then a lifetime of joy in your husband-and-prince's arms, as he enjoys you and your efforts to make yourself beautiful for him and pleasures you in turn."

Carmen simulated a smile for the kind woman. Even if she could confide in her, she wouldn't burden her with her despondency. Whatever awaited her with Farooq wasn't a lifetime of anything. She probably had until he was sated and avenged. There was no point in projecting how soon that would be.

As he'd said to her two days ago, there wasn't a choice here...

Mennah scampered off the sofa, wrenching Carmen to the present, and dashed toward the polished brass tray table laden with multicolored, hand-painted-in-gold tea glasses.

To her baby's chagrin, Carmen intercepted her, scooped her up, turned to Ameenah. "Okay, I'd say its time to bring in your team."

They were coming to childproof the living quarters, and to make adjustments to the bedroom suite per Farooq's instructions.

She hadn't spent the night there. She'd only taken a look inside. The sparsely furnished suite was as big as the whole apartment outside, with soaring domed ceiling, ringed by the same Arabian-style columns and arches, permeated by an over-powering male influence in every brushstroke and article. His.

She wondered about the "adjustments" he'd ordered. The place looked perfect as is. But she wouldn't be around to see them being installed, being busy starting the dressing up procedure.

She'd see them soon enough, though.

The wedding was in two hours.

She looked down at Mennah who was looking longingly at the glasses, lips drooping at the corners. "Don't be sad, darling. Everything I do is to keep you safe and happy. It's all for you."

"It's time, *ya Ameerati.*"

Carmen started. She'd known Ameenah would say that. It still jolted her. Time. It was time.

She was marrying Farooq. A real marriage. At least, real in form, in the physical side. It wasn't permanent, but who ever entered marriage positive it would last? People only assumed, *hoped* it would. It made no difference that she was entering theirs ahead in the game, without assumptions, without hope, knowing it wouldn't. She'd decided to make the best of it. While it lasted.

She was marrying him in a ceremony attended by the king of Judar, by world leaders. And she wasn't just some jittery, out-of-place, over-her-head waif.

Well, okay, she was. But that was only a part of her. The personal part, the one no one had to know about. She had more components to her. She was also the mother of Judar's princess. And she was a highly skilled professional, armed with every ability and knowledge to handle such a situation. In fact, it felt as if everything she'd learned and practiced in life had been pre-paring her for this moment, this event. As he'd said, who better than her? To navigate the rapids of an international gathering, bridge differences, meet disparate expectations?

No one, that was who.

She *would* honor Mennah, and her new position.

She would honor him.

Closing mind and ears to anything but this high note of her self-addressed pep talk, she walked out.

Ameenah walked behind her, resplendent in her bridal matron gown, carrying Mennah who looked heartbreakingly cute in a getup made in haste to match her mother's. Ameenah's daughters followed, heading the procession of her ladies-in-waiting, all stunning with their glowing olive complexion and their dark hair streaming down their backs, their lithe bodies wrapped in exquisite sarilike dresses in azures and golds that complemented her gown.

The wedding was taking place in the southern gardens, where the desert and sea winds remained calm as the night deepened. She'd been informed that Farooq would be waiting for her at the southern entrance to escort her to where the *ma'zoon* would write *el ketaab,* their public marriage certificate. She'd chosen not to have a proxy, to perform the rituals herself. Shehab and Kamal were the two required witnesses again…

Agitation and anticipation congealed. Air, the world, disappeared. *Farooq.*

He was standing at the wide-open doors. Waiting for her. He was obscured by distance, by shadows. But she saw him, felt him with everything in her. And all she wanted was to run to him, throw herself in his arms, tell him, show him, beg him…

Thunder assailed her the moment she descended the last step. The *zaffah,* the traditional bridal procession, a unique, instantly recognizable rhythm belted out on *doffoof,* huge tambourinelike instruments, for two bars before singers joined in, chanting the praises of the bride, congratulating her on her magnificent groom and wishing her eternal happiness. And bountiful progeny.

She managed not to falter, and after making sure the blaring beat hadn't startled Mennah, she kept walking, head held high, with quick, purposeful steps toward Farooq, who stood with his feet planted apart, his hands linked, waiting for her to have her *zaffah,* to come give him herself. As she couldn't wait to do.

When only two-dozen feet remained, he moved out of the shadows. Her heart stopped.

No deceleration, no warning. It just stopped.

And she no longer needed it to beat, to push blood to her brain, to keep her legs moving. They moved on their own, powered by everything about him that demanded her, at once. Her vision didn't dim. It remained clear and riveted on him.

If she'd thought he'd looked indescribable before, in suits, in any clothes, out of them, Farooq in traditional royal groom costume showed her what a loss for words, for *thoughts,* really meant.

All she could think was, he was dressed in blues and muted golds shades darker than those in her outfit. He matched her so much, she had to believe he'd done so on purpose.

Her agitation and pleasure sharpened to pain as she devoured every nuance of the heavy silk *abaya* as it hugged his shoulders, cascaded to his ankles, emphasizing his breadth and height. Its edges, shoulders and cuffs were heavily embroidered in gold and bronze thread and sequins in a paisley cashmere pattern. Underneath it, a striped top in the same colors buttoned down from his Adam's apple, stretched across his chest, crisscrossed by bronze metal belts. Another six-inch belt spanned his waist, anchoring ceremonial curved dagger and sword sheathed in gold scabbards over bronze pantaloons whose looseness hid none of the potency beneath.

This was Farooq as he really was, the heir to a legacy rooted in fables, a shaper of destiny, the embodiment of the desert and the sea, the incarnation of their might and wealth, their majesty and beauty.

And he was her groom, the man who'd given her what had made life real—the agony of loving him—and what had made it worth living, her miraculous Mennah. He was the man she still loved beyond sanity or hope.

He stood there, his eyes branding her as his. As she was, had been from the first moment.

Her heart had restarted at some point, propelling her toward him faster with each beat. His hand rose, asking for hers. She ran the last few steps, flew, both hands held out, grabbed his as if afraid he'd fade away.

"Carmen." She heard his rumble over the din, felt it in her bones, his astonishment, his possessiveness, his hunger as he crushed her hands in the assuagement of his reality.

Needing more proof, she burrowed into his side. His arm convulsed around her as the other ended the *zaffah* with a wave. He looked down at her, bombarding her with ferocity. She buried her face into his chest, seeking refuge from him in him.

His heart, his groan thundered below her ear. "Let's get this done before I give in, Carmen."

Without giving her time to wonder what he meant, he had her striding beside him on the royal-blue carpet, down the expansive path lined with stunning plant and flower arrangements ending in a dozen cream satin-covered steps. They climbed up to the *kooshah,* where bride and groom sit during the ceremony. Theirs was a massive gazebolike structure with clusters of exquisite Arabesque woodwork hanging from its eight corners like pendent stalactites, gilded on the outside, the color of cedar on the inside. Within its pillars was a huge curved cream-satin couch ensconcing an antique worked bronze table. The *ma'zoon* sat in the middle with their *orfi* marriage scrolls in front of him, and a book that looked like some ancient tome of prophecy open to empty pages where their destiny was still to be written.

The live music came to an end as Farooq led her to the edge of the stage and all her resolutions to be the seasoned professional boiled away. Being the designing mind behind such events was realms away from literally being centerstage in one.

Her arrhythmia somehow didn't shake her apart as she cast her gaze around the expansive gardens, even when it took a further plunge into irregularity. The gardens were decorated in the exact way she'd imagined and told Farooq about yesterday. Hundreds of lanterns undulated in the twilight breeze between symmetrically planted palm trees. Hundreds of torches flamed on top of polished brass poles, all intertwined between two hundred tables set in a level of luxury she'd only ever dreamed of achieving in her own enterprises, occupied by people who made the world go 'round.

And they were all looking at her. In resounding silence.

Her hand squeezed Farooq's. He squeezed back, leaned to put his lips to her ear. "Your beauty has stunned them, *ya jameelati.*"

Breath left her. Not at his assertion, as touched as she was by it, but at his endearment. Not because it was "my beauty," but because she'd given up on hearing one from his lips again. It was like gulping crisp water after months in the desert.

Then he murmured, "Let's work the crowd, *ya helweti.*"

Elation at yet another endearment, *my sweet,* bubbled over. She smiled with all her body, surged forward with him to wave to the attendees, who'd all stood up and started clapping.

Smiling wide, he winked. "Now let's play our trump card."

He turned and Ameenah came forward with Mennah, who launched herself into his arms. He held her up, showing her off, pride and love radiating from him. The crowd succumbed in collective to Mennah's cuteness and excitement, awing at the sight of her, chuckling at Farooq's intentional Lion King reference. Their clapping rose when he handed Mennah back to Carmen and bowed before her, branding her hand on both sides in kisses.

As he withdrew his lips, straightened, her heart stuttered, felt it would stop again, for real, if she lost contact with him.

She surged to maintain it, threw herself at him, Mennah and all. He went rigid. Silence descended.

She closed her eyes. *Oh* God. Way to be a professional

limpet. Had she deepened his anger at her? Did all those people who mattered to him and to Judar on so many levels think the crown prince had settled on an impulsive moron for a wife, casting doubts on his judgment, damaging his image…?

Agitation came to an abrupt end as Farooq swept her, Mennah and all, high in his arms. The crowd roared with approval.

Sagging in his hold in relief, she opened her eyes, sought his, found them roiling with hunger and delight.

"If you're trying to make your bill too huge to pay, you've only succeeded in enlarging the installments I'll exact from you. But now you have to cater to all those poor power brokers whose jaded senses you've jogged. They're clamoring for more."

He let her feet touch ground, gave her a slight push. He wanted her to go salute their guests alone, the so-called estranged princess laying claim to her rightful status.

Holding the waving Mennah tighter in her arms, she let her fingers and gaze trail off his, started across the stage, an out-of-body feeling coming over her. It was as if she was in the crowd watching that confident woman in the thousands of dollars outfit and priceless jewelry waving and smiling to the people who shaped and ruled earth as if she was one of them.

In the first row she recognized oil, shipping, and technology magnates. The German chancellor. The French president. The king and queen of Bidalya. And…was that the king of Judar…?

Sick electricity arced from her armpits, flooding her body. He looked so unwell, she almost hadn't recognized him. And he didn't look happy. Displeasure came off him in waves. There was no question in her mind. *He didn't want Farooq to marry her.*

Was Farooq going against his king's wishes? Or had the king given his consent on terms of it being a finite union? How finite?

And why was she wondering? She'd already known her days with Farooq were numbered. Again. Had she been fooling herself into thinking they might not be? Where had she learned that mutilating practice? When had she learned to hope?

A blacker wave of unease crashed into her. She traced its source to a man she'd seen only once. Tareq.

He'd seemed to suck up positive energy then, too, but she'd thought her condition when she'd stumbled into him during her life's darkest hour had imparted its oppression and grimness on him. It had seemed the only logical explanation when the man had gone out of his way to be accommodating when he'd found her staggering out of Farooq's skyscraper that night, weeping and lost. He hadn't probed when she'd said she needed to get away, had done all he could to help her. She'd never thought about why he had.

Now she felt his maliciousness focus on her, on Farooq, and she knew. He'd hoped it would hurt Farooq, or at least anger him greatly.

Insight became conviction. He'd introduced himself as Farooq's older cousin. That was why she'd accepted his offer of a ride. But that meant *he* must have been the first in line to the throne. And he'd been bypassed for Farooq. He Farooq's his enemy. He hated him, would do anything to hurt him. Would he go as far as physical harm…?

Suddenly she was suffocating with dread and hatred.

Farooq took Mennah from her, handed her back to Ameenah, and reached for her frozen-in-sweat hand, stilled its shaking. She found his gaze fixed on Tareq, his face turned to stone as he met his cousin's menace.

"Farooq…" She wanted to beg for reassurance, that he was safe, that Mennah was as he turned her to the *kooshah*, where Shehab and Kamal flanked the couch, in full traditional regalia. She caught their eyes, hers begging, for some reason believing they'd understand her fears, defuse them. They cast their gazes behind her, she just knew at Tareq. Then Shehab gave her a reinforcing glance, Kamal a ferocious one, as if each was telling her in his way not to worry.

Farooq's gaze was once more inscrutable as he seated her on one side of the *ma'zoon* before sitting on the other.

"Carmen, give me your hand," Farooq said, starting the ritual of *katb ek-ketaab,* literally writing the book, of matrimony. They'd hold hands, oppose thumbs, and the *ma'zoon* would place a pristine piece of cloth over their hands, place his on top and recite the marriage vows for each to repeat after him.

Overcome, by emotion, by everything, she gave him her hand.

Farooq stared at Carmen's hand. Was that…?

It was. His name. She'd written his name on her hand. And wait…that was his name, too. There. And there. It was everywhere. All over her hands. In Arabic and the other languages she spoke. He'd bet that Chinese script was it, too. Written in a way as to be the building blocks of the exquisite patterns, and to be almost indecipherable. He saw it right away.

It wasn't a custom here to kiss the bride. He'd make it one. He'd make kissing the bride within an inch of her life the new rage. He'd end up hauling her over his shoulder and giving the international assembly a reason to think Judar would one day have a king who would revert it to the days of desert raiders.

Everyone should be grateful he was suffering through the motions at all. The moment he'd seen her descending those stairs, with that distressing outfit hugging her lushness, constricting her waist, echoing her magnificent colors, intensifying them, he'd wanted to charge her, lug her back to their quarters, end the waiting and to hell with everything.

He would have done it and thought of his king and other guests only after he'd taken the edge off the hunger enough to regain coherence. Then she'd tampered with his desire further, as always doing the last thing he'd expected. She'd *run* to him.

Ya Ullah, she'd run, as if she was his old Carmen, as if he was everything she had or could ever want. She'd groped for his hand, cleaved to his side like a vital part of him that had been hacked out and then restored.

And now her hands. Those hands that had once weaved spells and wrung sanity from him were doing so again with the incantation of his name in all the tongues she commanded, in an unprecedented confession. As her offer of herself, her every act of generosity had once done.

This was no plea for a clean slate. This was a command for carte blanche. One he wanted to obey with everything in him. Especially now that his king had succumbed to Tareq's insistence on attending the ceremony and he'd seen how she'd looked at him.

Her reaction had been unmistakable. Revulsion. Dread.

Had Tareq been blackmailing her? Threatening her? This was a new motive he hadn't thought of before. One that would make her a victim rather than an accomplice. Dare he believe it? That this time she had no ulterior motive? That she'd always been coerced, that the only truth had been her desire for him?

The jewels of Carmen's eyes corroborated her hands' silent confession. Fanned the flames of hunger. And of hope…?

No. He hoped for nothing. But he hungered for everything.

He nodded to the *ma'zoon,* watched him place the monogrammed House of Aal Masood handkerchief over their hands, hers bearing her passive weapon of mass destruction, heard him clear his throat.

"*Somow'el Ameerah* Carmen, repeat after me…"

It was done. And he was trapped.

At his king's side. In the mire of protocol. Unable to roar to everyone that they'd done their bid for foreign policy, and to go away now so he could ravish his bride.

The bride who, besides entrancing the crowd en masse before proceeding to entrench her effect one-on-one, was in the advance stages of wrapping his king around her finger. The king who'd told him last night what a time bomb he considered her.

Having Carmen now was a necessary evil, he'd said, to

secure the succession, but didn't Farooq realize that, as a woman not of their culture and creed, she might be the lit fuse to set off the volatile mess Judar was mired in?

Then, ten minutes in her company and she'd had him laughing as he hadn't laughed in years. Two hours later, as they'd made the rounds of all the heads of state, he was showing her off as if she were one of his daughters.

Farooq had given Carmen two more hours to work her magic on the crowd, bringing poles together, riding the currents of the rife-with-potential-pitfalls situation, milking it for all the boons it could yield. In testimony to her effect, after talking to her at length in his mother tongue, an Argentinean magnate who'd formerly decided not to set his next worth billions IT project on Judarian soil had approached Farooq with his change of heart.

But even if she'd manage to negotiate an end to major conflicts if she circulated longer, he wasn't waiting one more second. He turned on the mike clipped to his *abaya*'s collar.

"My king, venerable guests…" Everyone turned to him. "I thank you for the honor of your presence and the generosity of your blessings. I hope you'll continue to enjoy yourselves longer, but I have an urgent matter to attend to…" He dragged Carmen to him, stabbed his fingers into her garnet waterfall beneath its flowing veil, crashed his lips down on hers. He invaded her, consumed her in the kiss he'd been depriving himself of, the one he intended to go down in history. He reeled with her reaction, taste, feel, with the incongruity of hearing hoots from such a congregation. Those people welcomed the spontaneity for once, didn't they? He kicked to the surface with all he had, swept the half-fainting Carmen up in his arms. "I'm sure you'll all see the pressing urgency of putting my estranged wife where she belongs. Back in my bed."

Ten

Carmen felt no heavier than Mennah, felt airborne, invincible, felt cherished and craved, and everything that wasn't real all the way to Farooq's quarters.

Or were they? She'd been lost in the tumult of marveling at his beauty as he swept through the palace, in the single-mindedness of his intentions and the way he'd announced them to everyone. Now she was no longer sure where he'd taken her. The sleeping quarters she'd seen this morning had been the utilitarian space of a man who had few needs and not much time for luxuries. This place was a cross between a sultan's chambers of erotic decadence and a bridal suite from another reality.

But it was the same place, if only judging by its structure. Not one piece of the furniture she'd seen remained. On the right wing was a sitting area of wine-red couches over acres of handwoven silk Persian carpets of complementing colors. On the left was a dining area for two with a polished hand-carved mahogany round table set with an incredible dinner. Separating the wings, from previously bare ceilings rained cascades of extensively pleated, cream-colored voile drapes that caught and suffused the lights from hundreds of candles burning at the base of each of the arabesque columns ringing the huge space. Sweet-spicy *ood* incense burned in urns below the arches, its fumes swirling up in the blazing candlelight like scented ghosts. In the background, evocative recorded music droned, on an instrument also called ood, Spanish guitarlike but with more exotic intonations, adding to the mystic lasciviousness that permeated the place.

Farooq crossed the intricate woodwork floor toward a square bed that spread below the dome, surrounded on two sides by drapes, with a gigantic mirror in a gilded, elaborately carved frame as headboard. It was the largest, thickest mattress she'd ever seen, layered in cream and white sheets, looking like a huge *mille-feuille,* with the last layer the frosting of a cream lace cover. Dozens of colorful pillows of all sizes were scattered all over it and around it, like fruits surrounding an indulgence.

She tried to cling to him, bring him down with her, on her, as he placed her on it. He pulled back. Her arms fell away, stinging with the need to be filled with his bulk, with the letdown. He circled the bed, then did something that sent her heartbeats scattering. He mounted it, stood there at its far end. Just stared at her. She couldn't take it, held out her arms again, begging for him, risking another rebuff.

It was as if a switch was hit, pushing everything inside him to maximum, the intensity emanating from him marrow-jarring.

Yet he still didn't move, stood there, containing it all, his body clenched with the effort, examining her abandoned pose.

He waited until she lowered her arms, her hands fisting on the hollow pain inside her chest, before he drawled, "What changed your mind, to borrow a question of yours?"

He meant about wanting him. She told him the truth, as she would from now on. "I haven't. I never said I don't want you."

His jaw tightened. "I remember statements to that effect."

"I only lied to you about that once, Farooq. Anything I said or implied since then was because it seemed best not to complicate matters by bringing up what I thought you no longer wanted from me."

"So you want me." She came up on one shaking elbow, reached out a hand in confession, in supplication. "No. I must have more than silent invitation and surrender. More than my name all over your hands. Say it, Carmen. I must have the words. The words you once lavished on me."

And she gave them to him. "I wanted you from the moment I saw you. I never knew there was wanting like that, that I was equipped to feel something so fierce, so total. I never stopped, and I can never stop craving you, Farooq. God knows how hard I tried. Whatever I said since we met again was me trying to spare myself pain and humiliation."

His pupils, his whole body expanded in affront. "You're saying I hurt and humiliated you?"

"No," she cried out. "You only ever gave me every satisfaction and consideration. Even when you found me again and had every reason to feel betrayed and insulted, to exact punishment, you still treated me with restraint, gave me rights another man would have considered forfeit. You even wanted to give me much more than I could ever accept. I wasn't protecting myself from you. I realize now I never feared you. I feared circumstances, reality, your complex status and existence, my own hang-ups. But I knew I would be injured anyway. I couldn't afford to get hurt when I must be the mother Mennah needs and deserves."

His teeth scraped together, his nostrils flaring. "So again I ask, what changed your mind?"

"Everything sank in," she said, coming to terms with her

own feelings and decisions. "The depth of your feelings and commitment to Mennah. Then last night I realized you still want me, and not just as Mennah's attachment, as you at first made it sound."

The ood trilling in the background launched into a haunting passage, as if scoring her words, underscoring the silence that expanded between them in their wake.

Still standing there like another wonder from the hyper-reality of this place, a colossus carved by gods of virility, he said, "Do you remember the night you walked out on me?"

"God, don't…"

He cut across her plea. "Do you remember what I said?"

She fisted her hands on the lace cover trying to alleviate the stinging that felt like her nerves had turned into hot needles, all trying to burst out of her skin.

"I remember what *I* said," she moaned. "Do you know how many times I wanted to take it back? Every moment I was myself, and not the single, working mother, that's how many times. Every time I imagined how I would explain my behavior then, how you trapped me when you wouldn't let me walk away without explanations, that I considered pretending to take your offer, pretend that had been my objective, but couldn't do that to you. Not after you gave me a glimpse into what being *you* means, what kind of segregation and alienation you live in, unable to trust anyone's feelings and intentions toward you…"

Something burst out of him, too furious and abrasive to be a laugh. "So you thought it better to let me think you were a promiscuous wretch than a mercenary bitch? You decided to stab my emotions as a man, my ego as a male, rather than consolidate my paranoia as a prince? Only you could think of something like that."

"At least I retained part of the truth," she quavered. "That my desire was real and for you, not what you can provide."

His hands fisted. "While it lasted, you mean."

So he still wanted more…assurance? No. That implied emotional involvement, and none of this had been about that on his side.

But…he'd said she'd "stabbed his emotions as a man." Did that mean…?

No. *No.* Don't even go there. Don't even think it.

But the way he'd said it all… "You talk as if you bought my act, when the first thing you said was that you saw through it."

"You keep putting the weirdest things in my mouth. When did I ever say anything to that effect?"

"You kept saying things like 'save it,' 'more acts' and commenting on my acting abilities."

"The act I was referring to was that of the unbridled lover who couldn't get enough of me. Now you tell me *that* was the truth. The only truth. I believed you the first time, every word, every touch instantly and completely. This time, I'm in need of proof."

And she wanted to give it to him, wanted to give him everything in her. If he wanted it. It didn't matter for how long.

She held out her arms to him again, shaking with the enormity of her love, the jump she was taking, the depths she was exposing. "Make your demands, Farooq. I'll meet them. Whatever they are."

He bared his teeth on a silent growl, his body tensing as if at the shock of a lash. Did her offer, the echo of his all those months ago, in words if not in meaning, hit him that hard? Because she was matching his material offers with the one thing she owned, could give, herself? Did he even want that much of her?

He still wouldn't move, his eyes becoming almost scary in their focus. "I asked if you remember what I said. Not what I said after your dropped your bomb. What I said when I came in. That I was almost afraid to touch you, that I thought it would take us to the edge of survival, after two days of deprivation." She lurched under the power of memory, the potential of reality. He started to move then, in steps laden with the danger of ebbing control, of near-explosion fierceness. "Use that insight of yours and picture how I feel now, what it will be like, after sixteen months."

Her senses ricocheted within a body that felt hollow. Every breath, every tremor, electrocuted her. Every heartbeat felt like a wrecking ball inside her chest. He kept coming, cruel in his slowness, blatant in his intentions.

"I don't need to picture anything," she gasped. "It's been tearing at me all that time, it's tearing me apart now. Please, Farooq, show me what the edge of survival feels like…"

He gave a rumble that traveled through the mattress then through her, made her feel she was lying on a livewire. Still rumbling, he stopped above her, looking at her like a lion deciding which part of his prey he'd devour first. Then he started to undress. The sheer injustice overcame her enervation, sent her surging up to snatch the privilege for herself.

He held out a warning finger. "Don't touch me, Carmen. It is no exaggeration, what I just said."

The one thing that made her abide by his admonition was realizing he wasn't undressing. He was just removing his ceremonial dagger and sword, his metal belts, like a warrior back from battle, relinquishing the evidence of one form of savagery, his eyes promising her another.

Throwing everything to the end of the bed, he kneeled beside her, let his hands hover over her, like that night, mimicking in pantomime all he'd do to her, all the liberties he'd take. Then he bent over her, his lips tormenting a flight pattern of their own.

And he told her. "I couldn't touch you for real, couldn't kiss you when we were alone. I had to remain distant, until I came to grips with the violence of my craving for you. But I can't. I never lose control. Unless it's you."

This was everything she could dream of, would risk everything for. *Her* Farooq back, confessing the depth of his desire.

Disregarding his warning, she lunged for him, hands trembling on the fastening of his pantaloons, the thousand buttons keeping his flesh away from her greed.

His growls detailed his enjoyment of her frenzy even as he ended it, grabbed her, flipped her on her stomach. Then he straddled her hips. She raised her head, met their images in the mirror headboard. He raised his eyes, meeting hers in the reflection. Instead of imparting a measure of detachment, the replicas moving in the coolness of glass sent her blood seething in her veins.

She cried out, arched her hips up, seeking more contact with him. He pushed her down, one hand flat on her back, his hardness digging into her buttocks, before he moved her again until she was lying sideways to the mirror, for a full-body view. He lay on top of her, keeping her eyes captive, grinding into her, mimicking what she was longing for him to do without the chafing barriers. Then he reared up, slowly unclipped the veil from her hair.

"I never liked red hair. But this…" He threaded his hands into it, raised the locks, let them fall. "This texture, this wave, this hue, that it's on top of *this* head…" His fingers dug into her scalp, massaged, had her thrashing beneath him. He suddenly bunched her locks, pulled on them as if they were reins.

She arched back, lips opening on the sharpness of stimulation, panting for his. He slammed into her buttocks, gave her a hand to kiss, to bite into, before he pushed her down again.

"Do you know what seeing you in that outfit did to me?" He began to unzip her corset top. Then he stopped. She saw his face seize in the mirror. She twisted around to get the reality, saw his raptness focused on the henna patterns on her back, felt his renewed rumbling forking through her. And he hadn't even seen their extent yet. Next moment the rumbling quaking her bones intensified as his fingers traced the spots where the patterns made up of his name clustered. He'd deciphered her homage.

She was elated now that he had. She should be alarmed that

she was tampering with the control of a being of such destructive potential, but she wasn't. He'd never lose control. Not that way. Not her Farooq. But he *was* losing his distance, his separateness to her power over him, to the sight of his name emblazoned all over her body. That was one of two things she wanted from life.

He flipped her onto her back, gloriously rough, dragging her top down to her waist, spilling her breasts into the palms they'd been made to fill, kneading them with a careful savagery that had her bucking beneath him. Her hands flailed, trying to tear his top open, needing the crush of his chest. He grasped both her hands in one of his, the other holding his top at the neck and shredding down. He tore off his *abaya,* pushed his tattered top wider, exposing the magnificent sculpture of his torso. She keened as her salivary glands stung. She needed her lips and tongue on his flesh, her teeth in it.

"There are more places I want my name on." He slid down her body, the silk of his body hair brushing her every inch into a distress of arousal. "Here." He gently bit each nipple in turn, had her crying out, before settling into a ruthless rhythm of suckling that had magma pouring from her core, until she was pummeling him for the release only the power of his possession would grant her.

He caught her clawing hands, slammed them to the bed in one of his, slid down as he bunched her *lehenga* up and her thong down to her feet. "And here…" He let go of her hands, held her feet apart, alternated kisses between them, suckled her toes, forcing her to withstand the sight, the sensations before moving up. "And here…" He bit into her calves, kneading them with his teeth as he trailed up to her inner thigh. "And here…" Her body contorted under his onslaught.

Suddenly he hissed like a geyser about to blow, his hands digging in her buttocks. He'd seen the henna patterns there.

On an explosive expletive, he knocked her legs wide with his shoulders, lunged between them.

She squirmed, trembled, tried to squeeze her legs closed. "You, please, I want you, *you,* inside me, now please now…"

He looked up at her, eyes like twin infernos, sable hair cascaded over his leonine forehead. Then with his mouth set in cruel intent, he slid up her body, igniting every fuse along the way until he lodged his hardness at her entrance through his clothes, had her whimpering, "Yes, yes, please, yes."

In answer he only knocked her clamping legs from around his hips, came over her, straddled her midriff, loosened his pantaloons enough to show her his shaft.

A clench of intimidation sank its talons into her gut at his girth and length, at his beauty and sleekness. She craved his invasion, not only for the ecstasy it forced from her flesh, but because when he occupied her, she was intimate with his power and maleness, the potency of his desire, with his essence. With him. Giving her pleasure without union now wasn't a reward but a punishment.

He held his shaft, doing what her hands, imprisoned by his thighs, burned to do, stroking himself inches from her lips. "Is this what you want most, Carmen?" Her nod was frantic, a tear slipping from one eye, trickling to her ear as she writhed beneath him, trying to free her hands, to get them on his flesh. "You told me you had your most intense orgasms with me inside you. Is that true, or were you catering to my ego?"

She renewed her efforts to escape the prison of his body, have him where she needed him, her heart stampeding with futility. "True…it's true, please, please…"

He tightened his waistband again, widened his thighs, let her pull her arms out only to clamp her hands, raised them for her to look at. "You think you can wear my name like this…" He dismounted her, twisted her toward the mirror to show her his hand slipping between the cheeks of her hennaed buttocks. "And this, and go unpunished, Carmen? For this you don't get what you crave most."

He pushed her onto her back, nudged her folds apart with deft fingers, before descending to replace them with his tongue.

He licked a taste, breathed her in, let his appreciation growl out over her engorged flesh, sending her screeching and scratching. He groaned his pleasured pain. "This is for every time you wrote my name on your delectable flesh. I'll torment you, like you tormented me every second of the past sixteen months."

Ignoring her protests, he took the lips of her core in a voracious kiss, tonguing her, thrusting light then hard, sweeping short then long, suckling, layering sensation until she was buried. He brought her to the edge, snatched her away, never pushing her over, too many times to count, no doubt the number of times his name marked her body.

When her breath fractured, her pleas stifled, and she lay beneath him paralyzed with hyperstimulation, he talked into her, sending the shock of each vibration, each syllable throughout her system. "Next time it's me who'll write my name all over you. But right here..." He pinpointed the bud where all her nerves converged, took it in a sharp nip. "I'll tattoo my name."

The discharge of all the pent-up stimulation was so explosive, she heaved in detonation after detonation until she felt her spine might snap.

He had no mercy, pushed three fingers inside her, sharpening her pleasure, lapping up its flood until her voice broke. He didn't stop even then, sucked every spasm and aftershock out of her, blasting her sensitized flesh with more growls. "And this is to get you ready for what you deserve for walking out on me." Two fingers sawed inside her spasming channel while one beckoned at her internal trigger, his thumb echoing the action on its mirror image outside. She writhed under the renewed surge, the need for release a rising crest of incoherence. She thrust against his hand until his rumbled *"Marrah Kaman"—one more time—*hurled her convulsing and shrieking into another orgasm.

He came up to loom over her, watching her trembling with what he'd done to her, watching his hand tracing the patterns of his name on her buttock. Mute, saturated with pleasure, hungrier for him than ever, she watched him, the emotions on his face coming too fast and thick for her to register, to decipher. To withstand.

Melting with the barrage, with needing him to end his punishment, give her the punishing ride she was dying for, she wrenched her eyes away, down. He was jutting against his pantaloons, the crown of his shaft straining beyond the waistband, wide and thick and daunting, dark and glistening with craving, throbbing with control. The moment he freed her hands to strip off her armbands, she lunged to snatch his pants down.

He caught her hands. "Even now you stand by your claims that you need me inside you for the most intense climax?"

She bucked her hips at him, begging. "I'm still conscious am I not? Still hungry, hungrier…" She was stunned to find her voice hoarse not gone. "I crave everything you do to me, your every touch turns me inside out with pleasure, but when you're inside me, it's…it's indescribable…"

Lava simmered in his gaze, the rest of him freezing. She made use of his stillness, skimmed stinging hands over the silk skin and hair-covered steel of his pecs, his abs, following the pattern with her lips and tongue while her hands delved beneath his waistband, closed on his engorgement.

He lay on his side, letting her worship him. He waited until she thought she'd fulfilled her hunger, was kissing the satin head, licking the precious flow of his arousal, let her get a full sample of his feel and taste and thickness as he thrust into the moist heat of her hunger, once, before he reared back, left her choking with chagrin and deprivation.

"This is my feast, Carmen. You are." He snatched a pile of pillows, arranged them, dropped her back on top of them, had her arched, prostrated for his domination with an urgency bordering on violence, kneeled between her spread thighs, took her buttocks in his hands, his fingers digging shards of pain and frenzy into her. "And this is just to take the edge off…"

"Just do it…tear into me, tear me apart…*please…*"

He did. He rammed into her. All his power and the accumulation of frustration and hunger behind the thrust. The head of his erection, nearly too wide for her, mashed against all the right places, abrading nerves into an agony of response, pushing receptors over the limit of stimuli they could take, the gush of sensation they could transmit. He'd forged halfway inside her when she screamed, arched up in a deep bow, going into a paroxysm as the world flickered out, diffused, only his beloved face in focus, clenched in pleasure, his eyes vehement with his greed for hers.

And what she'd heard was true. Sex *was* better after her operation, her great loss. Blindingly, excruciatingly better. Orgasm raged through her, discharging in blow after blow of pleasure so sharp it was agony.

She raved, begged. "Can't…can't…please…you…you…"

He understood. Gave her what she needed. The sight of his face seizing, the feel of him succumbing to the ecstasy she gave him, the hard jets of his climax inside her. They hit her at her peak, had her thrashing, weeping, unable to endure the spike in pleasure. Everything blipped, faded…

Heavy breathing and slow heartbeats echoed from the end of a long tunnel as the scent of sex and satisfaction flooded her lungs. Awareness trickled back into her body, which was a mess of tremors, so sated it was numb. She felt one thing, though. Farooq. Still inside her, even harder, larger. She opened lids weighing half a ton each, saw him swim in and out of focus, still kneeling between her legs, her hips on his thighs, one palm kneading her breasts, the other gliding over her shoulders, her arms, her belly.

"So it does take orgasming around me to knock you out."

"Told you so…" Her head flopped to the side, her heart following at the sight they made, the image of erotic abandon, half out of their wedding fineries, his ruined, their hair tousled, her face shell-shocked, his taut, savage, her position the image of wantonness, her arms thrown over her head, arched back over the pillows he'd piled beneath her, her hips jutting, her legs opened over his hips, his shaft half-buried inside her, stretching her glistening entrance, her lips wrapped around him in the most intimate kiss. And he was watching her watch them.

He gave her more to watch, thrust two more inches inside her.

"You were right…" she slurred at his deepening occupation, her tongue feeling anesthetized, swollen in her mouth. "This…is the edge of…survival. My heart…almost burst. I don't know if this—" a lethargic finger indicated her twisting tongue "—is from a stroke…or if the paralysis…will wear off. If this was just…to take the edge off the hunger…the main course might well be fatal."

He set his teeth as he rocked another inch inside her. "If ever there was a woman who can take a man to the limits of his mortality with her passion, it's you, Carmen. It's only fair I reciprocate in kind."

Her voluntary functions were shot to hell. Her thrust to accept more of him had to be some autopilot, set on Farooq. "We had…this conversation…before…"

"Your limited experience is irrelevant." He thrust deeper into her, the lubrication of their combined pleasure smoothing his advance. "You're a natural-born femme fatale."

Her hand moved under some external power, but with her hunger, trembled down the center groove of his abdomen to his shaft, to where they were merged. "Your femme fatale?"

"*B'haggej'Jaheem*—by hell, you are. *Mine.*" He ground deeper into her, reaching the point where the familiar expansion inside her turned into almost-pain. An edge of dominance, a sharpness of sensation that was glorious, addictive, overwhelming, even a little frightening. The idea of all that he was, melding with her, at her mercy as she was at his, filled volumes inside her, body and mind and soul. "Say it, *ya* Carmen. *Enti melki.*"

"*Ana melkak*…I'm yours, yours…Farooq, darling, please…"

At the word *darling* he snarled something colloquial she didn't get, took the edges of her *lehenga*'s zipper in both hands…and ripped. She lurched in mortification.

He growled again. "I'll have a dozen made for you, must see you…all of you…"

Still lodged inside her, he freed her from her torn clothes, his hands and eyes everywhere he exposed. She closed her eyes at the starkness of his appreciation, at the ferocity of anticipation. Now, he'd really make love to her…

He moved. But he wasn't feeding her more of him. He was leaving her body. Her eyes tore open in panic, whimpering at his loss, her fingers too feeble to stop him. Cold shuddered through her. But it wasn't that of losing her clothes or his heat.

His gaze on her lower belly was the source of frost.

"You have a scar."

Eleven

Carmen bit a lip that trembled out of control.

She couldn't talk about it. About her imperfections and losses. But oh God, he looked so…grim. Did he feel them? Did the external evidence of them put him off, now the edge had dulled?

"You had a Cesarean." She nodded. His eyes turned almost all-black. "Did it hurt?"

She tried to laugh, managed a sound of distress rather than mockery. "I clung to the drug-free route only until they told me Mennah was obstructed and was in fetal distress. Then I was screaming for them to give me every drug they had and to open me up. From then on, I can assure you I felt no pain."

"You know I meant afterward."

She knew. And she didn't want to answer. Didn't want to remember the pain that had made her weep as she'd nursed Mennah, the debilitation that had turned caring for her daughter, moving at all, into torture. She couldn't tell him any of it. He'd suspect that more than a surgical wound had caused her agony. And he'd be right. Her endometriosis had flared up to crippling levels until she'd given in, did the only thing that would put her back on her feet to be a mother for Mennah—removing the source of trouble. She'd had a hysterectomy three weeks after Mennah's birth. The reopened scar had hurt then, had taken weeks to heal. And she'd been unable to take painkillers while she nursed her baby.

"It hurt," he said when she didn't answer, his voice vibrating with conviction, with a fury over it. "And you didn't have anyone to take care of you, or Mennah for you. You *fool*."

He suddenly heaved up to his feet, tore his clothes off his body like a madman, every sinew and muscle straining as if against a crushing weight, his engorged manhood erect flat against his steel abs. He still wanted her.

Those difficult tears she'd learned to shed since she'd known him burned at the back of her eyeballs, two breaking the barrier of her resistance, corroding a path to her chin.

He descended on her like a great vulture, pulling her to him, slamming her against his overheated flesh, demanding, "Why the tears, *ya ghalyah?*"

Oh God. His endearment. The one he'd always called her. Precious. Treasured. He'd made it hers again. The sentinel tears were followed by a flood. "I thought the scar put you off, that I—I'm…"

"A fool a thousand times over." He gave her one quick shake, ending her doubts. "I crave nothing but you."

His teeth pressed into her lower lip, with enough force to still it, to show her the power of his craving. He groaned long and deep as he applied more pressure until she whimpered, opened her mouth, her hands clenching around his neck, her breasts crushed to his chest, cushioning him, one leg clamping his hip, a carte blanche for anything he'd do to her.

When her undulations against him became quakes, he suckled her lips into his mouth, in long, smooth pulls, drawing more plumpness into her flesh, running his tongue inside them, drawing more of her taste until her whimpers became incessant. Only then did he plunge into her with tongue and ferocity. He drained her, then tore his lips from hers, trailed them over her cheeks, jaw, neck, breasts, nibbling and suckling her to madness. Then he reached her scar.

What he did then almost ruptured her heart.

He pressed his face against it, nudging her like an affectionate lion, groaning. "This is where you gave me Mennah, the source of her miracle, and of the pain you endured alone. This binds you to me, makes you *aghla,* more precious, makes me want you more, when I didn't know there could be more wanting."

She hiccupped an intake of distress. It hurt beyond measure, whether she feared he didn't want her or she knew he did. Everything he did or said affected her with an intensity that ended up simulating pain. But it was worse now.

His lips were on her scar, paying homage, and for terrible moments, she felt a phantom womb convulse inside her. Primal longings burst there, to have his manhood driving into her as it once had, so huge and powerful it had breached her cervix, what remained of the core of her femininity, splashed his seed directly where the overriding forces of her love and his potency had smashed the odds, done the impossible, created the miracle of Mennah.

There would be no more miracles. Her potential had been amputated, and she'd been left clinging to her miracle with a desperation that might have suffocated her child, if Farooq hadn't found them.

The emptiness inside her hadn't hurt, had lain dormant, forgotten. But the wound had gaped with his reappearance, the loss damaging only with the yearning to be a whole woman for him.

He, as always, was the source of her agony.

And only he could make it bearable.

She grabbed him, tears splashing over him as she threw herself into the abyss of unrequited love.

"I feel so empty without you, darling," she choked. "I missed you…the emptiness is too huge, fill it—fill me, Farooq, again please…."

"Sahrah." He threw his head back at her invocation, calling her a witch on an elemental groan, his face twisting in carnal suffering as something seemed to shatter inside him. He plunged into her with all the force of the snapping momentum.

She screamed at the piercing fullness, beyond her capacity…tearing her apart… "Yes, Farooq, *yes…*"

But he rested inside her, possessed her lips in another exercise of abandon. She opened for his tongue, each plunge tightening her around his invasion in a vise until he growled, *"Ya Ullah,* so tight, so *right…"*

Next second, he was withdrawing from her depths.

The implosion was crippling. *"Farooq."*

In answer to her desperation he hauled her around him, bit her ear on a rough "Hang on" that had her digging her heels into his buttocks. He stood on the bed, stepped down from it, strode with her wrapped around him to the dining table set in the perfection of their wedding night dinner, set her on its edge. Then he reached behind her and sent everything crashing to the floor.

His violence jolted through her with a jumble of reactions. Consternation at his disregard for the things he'd destroyed, elation at his impatience to resume their merging, and fright.

"The glass…your feet…" she gasped.

He plastered her back to the cool mahogany, had her legs splayed, a hungry embrace for his bulk, her feet braced at the edge. "The wreckage is nowhere near me. From where I'm standing, the only injury I'm risking is a heart attack at your beauty, *ya jameelati.* Tomorrow I'll make an altar of this height and serve you on top of it." He plunged inside her again, filling her beyond her limits with every power and weakness. She was master and slave. Goddess and worshipper. His hands roamed over her, following the twin suns of his eyes, exacting every intimacy as he thrust inside her in an escalating rhythm, watching her climb, arch, seek. The volcanic core of an orgasm built inside her again and he came over her, gave her his weight to writhe under, his mouth to mate with, his fingers sliding between them, stimulating the focus of need, unlocking the code only he knew.

He gulped down every screech of her new climax, making it double as he exploded inside her, feeding her convulsions to the last twitches, pouring the fuel of his pleasure on hers.

It might have been another day, another age when she came back into her body, still keening, her teeth deep in his flesh, her most profound thanks for the torment and the satisfaction.

He extricated her fangs from his shoulder, his smile feral as he withdrew from her body. Even lost in the bliss and stupor of postorgasm devastation, she still moaned at his loss, at the sight of his erection still in full glory, glistening with the mixture of their pleasure.

He yanked her up, slamming her into his chest. "Don't worry. I'm far from finished with you."

He raised her up until her limp body hung above him at arm's height, kept her there looking down on him, half-fainting with satiation, still shuddering with aftershocks. Then he let her slide down his sweat-slick landscape, caught her lips. Just as she caught fire again, sought him, he caught her hands.

"I said *I* wasn't finished with you." With hands filled with cherishing power, he turned her, laid her facedown on the table, her bottom jutting off its edge, her toes barely touching ground. She discovered another mirror flanking the dining area. He'd positioned it for the best view of the next stage in her enslavement. "Now I'll find out how many times you have my name written in that maze. Here's one." He bent, nipped the tip of her shoulder blade. "Two." His blunt nail scratched half an inch beside it. "Three..."

She lay there, helpless, watching him own her in their re-flection, play her like a virtuoso, loving the game he'd invented, loving him as he reclaimed her every response and inch, sliding gossamer touches down her every sensitivity, sowing bites and suckles, knowing, pleasuring, punishing her every lightning-inducing switch until she felt her insides charring with the beauty, the expectation. The frustration.

So there was such a thing as torture by stimulation. Possibly death by arousal. He had unlocked her multiorgasmic potential, but surely those megaton orgasms should be all her nervous system could handle? How could she want more of him?

That's why it's called addiction, idiot. The more you have, the more desperately you want him.

When she felt she'd shudder apart she cried, "Just *take me.*"

"Take you, Carmen? You mean like this?" He slammed into her. She cried out at the abruptness of his invasion. He withdrew all the way out then slammed back, with even more power, forcing a sharper screech from her depths. "Or like this?"

"Farooq—yes!" She clawed at the smooth surface beneath her, putting all her strength behind thrusting back into his assault. She fought with him for deeper, harder, hating the in-equality of their positions.

Then he lay on her back, his hands around her, under her, completing his exploitation, stroking her, stoking her inside and out into another blinding orgasm. On the final shearing spasms he joined her, exploding into a roar of completion, his seed filling her to overflowing.

She lay pressed between now-warm, moist wood and warmer, moister living steel, full, fulfilled, wishing to remain fused with him forever. But he was ending it.

She felt him receding from her. In every way.

"Farooq?"

Farooq gritted his teeth at the tremolo of her call. At its power. She'd again offered herself, made him forget his resolutions. To keep it about carnal pleasures and nothing more. He'd even demanded confessions from her. And she'd freely offered them. *Ya Ullah,* the things she'd said...

And he still had no proof he could trust her. Yet he had. He'd believed her every word, every gasp and scream and tear.

Then he'd seen her scar and he'd been swamped. By the depth of the blessing she'd bestowed on him, what she'd had to endure to do it. Everything in him raged that he hadn't been there to hold her *ala kfoof er-raha*—on the hands of comfort and cosseting, his princess in his cocoon of pampering and protection. He'd wanted to develop temporal powers to wrench back time, go to her in her hours of need, absorb her pain and fear. He'd wanted to swear that next time he'd be there from the first second, for every heartbeat afterward. He hadn't.

He'd said enough. *Ya Ullah,* the things *he'd* said...

And beyond words, the way he'd lost all sense of self in her, surrendered to her as she'd dragged him into their dimension of carnal excess and sensory overload, spilled himself three times inside her in the delirium of ecstasy, each time with the image of all this pleasure forming another miracle like Mennah. She could already be pregnant again. The wish that she was, or soon would be, the need to tether her to him by any means, spread through him like a mind-altering drug...

La ya moghaffal—no, you fool. Stop.

He must decide how to proceed, couldn't go back and take her again. Not on her terms. He had to set new ones before he did. As he would. As he had to. His sac felt heavy and painful again, his erection straining, every inch stinging to feel her beneath him, around him. And that was only the physical part. Everything else in him was clamoring for her. Her voice, her eyes, her wit, her hunger. Her warmth and sincerity...?

He struggled to deny the pangs as he ignored her tremulous call, crossed his space to the bathroom. He felt her gaze following him, her confusion and hurt palpable.

He gritted his teeth against their influence, entered the

bathroom, crossed to the huge sunken tub, hit the heat-regulating buttons, started it. He'd soak. Until this seizure of hunger passed. Until she went to bed…

"Is this what I should expect from now on?"

Don't turn. Send her to bed. Don't look at her.

He turned, looked at her. He'd known he shouldn't have.

She was naked, as he'd left her, the cascade of her hair a burst of color under the spotlights among her paleness. She looked like a mermaid who'd suddenly grown legs and was thrown on land, unsure how to stand. Her voluptuousness bore the marks of his eroded restraint, her thighs slick with the ecstasy he'd found inside her, her shoulders hunched, her arms hugging her middle as if bracing against crippling pain.

"We have sex, then you walk away?"

She called the chain reaction of cataclysms they'd just shared *sex?* But then, he'd treated it as such.

"You expected cuddling?" he bit off, furious, with her, with himself. "Expected the old Farooq?"

He could swear he felt something inside her quiver before it shattered. Hope? For what? The clean slate she'd asked for? Or a renewed hold on him for a new plot?

Her eyes reddened. But their expressiveness, which for their six magical weeks and throughout this night had told him she was his in every way, was expunged, as if she'd ceased to…exist.

"I just needed to know what to expect. Now I know. When you get tired of me, will you let me move out of your quarters?"

"Who says I'll get tired of you?"

"The old Farooq. He gave me three months, of which I served half. Should I expect that after serving the other half, whatever fascination I hold for you will be depleted and you'll let me go, let me be Mennah's mother only?" As he'd thought in her apartment. A few lifetimes ago. "Or have you decided you have a taste for hurting and humiliating me after all?"

"Enough," he snarled. "You've changed your tune again,

I see. All through the night you've begged for me, been mine and now…"

"Now it doesn't matter what I am. It never mattered. To you or to anyone else. It's what *you* are that matters. What you do, what you decide. I'm not in your league, Farooq. You pointed that out to me early on. As if I needed to be told. You'll do what you want, and I have no say in the matter." Without warning tears splashed her face, her arms, the ground. "I only ask, for Mennah's sake…don't destroy me."

It was the most macabre thing he'd ever seen. Her face, as vacant as a corpse's, flooded in tears streaming from eyes so red he felt they'd start gushing blood any second.

This was real. Wasn't it? He could trust her. Couldn't he? He couldn't bear it if he was hurting her and she didn't deserve it. If she was and had always been his. If she loved him…?

He wanted to say…everything. But he couldn't. He had to make sure first. Because once he said it…*he'd be hers, too. Forever.*

He must find out if she was his, the same way. His heart and mind said yes. Now he had to await the verdict of time.

But he couldn't abide time now, couldn't bear her tears one more second. Couldn't stand to see her turning away after she'd given him the most sublime night of his life. After she'd given him all of herself. And tonight, she had. This he *was* certain of.

"Carmen, come here." She didn't stop. He strode after her, caught her at the threshold of his expansive bathroom, took hold of shoulders that slumped with defeat. "Come, Carmen."

Her tears flowed undeterred as she said, "Again? I'm sorry *somow'wak,* but this is probably beyond my physical abilities right now. I know you're used to making things happen with a word, and in my case, with a touch, but after sixteen months, and even though I begged you for every bit of it as you pointed out, having you three times will probably leave me unable to walk for a week."

And he laughed. Was there no end to her surprises?

Next second his laughter died. The burst of insight was blinding. She was trying to blind him to her tears, her weakness, using quips. Her wit was her only weapon against him.

Suddenly he hated that the power imbalance between them was so immense. He could balance it with three words. But those might unbalance it in his enemies' favor. And he wasn't just a man with his own heart, faith and life on the line. He would soon have Judar's, the whole *region's* fate resting on his clarity and decisiveness.

For now, he would obey, his instincts, not the murkiness of the doubts that had poisoned him for so long.

He cupped her face in his palms, damned himself when her teeth chattered as her features crumpled, her eyes those of a woman who would welcome the assurance of despair over the cruelty of hope.

"Your eyes are the first things that caught me, Carmen. Rivaling Judar's skies and seas in their openness, their depths. They make me see how the Arabian Nights tale in which the tears of a princess drowned a kingdom wasn't so ludicrous. Yours could drown a realm. I would kiss them away, stem the tears as I've been their source, but we have a saying here. *El boassah fel ain tefar'raa.*"

That stopped her tears. "A kiss in the eye separates?" He nodded. She hiccupped. "And you consider that a bad thing?"

"I can't think of a worse thing."

Her expression became lost. "Hot or cold, Farooq. Choose one temperature and stick with it. Please."

"I can't, when neither serves or applies. Scorching and incendiary still don't, *ya ajmal makhloogah.*" She moaned at his endearment, the most beautiful creature, squeezed eyes that leaked again. He bent, swung her up in his arms. "About not being able to walk for a week, who said you have to? Your feet won't touch the ground, *ya Ameerati.*" He took her to the sunken bath, descended into the perfect-temperature water.

Their groans of aching relief at its fluid embrace echoed each other. "As for your physical limitations, let's see how far we can stretch them…"

And he stretched them far, proved to her he could make her come again as he soothed the soreness he'd inflicted on her, stroking and suckling her to a dozen gentle orgasms before he let her melt back against him, drained but somehow awake in the warmth of water and intimacy. Then he took her back to their marriage bed, cuddled her as his heart dictated, not like the old Farooq would have, but as the new one who felt far more, far, far deeper.

As she slipped into sleep, he clung to her swollen lips one last time, told her all he could tell her at the moment.

"I will never get enough of you, Carmen."

"It's such a pleasure to see you and *Maolai* Farooq, so happy, *ya Maolati.*"

Carmen couldn't look at Ameenah. Mennah was standing, seemed determined to take her first step today. Maybe even right now.

Oh God, she had to call Farooq. "Ameenah, my cell, please, the one with the hotline to Farooq. And my video cam."

Ameenah zoomed out of the room. Carmen barely breathed, not daring to show any reaction to throw Mennah's concentration off. Ameenah was back in seconds.

Just as Carmen turned on her cam, was about to hit the dial button to summon Farooq with shrieks of urgency to see this milestone with her, Mennah sat down, crawled away and busied herself with the cubes Farooq had gotten her yesterday. He had then spent the entire evening playing with Mennah and Carmen.

Smiling in self-deprecation, at her still-booming heart, at the false alarm she'd been about to raise, she thanked God Mennah had pulled the plug on this situation when she had. Farooq had a vital state meeting, but at her word he would have dropped everything and come hurtling over here only to find a sitting daughter and a terminally embarrassed wife waiting for him.

Carmen looked at the broadly smiling Ameenah and sighed. "You were saying something when I sent you on that wild-goose chase?"

Ameenah repeated her previous statement, and Carmen only smiled. She was wrong. They weren't happy. They were delirious. At least, she was. He was…better than her old incomparable Farooq.

After their history-making wedding night, he'd seemed to let go, the bouts of anger and suspicion fading, his ups and downs becoming ups that kept only heightening. Their nights were intensifying infernos of ecstasy and abandon, and he no longer pulled away afterward, coming closer instead, letting down his guard until she felt he'd let her in all the way. Their days, which he designed with utmost care for leisurely family time with her and Mennah, followed a pattern of escalating joy.

It had been six weeks now, completing the time she'd thought she'd have before he had enough of her. But true to his word, he hadn't. He seemed to want more of her, and then more. In and out of bed.

They made heart-melting love and had recuperation-needed-afterward sex. They shared times that flowed from serious and contemplative to tender and bantering to teasing and hilarious. He started depending on her experience and counsel, delegated responsibilities to her, for the first time entrusting vital details to another. And in every possible situation, he was letting her skills and imagination soar to their full potential.

No, this wasn't happiness. This was bliss.

So much bliss that her heart hit the ground at random moments, with fear so brutal, she couldn't breathe.

When would it come to an end?

Then Ameenah added, "I only hope you won't let your happiness be affected when it's time for *Maolai* to do his duty."

And she knew. *Now* was when. She rasped, "What duty?"

Ameenah's eyes rounded with horror as she realized she'd slipped up, no doubt seeing her statement's impact on Carmen. "*Ya Elahi,* ana assfah—*Maolati samheeni,* I beg your forgiveness, I didn't mean to…"

Her heart started to implode. "Stop apologizing and freaking out, Ameenah. Now tell me what this duty is."

"If *Maolai* hasn't told you, it isn't my place—"

Carmen raised a hand. "It is your duty to do as I say, isn't it? Now I'm telling you to tell me."

After an oppressive minute, Ameenah said, "*Maolai* is to enter a marriage of state."

The world disappeared, the void outside joining the void inside, until she felt she would be no more…

"When?" Was that disembodied voice hers?

Ameenah was on the verge of tears by now. Carmen felt nothing as Ameenah choked, "No one knows. The bride hasn't even been picked yet."

"Why not?"

"It's a complicated story, and I'm not the one best equipped to tell it to you…"

Carmen interrupted her agitation. "You're my best friend around here, and if you won't tell me, I'll only be in the dark, and miserable. *Please*…tell me."

Ameenah finally nodded. "It started six hundred years ago…"

A bleeding huff burst out of Carmen. "God, it was preordained Farooq would marry someone else that far back?"

"It was that far back that the Aal Masoods ended the tribal wars and founded Judar. But ever since King Zaher fell ill, Judar's second-most influential tribe, the Aal Shalaans, started demanding their turn at the throne, threatening an uprising. Offering them settlements didn't work, and a forceful solution seemed the one remaining option. A solution that would lead to civil war. A war the Aal Masoods will do anything to prevent. Even if it means giving up the throne. Which would still tear Judar apart."

Carmen stared at her. Wow. Farooq couldn't be involved in anything that wasn't world-shaking, world-*shaping,* could he? Was it any wonder he'd shaken hers, shaped it?

Ameenah went on. "Then our neighboring kingdom, Zohayd, was dragged into the crisis. The Aal Shalaans form the ruling house and the majority of the population there, and they started pressuring King Atef to support their tribesmen's rise to Judar's throne. He refused. The Aal Masoods are his biggest allies and the reason behind Zohayd's and the region's prosperity, and their losing the throne would destabilize the whole region, maybe the world. His refusal was about to plunge Zohayd in civil war, too.

"But through the Aal Masood brothers' intensive negotiations, the Aal Shalaans accepted a peaceful solution. That the future king of Judar would marry the daughter of their noblest patriarch so their blood would enter the royal house of Aal Masood. The problem is, after much deliberation, that patriarch was determined to be the king of Zohayd himself, who has no daughter."

This kept getting better and better. Carmen felt twinges of hysteria rising through the numbness. "So now what?"

"They're in negotiations again," Ameenah rasped, as if confessing a crime. "Over picking another patriarch, I guess."

"And once this happens, Farooq will marry his daughter, to stop the whole region from going to hell in a handcart."

"Yes. But, *Maolati,* this won't affect you, you mustn't let it. You are the wife he picked himself, the one he loves."

She burst out laughing, shocking Ameenah like she'd once shocked her husband. This *was* a prime example of *sharr el-baleyhah ma yodhek*—the worst plights induce laughter.

She'd been tormenting herself with all the reasons it would end, and now she was going to lose him over something she couldn't have imagined. She couldn't even be angry that he'd married her knowing he'd take another wife. Farooq sure married only for momentous reasons. His daughter's future, now Judar's—the whole region's.

He'd marry another woman, come to *her* after copulating with that woman to produce the heir who'd avert civil wars…

She gestured for Ameenah to leave her, dropped her head to her knees, doubling over from the disemboweling pain. Jealousy. The one thing she hadn't suffered on his account. He'd been with her alone before. He had this integrity. But now, if all she felt for him was compounded by marrow-eating jealousy, her sanity *would* fray…

No. The moment he took another wife, she'd retreat from his life, become Mennah's mother only again. This meant one thing.

She had to take every breath she could of him, while she could, to hoard the memories for the nothingness ahead.

She pressed the dial button. Farooq answered before the second ring. "Carmen." His voice shook her with the intimacy he made of her name, the magic, with the roughness that carried his perpetual hunger. "What does *Ameerati el ghalyah* want?"

Desperation rose with the mercilessness of a sandstorm.

"I want *you*, Farooq. *Now.*"

Twelve

Farooq tore through the palace, had people dashing out of his way as they would out of the path of an out-of-control vehicle.

They were wise to recognize the danger in the eagerness that rattled his bones. Just as his opponents had. None had dared make their annoyance known when he'd walked out on the negotiations the moment Carmen had demanded him. Another first that only Carmen could induce. His Carmen. His.

Certainty had been blossoming during the last glorious six weeks. Endless details, momentous and trivial, all incontestable, had reinforced the verdict of his heart. She *was* his. Had always been. Tareq had lied. She'd never been his mole. The only solid evidence of that had been the words of a man who lived to lie. The rest was circumstantial, with a dozen explanations now that he believed his Carmen would never do anything that wasn't rooted in nobility and self-sacrifice. He had his proof in everything she was. He'd never bring it up, would never insult her with the inventions of the opportunistic pervert who'd claim-jumped her desertion, twisted it as he did everything to serve his purposes.

But Tareq no longer mattered. Nothing else did. Only Carmen.

Still…there was something about her that troubled him. Not him as Prince Aal Masood, but as her husband and lover. Something, an elusiveness, even through all her surrender and magnanimity, that stopped him from balancing the power between them once and forever. His mind had left the gravity of negotiations to ponder what else he could possibly need from her. Then she'd called, and he'd realized. This was what he'd been waiting for. For her to initiate intimacy, letting down the last barrier, trusting him unconditionally as he'd come to trust her. Did she also know that by doing so, she was invoking her ownership of him?

He stopped in front of their door, racked with emotions. He was ready to be claimed, body and soul, to relinquish all power to her. His voice, his fingers shook as he operated the door, posed on the threshold of the rest of his life.

He stepped inside and she sprang yet another surprise on him.

She charged him, climbed him, wrapped herself around him. He stood for a long moment, claimed, surrounded, deluged in her hunger, drowning in her ferocity. Then he staggered to their bed, his arms filled with happiness made flesh, made woman. His woman. He tried to lower her to the bed, but she twisted in his arms, made him change direction, take her on top.

He saw her then, rising above him, the flames of her hair scorching down on him, her body enveloped in another of those mind-messing creations that echoed her coloring, something semi see-through, stretched over her every perfection, showcasing her, hiding enough to send his imagination tearing through it. Which he would probably end up doing. He touched her and forgot how clothes where supposed to be taken off. But it was her face, her eyes, what he saw and felt there that sent his arousal shooting from distressing to life-threatening, catapulted his spirit on its first rocketing flight.

This. This was what he'd been born for. This woman. This being. This totality. *This.*

He took her lips, her tongue, letting her in, all the way, needing, living, *being,* in her, in their merging.

"All of you…I want all of you, Farooq…*all…*"

He drowned in the depths of her desire as she exposed him to its full measure, ignited fever all over him with touches and bites and suckles all the way down to the manhood he now knew had been created to mesh them together, to give her pleasure.

Then she devoured him. He let her, surrendered, spread himself for her to dominate, to pleasure, to drain.

His fingers shook in her hair, his body and heart in her power. After a life of sufficiency and restraint, of superiority, to feel such dependence was scary, transporting. Vital. He thrust his hips to her ravenous rhythm, sinking deeper into her hunger.

She drove her fingers into his buttocks, warning him not to draw away at his peak. "Give it all to me, darling…must have my fill…"

He had learned to give her this. He never had with others, just as he'd never foregone protection, both lines of intimacy he never wanted to cross. Until her, from the first night. In the past six weeks, she'd showed him beyond doubt there were no lines between them.

His hand convulsed in her hair as his loins exploded. She took his pleasure, lapped it up, climaxing, too, just from causing it, taking it, from rubbing against him to the rhythm of his release.

He snatched her up to his heart, communing in profound mouth-mating, sharing their descent. She reached for him again, knew she'd find him harder, crazed for more. She now knew that he achieved the heights of pleasure only inside her heat and giving, only in her pleasure.

She scampered over him, pushing him to his back, straddling him, looked at him through tears that bound him, turning her eyes to the seas he'd been lost in, never wanting to be found.

She held his erection against her scar, caressed him until he was thrusting against her in torment. She rose to scale his length, trembled so much she failed, cried out, "I *want* you, Farooq."

"Carmen, *ya ghalyah*...yes, want me..." He helped her, raised her, positioned himself at her entrance. "Feast on me, show me how much pleasure I give you..."

She took him in one downward stroke. A whiteout of sensation blinded him as her scorching honey engulfed him, his home inside her, his only home. His senses reignited when he felt himself deep within her.

"Farooq..."

He understood her frenzy, rose with her impaled on him, leaned against the mirror, held her buttocks in his palms. "Ride me, *ya rohi*. Take me and take your pleasure of me."

Her palms braced against the mirror, thighs trembling as she tried to rise his length. She'd managed to slide up only half of him when he engulfed one nipple while twisting the other.

Her palms slid off the mirror and she crashed on him, lodging him against her cervix, and wailed, *"Farooq...please..."*

"Lean on me, *ya habibati*." He placed her hands on his shoulders then held her hips and moved her up and down his length in leisurely journeys to the rhythm of his suckles and nibbles.

Then he told her. "Do you know how perfect you are? Do you feel what you're doing to me? I never dreamed pleasure like this existed. I never want to stop, stop pleasuring you, giving to you."

"I can't...Farooq...can't...it's too much..."

Again he understood, put his power behind her back as he rolled to ease her onto it in the middle of the mattress, spreading her knees wide-open with his bulk as he lunged forward, sliding up her flaming flesh. He undulated his hips, stretching her around his invasion yet again and stilled, throbbing in her depths, rising above her. "Heaven would be nothing to being inside you." He withdrew as he spoke. Then holding her streaming eyes, he growled, "Take me, Carmen, take all of me." And he rammed back into her.

She screamed, her inner muscles squeezing his length in a fit of release. He rode the breakers of her orgasm in a fury of rhythm, feeding her frenzy. It went on and on until he felt her heart stampeding beneath his palm, saw her tears thickening, feared he might be doing her damage.

"Come with me…"

Her sob as her seizure continued around him broke his dam. He let go, buried himself to her womb, wished he could bury all of himself inside her, and surrendered to the most violent orgasm he'd ever known, jetting his essence into her milking depths in gush after exhilarating gush, roaring his love, his worship.

"Ahebbek, aashagek, ya Carmen. Enti koll shai eli."

Carmen's consciousness didn't waver this time. The words exploding from Farooq's lips had blown it wide-open. Blown her away.

I love you, I worship you. You're everything to me.

She lay inert beneath his beloved weight, filled with him, with his roar, his words, their enormity mushrooming…

She felt him tear himself from her depths, pounce on her. *"Ya Ullah, Carmen…breathe."*

But she'd forgotten how. He shook her and air rushed in, almost bursting her lungs. She heard his choking relief, felt his kisses scorch off her skin, heard herself croak, "You said…said…"

"Ahebbek? Aashagek? Amoot feeki? And I *would* die for you."

"Stop, Farooq, stop…it's too much, too much…"

"You are too much. Everything you are, everything you make me feel. There's no one like you. You own me. *Enti habibati el waheeda, hob hayati. Enti hayati. Ana melkek."*

You're my only love, the love of my life. You are my life. I am yours. Too much. "But how…when…?"

"How can I not love you and only you? You are not tailor-made for me, you are created for me by God. As for when, from the first moment, and I fall in love with you again in every moment."

"But I never dreamed…"

"*I* never dreamed a woman like you existed. But you do, and you're mine as I'm yours."

You can't *be mine. If you are, how can I ever give you up?*

"Carmen, *ma beeki?*" The emotions turning his magnificent face incandescent dimmed. "You're not happy that I…?"

He stopped, as if he felt her anguish, and it hurt him.

She'd never let anything hurt him.

She surged into him, buried him under a storm of kisses and tears. "I'm *not* happy, *somow'wak.* Happiness is an emotion mere mortals induce, but you…you devastate me, transfigure me, overwhelm me. No. None of that does you justice. I'll have to invent new words to describe you, your effect, what you make me feel."

He surged up, his face a display of all she'd attributed to him. "And you dare wonder how I love you? It took all I had, trying not to love you. All my struggles made me love you more, *ya maboodati.*"

She collapsed over him, weeping again. He now thought them tears of jubilation. As they were. Jubilation with an expiration date. "Oh, darling…what I feel for you…that you feel the same way…then you call me your soul and your life, and now your goddess…you're messing with my life expectancy…"

"I'd give you mine. I'd give you all of it, *ya habibati.*"

She crashed her lips to his, silencing him. Every word, every expression on his adored face was impaling the spears into her deeper. She panted for mercy. *"Habibi, er-ruhmuh…"*

He crushed her to him, kissed her back as ferociously, inundating her with his euphoria until emotional passion caught fire and they were fighting for a faster descent into delirium.

It was dawn when the impetus of their hunger was satisfied. She lay cocooned in his strength, his cherishing arms. His love. It was still, would always remain too huge to encompass, that she inspired the same emotions, the same devotions in him.

But she didn't have always with him. She'd known that from the start. At first, because he was out of reach. Now, he was within reach, but would soon drift out of it again. But, like before, she'd think of the price later. She had now with him.

He rose above her, swept her with caresses, his love flaying her with its beauty, its power. "*Hayati,* whenever you feel ready, I want you to stop birth control. I can't wait to give Mennah a brother. Or a sister. Hopefully both."

She smiled at him, went through the motions until he wrapped himself around her, his hands caressing the abdomen he was certain would soon swell with his child again.

She waited until his breathing evened in sleep, then let his dreams detonate inside her, pulverize the now she had with him to ashes.

It had been three weeks since Farooq had confessed his love, asked her to stop birth control. She still hadn't confessed that she *really* didn't need it this time.

She couldn't cut her time with him short. She'd remain with him until he left her to take a wife who would give him more children. Give Mennah siblings…

Her phone rang. Thinking it must be a wrong number, she snapped it up to reject the call. No one but Farooq called her on this number, and he was in the shower.

Something made her press the answer button.

"*Ameerah* Carmen?"

Carmen's stomach lurched with instant dread and revulsion. She remembered that androgynous voice. Tareq.

He went on, not waiting for an answer. "I'll get to the point. I want to meet with you."

She found her voice. "No."

"Don't be so quick to refuse. I'm doing you a favor."

"Thank you, but again, no. Goodbye, Prince Tareq."

He gave up the polite act, flayed her with malignancy. "You and your bastard daughter were the only thing standing between me and the throne. But not anymore. Your days as princess are numbered. I would still have offered you a generous settlement if you left now so that I could claim the succession sooner, but now I'll wait until my cousin throws you away as the useless tramp that you are. Yes, I investigated you, found out your…medical history. So it's goodbye to you, *ya somow'el Ameerah.* And good riddance."

She hurled the phone away as if it was a scorpion, and ran.

Ameenah. She had to find Ameenah.

"Carmen…" Farooq called out after her as he came out of the bathroom. But she'd already closed the door.

His blood stirred again at the idea of catching up with her. But he had to put something on before he pursued her.

Huffing in frustration, he noticed her brick-red phone, their "hotline" phone, on the bed. She never went anywhere without it…

Something unfurled in his gut as he picked it up, accessed the call log. All his number. All but one.

He pressed the dial button. On the first ring a man answered.

"I knew you'd change your mind."

He terminated the call. Tareq.

She'd been talking to Tareq.

And he'd said, *Change your mind.* About what?

What did it mean?

He exploded to his dressing room. He must find her, talk to her. He wasn't letting Tareq, or doubts, come between them again.

* * *

"What's Tareq's story?" Carmen closed the door behind her and Ameenah, still struggling with the agitation of her brush with Tareq. "Why was he bypassed for Farooq?"

Ameenah looked up at her out-of-the-blue question. "Tareq was never named crown prince, even though, with the deaths of both of King Zaher's younger brothers, he was first in line. When King Zaher said he would bypass Tareq for *Maolai* Farooq, Prince Tareq called in all the favors his greatly loved late father had with the most influential members of the Tribune of Elders, to pressure the king into changing his choice. So, King Zaher resorted to a measure no one would contest— making *Maolai* Farooq his crown prince in effect, but saying he would give the title to his own male child, when he had one. However, our queen is too old to be that child's mother, so to have an heir, the king would have to take another wife."

Carmen frowned. "Why was that a problem? Polygamy is sanctioned in Judar."

Ameenah made a gesture unique to the region, one signifying *yes—but*. "It has strict rules and requires the consent of the first wife. A consent she gave. But the Aal Masood's, especially their kings, are monogamous, and King Zaher couldn't do that to his queen, even to stop Tareq's rise to the succession."

"Tareq has a lot against him, huh?"

"Among many of his excesses, he is said to…favor, uh, boys…"

Whoa. A pedophile. "Then I'm surprised there was ever any problem in bypassing him. I'm surprised he wasn't stoned."

"He would have been, if his guilt was proved in a court of law. But his connections in the Tribune of Elders prevented that. He then declared he'd be the first king of Judar who never married, couldn't care less who the throne went to after him. That won him the Aal Shalaan's unwavering support and protection. It was then that King Zaher came up with what would assure *Maolai* Farooq of securing the succession, a requirement no one could contest—having a wife and a child as proof of stability and commitment to family."

Her breath caught. "When was that?"

"Just over eighteen months ago now."

Just around the time she'd walked out on Farooq.

Realizations piled up inside her head.

The king wouldn't have made this decree if he hadn't been confident Farooq would be married at once. Farooq could have had a suitable wife lined up…but no. He wouldn't have been wasting time with her when he should have been securing a marriage to protect the throne from Tareq. That meant one thing.

He'd been about to offer her marriage.

Maybe even the same night she'd left. And unknown to both of them, her pregnancy would have clinched the succession at once. But she'd walked out. And Tareq had helped her disappear.

It all made sense. "What happened then?"

"Prince Tareq married at once, into the only family of the Aal Shalaans who would take him. But his wife didn't conceive, and it was rumored he was undergoing fertility treatments. Then she did get pregnant, twice, but miscarried and was diagnosed with a condition that would make it impossible for her to carry a child to term. Tareq divorced her, and he's now married another."

"But why? The succession is already Farooq's."

Ameenah winced. "He'd gotten the Tribune to amend the king's ruling. Now a male child is needed to settle the succession."

So that was why Farooq wanted—no, *needed* a male child, at once. And he must be secure thinking she was probably pregnant by now, had no reason to suspect she was damaged, barren…Oh *God.*

She couldn't tell him, couldn't bear to. But she had to do what she'd known needed to be done. Retreat from his life.

Before it was too late…

* * *

Carmen had gone out, had taken her car and banned her guards from joining her. He'd waited for her to come back, refusing to jump to conclusions again.

She came into their quarters, pale, subdued. He went to her, tried to take her in his arms. His heart squeezed when she avoided them, dread rising as she stumbled to the far side of the room, overlooking the sea.

Then she said, "I want a divorce, Farooq."

And there was nothing left. In existence. In him.

She wasn't finished. "I—I beg you not to let this affect Mennah, that you'll let her have her mother."

He discovered many things were left. There was agony and disillusion and despair. There was a woman who'd conquered him, who'd taught him the meanings of unity and destiny and bliss, only to gut him and throw him into hell.

"What is Tareq paying you? *How* is he making you do this to me?"

She jerked at his accusation, her shoulders shaking. Was she crying? Shocked?

She *must* be. Now she'd turn, explain this insanity away…

She turned. "It doesn't matter, Farooq. Just let me go."

No. No. He'd only accused her to hear her denial, would have believed anything she said. But what she'd said implied her guilt.

He advanced on her, sanity draining in every step. "If you can side with a criminal like Tareq when I made you my princess, gave you my love, *myself,* I can't trust you near Mennah."

Horror shredded her numb mask. "*No.* You know I'm a good mother…please…I'll do anything if you let me stay near her…"

He hit bottom, knew he'd do anything to hang on to her. Even use Mennah. "You want Mennah, you remain my wife."

"But I'll never give you more children," she shrieked.

"Why?" he thundered. "Because you won't sleep with me now that your mission is accomplished? Now that you broke me?

It was she who broke down, heaped to the floor. Her anguish pummeled them both. The moment he could move, breathe, her broken whisper paralyzed him again.

"I had endometriosis. Was declared infertile by a dozen specialists…Steve divorced me because I couldn't provide an heir to his family fortune. That was why I thought it safe to make love without protection…why I ran from you to protect my miracle baby. After I had her my condition became crippling and I couldn't afford the endless procedures and the incapacitation when I had to take care of her. This scar is not only from my C-section. It is where I had a hysterectomy."

He staggered, the bolt of horror almost felling him. He clutched his head. *"Ya Ullah, ya Ullah…"*

Horror became panic as Carmen withered before his eyes. She'd misunderstood, was staggering up, stumbling away.

He caught her, tears he'd only ever shed on his father's and mother's graves scouring his face.

"Stop wasting time on me, Farooq," she wailed. "You might have jeopardized everything because of me already. But I didn't know, or I would have told you, risked anything, even seeing this look—oh God—*tears* in your eyes…"

"You think it's sadness for myself? It's all for you, for what you went through without me by your side, what you lost, what you might not have lost if I was there, giving you all the time and support to explore treatment options. I *am* agonized, for your agony and absolutely unfounded insecurities. You are more than I dreamed to have. I would have chosen you even if you hadn't given me Mennah. I *do* choose you, over the world."

"You *can't,*" she screamed. "I thought I'd have more time with you, until you married the Aal Shalaan bride, but now you must marry any woman who can give you a male child before Tareq."

"You know everything…*ya Ullah…*" he choked.

Her nod was a quake. "That's why I didn't defend myself, so you'd leave me at once, while there was time to beat him to it."

"You'd do that for me? Paint yourself black…"

"I will do *anything* for you. You are my life. But I beg you, don't force me to stay near you, to see you in another woman's arms, see her get big with your child…"

She collapsed by degrees, clinging to him, ending up at his feet, racking sobs tearing her apart.

He stood paralyzed, a vise clamping his chest and back. This had to be how men lost their minds, had strokes and heart attacks. Being accosted by pain too big to encompass, loss too huge to endure. But no, he'd never lose her. Never.

"Carmen, ahleflek ya maboodati, I swear to you…"

What would he swear? That he didn't need a male child? That all she'd said wasn't true? It was. But it didn't have to be.

He swooped down, swept her up in his arms.

It was time to change a few truths.

"Carmen and I will not have more children, *ya Maolai.*"

Farooq had been about to demand an immediate audience with his uncle when the king beat him to it. He'd taken Carmen with him. Now she stood squirming in his hold, looking everywhere but at their king, who had eyes only for her, the new daughter he'd gained.

"I refuse the demand of providing a male heir for the succession. You must, too, or you'll be succumbing to Tareq's manipulation and to outdated notions. You yourself have no sons, and you are the happiest man I know with your wife and the daughters she gave you. You only worry about the succession because Tareq would make a disastrous king. I don't have that to worry about. I have my brothers as my successors, and I'm sure their children, when they one day have them, will be worthy successors, too."

Still casting his tired yet affectionate and compassionate

gaze on Carmen's bent head, the king said, "That's why I summoned you. I gathered the Tribune to debate the male child criterion. I reminded them a wife and child were proof of stability and responsibility, that the gender of the child is irrelevant and that we all know who between you and Tareq is king material. Things were up in the air until your latest intelligence on Tareq checked out as we convened. I presented the damning evidence but couldn't secure consent to a trial. I settled for banishing him from Judar and stripping him of his titles and wealth."

Still not daring to breathe, Carmen looked up at Farooq, who was clutching her as if he were afraid she'd dematerialize.

This meant…she had more time with him.

The king went on. "Now the succession is forever settled, you, my son, have to do your duty. I'm more sorry than I could express to ask you to do something I never could. But it's time for you to enter the marriage of state the peace treaty with the Aal Shalaans demands. I hoped we'd find another way, but it turns out King Atef has a daughter he never knew about from an American lover."

His gaze on Carmen grew more pained. "I know how painful this is, my daughter, but these are dangerous times, and if you love Farooq and have come to care for Judar, you'll consent to his second marriage."

"I—consent…" she rasped, tried to jerk free. Farooq's grip tightened. And she cried. "Just let me go, Farooq. Everything will be okay when I'm out of the equation."

Farooq clutched her harder. "I will *never* let you go, not in this life, and if I have any say, not in the next." She shook her head, splashing their arms with tears. "I never gave you a *mahr, ya rohi.* I couldn't decide on anything to do you justice. I just did." He turned to his uncle. "*Maolai,* I'm abdicating the succession to Shehab."

Farooq felt Carmen go rigid. His king's reaction was as dramatic. He looked…relieved. And Farooq understood why.

Even though he wanted Farooq to succeed him, he wanted him to be happy more. Wanted Carmen to be happy.

His answer seemed readymade. "I see this is your final decision, so I can only accept it. Just thank *Ullah* you have spare heirs as worthy as you of being king."

Carmen jerked out of his hold, in tears. "Are you both crazy? You're in the middle of a crisis that can change history and *you* say, I'm abdicating, and *you* just say, okay? No offense to Shehab, but how can anyone be as worthy as Farooq? I won't be the reason to deprive a nation of its most magnificent king…" She bit her lip. "No offense, King Zaher." She turned back to Farooq, the one to clutch him now. "You must fulfill your duty, remain crown prince, give Judar the marriage it needs. I take it back, Farooq, I take it back. I'll remain yours no matter what happens."

So there was more. More love. More wonder. Always would be with her. He hugged her off the ground. "*Ya rohi,* Judar's only loss today is losing you as its future queen. When I said I'm yours, I wasn't plying you with exaggerations. I was stating a fact. As unchangeable as my genetic code."

Her color neared that of her hair. "If you think you're proving anything to me, don't. This is bigger than us. I won't let you do something you'll regret—"

He silenced her with a kiss before he looked up, found his king watching them, moved but satisfied. He flashed him a smile. "*An eznak,* excuse me, *ya Maolai,* while I take this out of here. I believe this will end in a situation unsuited for your court."

Then he swept her away to their quarters as she protested and sobbed. He sat on their bed, dragged her on top of him, straddling his hips, and quieted her writhing into dwindling resistance.

"How about we make love first then argue later?" he purred.

"No. You must take it back before the king makes it public."

"Why must I, *ya hayati?* This is perfect. I rescued the succession from Tareq's claws. Now Shehab, who has never had a serious relationship and who won't mind marrying King Atef's daughter, will take it and her off my hands. I will become *his* crown prince, if one day he becomes king. I will remain second in line, as I lived most of my life. I've done my part for the throne, *ya roh galbi*. As for Judar, with you at my side—the best princess Judar will ever see—we'll accomplish great things."

"But you are the greatest man in the world, *ya habibi*. You'd be the best king. I think Shehab is great, too, but you, you…"

"I want only to be king of your heart."

Her weeping spiked. "Oh God…twenty-five years without shedding a tear, then I meet you and a lifetime accumulation floods out whether I'm happy or devastated. Now I'm both." She collapsed against his heart. "How is it possible that you love me as I love you? What have I ever done to deserve so much? How can I deserve it?"

"Just by being yourself, *ya rohi*. The most giving woman and mother, the most stimulating companion and the most addictive lover. No man, royal or otherwise, has ever dreamed of so much." He spread her on the bed. "About the addictive lover part…I need another fix…"

Hours later, he was lapping water over his armful of savagely pleasured and satisfied woman, murmuring his own pleasure into her clinging lips, over and over.

He'd finally convinced her that his abdication hadn't been an option but a necessity. Becoming king had been a duty, something he could relinquish. Being hers was his destiny.

"So what do you think of your *mahr?*"

She sighed her breath and taste into his mouth, the essence of love and satisfaction. "You had to go overboard, didn't you? Everything has to be world-shaking with you, doesn't it? I ask for one tiny clean slate, and you give up a throne for me."

He chuckled. Only his Carmen could talk like this, only her

words could make him feel like that. Invincible. Unparalleled. Blessed. "I take it you are impressed with my efforts?"

She traced patterns over his heart with fingers and lips. "If I was more impressed, you'd have to jump-start my heart."

"I trust you'll show proper awe and gratitude for the next sixty years or so?"

"You can certainly trust, *ya habibi.*" He knew nothing more certainly. That he could trust. Her. With his life. With everything. "And you know how inventive I can be."

"Indeed. I'm breathless to see, to experience, to thank the fates for your next brainstorm. Start inventing."

She twisted in the slickness of water and bubbles, gliding over his flesh, inventing new erogenous zones for starters, then proceeded to invent new reasons to love, new reasons to live.

As he knew she always would.

* * * * *

The Sheikh's Love-Child

KATE HEWITT

Kate Hewitt discovered her first Mills & Boon® romance on a trip to England when she was thirteen, and she's continued to read them ever since. She wrote her first story at the age of five, simply because her older brother had written one and she thought she could do it too. That story was one sentence long—fortunately they've become a bit more detailed as she's grown older. She has written plays, short stories and magazine serials for many years, but writing romance remains her first love. Besides writing, she enjoys reading, travelling, and learning to knit.

After marrying the man of her dreams—her older brother's childhood friend—she lived in England for six years, and now resides in Connecticut with her husband, her three young children, and the possibility of one day getting a dog. Kate loves to hear from readers—you can contact her through her website, www.kate-hewitt.com

PROLOGUE

I'M SORRY.

The two words seemed to reverberate through the room, even though the man who'd spoken them had gone.

I'm sorry.

There had been a touch of compassion in the doctor's voice, a thread of pity that had sent helpless rage coursing through Khaled as he'd lain there, prostrate, and watched the doctor shake his head, smile sadly and leave—leave Khaled with his shattered knee, his shattered career. His broken dreams.

He didn't need to look at the damning X-rays or medical charts to know what he felt—quite literally—in his bones. He was a ruined wreck of a man with an impossible, inevitable diagnosis.

Outside thick, grey clouds pressed heavily down upon London, obscuring the city view with their dank presence. Prince Khaled el Farrar turned his head away from the window. His fists bunched uselessly on the hospital bed-sheets as pain ricocheted through him. He'd refused pain killers; he wanted to know what he was dealing with, what he would be dealing with for the rest of his life.

Now he knew: nothing. No amount of surgery or physical therapy could restore his rugby career or his ruined knee, or give him a future, a hope. At twenty-eight, he was finished.

A tentative knock sounded on the door and then Eric Chandler, England's inside centre, peered round the doorway.

'Khaled?' He came into the room, closing the door softly behind him.

'You heard?' Khaled said through gritted teeth.

Eric nodded. 'The doctor told me, more or less.'

'There is no *more*,' Khaled replied with a twisted smile. He was still gritting his teeth, and there was a pale sheen of sweat on his forehead. The pain was growing, rippling through him in a tidal wave of increasing agony. His nails bit into his palms. 'I'll never play rugby again. I'll never—' He stopped, because he couldn't finish that sentence. To finish it would make it real, would open him to the pain and weakness. To admit defeat.

Eric didn't speak, and Khaled thought more of him for his silence. What was there to say? What pithy tropism could help now? The doctor had said it all: *I'm sorry*.

Sorry didn't help. It didn't restore his knee or his future as a healthy, whole man. It didn't keep him from wondering how long he had, how long his body had, before the illness claimed him and his bones crumbled away.

Sorry didn't do anything.

'What about Lucy?' Eric asked after a long moment when the only sound in the hospital room had been Khaled's raspy breathing.

Lucy. The single word brought memories slicing through him, wounding him. What could Lucy want with him now? Bitterness and regret lashed him, and he turned his head away, amazed that when he spoke his voice sounded so indifferent. So cold. 'What about her?'

Eric glanced at him in sharp surprise. 'Khaled—she—she wants to see you.'

'Like this?' With one hand Khaled gestured to his ruined leg. 'I don't think so.'

'She's concerned.'

Khaled shook his head. Lucy had feelings, maybe even love, for the man he'd been, not the man he was—and, far worse,

the man he would eventually become. The thought of her rejection—her pity, disgust—made his hands bunch on the sheets
again. 'And so are you, it seems,' he said coolly, and watched
Eric flush in anger. Every part of him hurt, from his shattered
knee to his aching heart. He couldn't stand to feel so much pain,
physical and emotional; he felt as if he would rip wide open
from its force. 'What is Lucy to you?' he demanded, knowing
he was being unfair, *feeling* unfair.

After a long moment Eric replied levelly, 'Nothing. It's
what she is to you.'

Khaled turned his head to stare blindly out of the window.
A fog was rolling in, thick and merciless, obscuring the endless
cityscape. He closed his eyes, pictured Lucy with her long
sweep of dark hair, her air of calm composure, her sudden
smile. She'd taken him by surprise with that smile; he'd felt
something turn over inside him, like fresh earth ready for
planting. When she smiled for him, he felt like he'd been given
a treasure.

She was the England team's physiotherapist, and she'd been
his lover for two months.

Two incredible months, and now this. Now he would never
play rugby again, never be the man he was, the man everyone
loved and admired. It hurt his ego, of course, but it also hurt
something far deeper, wounded him inside like a bruise on the
heart.

Everything had been snatched from him, snatched and
ruined.

He thought of his father's terse phone call, the life that awaited
him in his home country of Biryal. Another prison sentence.

Khaled knew this life, the life he'd won for himself, was over
now. There could be no going back. All of it, everything, was over.

Khaled opened his eyes. 'She's not that much to me.' It hurt
to say it, to act like he meant it. He turned his head away.
'Where is she now?'

'She went home.'

A single sound erupted from him, ringing with bitterness; it was meant to be a laugh. 'Couldn't stay around, could she?'

'Khaled, you were in surgery for hours.'

'I don't want to see her.'

Eric sighed. 'Fine. Maybe tomorrow?'

'Ever.'

The refusal reverberated through the room with bitter, ominous finality, just as the doctor's previous words had: *I'm sorry*.

Well, so was he. It didn't change anything.

Across the room, Khaled saw his friend freeze. Eric turned slowly to face him. 'Khaled…?'

Khaled smiled with bleak determination. He didn't want Lucy to see him like this, couldn't bear to see shock and dismay, fear and pity, darken her eyes as she struggled to contain the turbulent emotions and offer some weak, false hope. He couldn't bear to hurt her by knowing she was afraid of hurting him.

He couldn't bear to be so powerless, so he wouldn't. There was a choice to make, and in a state of numb determination he found it surprisingly easy. 'There is nothing for me here, Eric.' *No one*. He took a breath, the movement a struggle. 'It's time I returned to Biryal, to my duties.' What little duties he had that his father allowed him. For a moment he pictured his life: a crippled prince, accepting the pity of his people, the condescension of his father, the King.

It was impossible, unbearable, yet the alternative was worse—staying and seeing his life, his friends, his lover, move on without him. They would try to heal him with their compassion, and in time—perhaps not very much time, at that—he would see how his presence, his very self, had become a burden. He would hate them for it, and he would hate himself.

He had seen it happen before. He had watched his mother fade far too slowly over the years, the life and colour drained out of her by others' pity. That had been far worse than the illness itself.

Better to go home. He'd known he had to return to Biryal some day; he just hadn't expected it to be like this—limping back, wounded and ashamed.

The pain rose within him until he felt it like a howl of misery within his chest, iron bands tightening around his wasted frame, squeezing the very life, hope and joy out of him.

'Khaled, let me get you something. Some painkillers…'

Eric's voice was receding, Khaled's vision blacking. Still he managed to shake his head.

'No. Leave me.' He struggled to draw a breath. 'Please.' Another breath; his lungs felt like they were on fire. 'Don't…don't speak to Lucy. Don't tell her…anything.' He couldn't bear her to see him like this, even to know he *was* like this.

'She'll want to know—'

'She can't. It would…it wouldn't be fair to her.' Khaled looked away, his eyes stinging.

After a long moment, as Khaled bit hard on his lip to keep from crying out, Eric left.

Then Khaled surrendered to the pain, allowed the bitter sorrow and defeat to swamp him until he was choking with it, as the first drops of rain spattered against the window.

CHAPTER ONE

Four years later

LUCY BANKS craned her head to catch a glimpse of the island of Biryal as the plane burst from a thick blanket of cottony clouds and the Indian Ocean stretched below them, an endless expanse of glittering blue.

She squinted, looking for a strip of land, anything green to signal that they were approaching their destination, but there was nothing to be seen.

Breathing a sigh of relief, she leaned back in her seat. She wasn't ready to face Biryal, or more to the point its Crown Prince, Sheikh Khaled el Farrar.

Khaled... Just his name brought a tumbled kaleidoscope of memories and images to her mind—his easy smile, the way his darkly golden eyes had caught and held hers across a crowded pub after a match, the fizz of feeling that one look caused within her, the bubbles of anticipation racing along her veins, buoying her heart.

And then, unbidden, came the stronger, sweeter and more sensual memories. The ones she'd kept close to her heart even as she tried to keep them from her mind. Now, for a moment, she indulged them, indulged herself, and let the memories wash over her, making her blush in shame even as her heart ached with longing. Still.

Lying in Khaled's arms, late-afternoon sunlight pouring through the window, and laughter—pure joy—rising unheeded within her. His lips on hers, his hands smoothing her skin, touching her like a treasure, as their bodies moved, their hearts joined. And she'd been utterly shameless.

Shamelessly she'd revelled in his attention, his caress. She'd delighted in the freedom of loving and being loved. It had seemed so simple, so obvious, so *right*.

The shame had come later, scalding her soul and breaking her heart, when Khaled had left England, left her, without an explanation or even a goodbye.

She'd faced his teammates—who'd watched her fall hard, had seen Khaled reel her in with practised ease—and now knew he'd just walked away.

Lucy swallowed and forced the memories back. Even the sweet, secret ones hurt, like scars that had never healed, just scabbed over till she helplessly picked at them once more.

'All right?' Eric Chandler slid into the seat next to her, his eyebrows lifting in compassionate query.

Lucy tilted her chin at a determined angle and forced a smile. 'I'm fine.'

Of all the people who had witnessed her infatuation with Khaled, Eric perhaps understood it—her—the best. He'd been Khaled's best friend, and when Khaled had gone he'd become one of hers. But she didn't want his compassion; it was too close to pity.

'You didn't have to come,' he said, and Lucy heard the faint thread of bitterness in his voice. This was a conversation they'd had before, when the opportunity of a friendly match with Biryal's fledgling team had come up.

She shook her head wearily, not wanting to go over old ground. Eric knew why she'd come as much as she did. 'You don't owe him anything,' Eric continued, and Lucy sighed. She suspected Eric had felt as betrayed as she had when Khaled had left so abruptly, even though he'd never said as much.

'I owe Khaled the truth,' she replied quietly. Her fingers flicked nervously at the metal clasp of her seat belt. 'I owe him that much, at least.'

The truth, and that was all; a message given and received, and then she could walk away with a clear conscience, a light heart. Or so she hoped. Needed. She'd come to Biryal for that, and craved the closure she hoped seeing Khaled face to face would finally bring.

Khaled el Farrar had made a fool of her once. He would not do so again.

Khaled stood stiffly on the blazing tarmac of Biryal's single airport, watching as the jet dipped lower and prepared to land.

He felt his gut clench, his knee ache and throb, and he purposely kept his face relaxed and ready to smile.

Who was on that plane? He hadn't enquired too closely, although he knew some of the team would be the same. There would be people he would know, and of course the team's coach, Brian Abingdon.

He hadn't seen any of them, save Eric, since he'd been carried off the pitch mid-match, half-unconscious. He'd wanted it that way; it had seemed the only choice left to him. The rest had been taken away.

And what of Lucy? The question slipped slyly into his mind, and he pressed his lips together in a firm line, his eyes narrowing against the harsh glare of the sun.

He wouldn't think of Lucy. He hadn't thought of her in four years. It was astonishing, really, how much effort it took *not* to think of someone. Of her.

The silky slide of her hair through his fingers, the way her lashes brushed her cheek, the sudden throaty chuckle that took him by surprise, had made him powerless to do anything but pull her into his arms.

Too late Khaled realised he *was* thinking of her. He was indulging himself in sentimental remembrance, and there was no point. He'd made sure of that. He doubted Lucy was on that plane, and even if she was…

Even if she was…

His heart lurched with something too close to hope, and Khaled shook his head in disgust. Even if she was, it hardly mattered.

It didn't matter at all.

It couldn't.

He'd made a choice for both of them four years ago and he had to live with it. Still. Always.

The plane was approaching the runway now, and with a couple of bumps it landed, gliding to a stop just a few-dozen yards away from him.

Khaled straightened, his hands kept loosely at his sides, his head lifted proudly.

He'd been working for this moment for the last four years, and he would not hide from it now. He wanted this, he ached for it, despite—and because of—the pain. It was his goal; it was also his reckoning.

Lucy squinted in the bright sunlight as she stepped off the plane onto the tarmac. Having come from a drizzly January afternoon in London, she wasn't prepared for the hot, dry breeze that blew over her with the twin scents of salt and sand. The landscape seemed to be glittering with light, diamond-bright and just as hard and unforgiving.

She fumbled in her bag for sunglasses, and felt Eric reach for her elbow to guide her from the flimsy aeroplane steps.

'He's here,' he murmured in her ear, and even as her heart contracted she felt a flash of annoyance. She didn't need Eric scripting this drama for her. She didn't want any drama.

She'd already had that, lived it, felt it. Now was the time to stop the theatrics, to act grown up and in control. Cool. Composed.

Uncaring.

She pulled her elbow from Eric's grasp and settled the

glasses on her nose. Tinted with shadow, she could see the land-scape more clearly: a stretch of tarmac, some scrubby brush, a rugged fringe of barren mountains on the horizon.

And Khaled. Her gaze came to a rest on his profile, and she realised she'd been looking for him all along. He was some yards distant, little more than a tall, proud figure, and yet she knew it was him. She felt it.

He was talking to Brian, the national team's coach, his movements stiff and almost awkward, although his smile was wide and easy, and he clapped the other man on the shoulder in a gesture of obvious friendship and warmth.

With effort she jerked her gaze away and busied herself with finding some lip balm in her bag.

She hadn't meant to walk towards Khaled; she wasn't ready to see him so soon, and yet somehow that was where her legs took her. She stopped a few feet away from him, feeling trapped, obvious, and then Khaled looked up.

As always, even from a distance, his gaze nailed her to the ground, turned her helpless. Weak. She was grateful for the pro-tection of her sunglasses. If she hadn't been wearing them what would he have seen in her eyes—sorrow? Longing?

Need?

No.

Lucy lifted her chin. Khaled's expressionless gaze contin-ued to hold hers—long enough for her to notice the new grooves on the sides of his mouth, the unemotional hardness in his eyes—and then, without a blink or waver, it moved on.

She might as well have been a stranger, or even a statue, for all the notice he took of her. And before she could stop it Lucy felt a wave of sick humiliation sweep over her. Again.

She felt a few curious stares from the crowd around her; there were still enough people among the team and its entour-age who remembered. Who knew.

Straightening her back, she hitched her bag higher on her shoulder and walked off with her head high and a deliberate air of unconcern. Right now this useless charade felt like all she had.

Still, she couldn't keep the scalding rush of humiliation and pain from sweeping over her. It hurt to remember, to feel that shame and rejection again.

It was just a look, she told herself sharply. *Stop the melodrama*. When Khaled had left England four years ago, Lucy had indulged herself. She'd sobbed and stormed, curled up in her bed with ice cream and endless cups of tea for hours. Days. She'd never felt so broken, so useless, so *discarded*.

And now just one dismissive look from Khaled had her remembering, feeling, those terrible emotions all over again.

Lucy shook her head, an instinctive movement of self-denial, self-protection. *No.* She wouldn't let Khaled make her feel that way; she wouldn't give him the power. He'd had it once, but now she was in control.

Except, she acknowledged grimly, it didn't feel that way right now.

The next twenty minutes were spent in blessed, numbing activity, sorting out luggage and passports, with sweat trickling down between her shoulder blades and beading on her brow.

It was hot, hotter than she'd expected, and she couldn't help but notice as her gaze slid inadvertently, instinctively, to Khaled that he didn't look bothered by the heat at all.

But then he wouldn't, would he? He was from here, had grown up on this island. He was its prince. None of these facts had ever really registered with Lucy. She'd only known him as the charming rugby star, Eton educated, sounding as if he'd spent his summers in Surrey or Kent.

She'd never associated him with anything else, not until he'd gone halfway around the world, and when she'd needed to find him he'd been impossible to reach.

Even a dozen feet away, she reflected with a pang of sorrow, he still was.

Everyone was boarding the bus, and Lucy watched as Khaled turned to his own private sedan, its windows darkly tinted, luxurious and discreet. He didn't look back, and she felt someone at her elbow.

'Lucy? It's time to go.'

Lucy turned to see Dan Winters, the team's physician, and essentially her boss. She nodded and from somewhere found a smile.

'Yes. Right.'

Lucy boarded the bus, moving to the back and an empty seat. She glanced out the window and saw the sedan pulling sleekly away, kicking up a cloud of dust as it headed down the lone road through the brush, towards the barren mountains.

Lucy leaned her head back against the seat and closed her eyes. Why had she bothered to track Khaled's car? Why did she care?

When she'd decided to come to Biryal for the friendly match, a warm-up to the Six Nations tournament, she'd told herself she wouldn't let Khaled affect her.

No, Lucy realised, she'd convinced herself that he *didn't* affect her.

And he wouldn't. She pressed her lips together in a firm, stubborn line as resolve hardened into grim determination within her. The first time she saw him was bound to be surprising, unnerving. That didn't mean the rest of her time in Biryal would be.

She let out a slow breath, felt her composure trickle slowly back and smiled.

The bus wound its way along the road that was little more than a gravel-pitted track, towards Biryal's capital city, Lahji. Lucy leaned across the seat to address Aimee, the team's nutritionist.

'Do you know where we're staying?'

Aimee grinned, excitement sparking in her eyes. 'Didn't you hear? We're to stay in the palace, as special guests of the prince.'

'What?' Lucy blinked, the words registering slowly, and then with increasing dismay. 'You mean Prince Khaled?'

Aimee's grin widened, and Lucy resisted the urge to say something to wipe it off. 'Yes, wasn't he gorgeous? I didn't think I'd ever go for a sheikh, for heaven's sake, but—'

'I see.' Lucy cut her off, her voice crisp. She leaned back in the seat and looked out of the window, her mind spinning. The scrub and brush had been replaced by low buildings, little more than mud huts with straw roofs. Lucy watched as a few skinny goats tethered to a rusty metal picket fence bleated mournfully before they were obscured in the cloud of sandy dust the bus kicked up.

They were staying at the palace. With Khaled. Lucy hadn't imagined this, hadn't prepared for it. When she'd envisioned her conversation with Khaled—the one she knew they'd had to have—she'd pictured it happening in a neutral place, the stadium perhaps, or a hotel lounge. She'd imagined something brief, impersonal, safe. And then they'd both move on.

They could still have that conversation, she consoled herself. Staying at the palace didn't have to change anything. It wouldn't.

She gazed out of the window again and saw they were entering Lahji. She didn't know that much about Biryal—she hadn't wanted to learn—but she did know its one major city was small and well-preserved. Now she saw that was the case, for the squat buildings of red clay looked like they'd stood, slowly crumbling, for thousands of years.

In the distance she glimpsed a tiny town, no more than a handful of buildings, a brief winking of glass and chrome, before the bus rumbled on. And then they were out of the city and back into the endless scrub, the sea no more than a dark smudge on the horizon.

The mountains loomed closer, dark, craggy and ominous. They weren't pretty mountains with meadows and evergreens, capped with snow, Lucy reflected. They were bare and black, sharp and cruel-looking.

'There's the palace!' Aimee said with a breathless little

laugh, and, leaning forward, Lucy saw that the palace—
Khaled's home—was built into one of those terrible peaks like
a hawk's nest.

The bus wound its way slowly up the mountain on a
perilous, narrow road, one side sheer rock, the other dropping
sharply off. Lucy leaned her head back against the seat and suppressed a shudder as the bus climbed slowly, impossibly higher.

'Wow,' Aimee breathed, after a few endless minutes where
the only noise was the bus's painful juddering, and Lucy
opened her eyes.

The palace's gates were carved from the same black stone
of the mountains, three Moorish arches with raised iron-port-
cullises. Lucy felt as if she were entering a medieval jail.

The feeling intensified as the portcullises lowered behind
them, clanging shut with an ominous echo that reverberated
through the mountainside.

The bus came to a halt in a courtyard that felt as if it been
hewn directly from the rock, and slowly the bus emptied,
everyone seeming suitably impressed.

Lucy stood in the courtyard, rubbing her arms and looking
around with wary wonder. Despite the dazzling blue sky and
brilliant sun, the courtyard felt cold, the high walls and the
looming presence of the mountain seeming to cast it into eternal
shade.

Ahead of them was the entrance to the palace proper, made
of the same dark stone, its chambers and towers looking like
they had sprung fully formed from the rock on which they
perched.

'Creepy, huh?' Eric murmured, coming to stand next to her.
'Apparently this palace is considered to be one of the wonders
of the Eastern world, but I don't fancy it.'

Lucy smiled faintly and shrugged, determined to be neither
awed nor afraid. 'It makes a statement.'

Out of the corner of her eye she saw Khaled greeting some
of the team, saw him smile and clap someone on the shoulder,

and she turned away to busy herself with the bags. She'd barely moved before a servant, dressed in a long, cotton *thobe*, shook his head and with a kindly, toothless smile gestured to himself.

Lucy nodded and stepped back, and the man hoisted what looked like half a dozen bags onto his back.

'My staff will show you to your rooms.'

Her mind and heart both froze at the sound of that voice, so clear, cutting and impersonal. Khaled. She'd never heard him sound like that. Like a stranger.

She turned slowly, conscious of Eric stiffening by her side.

'Hello, Khaled,' he said before Lucy could form even a word, and Khaled inclined his head, smiling faintly.

'Hello, Eric. It's good to see you again.'

'Long time, eh?' Eric answered, lifting one eyebrow as he smiled back, the gesture faintly sardonic.

'Yes,' he agreed. 'Much has changed.' He turned to Lucy, and she felt a jolt of awareness as his eyes rested on her, almost caressing her, before his expression turned blankly impersonal once more. 'Hello, Lucy.'

Her throat felt dry, tight, and while half of her wanted to match Khaled's civil tone the other half wanted to scream and shriek and stamp her foot. From somewhere she found a cool smile. 'Hello, Khaled.'

His gaze remained on hers, his expression impossible to · discern, before with a little bow he stepped back, away from her. 'I'm afraid I must now see to my duties. I hope you find your room comfortable.' His mouth quirked in a tiny, almost tentative smile, and then he turned, his footsteps echoing on the stone floor of the courtyard as Lucy watched him walk away from her.

She murmured something to Eric, some kind of farewell, and with a leaden heart she followed the servant who carried her bags into the palace.

She was barely conscious of the maze of twisting passageways and curving stairs, and knew she wouldn't find her way out again without help. When the servant arrived at the door of a guest room, she murmured her thanks and stepped inside.

After the harshness of what she'd seen of Biryal so far, she was surprised by the room's sumptuous comfort. A wide double bed and a teakwood dresser took up most of the space. But what truly dominated the room was the window, its panes thrown open to a stunning vista.

Lucy moved to it, entranced by the living map laid out in front of her. On the ground, Biryal hadn't seemed impressive, no more than scrub and dust, sand and rock. Yet from this mountain perch it lay before her in all of its cruel glory, jagged rock and stunted, twisted trees stretching to an endless ocean. It wasn't beautiful in the traditional sense, Lucy decided, and you wouldn't want it on a postcard. Yet there was still something awe-inspiring, magnificent and more than a little fearsome about the sight.

This was Khaled's land, his home, his roots, his destiny. With a little pang, she realised how little she'd known him. She hadn't known this, hadn't considered it at all. Khaled had just been *Khaled*, England's outside half and rising star, and she'd been so thrilled to bask in his attention for a little while.

With an unhappy little sigh, she pushed away from the window and went in search of her toiletry bag and a fresh change of clothes. She felt hot and grimy, and, worse, unsettled. She didn't want to think about the past. She didn't want to relive her time with Khaled. Yet of course it was proving impossible not to.

She could hardly expect to see him, talk to him, and not remember. The memories tumbled through her mind like broken pieces of glass, shining and jagged, beautiful and filled with pain. Remembering hurt, still, *now*, and she didn't want to hurt. Not that way, not because of Khaled.

Yet she couldn't quite protect herself from the sting of his little rejection, his seeming indifference. A simple hello, after what they'd had? Yet what had she expected? What did she *want*?

They'd only had a few months together, she reminded herself. Only a few amazing, *artificial* months.

Four years later, that time meant nothing to him. It should mean nothing to her.

Shaking her head, Lucy forced herself to push the disconsolate memories away. She had a job to do, and she would concentrate on that. But first, she decided, she would ring her mum.

'Lucy, you sound tired,' her mother clucked when Lucy had finally figured out the phone system and got through to London.

'It was a long flight.'

'Don't let this trip upset you,' Dana Banks warned. 'You're stronger than that. Remember what you came for.'

'I know.' Lucy smiled, her spirits buoyed by her mother's mini pep talk. Dana Banks was a strong woman, and she'd taught Lucy how to be strong. Lucy had never been more conscious of needing that strength, leaning into her mother's as she spoke on the phone, her gaze still on that unforgiving vista outside her window. 'Tell me how Sam is.'

'He's fine,' Dana assured her. 'We went to the zoo this morning—his favourite place, as you know—and had an ice cream. He fell asleep in the car on the way home, and now he's got a cartload of Lego spread across the lounge floor.'

Lucy smiled. She could just picture Sam, his dark head bent industriously over his toys, intent on building a new and magnificent creation.

'Do you want to talk to him?'

'Just for a moment.' Lucy waited, her fingers curling round the telephone cord as she heard her mother call for Sam. A few seconds later he came onto the line.

'Mummy?'

'Hello, darling. You're being a good boy for Granny?'

'Of course I am,' Sam replied indignantly, and Lucy chuckled.

'Of course you are,' she agreed. 'But that also means eating your green vegetables and going to bed on time.'

'What about an extra story?'

'Maybe one more, if Granny agrees.' Lucy knew her mother would; she adored her unexpected grandson. A sudden lump rose in Lucy's throat, and she swallowed it down. She'd told herself she wasn't going to get emotional—not about Sam, not about Khaled. 'I love you,' she said.

Sam dutifully replied, 'Love you too, Mummy.'

After another brief chat with her mother, Lucy hung up the phone. Outside the sun was starting its descent towards the sea, a brilliant orange ball that set Biryal's bleak landscape on fire. Sam's voice still echoed in her ears, filled with childish importance, causing a wave of homesickness to break over her. Sam, Khaled's son. And she'd come to Biryal to tell him so.

CHAPTER TWO

THE next few hours were too busy for Lucy to dwell on Khaled and her impending conversation with him. Now that everyone was settled at the palace, she needed to visit the players who were suffering long-term injuries or muscle strain and make certain they were prepared for tomorrow's match.

The match with Biryal was a friendly and virtually insignificant, yet with the Six Nations tournament looming in the next few weeks, the players' safety and health were paramount. In particular she knew she had to deal with the flanker's tibialis posterior pain and the scrum half's rotator-cuff injury.

She gathered up her kit bag with its provisions of ice packs and massage oils, as well as the standard bandages and braces, and headed down the palace's shadowy corridors in search of the men who needed her help.

The upstairs of the palace seemed like an endless succession of cool stone corridors, but it would suddenly open onto a stunning frescoed room or sumptuous lounge, surprising her with its luxury. After a few minutes of fruitless wandering, Lucy finally located a palace staff member who directed her towards the wing of bedrooms where the team was housed.

An hour later, she'd dealt with the most pressing cases and felt ready for a shower. The dust and grime of travel seemed stuck to her skin, and she'd heard in passing that there was to be a formal dinner tonight with Khaled and his father, King Ahmed.

Lucy swallowed the acidic taste of apprehension—of fear, if she was truthful—at the thought of seeing Khaled again. It was a needless fear, she told herself, as she'd already decided she would not speak to him about Sam tonight. She wanted to wait until the match was over. And, since Khaled had already shown her how little he thought of her, she hardly needed to worry that he'd seek her out.

No, Lucy acknowledged starkly as she returned to her room, what scared her was how she wanted him to seek her out. The disappointment she'd felt when he hadn't.

Fool, she told herself fiercely as she stepped into the marble-tiled en suite bathroom and turned the shower on to full power. Fool. Didn't she remember how it had felt when she'd learned Khaled had gone? Lucy's lips twisted in a grimace of memory as she stripped off her clothes and stepped under the scalding water.

There must be a letter. My name is Lucy; Lucy Banks. I'm sure he's left something for me…

She'd tried the hospital, his building, the training centre where he'd worked out. She'd called his mobile, spoken to his friends, his neighbours, even his agent. She'd been so utterly convinced that there had been a mistake, a simple mistake, and it would be solved and everything would be made right. A letter, a message, would be found. An explanation.

There had been none. Nothing. And when she'd realised she'd felt empty, hollow. Used.

Which was essentially what had happened.

Lucy leaned her forehead against the shower tile and let the water stream over her like hot tears.

Don't remember. It was too late for that; she couldn't keep the memories from flooding her with bitter recrimination. Yet she *could* keep them from having power. She could be strong. Now.

At last.

Lucy turned off the shower and reached for a thick towel,

wrapping herself up in its comforting softness as she mentally reviewed the slim wardrobe she'd brought with her. She wanted to look nice, she realised, but not like she was trying to impress Khaled.

Because she wasn't.

In reality, there was little to choose from. She had two evening outfits, one for tonight and one for tomorrow. She chose the simpler one, a black sheath-dress with charcoal beading across the front ending just below the knee. Modest, discreet, safe.

She caught her hair up in a loose chignon and allowed herself only the minimum of eyeliner and lip gloss. Her cheeks, she noticed ruefully, were already flushed.

Outside night had fallen, silky and violet, cloaking the landscape in softness, disguising its harshness. A bird chattered in the darkness, and Lucy could hear people stirring in other parts of the palace.

Giving her reflection one last look, she headed out into the corridor.

Downstairs the front foyer, with its double-flanking staircases made of darkly polished stone, was bright with lights and filled with people. The combined presence of the England team and entourage as well as the palace staff created a significant crowd, Lucy saw.

She paused midway down the staircase, looking for someone familiar and safe. She saw Khaled.

He was taller than most men, even many of the rugby players, and he turned as she came down the stairs, alerted to her presence. How, Lucy didn't know, but she was rooted to the spot as his eyes held hers, seeming to burn straight through her.

Summoning her strength, she tore her gaze from his—this time *she* would be the one to look away—and continued down the stairs, her legs annoyingly shaky.

'You look like you need a drink,' Eric said, handing her

a flute of champagne. Lucy's numb fingers closed around it automatically.

'Thank you.'

'Have you spoken to Khaled?'

She glanced at Eric, saw his forehead wrinkle with worry and experienced a lurch of alarm. In the last few years she'd come to rely on Eric's comforting, solid presence. But his increasing concern over this trip to Biryal and seeing Khaled made her wonder just what he expected of their relationship.

Perhaps she was being paranoid, seeing things, feelings, where there were none.

Hadn't she done that with Khaled?

Still, Lucy acknowledged, taking a sip of cool, sweet champagne, she didn't want or need Eric's protective hovering. It made her seem and feel weak, and that was the last thing she needed.

'I haven't talked to him yet,' she told Eric. 'There's plenty of time.' She met his concerned gaze with a frown, although she kept her voice gentle. 'Please, Eric, don't coddle me. It doesn't help.'

Eric sighed. 'I know how much he hurt you before.'

Lucy felt another sharp stab of annoyance. 'That was before,' she said firmly. 'He can't hurt me now. He has no power over me, Eric, so please don't act like he does.' If she said it enough, she'd believe it. With another firm smile, she moved away.

A gong sounded, and Lucy turned to see a man standing in the arched doorway of the dining room. He was tall, powerfully built, with a full head of white hair and bushy eyebrows. She knew instinctively this was King Ahmed, Khaled's father.

'Welcome, welcome to Biryal. We are so happy and honoured to have England's team here,' he said. His voice, low, melodious and with only a trace of an accent, reached every corner of the room. 'We have worked hard to bring tomorrow's match to pass, and we look forward to thrashing you soundly!' King Ahmed smiled, and the English in the room dutifully chuckled. 'But for now we are friends,' Ahmed continued with a broad smile. 'And friends feast and drink together. Come and enjoy Biryal's hospitality.'

With murmurs of acceptance and thanks, the crowd moved as one towards the dining room. Ahmed took a seat at the head of the table, Khaled at the other end. Lucy immediately went for a safely anonymous place in the middle, and found herself sandwiched between Dan and Aimee.

The first course was served, Arabian flat-bread with a spicy dipping sauce of chillies and cilantro, and Lucy determinedly lost herself in mindless chitchat with her neighbours.

If her gaze slid to Khaled's austere profile once in a while, it was only because she was curious. He had changed, she realised as the bread and sauce was cleared and replaced with melon halves stuffed with chicken and rice, and seasoned with parsley and lemon juice.

The Khaled she'd known in London had been charming, arrogant, a little reckless. His hair had been thick and curly, his clothes casual and expensive. The man at the end of the table held only the arrogance and little of the charm. His hair was cut short, a scattering of grey at his temples. He wore the traditional clothes of his country: a white cotton *thobe* topped with a formal black *bisht*, a wide band of gold embroidery at the neck.

His eyes were dark and hooded, the expression on his face purposefully neutral. She remembered him smiling, laughing, always gracious and at ease.

But now, even as he smiled and chatted with his neighbours, Lucy saw a tension in his eyes, in the taut muscle of his jaw. He wasn't relaxed, even if he was pretending to be. Perhaps he wasn't even happy.

What had happened in four years? she wondered. What had changed him? Or perhaps he hadn't changed at all, and she'd just never known him well enough to realise his true nature.

Of course, she knew about his knee. She knew that last injury had kept him from playing. Yet she couldn't believe it was the only reason he'd left the country. Left her. All rugby players had injuries, sometimes so severe they were kept from playing for months or even years. Khaled was no different. With the right course of physiotherapy, or even surgery, he surely could have recovered enough to play again. Eric had told her as much himself, and as Khaled's best friend—not to mention the last person to have seen him—he should have known.

Just as Lucy had known he'd always had muscle pain in his right knee, and that the team physician as well as a host of other surgeons and specialists had been searching for a diagnosis. Lucy had treated him herself, given him ice packs and massage therapy, which is how it had all started…

I love it when you touch me.

They'd been alone in the massage room, and she'd been meticulously rubbing oil into his knee, trying to keep her movements brisk and professional even as she revelled in the feel of his skin. She'd been so infatuated, so hopeless.

And then he'd spoken, the words no more than a murmur, and she'd been electrified, frozen, her fingers still on his knee. He'd laughed and rolled over, his chest bare, bronzed, his muscles rippling, and he'd captured her fingers in his hand and brought them to his lips.

Have dinner with me.

It hadn't been an invitation, it had been a command. And she, besotted fool that she was, had simply, dumbly nodded.

That was how it had begun, and even now, knowing all that had and hadn't happened since, the bitterness couldn't keep the memory from seeming precious, sacred.

She forced her mind from it and concentrated on her food. Yet she felt the burdensome weight of Khaled's presence for the entire meal, even though he never once even looked at her. She breathed a sigh of relief when the last course was cleared away and King Ahmed rose, permitting everyone else to leave the table.

Of course, escape didn't come that easily. With a sinking heart Lucy saw Ahmed lead the way into another reception room, this one with stone columns decorated in gold leaf, and gorgeously frescoed walls. Low divans and embroidered pillows were scattered around the room and Lucy's feet sank into a thick Turkish carpet in a brilliant pattern of reds and oranges.

A trio of musicians had positioned themselves in one corner, and as everyone reclined or sat around the room, they began their haunting, discordant music.

A servant came around with glasses of dessert wine and plates of pastries stuffed with dates or pistachios, and guests struck up conversations, a low murmur of sound washing through the crowded space.

Lucy dutifully took a cup of wine and a sticky pastry, although her stomach was roiling with nerves too much to attempt to eat. She balanced them in her lap, the music jarring her senses, grating on her heart.

Khaled, she saw, was sitting next to Brian Abingdon, a faint smile on his face as his former coach chatted to him—although even from a distance Lucy could see the hardness, the coldness, in his eyes. She could feel it.

Did anyone else notice? Did anyone else wonder why Khaled had changed? He'd brought them here; Lucy knew he'd orchestrated the entire match. Yet at the moment he looked as if he couldn't be enjoying their company less. Why did he look so grim?

Lucy took a bite of pastry, and it filled her mouth with cloying sweetness. She couldn't choke it down, and the incessant music was a whining drone in her ears. She felt exhausted and overwhelmed, aching in every muscle, especially her heart.

She needed escape.

She put her cup and pastry on a nearby low table and struggled to her feet. Almost instantly a solicitous servant hovered by her elbow, and Lucy turned to him.

'I'd like some fresh air,' she murmured, and, nodding, the servant led her from the room.

She followed him down a wide hallway to a pair of curtained

French doors that had been left ajar. He gestured to the doors, and with a murmur of thanks Lucy slipped outside.

After the stuffy heat of the crowded reception room, the cool night air felt like a balm. Lucy saw she was on a small balcony that hung over the mountainside. She rested her hands on the ornate stone railing and took a deep breath, surprised to recognise the scents of honeysuckle and jasmine.

The moon glided out from behind a cloud and, squinting a bit in the darkness, Lucy saw that the mountainside was covered in dense foliage—gardens, terraced gardens, like some kind of ancient wonder.

She breathed in the fragrant air and let the stillness of the night calm her jangled nerves. From beyond the half-open doors, she could still hear the strains of discordant music, the drifting sound of chatter.

I didn't expect this to be so hard. The realisation made her spirits sink. She'd wanted to be strong. Yet here she was—unsettled, alarmed—and she hadn't even spoken to Khaled, hadn't even told him yet.

And what would happen then? Lucy didn't let herself think beyond that conversation: message delivered…and received? She couldn't let her mind probe any further, didn't want to wander down the dangerous path of pointless speculation. Perhaps it was foolish, or even blind, but she knew the current limitations of her own spirit.

Footsteps sounded behind her, and Lucy straightened and turned, half-expecting to see Eric frowning at her in concern once more.

Instead she saw someone else frowning, his brows drawn sharply together, his eyes fastened on hers.

'Hello, Khaled.' Lucy surprised herself with how calm and even her voice sounded. Unconcerned, she turned all the way round, one hand still resting on the stone balustrade.

'I didn't think anyone was here,' he said tersely, and Lucy inclined her head and gave a small smile.

'I needed some air. The room was very hot.'

'I'm sorry you weren't comfortable.' They were the words of a cordial host, impersonal, distant, forcing Lucy to half-apologise.

'No, no. Everything has been lovely. I'm not used to such star treatment.' She paused, and gestured to the moonlight-bathed gardens behind her. 'The palace gardens look very beautiful.'

'I will have someone show you them tomorrow. They are one of Biryal's loveliest sights.'

She nodded, feeling somehow dismissed. There was a howl inside her, a desperate cry for understanding and mercy.

After everything we had...

But in the end, it—she—had meant nothing to Khaled. Why couldn't she remember that? Why did she always resist the glaring truth, try to find meaning and sanctity where there had been none? 'Thank you,' she managed, and then lapsed into silence as the night swirled softly around them.

Khaled said nothing, merely looked at her, his gaze sweeping over her hair, her face, her dress. Assessing. 'You haven't changed,' he said quietly, almost sadly.

Surprised by what felt like a confession, Lucy blurted, 'You have.'

Khaled stilled. Lucy hadn't realised there had been a touch of softness to his features in that unguarded moment until it was gone. His smile, when it came, was hard and bitter. 'Yes, I have.'

'Khaled...' She held one hand out in supplication, then dropped it. She didn't want to beg. There was nothing left to plead for. 'I'd like to talk to you.'

Khaled arched one eyebrow. 'Isn't that what you're doing?'

'Not now,' Lucy said, suddenly wishing she hadn't started this line of conversation. 'Tomorrow. I just wanted you to know... Perhaps we could arrange a time?' Her voice trailed away as Khaled simply stared, his lips pressed in a hard line, a bleakness in his dark eyes.

'I don't think we have anything to say to each other any more, Lucy.' Startled, she realised he sounded almost sad once more.

'You may feel that way, but I don't. I just need a few minutes of your time, Khaled. It's important.'

He shook his head, an instinctive gesture, and Lucy felt annoyance spurt through her. She hadn't come to Biryal to be rejected again, and for something so little. Was he not willing to give her anything? Would she always feel like a beggar at the gates when it came to Prince Khaled el Farrar?

'A few minutes,' she repeated firmly, and without giving him time to respond, or time to betray herself with more begging, pleading, she moved past him. Her shoulder brushed his and sent every nerve in her body twanging with feeling as she hurried back into the palace.

Lucy didn't sleep well that night. She was plagued with half-remembered dreams, snatches of memory that tormented her with their possibility. Khaled inhabited those dreams, invaded her heart when her body and mind were both vulnerable in sleep. Khaled, laughing at a stupid joke she'd told, his head thrown back, his teeth gleaming white. Khaled, walking off the pitch, his arm thrown casually yet possessively over her shoulders. *My woman.* Khaled, smiling lazily at her from across the lounge of his penthouse suite.

Come here, Lucy. Come to me.

And she had, as obediently as a trained dog, because when it came to Khaled she'd never felt she had a choice. What hurt more than her own foolish infatuation was Khaled's easy knowledge of it. He'd never doubted, never even had to ask.

Muttering under her breath, Lucy pushed the covers off and rose from the bed. The sun had risen, fresh and lemon-yellow in a cloudless sky, and she was relieved to be free of her dreams, for the new day to finally begin.

The day she'd been waiting for since she'd heard of the match with Biryal. The day Khaled would find out he was a father.

As she dressed in her physio scrubs, she found her mind sliding inexorably to the question of how Khaled would react to the news, wandering down that dangerous path. Would he deny it? Deny responsibility? Lucy couldn't see many other possibilities. You couldn't trust a man who walked out; it was a lesson she'd learned early. A lesson her mother had taught her. And, after the way Khaled had walked out on her, she couldn't imagine him taking an interest in his bastard child.

She didn't want him to; that wasn't the point. The point, as she'd explained to her mother and to Eric—who'd both disapproved of her intention to come to Biryal—was for Khaled to know the truth. He had a right, just as she felt she'd had a right to a goodbye all those years ago. And now she had a right as well: to finish with Khaled once and for all. To know it was finished, to feel it. To be the one to walk away.

Turning from her own determined reflection, Lucy left her bedroom in search of the others.

Biryal's new stadium, completed only a few months before, was an impressive structure on the other side of Lahji with a breathtaking view of a glittering ocean. All modern chrome and glass, it was built in the shape of an ellipse, so the ceiling appeared to hover over the pitch.

As Lucy arranged her equipment in the team's rooms, she saw the stadium was outfitted with every necessity and luxury. Khaled clearly had spared no expense.

'It seats twenty thousand,' Yusef, one of the staff who had shown them to the rooms, had explained proudly. Considering Biryal's population was only a few hundred thousand, it seemed excessive to Lucy. The building also jarred with Lahji's far humbler dwellings. Yet she had to admit the architect had designed it well; despite its modernity, it looked as if it belonged on the rocky outcropping facing the sea, as if about to take flight.

Lucy was used to before-game energy and tension, although the match with Biryal did not have the high stakes most matches did. There was something else humming through the room, Lucy thought, and she knew what it was.

Memory.

At least a third of the team had played with Khaled, seen him fall on the pitch. Had felt the betrayal of his abrupt and unexplained departure. The reason Brian Abingdon had agreed to this match at all, Lucy suspected, was because of Khaled and the victories he had brought to England's team in his few years as its outside half.

As the match was about to start, Lucy found herself scanning the crowds for a glimpse of Khaled. Her eyes found him easily in the royal box near the centre of the stadium. As usual, he looked grim, forbidding.

The match started without her realising, and almost reluctantly she turned to watch the play. After a few moments a man came to stand next to her, and out of the corner of her eye she saw it was Yusef.

'The stadium's full,' she remarked, half-surprised that twenty-thousand Biryalis had come to watch.

'This match is very important to us,' Yusef replied with a faint smile. 'Although it's small to you, this is one of Biryal's first matches. The team was only organised two years ago, you know.'

'Really?' Lucy hadn't realised the team was quite so recent a creation, although perhaps she should have. Biryal was a small country, and there was no reason for it to possess a national rugby team.

No reason save for Khaled.

'Khaled began it,' Yusef explained, answering the half-formed question in Lucy's mind. 'When he returned from England. Since he couldn't play himself, he did the next best thing.'

'He couldn't play himself?' Lucy repeated, a bit too sharply. Yusef glanced at her in surprise.

'Because of his injury.'

'He'd always had trouble with his knee,' Lucy protested, and Yusef was silent, his expression turning guarded and wary.

'Indeed. Prince Khaled arranged for the stadium to be built as well. He hired one of the best architects, helped with the design himself.'

Lucy knew there was no point in pressing Yusef for more information about Khaled's injury, even though her mind spun with unanswered questions and doubts. She smiled and tried to inject some enthusiasm into her voice. 'It was clearly an ambitious project, especially when Biryal could benefit from so much.'

Yusef gave a little laugh, understanding her all too well. 'We are a poor country in the terms you understand,' he agreed. 'And Prince Khaled realises this. He understands our nationalistic pride, and he built us something we could show to the world. You might think we'd benefit from more hospitals or schools, but there are other ways of helping a country, a people. Of giving them respect. Prince Khaled knows this.'

He smiled, and Lucy found herself flushing. Had she sounded so snobbish, so judgemental? 'Besides,' Yusef continued, 'Rugby will bring with it more tourism, and with that a better and stronger economy. Prince Khaled has taken this all into consideration. He will be a good—a great—king one day.'

A king. King Khaled. The thought was so strange, so impossible. The Khaled she'd known would never have been a king. She'd barely been aware he was a prince. He'd simply been Khaled—fun, sexy, charming Khaled. Hers, for a short time.

Except, of course, he really hadn't been.

Lucy glanced up at him and saw Khaled lean forward, one white-knuckled hand clasped in the other, watching the match with an intent ferocity. She wondered what had brought him to this moment, what had made him work so hard. What made him look so…unhappy.

Since he couldn't play himself… Was that really the truth? Was that the reason he'd left so suddenly? And did it really make any difference? Lucy wondered sadly. If he'd loved her, as she'd loved him—had thought she'd loved him—he would have shared such important, life-changing information with her. He would have wanted her to be there.

She'd tried to be there, God knew. She had been turned away from the hospital when a nurse had flatly explained that Prince Khaled had requested no visitors. No visitors at all.

A cry rose from the crowd, and Lucy saw that Biryal had scored. She narrowed her eyes, noticing that Damien Russell, the team's open-side flanker, was limping a bit, and went to get one of her ice packs.

The next hour was spent fulfilling her duties as team physio, checking injuries, watching for muscle strain, fetching the tools of her trade. She kept her mind purposely blank, refused to think of Khaled at all, even though her body hummed with awareness, ached with tension.

The match seemed to go on for ever. For a fledgling team, Biryal was surprisingly good—thanks to Khaled and his insistence on one of the best coaches in the game, Lucy suspected. She also suspected the England team wasn't trying as hard as it might, wanting to save its energy and stamina for the more important matches coming up in the Six Nations.

And then finally it was over. John Russell, England's outside half, spun away from an opposing player in a daring move that sent a ripple of awareness through the stadium like an electric current. When he went on to score, the stadium erupted in cheers.

For a moment, Lucy was startled; Biryal had lost, yet they were cheering.

'Close match,' Yusef murmured. 'And, as you just saw, won by one of Prince Khaled's signature moves.'

Of course. Lucy had recognised that half-spin; now she knew why. Khaled had invented it. How many times had he been photographed for the press in that almost graceful pirouette?

And now England had taken that from him too.

Lucy didn't know why that thought slipped into her mind, or why she suddenly felt sad. She didn't know what Khaled felt, although she could see him smiling now as he walked stiffly towards the pitch to shake hands with the players.

He was limping. The thought sent a ripple of shocked awareness through her. Khaled was *limping*, although he was trying not to show it. Just as Yusef had intimated, his old injury must have been a good deal worse than anyone had thought.

Than she had thought—and she had been his physiotherapist! Shouldn't she have known? Shouldn't she have guessed?

Shouldn't she have understood?

Lucy shook her head, wanting to stem the sudden, overwhelming tide of questions and doubts that flooded through her. She didn't want to have sympathy for Khaled, not for any reason. It would only make this trip and everything else harder.

The stadium was in its usual post-match chaos, and numbly Lucy went about her duties, checking on players, arranging care.

At some point Aimee told her there was another party tonight at the palace, a big celebration—for, even though Biryal had lost, they'd played such a good match that it felt like a victory.

Lucy listened, nodded, smiled. Somehow she got through the rest of the afternoon, though both her body and mind ached. She'd never wanted to talk to Khaled more, even as she dreaded it.

Yet he was as inaccessible as he'd been since she'd arrived in his home country, and she wondered if he would ever grant her the opportunity of a moment alone—or if she would have to make one.

From the top of the foyer's staircase Lucy heard the drifting sound of a classical quartet; there would be no discordant music tonight. Tonight, she saw as she came down the stairs, was a show of wealth as well as a celebration. White-jacketed waiters circulated through the palace's reception rooms with trays of champagne and hors d'oeuvres, and King Ahmed stood by the front doors that were thrown open to the warm night air, dressed Western-style in a tuxedo.

Lucy ran her palms down the sides of her evening dress, an artfully draped halter-neck gown in cream satin. It was the most formal piece of clothing she owned, as well as the sexiest, even though the draped fabric didn't cling or reveal, simply hinted. With her hair pulled back in a slick chignon, she felt glamorous—as well as nervous.

Judging from the crowds below her, she wasn't overdressed; Aimee's pink-ruffled concoction made her own gown look positively plain. But she felt it. She felt like she was parading herself for Khaled, never mind every other man who turned with an admiring glance as she came into the foyer.

A few glasses of champagne later, her bubbling nerves had begun to calm. Lucy circulated through the crowd, smiling, chatting, laughing, looking.

Where was Khaled? She wanted to see him now, she wanted that conversation. Fortified with a bit of Dutch courage, she was ready, and she simply wanted it to be over.

Yet he was avoiding her, he must be, for as she wandered through the crowded reception rooms she couldn't find him anywhere.

Disappointment sliced through her as she surveyed the foyer once more. It was getting late, and her head ached from the more-than-usual amount of champagne she'd consumed. Yet she was leaving tomorrow morning, and this was her last chance. Her only chance.

Lucy's face felt stiff from smiling, and fatigue threatened every muscle of her body. She felt anger too, a surprising spurt of it. Khaled had known she wanted to talk to him. She'd told him it was important, yet now he was avoiding her.

Or did he just not care at all?

Shaking her head, Lucy turned towards the stairs. Fine; if Khaled was going to act this way again, then he didn't deserve to know about his son. *Message forgotten.*

Angry, annoyed and hurt, Lucy stormed down the hallway towards the maze of rooms in the back of the palace. Over the thudding of her heart and the silky swish of her gown, she heard another, surprising sound.

A moan. Of pain.

She stopped, waited. Listened. And she heard it again, a low, animal sound.

After a moment's hesitation, her medical training coming to the fore, she knocked once and then pushed open the door from behind which had come those terrible sounds.

Another moan, coming from the hunched figure on the edge of the bed.

'Can I help...?' she began, only to have the speech and breath both robbed from her as the figure looked up at her with pain-dazed eyes.

It was Khaled.

CHAPTER THREE

THEY stared at each other for a long, frozen moment before Khaled jerked his head away.

'Leave me…' he gritted, his teeth clenched, sweat pearling on his forehead. Lucy ignored his plea, dropping to her knees in front of him.

'Is it your knee?'

'Of course it is,' he retorted. Both white-knuckled hands were curled protectively around his leg. 'It's just acting up. Leave me. There's nothing you can do.'

'Khaled—'

'There's nothing I want you to do,' Khaled cut her off. Lucy looked up at him, and saw misery and fury battling in his eyes. 'Go.'

'You must have painkillers,' Lucy said firmly. 'Let me get them for you.'

Khaled was silent, and Lucy felt the struggle within him, although she didn't fully understand it. Finally he jerked a shoulder towards the bedside table, and Lucy went quickly to rummage through it. When she found the small brown bottle, she experienced a jolt of alarmed surprise: it contained a powerful narcotic. A prescription for a powerful narcotic.

Wordlessly she checked the dosage label, and shook two pills out into her hand. She fetched a glass of water from the en suite bathroom and handed both to Khaled, who took them silently.

A few moments ticked by in taut silence and then Khaled eased back onto the bed, his hands braced behind him. 'Thank you,' he said stiffly. 'You can go now.'

'The narcotic doesn't take effect that quickly.'

'It doesn't matter.'

'I can't leave you in such a vulnerable state,' Lucy replied. 'As a medical professional—'

'Oh, give it a rest,' Khaled snapped. 'You don't think I know what I'm doing? You don't think I've been dealing with this for four years?' He glared up at her, his eyes flashing fury. Lucy took a step back.

'Khaled—'

'Go.' It came out as a roar of anguish, a plea, and Lucy almost, *almost* went. But she couldn't leave him like this, couldn't walk away from the pain in his eyes and the unanswered questions in hers.

So she sat across from him on a low, cushioned stool and waited.

After a long moment Khaled let out a ragged laugh. 'I dreamed of seeing you again, but not like this. Never like this.'

Shock rippled through her, cold and yet thrilling. 'You dreamed of seeing me again?' she repeated, the scepticism in her voice obvious to both of them.

'Yes.' Khaled spoke simply, starkly, before he shook his head. 'But I don't want you here now, Lucy. Not like this. So go.'

'No.'

He let out an exasperated sigh. 'You know I can't make you go.'

'No.'

'But I would if I could.'

'I gathered that.' She paused, sifting the memories and recollections in her mind. 'Has your knee been bothering you the whole time we've been here?'

'It's just a flare up,' he said flatly, but Lucy thought she understood why he'd looked so grim. He'd been in pain.

Another few moments passed; the only sound was Khaled's ragged breathing. Finally he pushed himself off the bed and limped stiffly to a table by the window, where Lucy saw a decanter of whiskey and a couple of tumblers.

'You shouldn't drink that on top of a narcotic,' she said as Khaled poured himself a finger of scotch. He smiled grimly as he tossed it back and poured another.

'I have a strong stomach.'

Lucy watched him quietly for a moment. 'Everyone was told your injury wasn't too serious,' she finally said. 'Yet obviously it is if you're still suffering.'

Khaled shook his head, the movement effectively silencing her. 'I told you, this was nothing more than a flare up.'

'How long do they last?'

He turned to face her, a smile twisting his features. 'You're not my doctor, Lucy.'

'Are you having some form of physiotherapy?' she pressed, and he poured some more whiskey.

'Yesterday you said you wanted to talk to me. Now seems like a good opportunity.'

'Why, Khaled?' Lucy asked softly. 'Why did no one know the truth?'

'Why,' he repeated, swinging round to face her, 'don't you tell me what I supposedly need to know and then get out?' He took a deep swallow of his drink. 'I'd like to be alone.'

Lucy hesitated. This wasn't exactly the way she'd wanted to have this conversation, yet she recognised that there might not be another opportunity. She drew a breath and let it out slowly. 'Fine. Khaled...when you left England four years ago I was pregnant.' She saw a current of some deep, fathomless emotion flicker in Khaled's eyes before he stilled, became expressionless. Dangerous.

There was no way she knew of to make this information

more palatable, less surprising, so she ploughed on. 'You have a child, Khaled. A son.'

The silence ticked by for a full, taut minute. Khaled just stared at her, a blank, unnerving stare that made Lucy want to explain, apologise, but she did neither. She just waited.

'A son,' he finally repeated, his voice still so terribly neutral. 'And you did not seek to apprise me of this fact until now?'

'Actually, I did.' Lucy kept her voice even. Now that she'd told him, now that he knew, she felt calm, composed. In control. All the things she'd wanted to be all along—all the things she'd wanted to be four years ago. 'I didn't realise I was pregnant until after you left,' she continued. 'And, when I did, I tried to get in touch with you. Your mobile number had been disconnected—'

'That's all?' Khaled bit out. 'One attempted phone call?'

'Not quite,' Lucy returned coolly. 'I sent an e-mail to you in Biryal. I got the address off the government website—'

'You sent an e-mail to a generic government e-mail address and expected me to get it?' Khaled interjected, raking a hand through his still sweat-dampened hair. 'With the kind of information it contained, it was undoubtedly dismissed as a tabloid's ploy or the ravings of a scorned mistress.'

'And isn't that what I was?' Lucy flashed, her own temper rising to meet his. 'Except I didn't happen to be raving.'

They glared at each other for a long moment and then with a sudden, ragged sigh Khaled turned away. 'What's his name?' The question surprised Lucy, softened her.

'Sam.'

'Sam,' he repeated, and there was a note of wonder in his voice that made him seem somehow vulnerable, and made Lucy ache.

'He's three years old,' she continued quietly. 'He had his birthday four months ago.'

Khaled nodded slowly, his eyes on a distant horizon. From downstairs there came a sudden burst of raucous laughter that felt like an intrusion in the sudden cocoon of warmth Sam's name had created.

Khaled straightened. 'I'll have to have a DNA test done.'

Lucy blinked. It was no more than she expected, but still it hurt. 'Fine.' She drew a breath. 'Khaled, I didn't tell you about Sam because I wanted something from you. You don't need to worry—' She broke off because Khaled was staring at her in what could only be disbelief, his eyes narrowed, his mouth no more than a thin line.

'Worry?' he repeated softly, and Lucy shrugged, the movement defensive.

'Worry that I came here asking for money or something. Sam and I are fine. We don't need—'

'Me?' he finished, and Lucy felt a chill of apprehension. This wasn't what she'd expected, what she'd *wanted*.

'We're fine,' she repeated firmly, and Khaled shook his head.

'Every boy—every child—needs his father.'

'Plenty of children are raised without one.' Like she had been. Children didn't need fathers—not ones who walked away, at any rate. She swallowed, her throat suddenly tight, and met his gaze. She saw sparks firing the golden depths of his eyes.

'Are you trying to tell me that you don't *want* me in my son's life?'

His words were almost a sneer, a condemnation and a judgement. Lucy threw her shoulders back and lifted her chin. She was ready to fight. God only knew, after four years of living with so many unanswered questions, the broken pieces of a shattered existence—not to mention of her heart—she was ready. 'Yes, I am saying that. You haven't exactly proven yourself reliable, Khaled. The last thing I want is for Sam to come to know you, love you, and then for you to do another disappearing act.'

The skin around Khaled's mouth had turned white, his eyes narrowed almost to slits. 'You are insulting me,' he said in a dangerously quiet voice.

'Is it an insult?' Lucy arched one eyebrow. 'I rather thought I was telling the truth.'

Khaled muttered a curse under his breath, then stalked back to the table by the window to pour himself another drink.

'I think you've had enough, considering you're on medication.'

'I haven't even begun,' Khaled snarled, his back to her. 'And I don't need any advice from you.'

'Fine.' Lucy's heart thudded but she kept her voice cool. Still her fingers curled inwards, her nails biting into her slick palms.

What did Khaled want?

His back and shoulders were taut with tension and fury as he tossed back another finger's worth of whiskey. Lucy was suddenly conscious of how tired she was; her mind spun with fatigue, every muscle aching with it.

'Why don't we continue this conversation tomorrow?' she said carefully. 'I don't leave until noon. I think we'd both be in a better frame of mind to consider what's best for Sam.'

'Fine.' His back still to her, Khaled waved one hand in dismissal. 'We can have breakfast tomorrow. A servant will fetch you from your room at eight.'

'All right,' Lucy agreed. She waited, but Khaled did not turn round. 'Till tomorrow, then.' She walked towards the door, only to be stopped with her hand on the knob by Khaled's soft warning.

'And, Lucy…' He turned round, his eyes glittering. 'We'll *finish* this conversation tomorrow.'

The door clicked softly shut and Khaled raised his glass to his lips before he thrust it aside completely with a muttered oath. It clattered on the table and, pushing a hand through his hair, he flung open the doors that led to a private balcony.

Outside he took in several lungfuls of air and let it soothe the throbbing in his temples, the still-insistent ache in his knee. He hadn't had a flare up like the one tonight in months, years…and Lucy had seen it. Seen *him*, weak, prone, pathetic.

He'd never wanted that. He'd never wanted anyone—especially her—to know. Hadn't wanted the pity, the compassion that was really condemnation. He didn't want to become a burden, as his mother had, to her own shame and sorrow.

It was why he'd left, why he'd taken the decision out of Lucy's hands. It was the only form of control he'd had.

Yet now he realised he would have to put that control aside. Things would have to change. *He* would have to change. Because of Sam.

Sam...

The air was sultry and damp; a storm was coming. He felt as if one had blown through here, through his room, his life, his heart.

Sam. He had a son. A child; flesh of his own flesh. A *family* at last. It was an incredible thought, both humbling and empowering.

A three-year-old son who didn't even know of his existence. Khaled frowned, guilt, hurt and anger all warring within him. He wanted to blame Lucy, to accuse her of deceiving him, of not trying hard enough to find him, but he knew that would be unfair. He had not wanted to be found.

He had pushed her out of his mind, his heart, his whole existence, and thought things would stay that way. He'd made peace with it, after a fashion. He'd certainly never planned on seeing her again.

Loving her again.

For a moment, Khaled allowed himself to savour how she'd looked—kneeling before him, the sweep of her glossy hair, her slender, capable hands that had once afforded him so much pleasure. He remembered the way that satin dress had clung to her curves, pooled on the floor, and even in the red haze of pain he had a sharp stab of desire.

Desire he wouldn't—*couldn't*—act upon. Yet neither could he deny that Lucy was in his life once more, and now he would not let her leave it. He wouldn't leave, because things were different.

Sam had changed everything.

* * *

Exhausted, Lucy entered her bedroom and peeled off her evening gown, leaving it in a puddle of satin on the floor. She knew she should hang it up, keep it from creasing, but she couldn't be bothered. Her mind and body cried out for sleep, for the release of unconsciousness.

For forgetfulness…for a time. A few hours; that was all the respite she'd been given.

And then tomorrow the reckoning would come.

What did Khaled want?

Just the question sent her heart rate spiralling upwards, her breath leaking from her lungs. She hadn't anticipated him wanting anything. She'd planned, hoped, *believed* that after today she would walk away, free.

Yet now she realised she might have entangled herself in Khaled's snare more firmly than she had before. Now perhaps Sam was entangled too.

What did Khaled want?

And had she been so naïve—stupid, really—to think he wouldn't want anything?

That he wouldn't want his son?

But he didn't want me.

She slipped under the covers and pressed her face into the pillow, trying to stop the hot rush of tears that threatened to spill from behind her lids.

She didn't want to cry now. She didn't want to feel like crying now.

Yet she did feel like it; she craved the release. She wanted to cry out in fear for herself and for Sam, and in misery for all she'd felt for Khaled once and knew she could not feel again.

And, surprisingly, she felt sad for Khaled. What was he hiding? Lucy couldn't tell what kind of injury had him in its terrible thrall, but it was serious. More serious than she could treat as a physio-therapist. It was the kind of injury, she suspected, that could keep him from playing rugby ever again…no matter what Eric had said.

Had he left England because his rugby career was finished?

And why would that have meant *they* were finished? The only answer, even now, was that she simply hadn't meant enough to him. Not like he'd meant to her.

Her mind still spinning with too many questions and doubts, her heart aching like a sore tooth with sudden, jagged, lightning streaks of pain, she finally fell into a restless and uneasy sleep.

Lucy hadn't even risen from bed when she heard a perfunctory knock on her bedroom door the next morning. With a jolt she realised it was already eight o'clock, and Khaled's servant had come to fetch her.

'Just a moment,' she called out, throwing off the sheets and reaching hurriedly for clothes. Unshowered, groggy from sleep, she knew she'd be at a disadvantage for her breakfast with Khaled.

Calling out an apology, she quickly splashed water on her face, brushed her teeth and indulged herself in a touch of make-up.

She didn't need any disadvantages now.

Opening her door, she saw Yusef, the palace staff member from the stadium yesterday.

'Good morning, Miss Banks,' he said smoothly. 'Prince Khaled is waiting.'

Wordlessly Lucy followed him down the corridor, and then another, and yet one more, until she was hopelessly lost. Finally Yusef brought her through a pair of double doors to a wide, private terrace overlooking the gardens she'd glimpsed by moonlight two nights before.

Khaled stood as she approached. He was, she noticed a bit sourly, dressed in a crisp, white shirt and immaculately ironed chinos, his hair still damp from a shower. He looked fresh and clean, the picture of good health, his skin a dark golden-brown, his teeth flashing white.

Lucy's heart gave an unexpected lurch at the sight of him. When he smiled, he reminded her of the man she'd known, the man she used to love. The rugby star, the player.

The man who had broken her heart.

There was, she thought, no sign of the pain-wracked sufferer she'd seen last night. Even Khaled's limp was virtually unnoticeable as he walked round the table to pull out her chair.

'Did you sleep well?' he asked, and Lucy grimaced.

'Not particularly.'

'I'm sorry to hear that.' Khaled moved back to his own chair and picked up a porcelain coffee-pot stamped with the Biryali royal emblem. 'Coffee?'

Yusef, she realised, had quietly, discreetly disappeared. They were alone.

'Please.'

Khaled poured the coffee, and before she could ask he handed her cream. 'I remember how you like it.'

'Thank you,' Lucy murmured, flushing. She poured a generous amount of cream while Khaled watched with a faint smile.

'Do you still take half a teaspoon of sugar?'

'No,' she said, somewhat defiantly, even though she did. She didn't want him to be like this: confident, charming, urbane. In control. The way he'd been four years ago, when he'd reeled her in and she'd fallen so hard.

Almost savagely she thought she preferred the pain-ridden man she'd encountered last night. He'd been vulnerable; he'd needed her. This man didn't. This man expected her to need him.

Khaled just smiled and took a sip of his coffee, which Lucy saw he still drank black. She stirred the cream into her own coffee as she gazed out over the terraced gardens. Compared to the rest of the island with its craggy rocks and seemingly endless scrub, the gardens were luxuriously verdant, thick green foliage and bright bougainvillea tumbling over the landscaped ledges. Lucy could hear the bright tinkling of a nearby fountain, although she couldn't see it.

As if reading her thoughts, Khaled said, 'There are many hidden delights in the palace gardens. I will give you a personal tour.'

'I'm sorry,' Lucy replied, her voice scrupulously polite. 'I won't have time.'

Khaled merely smiled, arching one eyebrow in such blatant scepticism that Lucy's heart lurched again, unpleasantly, and she set her cup back in its saucer with a clatter.

'What do you want, Khaled?' It was the question that had been tormenting her since last evening, when she'd realised with a growing dread that Khaled wasn't going to go his own way, or let her and Sam go theirs, as she'd so naïvely, stupidly, anticipated.

Khaled took a sip of coffee. 'That is an interesting question,' he mused. 'And one I will be glad to answer. But first…' He set his cup down and gave her a long, level look. 'I'd like to know what *you* want.'

'Very well.' Lucy licked her lips and took a breath. 'I want to return to England this afternoon. I want to get back to my son, and my life as it's been, with nothing changed. And I want to forget we've ever even had a conversation.'

As she said the words, Lucy realised how harsh they sounded, as well as how much she meant them. And, gazing at Khaled, who had not spoken or even changed expression, she realised how unlikely it was for anything she wanted to come to pass. 'You asked,' she said with a shrug, and took a sip of coffee.

'So I did.' Khaled rubbed his jaw with one long-fingered hand, his expression fixed on the distant mountains. Somewhere in the garden a bird shrieked, and then Lucy heard the rustle of wings as it took flight. 'These things you want,' Khaled finally said, his voice mild, 'necessitate the absence of my presence in my son's life.'

Lucy swallowed. 'Yes.'

'Does that seem fair to you?' He sounded genuinely curious. Lucy swallowed again.

'It's not about what's fair, it's what's best for Sam.'

'And you think it's best for Sam not to know his father? His father who wishes to know him, love him?'

Lucy felt the fear and fury rise within her like a great dormant beast, though even now it was tinted with a fledgling, uncertain hope. *His father who wishes to know him, love him.* She'd never had that. Sam had never had that. Yet the thought of Khaled in that role was impossible, frightening. Dangerous. She glared challengingly at him. 'And is that what you think you are? What you want?'

'Yes.' The single word was so sincere, so heartfelt, that it left Lucy temporarily speechless. She believed him, accepted that single word, and it left her blindsided.

She lowered her gaze to the table and focussed on the intricate scrollwork on her sterling-silver fork. Even so, her eyes filled and her vision blurred. She blinked back the treacherous tears. 'I find that hard to believe,' she said in a low voice, even though that wasn't quite what she meant. She found it hard to trust—trust that he wouldn't let Sam down, that he wouldn't let *her* down. Again.

Khaled was silent; it felt as if the whole world was silent, except for that faint, musical tinkling of the distant fountain.

'You have a very low opinion of me,' he finally said, his voice as low as hers. 'To say such a thing and, worse, to believe it.'

Lucy's heart twisted. She didn't want to feel guilty, and so she wouldn't. 'And why shouldn't I have a low opinion of you?' she asked. She looked up, met Khaled's hard gaze. 'You left, Khaled. You left me without a word or an explanation, without even the briefest of goodbyes. Why shouldn't I think you would do that to Sam?'

Khaled's fingers clenched around the handle of his coffee cup, and Lucy saw his knuckles turn white. 'Are you going to judge me on the basis of that one action, Lucy?' he asked. 'One decision?'

Lucy gave a short, abrupt laugh of disbelief. 'You speak as though it was one misstep, Khaled. A mistake, or a little slip. That one *decision* defined everything. It defined you to me, and what you thought of me. Of our relationship.'

Khaled stilled, his fingers loosened. 'And what did I think of you?'

She shook her head. Now that they'd begun, she felt compelled to tell the truth. She was past blushing or tears, humiliation or hurt—for the moment, at least. 'I shouldn't even say we had a relationship, because we obviously didn't. We had an affair. Torrid. Tawdry. And it wasn't worth enough for you to even let me know you were leaving the country. *For good.*'

Khaled rotated his cup between his long, brown fingers, and Lucy stared, strangely mesmerised by the simple action. His fingers were so familiar to her—they'd touched her, caressed her—and yet they were so strange. He was a stranger, and she wondered if he always had been.

'I realise I hurt you,' he murmured. 'But that is past us now, Lucy. For our son's sake, it has to be.'

It wasn't an apology, not even close. Even now he couldn't explain. He couldn't say sorry. 'That's not true, Khaled. I agree I may have to put my own feelings aside, but your past behaviour has given me no reason to trust you with Sam.'

She spoke flatly, her expression and voice both bleak, and yet it was as if she'd brandished a knife. The tension that suddenly stilled the air could have been cut. With chilling precision, Khaled set his cup back down on its saucer; when he spoke his voice was just as cold as that careful action.

'I'm afraid,' he said, 'you do not have the luxury of such feelings. And this decision, Lucy, is not yours alone to make.'

His words trickled icily into her consciousness, realisation pooling with dread in her stomach.

'Are you threatening me?'

'I'm stating facts. If the DNA test reveals what I believe it shall, Sam is as much my son as yours, and I have as much right to his time and attention as you do. And,' Khaled continued, his voice soft, chilling, 'I think you'll find I have far more resources than you do to see I am granted custody of my own child.'

Lucy's vision swam. She tasted bile in her throat, on her

tongue, and forced it down. She blinked, tried to focus, to think, but all she could hear or feel was Khaled's threat echoing sickly through her head and heart.

Resources. Custody. He was talking about legal action.

Lucy rose unsteadily to her feet. With a few shaky steps she made it to the balcony, her fingers curling around the railing as she took several deep breaths of fragrant air.

If Prince Khaled el Farrar of Biryal went against her in a custody battle, Lucy was sure she'd lose. At best, she'd gain partial custody, or perhaps only visiting rights.

She choked back a gasp of horror, of terror, and heard Khaled rise from the table behind her. She felt his hand solid and firm on her shoulder and managed to choke out, 'Don't touch me.'

After a moment, he removed his hand; her shoulder burned. 'Lucy,' he said quietly. 'I don't want to threaten you. I don't know what kind of man you think I am—' He broke off, sighing wearily. 'No, I do know, and it seems it is a virtual monster—unfeeling, cruel.'

'You aren't giving me many reasons to believe otherwise,' Lucy retorted.

'And what recourse have you given me?' he countered. 'You came to Biryal, it seems, with the specific purpose of finding me, telling me about our child. Yet now you act as if I have hunted you down and forced the information from you! Why did you tell me, if you didn't want anything from me? You could have kept the information to yourself.' His voice rang with bitterness. 'You've managed to do that for nearly four years.'

'I didn't think you'd want him!' The words were ripped from her lungs, her heart. She felt tears crowd her eyes again and dashed them away angrily. 'Why should I think you would? You walked away from me quickly enough.'

'Sam is my *child.*'

'As opposed to just your lover.' She nodded with a mechanical jerking of her head. 'Yes, I understand. Clearly I rated myself too highly.'

'If you thought you could tell me I had a child and expect no repercussions at all, then you were naïve,' Khaled told her brusquely. 'A fool.'

'Yes, I realise that now,' Lucy replied dully. She felt weary, all the fight gone out of her, leaving her with nothing but an aching, accepting despair. 'I was always a fool when it came to you,' she added with a bleak, humourless smile. She moved back to the table and sat down. She took a sip of coffee. It was cold.

Khaled leaned against the balcony, watching her with cool speculation. Lucy put her coffee cup down and forced herself to continue. 'I don't have much experience of fathers,' she said, her voice flat and unemotional even though her heart was twisting painfully. 'My own divorced my mother when I was six, and the last time I saw him was when I was nine.' She had a sudden vision of his quick, easy smile, his promise that he'd see her soon—and then the waiting. So much waiting, followed by a deep, echoing despair when he hadn't come.

She pushed the memory away, managing a watery smile as she looked up at Khaled; his expression did not change. 'If I indulge myself in a bit of pop psychology, I suppose I could say I thought you'd be just like him. He left my mother without a backward glance, and he had no interest or time for me either.'

Khaled was silent for a long moment, and Lucy looked away. 'I'm sorry for that,' he finally said. 'But I am not your father, and I have no intention of walking away from Sam now that I know about him. I will be in his life, Lucy, and, the more we can work together to love and support him, the happier I believe we will all be.'

Lucy nodded; her heart still felt leaden. She supposed she should be grateful for Khaled's reasoned response. Despite the way he'd treated her, she believed now that he wouldn't let Sam down. She had no choice. And despite his earlier veiled threats she didn't think he'd try to take Sam away from her completely. Still, it was too hard, too new, too *much*. She hadn't expected this, hadn't wanted it, even if that made her a blind fool.

'Let's eat,' Khaled said, his voice almost brusque. 'You look too thin.'

Lucy smiled wryly. 'Life with a busy three-year-old makes it easy to skip meals sometimes.'

'You must take care of yourself. How can you take care of Sam otherwise?'

Lucy did not respond, yet silently she wondered if she could now expect more of these imperious commands. This was Khaled the prince, the future king, not the feckless rugby star.

Yusef must have been waiting for some kind of summons, for it only took a single flick of Khaled's wrist for him to wheel in a silver domed trolley. Lucy watched as he placed several dishes on the table: scrambled eggs, bacon, sausage, stewed tomatoes, sautéed mushrooms.

'I forgot how much you liked the full fry-up,' she said, and just the words caused a shaft of memory to pierce her: scrambling eggs in Khaled's kitchen, barefoot, dressed only in his rugby jersey, laughing as she teased him that he never used his expensive pots and pans.

Did Khaled remember? Was that memory as precious to him as it was to her?

Watching as he served them both eggs—his face impersonal, blank—she knew it was not. He probably didn't even remember it at all. The weeks they'd had together were as incidental and unimportant as the other days, weeks or months he'd had with no doubt dozens of other women. The only difference was that their weeks together had resulted in a child: Sam.

They ate in silence for a few moments, and Lucy found her appetite had returned as she dug into her eggs and bacon. Yet questions still crowded her mind, worked their way up her throat.

What now? What next?

She knew what Khaled wanted, but what did he expect?

Yusef had cleared their plates and brought fresh coffee when Khaled told her.

'I've made arrangements for us to fly back to England together, on the Biryali royal jet.'

Lucy's mouth dropped open. 'But—'

'We leave tomorrow. We can have the DNA test done, and then I'd like to spend a few days with Sam in London, in his familiar surroundings. When he is comfortable and used to me, I'll bring him back to Biryal.'

Lucy was still struggling for words. 'Biryal? You want to bring him *here*?'

Khaled raised his eyebrows and took a sip of coffee. 'This is my home, and therefore it must also be his home for at least part of the year.'

'But...' She shook her head, realising sickly that she should have anticipated this. What had she expected—that Khaled would come to London for weekend visits or take Sam to the zoo and the seaside once every few months? Had she actually thought it could be so simple? 'Biryal is so...' She couldn't imagine Sam here, in this rugged and unforgiving land, in this palace.

Terror struck Lucy's soul as she realised the implications of that word, of who Khaled was: palace. Prince.

Prince Sam.

Khaled watched her carefully, and for a moment Lucy thought she saw compassion flicker in the golden depths of his eyes. 'Sam is my heir, Lucy,' he said. 'One day he will be king.'

'But—but he's illegitimate,' she protested, trying to sound reasonable. To feel reasonable. 'If you marry—have other children—'

He shook his head. 'It is Biryali tradition that a king may choose which son he wishes to succeed him, legitimate or otherwise. As long as there is a son, it doesn't matter which.'

'But you may have other sons,' Lucy insisted, even though

the thought of Khaled with a wife or other children was unpleasant to contemplate. But it was better than considering the massive life changes that would lie in store for Sam…and her.

'There won't be other children,' Khaled told her flatly. 'And, in any case, I choose Sam.'

Fear clutched at her and she shook her head frantically. 'But I don't want Sam to be king!'

'One day he will be,' Khaled replied steadily. 'It is his legacy, his destiny, as it is mine.'

Lucy pressed her palms to her eyes, blotting out the world and its horrible reality for a few merciful seconds. Why hadn't she considered this? Why hadn't she thought more carefully about the Pandora's box she'd be opening when she told Khaled about Sam?

Because, she realised with sudden, stark clarity, *you wanted him to know. You wanted to see him again.*

And she wanted Sam to have a father, unlike her.

Had she expected this, secretly hoped for this, when she'd decided to tell Khaled? The heart was deceitful, yet it shamed her to think she'd been so willfully blind to her own secret desires. She'd convinced herself that coming to Biryal, telling Khaled about Sam, was right. Her duty.

Yet now she wondered if she'd just done it for her own selfish reasons—because she'd *still* wanted to see Khaled. To be with him.

And who would suffer because of it? They all would, she supposed bleakly, and perhaps Sam most of all.

CHAPTER FOUR

THE Biryali royal jet took off from the island into a sky of cloudless blue, the sea smooth and winking with sunlight below. Lucy leaned her head back against the luxurious leather seat and closed her eyes.

The last twenty-four hours had been completely draining. First there had been the breakfast with Khaled, when her world had slipped on its axis, and she'd realised—and accepted—that nothing would be the same. Not for her, not for Sam. And, she added fairly, not for Khaled.

Her reluctant agreement to accompany Khaled on the Biryali jet and return home a day later than she'd planned had led to a flurry of activity.

First, the England team's travel coordinator had had to be told. This had led to everyone else in the team's entourage knowing her changed plans almost immediately, and within the hour Eric had been knocking on her door.

'You're staying? With Khaled?' he demanded as soon as Lucy opened it, and she'd sighed wearily.

'Yes, Eric. It turns out Khaled wants to be involved in Sam's life.'

'And you're permitting this?' Eric's eyes had narrowed. 'You want this?'

Did he sound jealous? Lucy had shrugged impatiently. 'I don't really have much choice. And Khaled has a right to know his son—' She broke off, not wanting to finish that sentence: *even if I don't want him to.*

'And what about you? Do you want to be with Khaled?'

Lucy had found herself flushing, much to her irritation. 'That's none of your business.'

'Isn't it?' Eric had asked quietly, and Lucy had felt a flash of alarm.

'Eric—'

'Never mind.' He'd held up one hand to stop her from speaking. 'I don't really want to know.' He'd turned to go. Lucy had suddenly blurted, 'Why did you tell me Khaled would recover from his knee injury?' Her voice had rung out in accusation. 'He's still clearly in a lot of pain. That injury is more serious than anyone ever imagined.'

'I did what Khaled wanted me to do,' Eric had replied after a moment. He'd looked disappointed, defeated. 'I'll see you back in England, Lucy.'

There had been other difficult conversations before their departure, although Lucy had not been privy to them. Khaled had broken the news to his father that he had a son, an illegitimate one, and that he was going to England to see him.

Lucy didn't know how King Ahmed had reacted to such surprising news, but she supposed she could guess. Khaled had emerged from the reception room tight-lipped and white-faced, and the palace had seemed alive with speculative whispers.

She'd retreated to her room, too tired and overwhelmed to face even one more sliding, sideways glance.

Now that was all behind her—for now. They'd left Biryal for England, but for how long? How long would Khaled be willing to pretend at being happy families in London? Would he tire of her, of Sam? Did she want him to?

The thoughts and desires of her mind and heart were so tangled, so twisted. She didn't know what she wanted.

She wanted to be safe. The thought slipped, unbidden, into

her mind. She wanted Sam to be safe. She wanted her heart to be safe.

Was it already too late?

Cool fingers tapped her hand and her eyes flew open. Khaled was leaning across the aisle towards her, a faint smile on his face.

'Would you like a drink?'

Wordlessly, Lucy nodded. He was close enough that she could see the gold flecks in his eyes, the faint stubble on his chin. When she inhaled, she breathed in the scent of him, a strong, woody aftershave, and something else indefinable— something that she remembered as just being him. 'Yes, thank you,' she finally managed. 'An orange juice, please.'

Khaled raised one hand—an imperious gesture, if there ever was one—and an attendant hurried forward. He murmured something in Arabic, and then sat back in his seat.

'You are all right?'

'I'm fine,' she assured him.

'I realise much has changed for you in the last few days,' Khaled went on as if she hadn't spoken. 'And it must be difficult for you.'

'Thank you for that sensitivity,' Lucy replied, her tone containing a touch of acid. Khaled smiled faintly.

'You're welcome.'

Lucy turned away from Khaled, towards the window. She had so many unanswered questions, but she wasn't ready to ask them, or to hear Khaled's answers.

It was astonishing, she reflected numbly, how quickly and utterly her life had changed. And now that it had she couldn't believe she'd actually ever thought or hoped it wouldn't. Yet, even as she struggled to grasp the enormity of the changes ahead of her and Sam, another part of her shied away from confronting the reality. One step at a time. One day at a time. One minute at a time if necessary.

'Where is Sam staying now?' Khaled asked, breaking into

her spinning thoughts. Startled, Lucy turned to him and nearly jostled the glass of chilled juice the steward had discreetly left on the coffee table by her elbow.

'With my mother.'

Khaled nodded. 'He likes it there?'

'Yes. Mum is very close to him. She's been a tremendous support since Sam was born.'

Khaled slid her a thoughtful glance, his eyes dark and hooded. 'I suppose it was very difficult for you, a single mother with a demanding career.'

'Yes, but Sam has always been worth it.'

'Does your mother take care of him when you work?' Khaled's voice had sharpened slightly, though with curiosity or judgement Lucy could not say. Still, she prickled uncomfortably, ready for a fight.

'Sometimes. He's in a nursery now that he's three, and before that I had a part-time nanny.'

Khaled nodded, his lips pursed, and Lucy steeled herself for another imperious interdict. Would Khaled tell her she couldn't work, or that he wanted to vet the staff that took care of his son?

And what would happen if—when—he took Sam to Biryal?

Don't think of it, she told herself. *Not yet; it's too much. One day, one minute, one second at a time.*

'You'll fetch Sam from your mother's tomorrow?' Khaled asked, and Lucy nodded. 'Then I'll leave the two of you to settle yourselves. The next day, when he's back home, I'll come and see him.' He paused, rubbing his chin. 'You don't need to tell him who I am right away. Wait until he's comfortable with me.'

How long would that take? It was difficult to imagine Khaled with a child, his child. Would he charm Sam? Would he tire of him? The fear gnawed at her, ate away at her insides.

When would he leave?

It was stupid to be afraid of his leaving, when that was what she'd wanted all along: to be left alone. Yet already the thought of his rejection made her insides twist and roil. *Stupid.*

'That sounds sensible,' she finally said, and took a sip of juice.

Eventually she fell into an uneasy doze, only to be woken when the attendant began to serve dinner.

'Will you have wine?' Khaled asked as the steward prepared to pour, and, still befuddled by sleep, Lucy nodded.

The wine was rich and red, and glinted in the dimmed lights of the cabin. Lucy felt as if she were in a fancy restaurant rather than on an aeroplane. The table between their seats had been laid with a linen tablecloth and napkins, winking crystal and creamy porcelain plates.

Outside the hard, blue sky was replaced by endless black, lit only by the plane's wing lights. The attendant served a salad of baby spinach leaves with roasted peppers and pecans, and then retired to the rear of the cabin. Khaled lifted his glass, smiling faintly.

'To our future.'

Lucy's fingers felt cold as they curled around the stem of the glass; she raised it to her lips. *Our future*. Khaled's meaning couldn't have been plainer: he was staying in her life, in Sam's life. They *had* a future.

What would it be like, Lucy wondered, to see Khaled on a regular basis? To have a relationship, a future with him, even if it wasn't the one she'd once imagined?

How long would it last? How long did she *want* it to last? The prospect of inviting him into her life once more terrified her. What she couldn't do was invite him into her heart.

Except she wondered how much choice she really had when it came to Khaled. She'd been so weak before. She wanted to be strong now, to keep him at a distance, but could she?

Would he leave her broken-hearted again—or worse, break the heart of her son?

'What are you thinking?' Khaled asked, his voice low and husky with suppressed laughter. 'Your forehead is crinkling as if you're trying to work out a rather difficult maths problem.'

'No, nothing like that.' Lucy took a sip of the rich, red wine and let it slip like liquid velvet down her throat, firing her belly. 'Just…thinking.'

'It is bound to be awkward for us at first,' Khaled said, also sipping his wine. 'Considering our past. But I'm sure, for Sam's sake, we can move past whatever we felt for each other.' His voice was so neutral, so bland and indifferent, that Lucy couldn't keep from giving a rather sharp laugh.

'That's a good way of putting it—"whatever we felt for each other".'

Khaled frowned. 'What are you implying, Lucy?'

She shrugged and took another sip of wine. 'Only that we rather obviously felt different things. But you're right, Khaled, it will be awkward, and we can move past it. I have already.' She smiled with bright determination, knowing she sounded too defiant, too childish, but not caring.

Whatever we felt for each other. Ha! She knew what he'd felt: nothing.

'You think I didn't care for you?' Khaled said slowly, and now he was the one who sounded like he was working out a maths problem.

'I'd say you spelt that out quite clearly when you left,' Lucy replied shortly. 'Wouldn't you?'

Khaled looked away, and Lucy saw the tension in his jaw, his powerful shoulder. 'There were reasons why I acted the way I did.'

'What—your knee?' Khaled stiffened, and Lucy ploughed on with relentless determination. 'Obviously your injury was more serious than anyone supposed, Khaled. I see that now, and Eric told me you didn't want anyone to know. But, even so…' She took a breath, feeling the hurt once more, so fresh and raw. 'Even so, you didn't have to…to take your bat and go home!' He jerked, turning back to her, his eyes narrowing dangerously. 'If you were hurt, I wanted to be with you,' she said quietly. 'Comfort you. *Help* you.'

'Help me,' he repeated, and it sounded like a snarl. A sneer.

'Yes,' Lucy agreed. She sat back, tired and defeated once more. What was the point of remembering, rehashing, the past now four years later? Four years too late. It didn't change things. It just made them hurt again. Hurt more. 'But obviously you didn't want that from me,' she finished, setting her glass on the table. 'And I accepted that, and moved on. So.' She forced herself to look up, and even to smile. 'That's why we can get past the awkward bit. For Sam's sake…and for our own.'

Khaled gave a little laugh and shook his head. '*Obviously* we felt different things. *Obviously* I didn't want your help. It's so very clear in your world, isn't it, Lucy? You have all the answers without having asked any of the questions. So very black and white.' He gave another little laugh, the sound taut with bitterness, and Lucy stared at him in surprise.

'Then tell me—' she began, but Khaled cut her off.

'No matter. I am glad we are in agreement. The past is finished, and we can move on.' He lifted his glass in a mock toast before taking a sip. 'In fact, I think we have already.'

By the time the plane landed at Heathrow, Lucy was exhausted. Khaled, she noticed, looked tired as well; his face had the greyish tinge of fatigue, and she wondered if his knee was paining him again. How long did these flare ups last?

They didn't speak as they left the plane. Khaled issued a few terse instructions to a hovering attendant regarding their luggage and then gestured to a dark sedan idling by the kerb.

Lucy climbed in, grateful for the comfort, and Khaled followed. 'What is your address?' he asked, and Lucy gave it to him.

She didn't particularly relish the thought of Khaled seeing her rather humble Victorian terrace on the outskirts of London. It was far from what he was used to, whether it was the Biryali palace or his luxury flat in Mayfair. She thought of the days and nights she'd spent in that flat, and forced the memory from her mind.

'Where will you be staying?' she asked as the car pulled away from the kerb. 'Do you still have your flat?'

'No. I sold it.' Khaled's voice was brusque, and with a pang of surprise Lucy realised he hadn't been back to England since his accident. Since their break-up. What did he think or feel, coming back here? Did the rain-slicked pavement and cold, damp air bring back a flood of memories of his time on the team, or his time with her? 'I'm staying at a hotel,' he continued. 'I'll give you all my contact information.'

They didn't talk for the rest of the trip, which was just as well, as Lucy's eyes were fluttering with exhaustion when the car pulled up to her house.

'You don't need to...' she began, but Khaled had already opened his door and was striding around to open hers.

Lucy slipped out and fumbled for the keys in her handbag as the driver retrieved her luggage.

It felt awkward and strangely intimate to be standing in the moonlight outside her front door, Khaled gazing down at her with his usual, unfathomable expression. It felt, she thought with an amusement born from exhaustion, like a date.

'You're seeing me to my door?' she asked, and Khaled frowned.

'I have a responsibility to keep you safe.'

Since when? Lucy wanted to ask. When had she become his responsibility? She opened her mouth to make some querulous reply, then closed it again. What was the point? It was too late for arguments, in more than one respect, and she was too tired anyway.

'Goodnight,' she said, and Khaled thrust a stiff white card into her hand.

'There is all my information. Call me any time, for any reason.'

Lucy raised her eyebrows as she glanced down at the impressive list of contacts: e-mail, mobile, hotel number, suite number. For once, she thought sardonically, Khaled wanted to be found.

'Thanks,' she said, and, with him still standing there on her front stoop, she slipped inside and closed the door.

* * *

She surprised herself by sleeping well and dreamlessly, waking only when pale January sunshine was streaming weakly through her bedroom window.

Sam. Today she would see him. Even though she had to travel all too frequently, Lucy had never got used to time away from her son. She was thankful for her mother's glad readiness to take him, and Sam's happiness in going.

Yet all that would change…

As she showered and dressed, Lucy forced herself to address the practicalities. The possibilities. Back in England, with a good night's sleep behind her, she felt able to face the enormous changes that were in store for her and Sam, even if she didn't know exactly what they were.

One thing she did know, and planned on telling Khaled, was that Sam would not be going to Biryal without her. Not until he was older, anyway. A lot older.

Lucy paused mid-stroke in brushing her hair and gazed at her reflection in the mirror. Her eyes were dark and wide. What if Khaled wanted Sam for weeks, months, at a time? Half the year? How could she have a life for herself in Biryal for that amount of time? How could Sam?

And how could she bear seeing Khaled day in and day out? Perhaps she would become used to it, she thought. Perhaps they would become familiar—friends, even.

The idea felt not only impossible, but unpleasant. She didn't want to be friends with Khaled. She'd once wanted so much more.

Yet she didn't any more.

Did she?

The question made Lucy close her eyes. *No, no, no, no, no, no…*

She couldn't want that. Yes, she was still attracted to him; she was honest enough to admit that, and felt the electric tug of longing deep in her belly. But love? No. The man she'd loved didn't exist. She'd thought he was caring, not just charming.

She'd believed there was something deeper underneath that reckless, roguish charm, yet there hadn't been.

Had there?

The Khaled she saw now was so different from the one she'd known, and yet she didn't think she liked this version any better. At the core, he was still the same—arrogant, powerful, uncaring.

With a sigh Lucy turned away from her reflection. She wasn't going to think about Khaled; now she only wanted to think about—and be with—Sam.

'Mummy!' He hurtled himself into her arms, his small, sturdy body warm and comforting against hers. Lucy buried her face in Sam's soft hair for a moment, then pulled back to look at him.

'Any new scrapes?'

Sam showed her a skinned elbow with pride, and Lucy smiled. 'Doesn't look fatal,' she said, pretending to examine it with professional seriousness. 'Do you think you'll live?'

'It's just a scrape,' Sam said scornfully, but he was grinning. He loved this game.

'How was your trip?' Dana Banks gave her daughter a quick hug before looking over her with critical concern. 'Lucy, you look completely worn out.'

'I feel it,' Lucy replied with a wry smile. 'It's that jet lag.'

'Is that all?' Dana asked, eyebrows arched, and Lucy gave a small smile and shook her head, the understood signal that they were not to talk of this in front of Sam.

'Mummy, did you bring me a present?' Sam asked, pulling on her sleeve. Lucy looked down at her son with a jolt of sudden realisation. He had Khaled's eyes—the long lashes, the almond shape, the darkly golden irises. How could she not have seen it before?

But of course she had; she'd just never acknowledged it, admitted it. She'd spent four years trying *not* to think of Khaled, and now she found he was constantly in her thoughts.

'I'm sorry, sweetheart,' she said, dropping a kiss on the top of his head even as he started squirming away. 'There was no time. But I do have a present, of sorts. A surprise, at least.' Lucy's eyes met her mother's over the top of Sam's head. 'A new friend is coming to visit tomorrow. He's going to take us out.'

'Where?' Sam asked eagerly. 'To the zoo?'

'Haven't you just been to the zoo?'

'I want to go again!'

Lucy chuckled and released Sam, who began racing around the room. He had so much energy, her boy. 'Perhaps. We'll have to see.'

Sam peppered her with more questions until, bored, he finally went out to the garden. Dana took the opportunity to put the kettle on and ask Lucy a few questions herself.

'A new friend?' she repeated, handing Lucy a mug of tea. 'Is that who I think it is?'

Lucy sighed. 'Yes. Khaled came back to England with me. Or, rather, I came with him on the Biryali royal jet. He wants to be involved in Sam's life.'

'Oh, Lucy.' Dana's eyes widened with concern. 'You didn't expect that, did you?'

'No,' Lucy admitted ruefully. 'I didn't. But I should have.' She took a sip of tea, shaking her head. 'I think I believed that telling Khaled about Sam would give me some kind of closure. Pitiful, I know, that after four years I still need it.'

'You never had it,' Dana interjected quietly.

'And I'm not getting it now.' Lucy smiled bleakly at her mother. 'Khaled's indicated that he won't settle for a few trips to the zoo. He doesn't just want to be in Sam's life. He wants to be Sam's father.'

Dana looked sceptical. 'And you think he'll keep feeling that way, once the novelty has worn off? He hasn't given you any reason to trust him in the past.'

'I know.' Lucy gazed out of the kitchen window. Sam was doing laps of the garden, absolutely fizzing with energy. 'He's a different man now,' she said slowly. 'Or at least he seems like it. He isn't carefree any more. Life seems to…weigh him down. And he takes his responsibilities very seriously.'

'He's grown up, then,' Dana said with an edge to her voice, and Lucy smiled wryly.

'Maybe.' Her mother had every right to be wary. Khaled hadn't proved himself reliable four years ago, just as Dana's own husband, Tom Banks, hadn't when Lucy was a child. Her memories of her dad were vague at best—a few treats, a few hugs, standing at the window waiting for him to fetch her…

And then one day he never came.

Lucy swallowed, surprised that such an old, faded memory still had the power to hurt. Khaled's re-entry into her life had brought up too many ghosts, too many scars. Too much fear.

'And how do you feel about all this, Lucy?' Dana asked gently. 'You could fight him, you know.'

'The Crown Prince of Biryal?' Lucy raised her eyebrows. 'If we ever took this to court, Khaled could wipe the floor with me, Mum. I haven't got the resources he has, and he told me as much.'

'He *threatened* you?'

'No.' Lucy let out a breath. 'Although it felt like a threat at the time. But I was telling him I didn't want him in Sam's life.'

'And now?'

Lucy sighed. Her thoughts and feelings were still so hopelessly tangled. 'I don't know,' she admitted after a moment. 'I honestly don't know what I want. I thought I didn't want anything from Khaled, or to see him again, but then why did I tell him about Sam?'

'Because you're a good person,' Dana returned robustly. 'And you felt he had a right to know.'

'But, if he has a right to know, then he also has a right to be part of Sam's life,' Lucy countered. 'And I think part of me knew that all along. I think part of me—even if I've been trying to deny it to myself—wants Khaled in Sam's life.'

Dana's eyes were shrewd, even though her voice was gentle. 'And what about in *your* life?'

Lucy swallowed and looked away. That, she realised despondently, was a question she wasn't ready to answer.

Sam was up early the next morning, eager for his surprise friend. Khaled had rung last night, and they'd agreed on a day's outing to the zoo followed by a children's tea back at Lucy's house.

A whole day with Khaled. A whole day, Lucy thought with a sense of disbelief, as a family.

Even though Khaled wasn't due until nine o'clock, she kept glancing out of the window all morning. Sam was perched on the sofa, informing her in a piping voice of every car that came crawling down the street.

Lucy's nerves were taut, ready to break, and Khaled hadn't even arrived yet.

She checked her appearance in the mirror once more, nervously smoothing her hair behind her ears, making sure that her pale pink V-neck jumper didn't have any stains from breakfast.

Sam turned to watch her. 'You look nice, Mummy.'

'Thanks, darling.' Lucy gave her son a quick, distracted smile. Why was she so nervous? Why had she spent twenty minutes deciding what to wear, how much make-up to put on?

Why did she care?

She didn't want to care. She wanted to be cool, composed. In control.

All those things she'd told herself she would be when she went to Biryal, when she saw Khaled again.

Now she felt them hopelessly, helplessly, slipping away.

As the sedan pulled to a stop in front of the small terraced house, so like the dozen others on the narrow, suburban street, Khaled felt his heart leap in his chest.

Today he would meet his son. What would he look like? Sound like? Be like?

His mind whirled and wondered at the possibilities.

Sam.

Lucy.

She crept into his thoughts, slipped under the mental defences he'd erected over the years.

Lucy.

She was so much the same, he thought. She looked the same, with that luxuriant sweep of hair that made him itch to tangle his fingers in its richness, draw its silkiness against his lips as he'd once done with such casual, easy liberty. Now it was forbidden, and all the more tempting.

He loved the way she straightened her shoulders and lifted her chin, unafraid and defiant. The way sparks shot from her eyes, the colour of dark chocolate.

He loved the feel of her body, soft and pliant, against his— and he hadn't felt that in four years. Yet now the memory tormented him, and he wanted to feel it again. 'Wanted' wasn't even a strong enough word; he craved it. Needed it as much as a man needed a drug—or other medication.

Touching Lucy would be the most powerful prescription of all.

His knee ached, a cruel reminder of his own limitations, his weaknesses, and worst of all his inevitable decline. Lucy, he told himself yet again, was off-limits. She had to be, for Sam's sake, for his own.

For hers.

He'd hurt her, Khaled knew. He'd seen it in her eyes, heard it in the jagged edge of her voice, and he realised he hadn't let himself consider how *much* before. He'd thought only of what he'd spared her, spared himself.

Yet now she seemed determined to put the feelings she'd had for him aside, relics of an irrelevant history. He'd intended on doing the same, yet now he felt himself craving more. Of Lucy.

He hadn't expected the intensity of need, of desire, when

he'd seen her. He hadn't expected to feel unmanned, weak and desperate for her touch, her smile.

Her love.

Like Lucy, he'd wanted to put their relationship behind them, relegate it to 'pleasant anecdote' status. He wanted to forget how much he'd loved her.

Yet now he was afraid he couldn't.

His knee throbbed again; he'd refused painkillers that morning as they tended to make him drowsy. He wanted to be at full capacity for Sam. For his son.

As he exited the sedan and walked up to Lucy's door, he heard a sudden squeal from the front window. Khaled saw a dark tousled head disappear behind a sofa before he heard the impatient rattling of the doorknob.

'He's here!'

Smiling, his heart expanding with joy, Khaled prepared to meet his son.

Her fingers fumbling on the lock, Lucy hastened to answer the door. She opened it, and there he was—Khaled.

Why did it feel so different now, so much more intimate? Perhaps it was Sam's presence; perhaps it was simply because something had shifted or settled.

He'd been accepted.

She smiled and said quietly, 'Hello, Khaled.'

'Hello, Lucy.'

Sam's earlier excitement had suddenly turned into shyness, and he now hid behind Lucy, one arm wound around her leg.

Lucy was afraid Khaled would be displeased by their son's reticence, but he merely crouched down so he was eye-level with Sam.

'Hello, Sam. My name is Khaled, and I'm a friend of your mother's.'

Sam's eyes were dark and wide, as dark and wide as Khaled's, and he popped a thumb in his mouth, sucking industriously for a moment before he removed it and said, 'That's a funny sort of name.'

'Sam!'

'It is, isn't it?' Khaled agreed. 'It's an Arabic name. I come from an island country on the other side of the world. It's called Biryal.'

Lucy tensed, waiting, but Khaled said no more. Shrugging in acceptance, Sam asked, 'How did you know my name?'

'Your mother told me. She's told me a bit about you.'

'And we're going to the zoo?'

'Yes, if you'd like to.'

Sam nodded vigorously, and, smiling, Khaled stood up. Lucy caught a whiff of aftershave, that familiar cedar scent mingled with the musk that was just him, and her breath caught in her throat.

'Would you like a coffee first?' she asked. She tucked her hair behind her ears once more, a nervous gesture if there ever was one, and strove to find the composure that had been her armour, her defence, for so long.

'That would be lovely, if Sam doesn't mind postponing our trip for a few minutes?'

Sam looked ready to pout, and Lucy said quickly, 'Of course he won't. Sam, why don't you show Khaled the zoo you made out of Lego yesterday? I'm sure he'd love to see it.'

'I would,' Khaled said gravely, and, his shyness abandoning him, Sam tugged on Khaled's hand and led him to the lounge.

Lucy watched Khaled's long fingers curl around her son's, his eyes suspiciously bright, and something inside her broke. It was a good break, a healing one.

How could she ever have fought this? How could she have ever thought Sam and Khaled didn't need this?

That she didn't?

She swallowed the lump in her throat, annoyed by her own heightened emotions, and hurried to make the coffee.

She couldn't keep herself from eavesdropping on Sam and Khaled's conversation as she spooned the coffee into the cafetière. Sam was chattering away, completely comfortable now, pointing out all the little plastic animals he'd placed carefully on the floor, each one in its own little Lego pen. It had taken most of the afternoon yesterday, and Lucy had already heard the very detailed explanations of his architectural design.

'And that's a zebra…they're stripy. Have you seen one before? Do you know what they look like?'

'Yes, I have. You're right; they are stripy.'

Lucy smiled to herself, amazed and gratified that Khaled was humouring her son, that he knew how to. That he wanted to.

She poured the coffee and entered the lounge, stopping at the sight of Khaled stretched out beside Sam on the carpet, studying the Lego zoo with intent seriousness.

'Here's your coffee.' She held the mug out awkwardly, still not used to the enforced intimacy of their situation. She wondered if she ever would be.

'Thanks.' Khaled stood up—stiffly, Lucy noticed. She almost asked about his knee, but then decided not to. Khaled had made it clear that he didn't like talking about his injury.

'Can we go now?' Sam asked, and Lucy smiled.

'I've just given Khaled his coffee, sweetheart. Why don't you play for a few minutes and then we'll go?'

Sam started to pout—three-year-olds, Lucy had noticed, were so good at that—but Khaled rescued the moment by picking up a discarded giraffe. 'I think this one needs a pen.'

Sam hesitated, and then took the plastic animal from Khaled and began to construct a pen out of Lego.

Lucy cradled her mug between her hands and watched Khaled covertly over the rim.

Sleep had restored him, as it had her, and he looked awake and relaxed. He looked good, Lucy admitted, letting her gaze become bolder, sweeping over his familiar features that still somehow seemed so strange.

'You cut your hair.' The words popped out, and Lucy bit her lip. Khaled gave a wry smile.

'The son of a king must have a different appearance from a rugby player.'

'I never thought of you as the son of a king,' Lucy admitted. 'You were just Khaled, rugby star.'

'Yes, I was, wasn't I?' There was a faint edge to his voice that Lucy couldn't understand. 'I never thought of myself as the son of a king either,' Khaled added, and took a sip of coffee.

Lucy frowned. 'But surely you knew you'd have to return to Biryal? You've been the heir your whole life.'

Khaled paused, his expression both shadowed and thoughtful. 'In a manner of speaking. My family has always been royal, but Biryal was a British protectorate until the early 1960s. Then they gave us back our independence, and my father was poised to become king in the true sense. Unfortunately, his cousin Ghassan seized the throne while my father was travelling from Yemen to take it himself. The British supported Ghassan because it was easier and they didn't want a civil war. They'd just withdrawn all their troops, after all. My father fled back to Yemen, where I was born and grew up.'

It was like something out of a history book or even a film, Lucy thought. 'How long was Ghassan king?'

'Twenty years, until he died without heirs. Then my father finally gained his throne.' Khaled shook his head. 'By that time he was bitter and suspicious of everyone.' He paused, his gaze sliding away from hers to a dark memory. 'Even me.'

'You mean he was afraid that you would seize the throne?'

'Or that rebel insurgents would use me as a puppet.' Khaled shrugged. 'I'm not sure what my father was thinking, but he wanted me out of the picture—which is why he sent me to boarding school in England when I was seven. Then university, and then I played rugby, which he encouraged. Anything to keep me from home.' He spoke flatly, but Lucy still sensed the bitterness underneath.

'So why did you go back?' Lucy whispered. She was appalled by what sounded like a loveless childhood.

'I knew I would have to go back eventually. And when I was injured it seemed like the time had finally come.' He paused, taking another sip of coffee. When he spoke again, his voice was careful, deliberate. 'A few weeks after my return, my father had a heart attack—a minor one, but it made him realise his own mortality, and he realised I was his heir, not a usurper. So he made a place for me, albeit a small one, and I accepted my royal duties.' He put his empty mug on the coffee table and smiled at Sam. 'Shall we go?'

Lucy was still mulling over all that Khaled had told her as they headed outside to the waiting sedan. It was more than she'd ever known before, more than he'd ever told her before. More than she'd ever asked.

The knowledge—and her own previous ignorance of it—unsettled her. Made her wonder.

She glanced over at Khaled; his face was averted from hers as he looked out of the window. She let her gaze rove over his strong profile, the hard lines of his cheek and jaw, and felt a pang of sorrowful curiosity.

Who are you?

Sam, sandwiched between them, started to wriggle, and she spent the rest of the trip distracting him. Yet, even so, her mind and eyes would wander back to Khaled and she realised she wanted to know the answer to that question.

CHAPTER FIVE

SAM was, as always, enthralled with the zoo. He insisted on being Khaled's personal tour-guide, dragging him by the hand to the Butterfly Paradise and rainforest lookout, and of course his favourite, the spiders.

Lucy shuddered as they stood in front of a glass case housing some alarmingly large and hairy tarantulas.

'You like spiders?' Khaled asked Sam, whose nose was pressed against the glass.

'Big, hairy ones,' Sam confirmed.

'There are some big spiders in Biryal,' Khaled told him. 'Some of the largest in the world. They spin yellow webs, sometimes several metres wide.'

'Really?' Sam's eyes had grown huge, and Lucy couldn't help but wince. Spiders were not exactly a compelling reason to return to Biryal—not for her, anyway. She couldn't think of *any* compelling reasons to return to Biryal…except for Sam. Instinctively her gaze slid to her son, so innocent of the changes in store for him, and something in her tightened.

Khaled glanced at her over Sam, his eyes laughing. 'Don't worry, Lucy, they're harmless.'

'Mum doesn't like spiders,' Sam confided, and then he was tugging on Khaled's hand again, leading him off to the Gorilla Kingdom.

By the end of the day they had tramped through the entire

zoo and seen most of the animals at least twice. Sam, exhausted and sticky with ice cream, fell asleep in the car with his head against Khaled's shoulder.

'He's taken to you,' Lucy said quietly, watching the two of them, her heart constricting at the sight.

Khaled smiled down at his son. 'I'm glad.'

'So am I,' Lucy admitted, and Khaled glanced up at her, his eyes gleaming.

'Are you?'

Lucy looked away, unable to meet that compelling golden gaze, a gaze that seemed to dive right inside her and clutch at her heart. 'Yes. Sam deserves to know you…and you deserve to know him.'

They didn't speak again until the car pulled up in front of Lucy's house, and she instinctively reached for Sam.

'I'll take him.' Sam was still slumped against Khaled, and he put his arms around him, ready to scoop him up.

'Are you sure?' Lucy asked. 'Can you manage…?' She trailed off as every muscle in Khaled's body stiffened, his arms still cradling Sam.

'I think I can carry my own son,' he said, the words cold and stiff. Wordlessly, Lucy slipped from the car.

Khaled carried Sam inside—limping slightly, Lucy noticed—and she motioned to the sofa. 'You can lay him there. He'll need to wake up soon or he won't go to bed tonight.'

'We can't have that.' Gently Khaled laid Sam down, smoothing the soft, dark hair from his forehead, before stepping back. 'He looks like me, like I was as a child.'

'Yes, I noticed that.'

'The DNA test will be no more than a formality.'

'Right.' Lucy escaped into the kitchen, concentrating on fetching things for tea. 'Just yesterday I realised he has your eyes,' she called back, trying to keep her voice friendly and light.

Khaled came in, propping one shoulder against the door-frame. 'You didn't notice before?'

Lucy hesitated, her back to him. 'I must have done,' she confessed. 'Even if I didn't admit it to myself.'

'Were you so determined to forget me?' Khaled asked softly. 'Forget us?'

Lucy felt an ache deep inside at his words, at their sorrow. 'Weren't you?' she said, and busied herself with filling a pot with water. 'I hope spag bol is good enough for you. It's Sam's favourite.'

'Sounds delicious.' Khaled was silent, watching her, and Lucy felt like she couldn't breathe for the tension uncoiling in the air, drawing her inexorably to him, even though neither of them moved.

Don't do this, she wanted to say, to cry. *Don't make me want you again. Don't make me remember how it was. I'm different. You're different. We can't...*

'Lucy.' Khaled's voice was low, insistent and sure. Lucy kept her head averted.

'Could you get some salad from the fridge? I try to make Sam eat some greens.'

Wordlessly Khaled went to fetch the lettuce. This was so cozy, Lucy thought, reaching for some tomatoes. It was so domestic, so normal.

And yet the heightened atmosphere, the tension in the room and in her belly, didn't feel normal at all.

Khaled didn't say anything more, and Lucy was grateful for the reprieve. Yet she knew the tension between them couldn't be ignored, not for ever. Not now that there *was* a for ever, or at least a very long time, with Sam between them.

'Mummy...' Sam, tousle-haired and sleepy-eyed, stumbled into the kitchen, rubbing his face with his fists. 'Is Khaled still here?'

'Yes, Sam,' Khaled said and Sam dropped his fists to stare at him with obvious delight.

'Are you staying overnight?'

Did Lucy imagine the tiny, charged hesitation before Khaled

answered? She wasn't sure. 'No, Sam. But perhaps I can see you again tomorrow?'

'I have to work tomorrow,' Lucy interjected. 'We're getting ready for the Six Nations—'

'Yes, I know.' Khaled's expression had darkened, but for Sam's sake he merely shrugged. 'We can talk about it later.'

Oh, and *that* was a conversation she was looking forward to, Lucy thought with just a little venom. No doubt Khaled would impose some of his royal decrees on her life and her job. And what could she do about it, when he had the threat of bringing a custody suit—and winning it—to hang over her?

Fortunately the rest of the evening passed in idle pleasantries, for Sam's sake, and Khaled even helped with bath time. Lucy watched him perched incongruously on the edge of the tub, his shirtsleeves rolled up to expose strong forearms, and felt a lurch inside her.

She was tired of this feeling creeping up on her—the feeling that nothing could be the same, that she now wanted something, a life, she'd never hungered for before.

Before Khaled. Before he'd come into their lives and acted like he belonged there, carving a place in Sam's heart in the space of a day, acting so natural and normal and *right*, somehow—and he wasn't.

It wasn't.

This couldn't last; it wouldn't last. At some point it would break down, break apart, and Khaled would walk away.

And break your heart.

No. She would not let herself think like that. Her heart was not involved. Not at all. She would not allow it to be.

Yet as soon as Sam was settled in bed the tension returned, taut and heavy with silent expectation. Lucy came downstairs after tucking Sam in, to see Khaled stretched out on the sofa scanning yesterday's newspaper. The room was lit only by a single lamp, the curtains drawn against the night. Khaled looked so comfortable on her sofa, Lucy thought with a touch of resentment, so big, strong and sure. Like he owned it, owned this house, owned every situation he'd ever been in. She was reminded forcefully of the charming, arrogant man she had loved, who had broken her heart. She didn't like that man. She didn't want him in her lounge or lying on her sofa. She didn't *want* to want him.

Yet she did.

'Would you like a coffee or tea?' she asked, and the ludicrous phrase 'or me?' popped into her mind. She pushed it away.

Khaled looked up. 'Coffee, if you're making it.'

She nodded mutely before going into the kitchen to boil water, spoon coffee, get out mugs. Mechanical actions that kept her from thinking, from picturing Khaled on the sofa—stretched out, his eyes glinting in the lamplight—from remembering how darkly golden his skin was, his muscles hard and chiselled from rugby, so hard against her own softness. Would he look the same? Feel the same?

It wasn't working, Lucy realised as she put two mugs and a plate of shop-bought biscuits on a tray. She *was* thinking and picturing. Remembering.

'Here we are.' She kept her voice brisk and her smile sunny as she set the tray on the coffee table. Khaled sat up, murmuring his thanks, his left leg stretched out stiffly.

Lucy handed him his coffee. 'Have you taken your medication today?'

'I don't need it,' Khaled replied shortly.

'Is your knee still flaring up?'

'A bit, but I can handle it.' His dark eyes clashed with hers, filled with warning. 'Don't talk to me as a therapist, Lucy.'

'Then as what?' She'd meant the question lightly, but it came out as more of a demand.

'How about as a woman?' Khaled said. His eyes had suddenly turned heavy-lidded, his smile languorous, and Lucy knew what that meant.

Come here, Lucy. Come here to me.

And she'd come. God help her, she'd always trotted to him with the pathetic obedience of a little lapdog.

'Although it's a difficult question, isn't it, Lucy?' Khaled continued lazily. 'How are we to relate to one another? What can we be to one another?'

'Nothing,' Lucy replied, and was glad her voice didn't waver. She was already feeling the tug of sensual hunger deep in her belly, sending a wave of need crashing through her.

'Nothing?' Khaled repeated musingly. He reached out and threaded his fingers through Lucy's hair. The slight, simple touch nearly had her shuddering. How had she ever forgotten the kind of effect he had on her? It was more powerful than any drug or medication that could be prescribed.

She'd been a slave to it, to him, helplessly bound by her own attraction, her own need. And it was happening again; she was still, unmoving, letting him touch her.

Wanting it…

Khaled rubbed her hair between his fingers, his expression almost harsh with desire. 'I've wanted this for a long time,' he murmured. 'I've dreamed of it, of touching you…'

Had he? Lucy wondered fuzzily. How was that possible, when she was so certain he'd completely forgotten her?

He had to have forgotten her, for nothing else made sense. 'Khaled…'

'Say my name,' Khaled commanded, his voice ragged. 'Say it again. I love it when you say my name.'

'Khaled…' she said again, desperately, for they had to stop this madness before it got too far.

Then his fingers slipped from her hair to her face, cradling her cheek, using the motion to draw her towards him. And Lucy went, drawn by her own need and desire, until she was half on her knees next to him on the sofa, every nerve, sense and sinew straining towards him.

'*Lucy.*' He spoke with a needy desperation that surprised her, for she'd never thought of him needing anything. Needing her. Yet at that moment, seeing his eyes clenched shut as he drew her to him, she felt as if he needed her very much.

And she needed him.

His other hand came up to cradle her face and draw her towards him, her hands braced against his shoulders as his lips hovered over hers. 'Lucy.'

Her lips parted, waiting, wanting—and then he kissed her.

It was softly at first, little more than a brush, a kiss that said, 'hello, do you remember me?'

And she did. Her lips parted under his, her mouth opening in invitation and acceptance.

Khaled deepened the kiss until the sensation of his touching her, tasting her, flooded her whole body; she melted towards him, his arms coming round to draw her in closer, fitting her so neatly, so perfectly, against him. Her head fell back and he kissed her lips, her cheek, her throat, behind her ear, as she moaned, remembering how he'd known that place turned her helpless.

Her hands drove into his hair, caressed the nape of his neck, the curve of his shoulder, before resting against the hard plane of his chest. Her hands remembered how he felt, all the hidden places, the way she'd touched him with such pleasurable abandon.

Somehow they'd both moved and were now stretched out along the sofa, Khaled half on top of her, his body braced on one forearm. It was a position that allowed Lucy to feel his whole body against hers, and one leg almost of its own accord twined around his.

Khaled groaned against her lips and captured her mouth once more in a kiss as his hands drifted down, leaving fire wherever they touched.

Stop. They had to stop. Her mind kept repeating this litany even as the rest of her resolutely ignored it. She wanted this. She wanted it more than she'd ever realised. So now that it was happening she wondered how she'd existed for so long without Khaled, without his touch, his love.

But he doesn't love you.

And suddenly her body was recalling another memory, the pain and shame she'd felt wash through her when the doorman at his building had told her he'd left.

Is he coming back?

No, miss. He has left the flat. There's no forwarding address.

There must be a letter…

No, miss. I'm sorry.

Lucy flattened her hands against Khaled's chest and pushed. 'We can't do this.'

He stilled above her, and she was afraid that he would try to seduce her—afraid because she didn't think she could resist.

A long, taut moment passed and then Khaled rolled off her into a sitting position. His hair was mussed, and a faint flush stained his cheekbones. Both of their breathing was ragged.

'You're right.'

Disappointment and, worse, rejection sliced through her, mingling with the unfulfilled desire coursing through her. She pushed the feelings away. 'We can't have a physical relationship, Khaled,' she said, and was amazed at how strong and sure her voice sounded. Inside she felt a mess. Her lips were swollen, and her body tingled where he'd touched her. 'For Sam's sake we need to stay…professional.'

'Professional?' Khaled arched one eyebrow. He looked remarkably recovered from their kiss, and Lucy saw a new hardness in his eyes that she didn't like. 'Is that really possible, Lucy?'

'Friends, then,' she said with an edge of sharpness. 'Acquaintances, colleagues—use whatever term you prefer, Khaled. But I can't have a physical relationship with you again. I won't.'

'Just for Sam's sake?' Khaled asked softly. 'Or for your own?'

'Both,' Lucy replied flatly. She could be honest, even if it humiliated her. 'You hurt me four years ago, Khaled. I thought I loved you, and when you left it damn near destroyed me.' She felt a blush staining her cheeks, and tears stinging her eyes. Memories could hold such power; they could hurt so much. She blinked back the tears and willed the blush to recede.

'You *thought* you loved me?' Khaled queried. His voice was soft, yet it still held a dangerous thread of steel.

'Yes, *thought*. I realise now that what I believed was love was no more than a girlish infatuation. A crush, pure and simple.'

'A crush,' Khaled repeated neutrally, and Lucy found herself compelled to explain.

'I was dazzled by you. You were England's rugby star, adored by the press, surrounded by fans—many of them women. I never thought you'd even look once at me.'

'I see,' Khaled replied after a moment, and Lucy thought she heard a bleakness in his voice that she didn't understand. 'I see,' he repeated, almost to himself, 'what kind of man you loved.'

'*Thought* I loved,' Lucy corrected.

Khaled's answering smile was hard and cold. 'Right.'

For a moment Lucy felt like apologising, feeling almost as if she'd hurt him somehow. Yet she couldn't have hurt him, because he'd never cared. Not like she had. Perhaps his ego was dented, she thought cynically. Perhaps he didn't like the fact that she was no longer the woman she'd once been…even if he was still the same man.

For he was the same man, she realised. His hair was shorter, his face harder, and he'd clearly had some tough experiences in the last four years—but underneath? Lucy shook her head. Still the same arrogant charmer who thought he had the world and all of its women at his feet.

'Well.' Khaled stretched, running his fingers through his hair, and gave a little shrug and a smile. 'Well, it's all past history now, isn't it?' he said in a tone that relegated their relationship to some kind of trivial anecdote.

Lucy forced herself to smile back. 'Yes. Past history.' Although it hadn't felt all that 'past' a few moments ago when she'd been lying under him.

A momentary lapse. A blip. Something they had to get out of their systems. That was all it had been, all it could be.

'You mentioned you have to work tomorrow,' Khaled said, his voice turning brisk and businesslike. 'What were you planning to do with Sam?'

'He has nursery in the morning, and my mother can pick him up—'

'I'll do that. Sam and I can spend the afternoon together.'

Lucy hesitated. She wanted to resist, yet she also knew Sam would love spending the afternoon with Khaled. And wouldn't it be better for him to get used to Khaled sooner rather than later?

'Trying to think of an excuse to say no?' Khaled mocked gently. 'Get used to it, Lucy. I'm staying in Sam's life.'

'Are you?' The question slipped out involuntarily and Khaled's face darkened. 'Why?' she pressed. 'I mean, why do you want him so much? I never thought you'd—'

'Care?' Khaled finished for her. 'Yes, I know. I'm amazed that you spent as long as you did with me, considering your low opinion. But the fact is I take my responsibilities seriously.'

'Sam doesn't have to be your responsibility,' Lucy interjected and Khaled gazed at her coolly.

'But he is.'

'If you're going to be in his life, I want him to be more than a *responsibility*,' Lucy said in a low voice. Khaled made a grunt of disgust.

'Do you think I'm here out of some sense of duty? If that was all it was, Lucy, I could have written a cheque. I want to be in Sam's life because he's my son, and I'm his father, and families are meant to be together. To love each other.'

'Like yours?' Lucy snapped, and then bit her lip as she saw Khaled's expression close once more.

'No, not like mine,' he replied after a moment. 'My own experience is all the more reason to give Sam a proper family. And I'd have thought you'd want the same for him, considering the absence of your own father—'

'I was fine without my father!' Lucy flashed.

'Were you?' Khaled queried softly. 'I wasn't.' He stood up, effectively finishing the conversation. 'Why should I not spend time with Sam?'

Lucy nibbled her lip, disarmed by the simple question. 'Fine,' she said at last. 'I'll call the nursery so they can expect you at noon.'

'Good.' Khaled paused, and Lucy braced herself for what was coming. Somehow she knew it wouldn't be good. 'I can spend a week in England,' he said. 'And then I want to bring Sam back to Biryal.'

Lucy jerked back. 'A week? That's no time at all!'

Khaled shrugged, every inch the regal prince who barked orders and didn't wait for them to be obeyed, who just knew that they would. 'It will have to be enough.'

'He doesn't even have a passport,' Lucy argued, grabbing onto perhaps the most irrelevant detail. 'Or proper clothes.' No, that was even more irrelevant.

Khaled shrugged again. 'We can have the passport expedited, perhaps through the Biryali embassy. As my son, he is a Biryal national.'

'Is he?' Her lips felt cold and numb, and her arms came around herself as a matter of instinctive protection. She dropped them. 'Khaled, I don't like this. It's too soon. Sam doesn't even know you're his father.'

'We'll tell him when the time is right. Meanwhile, I'm sure he will be excited to learn of a holiday to a new and exciting destination.' Khaled smiled faintly. 'One with spiders.'

She didn't need a reminder of those. 'I want to come with him.'

Khaled was silent long enough for Lucy to glance at him and

see his eyebrow arch speculatively. He looked almost smug, and with a jolt she wondered, *Is this what he'd wanted?*

'Fine,' he finally replied with a shrug. 'But what about your job?'

Lucy gritted her teeth. 'I suppose I'll have to take a temporary leave of absence.'

'At such a critical time?' Khaled pressed, and Lucy knew it was hopeless.

Hadn't she known everything would change once they started down this path? Sam's life, her life, her job. She forced herself to shrug. 'Let me worry about my job, Khaled. It's not your concern.'

'Very well. But we are leaving in a week…regardless.' He stood up, and for a second his leg buckled underneath him.

Lucy sprang up, one hand reaching to steady his elbow, but Khaled jerked away.

'Khaled—'

'I'm fine.' His voice was terse, his face momentarily clenched with pain. 'I'm fine,' he repeated, and stiffly he walked to the door. 'I'll see you tomorrow, Lucy,' he said, and then he was gone.

I was dazzled by you. You were England's rugby star…I thought I loved you.

Lucy's words, so honestly given, hammered relentlessly through Khaled's head and in his heart. She hadn't even loved him, and the man she'd *thought* she loved… He wasn't that man any more.

He leaned his head against the car's leather seat as his driver pulled away from Lucy's house onto the darkened street. Pain racked his body, but worse was the desolation that swept him as he considered Lucy's words.

He didn't want to feel that consuming emptiness again. It reminded him of the bleakest time in his life: alone in his hospital bed, refusing visitors, because for anyone—for

Lucy—to have seen him like that—helpless, hopeless, with a crippling diagnosis—was more than he'd been able to bear. More than Lucy could have borne, even if she'd thought she could…

He'd seen what his kind of long-term diagnosis did to someone. He'd watched his father gaze at his mother, first in compassion, then pity, then disgust, and finally resentment and hatred. Oh, he'd disguised it, of course; his father had always been solicitous. But Khaled had seen it, his mother had seen it, and in the end it had caused her to wither away and die from despair rather than disease.

He wouldn't let that happen to him; he wouldn't let it happen to Lucy.

And it still wouldn't, he reminded himself with harsh determination. He'd allowed himself a few moments of weakness. Lord, how he'd wanted, needed, to touch her! Even if he couldn't have her for more than that moment.

He closed his eyes, battling against the images that danced through his mind anyway, enticing, impossible: Lucy in his bed. Lucy on his arm. Lucy as his wife, with Sam, a proper family…

The family he'd never had.

The family he couldn't have.

Lucy didn't want him. She didn't want Khaled the cripple, she wanted Khaled the rugby star. The man he'd been—laughing, charming—the world as his oyster. That was the man the world had courted and admired, the man everyone had loved. The man Lucy had loved.

Not as he was now, both weakened and hardened. Weakened by his illness, the endless surgeries and rounds of therapy, the loss of the career he'd found his whole self in; hardened by his father's constant mistrust and suspicion, his grudging admission of Khaled's rights as prince, by four years of fighting for just one corner of the kingdom that would one day rightfully be his.

And Sam's. This was all for Sam's sake. The pain he'd have

to endure living with Lucy—seeing her, needing her, and not having her, was for Sam. His son.

And that made it worth it, Khaled told himself. It had to.

A sudden, insistent trill had him flicking open his mobile. His mouth hardened into a grim line as he saw who was ringing him; it was the Biryali palace's private number. His father. It was a conversation he'd been avoiding, and yet one he knew was inevitable. Setting his jaw, Khaled opened the connection and spoke into the phone.

The next few days passed in a flurry. It was strange, Lucy thought, how quickly Khaled had settled into their lives, how Sam—and even Lucy herself—had begun to expect his presence. Somehow the new had become routine. Lucy would set a third place at the table, and Sam would perch on top of the sofa, looking for Khaled's sedan to come stealing softly down the street.

And yet, as each day slipped past, Lucy knew she needed to brace herself for irrevocable change. Sam and Khaled had both submitted to the DNA test, which had confirmed what had already been glaringly obvious. She'd taken Sam to the Birayli embassy, and with Khaled's assistance a passport had speedily been arranged.

She spoke to the HR manager at work, and was reluctantly given a fortnight's absence.

'I suppose it's important?' Allie the manager asked with a raised eyebrow, and Lucy had smiled thinly.

'Yes. Rather.'

Nothing was more important than Sam.

Questions niggled at her with insistent worry. How long did Khaled want Sam in Biryal? How often did he expect him to visit? It was a fourteen-hour flight; it was halfway around the world. For Sam's sake, he couldn't keep bouncing between England and Biryal; some kind of compromise would have to be made.

She just didn't want to be the one to do it. Already her life had bent and stretched to a nearly unrecognisable shape; any more and Lucy was afraid it would break. Or that she would.

She knew she should consult a solicitor, or come to some formal custody arrangement with Khaled, yet she was unwilling to be the first to do so. Right now things were calm, cozy even, and though she knew it couldn't last part of her wanted it to.

Yet how long did anything last?

And then suddenly, too soon, it was over, and a new phase began…Biryal.

'This is the best aeroplane ever!' Sam bounced in his seat, gazing round the sumptuous luxury of the Biryali royal jet with obvious delight.

Lucy leaned back in her own seat, her fingers nervously clicking and unclicking the metal clasp of her seat belt.

Smiling at Sam, Khaled reached over and covered her hand with his own. 'You're going to drive me crazy with that noise,' he said, and Lucy gave a nervous little smile.

'Sorry.'

'Why are you so jumpy?'

She shook her head, unwilling, unable, to explain. Why was she so nervous? Why did going to Biryal feel like some kind of monumental, irrevocable step, so much more so than having Khaled in her life? Now she would be in *his*, and she didn't know if there was a place for her.

'Sam will love Biryal,' Khaled said firmly. 'Don't worry.'

Lucy bit her lip and said nothing. Was that what she was afraid of—that Sam would love Biryal and his new life there more than the one she'd been able to give him? Was she actually *jealous*?

Lucy leaned her head back against the seat and closed her eyes. The plane began to taxi down the runway, and within minutes they'd left the dank fog of London for cloudless blue sky.

Sam had started to fidget, and she busied herself organising him with an array of toy trains, glad to avoid talking with Khaled for a little while.

But of course she had to talk to him; she'd come to the conclusion several sleepless nights ago. Life was spiralling out of control, and it needed to stop. She needed stability. Safety. Security. And the only way to gain them was by talking to Khaled.

She waited until Sam had fallen asleep in his seat, exhausted from so much excitement, curled up with a fleecy throw tucked around him.

Khaled was sitting near the front of the plane, some papers spread out before him on a table. Lucy moved to sit across from him.

'What are you doing?'

'Work.' Khaled smiled faintly and shrugged. 'Trying to make Biryal a bit more of a tourist destination, and in so doing boost our revenue.' He tapped the papers in front of him with a gold fountain pen. 'These are plans for a luxury resort on the island—tasteful, in keeping with Biryal's untouched beauty.' There was a trace of irony to his voice, and he laughed aloud at Lucy's expression. 'You don't think Biryal beautiful? But it is. This trip, I will make it my personal duty to show you all of its glory.'

'That should be interesting,' Lucy murmured. She pleated her fingers together, nerves starting to jump as she considered what to say. How to explain...

Khaled touched her hand. 'Lucy, what is it?'

That was an opening if ever there was one. Lucy smiled with bright determination. 'Khaled, we need to talk. We need to make some kind of plan for Sam's future. One that is sustainable for both of us, and of course for him.' She took a breath. 'I think we should see a solicitor.'

Khaled leaned back in his seat, his eyes darkening to a deep bronze. 'A formal custody arrangement?'

'Yes.'

'I see.'

Lucy knew he was at his most dangerous when his voice turned mild, but she pressed on anyway. 'It makes sense. I think a formal arrangement will give us all a sense of stability—peace, even.'

'Do you?' Khaled turned back to his papers, seemingly done with their conversation.

Frustration bubbled inside her. 'Yes, I do, Khaled. I've been flexible now, in the beginning, so you have a chance to get to know Sam. But we can't go on spending a few weeks in Biryal, a few weeks in London. I have a job, and next year Sam will start school. It makes sense,' she ploughed on, even though Khaled had not looked up from his damn papers, 'to have a plan. Perhaps he could spend a portion of his school holidays in Biryal.'

Khaled sighed and finally looked up. 'Indeed, a plan makes sense. But do you intend to speak to a solicitor on Biryal, Lucy? Because I don't think you'd be pleased with the outcome.'

Lucy stiffened. 'Is that a threat?'

'No, of course not. Just a statement of fact.' He paused, his head tilted thoughtfully to one side, his eyes intent on hers yet suddenly filled with a dangerous languor. 'The last week has been pleasant, has it not?'

'Yes,' Lucy admitted reluctantly. 'But that sort of arrangement can hardly continue.'

'Can't it?' Khaled turned back to his papers, brisk and dismissive once more. 'There is no point discussing this now. We can't even think of a solicitor until we return to London.'

Lucy didn't miss the 'we'. Would Khaled be following them like a shadow? 'When will that be?'

Khaled shrugged. 'You took a fortnight's leave of absence. We can think about returning then.'

Think about it? Lucy wanted hard facts, clear answers, yet she knew there was no point pushing for them now. Push Khaled, and he would just become more intractable, more imperious. It was better, Lucy decided, to spend a few days in Biryal, act amenable and then insist on a firm return date.

What other choice did she really have?

With a sigh she went back to her own seat and closed her eyes, determined to catch some sleep while Sam was still napping and to forget the worries and uncertainties that had dogged her since Khaled had come back into her life.

Khaled watched Lucy settle into an uneasy sleep. His own body and mind were too restless even to think of sleeping, and his knee ached abominably.

He gazed out of the window at the fathomless night sky, and recalled the terse conversation with his father just a week ago.

'The reporters are circling, Khaled. They scent carrion. You cannot allow these rumours to continue.'

'They will die down.'

'That is not good enough!' King Ahmed's voice had been savage. 'I did not wait two decades to win my kingdom only to hand it to a son who will tarnish the honour of our heritage and our land with rumours and half-truths too tawdry to be believed.'

'My son,' Khaled had replied through gritted teeth, 'is not tawdry.'

Ahmed had ignored this, as he'd ignored every reasoned argument Khaled had ever made. If it did not suit him to hear, he did not listen. 'You know what you have to do,' he'd told Khaled, 'To make this right. One way or the other... Take her or leave her, but it must be resolved.'

Khaled's hand had tightened slickly around his mobile. 'And do you have an opinion either way?' he'd asked sardonically.

Ahmed had been silent for a long moment. 'No, I don't,' he'd replied finally. 'For, when you take the throne, I shall be dead and it will not matter to me.'

And that was the crux of his father's sensibility, Khaled

thought as he'd severed the connection—utterly self-centred, utterly dedicated to his own purpose, his own rule, without any thought of the legacy he might leave for his country or for his son.

He would not be that way with Sam, Khaled vowed. Sam would be his son in every respect; he would grow up at his side, learning the ways of the kingdom, his own sacred place. He would be respected, valued, loved.

One way or the other…it must be resolved.

Ahmed's words echoed in Khaled's mind, forcefully reminding him that he had a duty, a duty as both prince and father. Now, on the plane, he found himself considering it with both desperate hope and dread. Would Lucy despise him? Pity him?

Or could she *possibly* come to love him—*him* the man he was now?

Twelve hours later the plane taxied to a halt in front of Biryal's airport. Glancing outside at the hard, bright sky, Lucy was amazed that it had only been a little over a week since she'd last been here. It felt like an age, a lifetime.

She scanned the tarmac, surprised and more than a little discomfited to see a crowd of people. Was this the royal welcome?

'Who are all those people?' she asked Khaled, who glanced out of the window, his expression turning ominously dark.

'Journalists, by the look of it.'

'Journalists?' Lucy repeated incredulously. 'Does Biryal have so many?'

He smiled faintly, although his eyes were still hard. 'Indeed not. There is only one newspaper here. Besides, the Birayli journalists wouldn't dare to inconvenience the royal family by showing up at an airport like this.' He frowned. 'Undoubtedly they are from other countries. I think I see a French photographer I recognise there.'

'French…?' Lucy peered out of the window again and saw from the television cameras and microphones that Khaled was indeed correct; it was a mini–United Nations out there.

Lucy was used to the press, having spent her working life among professional sports teams, but it had never been so relentlessly focussed on her. Now she found her mouth turning dry and her heart rate going up a notch or two.

'Why are they here?'

'Someone tipped them off,' Khaled replied. 'Leaks to the press are almost always unavoidable.'

'But why are they so interested?' Lucy pressed, and Khaled glanced at her, his second's hesitation making Lucy wonder. Suspect.

'Because I am the prince of this country, Lucy, and Sam is my newly discovered heir. You might not acknowledge it as such, but it is a momentous occasion. And a big story for them.' He jerked a thumb towards the crowded tarmac. 'You've faced the press before. Can't you manage it now?'

'Sam...' Lucy glanced at Sam, who had managed to stay asleep through the bumpy landing.

'I'll carry him,' Khaled replied. 'I don't want any photographs of him released at present.'

Now she really felt like things were spinning out of control. Was this why she'd been afraid to come to Biryal—because here Sam wasn't just Khaled's son but his heir-apparent? The thought made her nauseous and for a moment the cabin spun.

'Lucy,' Khaled said warningly, 'pull yourself together. This is your life now. It is Sam's life.'

For the first time, Lucy truly wished she'd never told Khaled about Sam. Yet even as the thought sprang to her mind her heart retracted it. Khaled was gathering a sleepy Sam into his arms, and the look of tenderness softening his features was unmistakable.

'Ready?' Khaled asked, and Lucy nodded.

Sam had wound his arms around Khaled's neck with trusting ease. 'Are we here? Are there spiders?' he asked sleepily, and, smiling, Khaled tucked Sam's head against his shoulder so the little boy wouldn't be seen.

'We're here, sport, and I promise to show you the spiders soon. When your mum's not around to be frightened by them.' He smiled at Lucy, who tried to smile back, and almost managed it.

She felt perilously close to tears, caught between the strain of the press's scrutiny and the tenderness Khaled showed towards Sam. It was too much, an emotional overload.

'Right. Let's go.'

One of the stewards opened the aeroplane's door, and Khaled stepped out into the bright glare of sunlight and what felt like a thousand flashing cameras. Lucy followed him.

The questions fired at them like bullets, and Lucy heard at least a dozen different languages, each one incomprehensible. Then a question came in English, one she heard all too clearly.

'Prince Khaled, when is the wedding date?'

CHAPTER SIX

WEDDING. The word echoed through Lucy as she stared, horrified, at Khaled.

Khaled, however, didn't answer that question—if he'd even heard it. He simply ploughed through the crowd, his head lowered, protecting Sam. Lucy followed.

They made it into a waiting sedan, and Lucy pressed back against the seat, grateful for the protection and privacy of the darkly tinted windows.

Sam struggled to sit up, looking about him with bright-eyed curiosity. 'Who were all those people?'

'A welcoming committee,' Khaled said dryly, and the sedan pulled away from the airport.

She wouldn't ask Khaled about that ridiculous question now, Lucy decided. She'd wait until tonight, when Sam was asleep and they had a moment's privacy. Besides, it was undoubtedly just a stupid rumour. She had enough experience with the press to know they made up the most ridiculous things.

Except it had sounded as if the journalist knew about the wedding, and just wanted a set date. The question hadn't been 'are you getting married?' but 'when'.

As if it were a foregone conclusion.

Stop, Lucy told herself. You're tired and overwrought and imagining things—just like the journalists had to have been.

The rest of the short trip to the palace was occupied by

Sam's incessant questions as he pressed his face to the window and demanded to know how high the mountains were, were those buildings really made of mud, and where *were* the spiders?

Khaled answered each question with laughing patience, until finally the car pulled to a halt in the palace courtyard.

The palace was just as impressive and forbidding as it had been a week ago, and this time Lucy felt even more like a prisoner. The gates closed behind them, and she was conscious of a sudden sense of loneliness. The last time she'd been here, she'd been part of a lively entourage, a diplomatic event. Now she was alone, in Khaled's own country. At his mercy.

Khaled was holding Sam's hand, drawing him into the palace, and Lucy told herself to stop being so horribly melodramatic. There was something gothic and even frightening about the palace, yes, but it didn't mean that was the reality.

The reality, she told herself firmly, was that Khaled was getting to know his son and vice versa. They would have a few weeks' holiday—just as Khaled had suggested—and then return to London.

If she told herself that often enough, Lucy thought grimly, perhaps she would begin to believe it.

Pasting on a bright smile, she followed Khaled and Sam into the palace.

'So.' King Ahmed stood in the foyer, dressed in a pure white *thobe* which made a stark contrast to Khaled's casual Western clothes. His dark eyes swept over Sam's small figure. 'This is the child.'

Khaled laid a proprietary hand on Sam's shoulder. 'Sam, meet my father, King Ahmed.'

'King?' Sam repeated, his eyes rounding in wonder.

'Yes, and I'm Prince Khaled, although you don't need to call me that.' Khaled's voice was light, his hand still resting on Sam's shoulder, and Lucy's hands clenched into fists.

Great. Sam undoubtedly felt like he'd stepped into a fairy

tale. He looked round the ornate reception room with its frescoed walls and pillars covered in gold leaf and breathed a single, happy sigh, his fingers twining with Khaled's.

Ahmed's gaze slid from Sam to Lucy. 'And you are Sam's mother.' His mouth twisted in something close to a smile, cynical though it was. 'My son's bride.'

Lucy stared. *Wedding. Bride.* Something was going on, something she didn't understand, didn't even want to think about. She opened her mouth—although as to what she was going to say she had no idea—but Khaled cut her off before she uttered a word.

'Lucy is tired from such a long journey,' Khaled said smoothly. 'As we all are. I'm sure we'll look forward to chatting and getting to know each other over dinner, Father.'

Ahmed jerked his head in a terse nod of acceptance, and Khaled brought his hands together, touching them to his forehead in the classic gesture of obeisance. Then, with one hand returning to clasp Sam's, he took Lucy's elbow and guided her from the room.

She followed him through the twisting corridors to an upstairs hall of bedrooms. 'You and Sam can stay here,' Khaled said, stopping in front of a doorway. 'I'm right down the hall if you need me.'

Lucy didn't even glance in the bedroom. 'Khaled, what was your father talking about, calling me your—'

'You're tired,' Khaled cut her off. 'Have a rest, and we'll speak later.'

Frustration bubbled inside her. 'I don't want to rest,' she hissed. Sam tugged on her hand, eager to explore their new bedroom. 'I want to know what's going on,' Lucy insisted, keeping her voice low for Sam's sake.

'Now is not the time.' Khaled's voice and expression were both implacable. 'Rest, Lucy, and later I will answer whatever questions you might care to ask.'

'Trust me,' she replied through gritted teeth, 'there are quite a few.'

Khaled smiled faintly, a little sadly even, and to her surprise he brushed her cheek with his fingertips, causing an electric shock of awareness to ripple inwards from her skin. 'I'm sure there are.'

Then he disappeared down the corridor, and Lucy followed Sam into their bedroom.

No luxury had been spared, she soon saw. There were two bedrooms, each with a king-size bed, and a sitting room connecting them. Each room had a pair of French doors that led out to a shared terrace twice as large as her garden back home.

Sam hung over the balcony, gazing in rapt wonder at the view of the gardens. Lucy saw a swimming pool on its own landscaped ledge glinting in the distance.

Clearly so did Sam, for he breathlessly asked, 'Can we go swimming? Can we?'

'Later,' Lucy promised, pulling him back from the railing. Even though she'd been spoiling for a fight with Khaled, she reluctantly recognised the wisdom of his words. She was exhausted, and so was Sam. 'I'm not even sure what time it is back home, but I think we both need a rest.'

Sam was surprisingly unresistant to the idea of a nap, and within a few minutes Lucy had settled him in one of the bedrooms. He looked so small in the huge bed, his hair dark against the crisp, white pillow. Lucy sat on the edge of the bed, stroking his hair as he drifted to sleep, until her own fatigue drove her to the other bedroom and the sanctuary of sleep herself.

She awoke several hours later, the sky outside just darkening to violet. A cool breeze blew in from the French doors, ruffling the gauzy curtains. The only other sound was the lazy whir of the ceiling fan.

Lucy rose from the bed and checked on Sam, who was still sprawled in the middle of the wide bed, fast asleep. Smiling at the sight, she went to have a shower and dress for dinner while she could.

An hour later, both she and Sam were washed and dressed and ready to head downstairs.

'You both look refreshed,' Khaled said as they came down the stairs into the foyer.

'Thank you,' Lucy murmured, and couldn't help but notice that he also looked much refreshed—and irresistible. Her heart gave an extra two bumps as her gaze swept over him. He wore a crisp white shirt, open at the throat, and somehow she couldn't quite tear her gaze away from that smooth column of brown skin. The memory of kissing his pulse there sent heat flaring to her cheeks. She forced herself to look away.

Khaled stretched out a hand to her, and after a second's hesitation Lucy took it. She shouldn't like the way his hand felt encasing hers, cool and dry and strong. She shouldn't feel bereft when he let go to tousle Sam's hair.

She shouldn't want this…again.

Ahmed stood in the doorway to the dining room, his manner stiff and formal as he greeted both Lucy and Sam.

A few minutes later a servant ushered them to their places at the vast table. A week ago it had held places for twenty, but now one end was set only for four.

'This has all come as a surprise,' Ahmed said, smiling slightly as the first course was served. Sam looked down at the unfamiliar food—*marag lahm*, a meat soup—and grimaced. Lucy laid a warning hand on his shoulder. 'I had no idea my son was hiding such secrets.'

'It was a secret to him as well until recently,' she said, meeting Ahmed's gaze directly. She refused to be intimidated. She thought of how Khaled had spoken of his father, of his endless, senseless suspicion of his own son.

'And not something that should be discussed at present,' Khaled interjected mildly, although his pointed glance at Sam was clear enough.

Ahmed's lips thinned. 'I see.'

Sam wriggled impatiently. 'I don't like this,' he said in a whisper that carried through the entire room. 'I want pizza.'

'I'm afraid we do not have English food,' Ahmed said shortly. 'In Biryal, boys eat what they are given and are glad.'

Sam stiffened under Lucy's hand and she saw him bite his lip, near tears at the strangeness of everything, as well as Ahmed's terse reproof. The fairy tale was unraveling, she thought.

'Biryali boys eat Birayli food,' Khaled agreed, smiling at Sam. 'And English boys eat English food. Do you know which you are, Sam?'

Sam, still biting his lip, shook his head uncertainly.

'You're both,' Khaled explained gently, and Lucy's heart rate kicked up a notch. 'You're Biryali *and* English.'

'Am I?' Sam said, caught between excitement and uncertainty.

'Yes. And while you're here, perhaps you can eat both Biryali and English food. This soup,' Khaled continued, taking a small spoonful, 'is actually quite tasty. It's just meat, the same kind of meat as in hamburgers.'

Sam did not look convinced, but to Lucy's surprise he dutifully took a bite, wrinkling his nose before he shot Ahmed a nervous glance.

Smiling, Khaled leaned over and whispered, 'Not too bad, eh?'

Actually, Lucy thought over an hour later, it *was* too bad. The whole meal had been interminable, with Sam's squeamishness over the food and Ahmed's terse conversation. He'd fired sudden, staccato questions at Sam or her, or even Khaled, who managed to keep his equanimity for the entire meal.

Lucy's started to fray. She felt strange, tired and near tears, and she wanted desperately to be in her own house, her own bed, with a large glass of wine and a good book.

Khaled must have sensed something of what she felt, for as soon as the last course was cleared he excused both Lucy and Sam from the table and led them back to their rooms.

'I'm not tired,' Sam insisted, but Khaled hoisted him on

his shoulder as he carried him upstairs, sending him into a fit of giggles.

'But you have a big day tomorrow, Sam. I want to show you our lovely pool—that is, if you like swimming?'

'I do!'

'And I promised to show your mother the garden, and of course there are…' Khaled paused dramatically. 'The spiders.'

Sam squealed in delight, and, tickling him, Khaled brought him into the bedroom. Servants had tidied the mess of clothes Lucy had left about, and the beds were turned down and the lamps dimmed, creating warm pools of light and shadow.

With Khaled's encouragement, Sam soon had his teeth brushed and his pyjamas put on, and Lucy tucked him in bed.

'I like it here, Mummy,' he said sleepily, his thumb creeping towards his mouth. 'Let's stay for ever.'

Lucy managed a laugh, despite the feeling of a fist squeezing her heart, draining it of its joy. 'That's a rather long time, Sam.'

'I know,' he said. His eyelids started to flutter, and Lucy watched him for a few moments before she slipped quietly from the room.

Khaled was in the sitting room, stretched out on the sofa, looking relaxed and comfortable. It was, Lucy knew, finally time to talk.

Yet, now that they were alone, she found herself strangely, stupidly tongue-tied. All she could think about—all she could *remember*—was the last time they'd been alone, when Khaled had reached out and touched her, and she had gone so willingly to him. As she always had.

Here: take me. Love me.

Use me. And then leave.

She moved around the room, mindlessly plumping pillows and aligning Sam's shoes so they were perfectly straight, until in exasperation Khaled finally said, 'Lucy?'

She turned. 'What?'

'You told me you had questions?' There was a lilt to his voice, and he smiled. Something about his absolute, easy confidence annoyed her, finally spurring her to action, to words.

She planted her hands on her hips. 'Why did those journalists ask when the—*our*—wedding was? Why did your father refer to me as your bride?'

Khaled's smile widened; it was almost lazy. 'Because they all think we're going to get married.'

Lucy's eyes narrowed. 'And why would they think that, Khaled?'

He shrugged. 'Because in this country, as in many others, if a man and woman have a child marriage is the expected outcome.' He paused thoughtfully. 'Of course, marriage usually precedes children, but…'

'That's not true.' Khaled arched an eyebrow, waiting, and Lucy shook her head. 'Plenty of men, even in countries like Biryal, have illegitimate children. Mistresses. Harems, for heaven's sake. That doesn't mean they marry their—their *concubines*!'

Khaled smiled and his voice turned suggestively soft. 'Are you calling yourself my concubine?'

'*No.*' Lucy glared at him. 'I'm just pointing out that just because we have a child doesn't mean that people would expect us to marry.'

'True, but in this case, when Sam is my named heir…' He trailed off, shrugging a bit, and Lucy felt herself turn cold.

'Have you made that public knowledge?'

'Of course.'

'Of *course*?'

Khaled shrugged again, the movement more expansive, and yet somehow still indifferent. 'If I had not, Biryal—not to mention the tabloids—would be rife with rumour and speculation. Sam's place as my heir would be suspect. I will not have his position or inheritance jeopardised.'

Lucy let the words trickle into her consciousness like cold

water dribbling down her spine. After a moment she sank slowly onto the sofa opposite Khaled. 'I didn't sign up for any of this,' she said, her voice little more than a whisper.

A flicker of sympathy lit Khaled's eyes and then turned to cold ash. 'Perhaps not, but you should have considered the implications of telling me about Sam.'

'I just thought…' Lucy stopped. Her brain felt fuzzy with both fatigue and sorrow. 'I don't know what I thought,' she finally said with a little shrug of self-defeat. 'I'd convinced myself you wouldn't care about Sam, that you'd walk away.'

'Like I walked away from you?'

'Yes.' She looked up and met his hard gaze. He didn't look repentant, more resolute than anything. 'And yet I'm honest enough to realise I would have been disappointed if you'd done that,' Lucy admitted quietly. 'I realise that now, seeing you with him. I want Sam to have a father. A good one, more than I've ever had—or you've had, for that matter.'

'And he will.' Khaled's voice and gaze were both steady.

'How?' Lucy's voice broke, and she covered her face with her hands, taking in a few deep breaths. She didn't want to cry, not in front of Khaled. Not at all. But she couldn't take this— all this sudden change, the way her life and Sam's life were sliding out of control, out of context. Both were unrecognisable.

'You could marry me.'

Any threat of tears evaporated in the face of complete incredulity. Lucy dropped her hands. 'Are you *insane*?'

Khaled's smile was crooked and somehow strangely vulnerable. 'No, eminently sensible, I should think.'

'Marry you?' Lucy shook her head, scarcely able to believe he'd even suggested such a thing. 'Those were just *rumours*!'

'And don't rumours hold a thread of truth?' He was smiling, that fluid mouth she knew so well tilted up at the corners, yet his gaze was golden and intent.

'You certainly didn't deny the rumours,' Lucy said slowly.

'You didn't answer the journalists, *or* correct your father.' Realisation was dawning, creeping over her mind the way the sunlight peeked over the horizon, then flooded the world with harsh light. 'These rumours hold more than a thread of truth, don't they?' Khaled didn't answer; his expression didn't even flicker. If anything it became more resolute. 'Don't they?' she repeated more loudly.

He raised a finger to his lips. 'You'll wake Sam.'

At that moment, Lucy didn't care if she woke the entire palace. Realisation was now as bright as the sun at midday, glittering with relentless heat. 'And you're still not denying them. Tell me I'm wrong, Khaled. Tell me I'm paranoid and ridiculous and absurd—*tell me you didn't tell people we're getting married.*'

'Well.' His mouth crooked upwards once more, and his eyes gleamed. 'You're putting me in a rather difficult position. I'm afraid I can't say any of those things.'

Looking at him lying there, relaxed, confident and smiling, Lucy was forcefully reminded of the man who'd left her in London. Reminded of the reckless, feckless charmer she'd been in love with, the man who'd left her without a word—and she felt a hard, cold fury lodge in her stomach like a ball of ice.

'How?' she whispered. 'How could you play with my life—with Sam's life—without even a scruple? To suggest something so absurd—'

'Is it?' Khaled cut her off softly. He leaned forward, intent once more. 'Is it so absurd, Lucy? Or is it, in fact, sensible?'

Sensible. The word stopped her short. Sensible, as opposed to romantic. A sensible marriage, a way of uniting their awkward little family, uniting the kingdom of Biryal if it came to that. No more custody battles, no more arguments about the future, how Sam would spend his time or his life. No awkward questions, no uncomfortable negotiations.

No possibility of distancing herself or keeping her heart safe. No stability. No trust.

She didn't need to hear his arguments. She knew them, felt them. Of course it was sensible. Who had suggested it first, Lucy wondered—Ahmed or Khaled? Some royal advisor with diplomacy in mind? Fortunately she wouldn't be swayed by such sensible arguments. She didn't even need to consider them. 'Sensible, perhaps,' she said coolly. 'Possible, no.'

'Why not?'

'Because I don't want to marry you,' Lucy said flatly. 'I don't want to live in Biryal as your—your queen, I suppose, and give up my job, my life, my whole identity.'

'Did I say it had to be like that?' Khaled's voice was mild, but his eyes flashed. So did Lucy's.

'You didn't need to.'

'More assumptions,' Khaled said with the hint of a sneer. 'Everything is so *obvious*.'

Lucy glared at him. 'Sometimes it is, Khaled. Sometimes it's *very* obvious. And, anyway, we don't need to argue about it because I don't love you. You don't love me. Full stop.' Why did it hurt to say that?

'Is that obvious as well?' His voice was no more than a whisper, a hiss of breath, a lilt of suggestion, yet it stole around Lucy's heart and squeezed it. Painfully. Suddenly she couldn't answer, couldn't speak, couldn't even think.

Yes. Yes, it was. It had to be.

Khaled rose from the sofa. He walked towards her with careful, calculated steps. 'You told me you *thought* you loved me,' he said, his voice still that entrancing whisper. 'Do you think you could love me again?' He stood in front of her, close enough to see his chest move as he drew a breath, and her eyes fastened on the bit of brown skin bared by the neck of his shirt.

Why couldn't she stop looking at that little bit of skin? Stop imagining, remembering, how it felt against her fingers, her lips…

'I don't want to love you again,' Lucy said. She leaned back against the sofa, not wanting Khaled to come closer—for if he reached out just one hand, one finger, and touched her…

She didn't know what would happen. She didn't know what she'd say yes to. And Khaled knew that, knew his power over her, always had.

He lifted a hand and Lucy flinched, bracing herself for the softly cruel invasion that the merest caress could cause. But he didn't touch her; the threat, the promise hovered in the air between them, made her both yearn and fear.

'Don't,' she whispered brokenly. 'Don't, *please.*'

For a moment Khaled's hand hovered, his fingers outstretched, his face made harsh with—what?—desire or desperation. Then he shook his head, as if clearing it, and dropped his hand.

'No, you're right. I shouldn't. We can't…' He stopped, swallowed. 'We can't love each other, can we?' He turned away, and Lucy was gripped with the desperate urge to run to him, comfort him. To admit the truth: *I loved you then…and I'm afraid I could fall in love with you now.*

Somehow she managed to resist that devastating urge and stay silent, motionless. His back to her, his shoulders stiff with tension, Khaled resumed speaking in a brisk, neutral voice.

'But we can still be sensible.'

'Sensible?' Lucy repeated, laughing without humour, memory giving rise to rage. 'I'll tell you what's *sensible.*' Khaled's eyes narrowed, darkened, and, empowered by her own memory and anger, Lucy continued.

'I trust you not to hurt Sam, because he means something to you. Because you care. But I don't trust you not to hurt me, Khaled.' Khaled's mouth tightened, his hands clenched into fists at his sides. Lucy didn't care. No, she realised distantly, she did care—and she *wanted* him to be angry. She wanted him to hurt. She wanted him to hurt like she had done four years ago, like she'd always wished he had. Yet then she hadn't been worth enough to cause him a moment's anxiety or pain.

Was that obvious as well?

Yes, it was. He could hint now, he could act misunderstood

and hard done by, but she knew the truth. The truth was in the blank, unending silence she'd been faced with four years ago.

No miss. I'm sorry.

She half rose from the sofa, a vengeful fury come to life, given wings. 'I don't care what secret reasons you had to leave four years ago. Nothing—nothing—excuses what you did. Not in my mind. Not in anyone's. Not if you loved me, like you hint now that you did. You didn't.'

Khaled's face remained expressionless, yet it *felt* as if he'd flinched. Lucy drew a breath, determined to continue. 'And that one little mistake, Khaled? It was big. The kind of man who does that doesn't deserve a second chance in my mind. He doesn't get one.' Her breath came in tearing gasps, as if she'd been running, and pure adrenaline surged through her, fuelling her fury. When it was gone, what would be left? She didn't want to know. She certainly didn't want to feel it.

'I see.' Khaled's voice was cool; everything about him, from his hard eyes to his thin-lipped mouth, was remote. Had she hurt him? Lucy couldn't tell. She wasn't sure she wanted to know. 'In that case, if there can be no second chances for us, perhaps you can at least think of a first one for Sam.'

'What?'

'The stigma of bastardy,' Khaled informed her coolly, 'can stick, even to a king.'

Lucy's mouth was dry, and she strove to keep her voice even. 'But surely you knew that when you decided to make Sam your heir?' To disrupt his life. Ruin it, even. 'You didn't have to.'

Another shrug; such an uncaring little gesture. It made Lucy want to scream and stamp her feet, to shake him and make him feel as twisted and racked with pain as she was, as he had been the night she'd seen him in his bedroom, bent over his damaged knee.

Why did *that* man seem so different from this one? How could they be the same?

Which one was real?

'As I said, marriage would be a sensible option for both of us,' Khaled said. He sounded as if he were summing up a business report. 'As well as for Sam. Love need not be involved. It usually isn't in these kinds of marriages.'

Lucy blinked. 'And why should I even think of it?' she demanded. 'What's in it for me?'

Khaled subjected her to a long, level look. 'Perhaps nothing, since you seem determined for it to be so. It's what's in it for Sam that should make you reconsider the flat refusal you just gave me.' He stepped away from her, the movement stiff, awkward, even. Lucy wondered if his knee hurt him again. Now was not the time to ask. She didn't even want to care about the answer. 'Tomorrow we will spend some time together, with Sam, as a family. Perhaps that will help you in your…deliberations.'

He walked with that stiff, uneasy gait to the door, and Lucy thought he meant to leave her without a backward glance, like a haughty parent leaving a chastised child.

Then he turned round. He smiled; it was barely more than a flicker across his face, yet somehow it changed his whole countenance. It changed everything.

There was something tender, sweet and vulnerable about that tiny smile, something that made Lucy wonder about everything she'd assumed—everything that had seemed *obvious*. Something that even made her want to be wrong.

'Goodnight, Lucy,' Khaled said softly, and then he really was gone.

His knee felt like it was on fire. Khaled walked stiffly down the hall to his own bedroom, furious with his body's weakness as well as his mind's. His heart's.

He wanted Lucy. He wanted her to love him, and yet he knew she didn't. She couldn't.

Not the wreck of the man he was now; not even the rugby star he'd once been. She didn't love him at all.

Do you think you could you love me again?

Khaled closed his eyes, shamed by the memory of his own naked need. And she had told him plainly. She didn't even *want* to love him.

Was it because he'd hurt her? Khaled wondered bleakly. Or because she'd never loved him in the first place? Did it even matter?

He'd accepted his father's suggestion of a marriage of convenience because it had made sense. It made Sam safe in a family that was whole, not disjointed and conflicted by the turbulent resentments of four years ago.

Or would those remain?

Would Sam notice?

Khaled shook two pills into his hand and swallowed them dry. How long would it take, he wondered, before Lucy hated him? Perhaps she hated him already. Simple lust didn't change that.

And yet still he had gone forward—announcing the marriage to the press, steamrolling the impossible plan into being—because he wanted her. Needed her.

And, no matter the cost to either of them, he would have her.

Khaled flung himself into a chair, the prescription drug stealing sweetly through his body, bringing temporary relief to his knee even though he still felt swamped with pain.

Was he really so selfish, so greedy, that he would force Lucy to marry him, bring them both pain and misery, simply because he wanted her so much?

He could pretend it was for Sam's sake—he could almost make himself believe it—but his heart knew the truth.

It was for his sake… And it might well be his damnation.

CHAPTER SEVEN

LUCY slept badly that night. She could have blamed it on Sam, who woke several hours after he'd first gone to sleep, his body clock hopelessly out of sync—but in truth she'd been wide-eyed and awake before Sam had ever uttered a sound.

It wasn't Sam keeping her awake; it was Khaled.

She felt tangled up inside, memories, beliefs, hopes, suspicions all twisted. She didn't know which was true, what to trust. Who to trust.

Is that obvious as well?

Could you love me again?

Sensible.

Lucy groaned aloud, sleep no more than a distant memory. Outside stars glittered in a velvety black sky, and the breeze wafting through the French doors was a soft, sultry blanket around her.

What kind of man was Khaled? Was he the reckless, uncaring playboy she'd so stupidly given her heart to? Or was he a man shaped and strengthened by life's trials, a man she could love now, love deeply, not with the silly, desperate infatuation of four years ago?

With the love of a woman, rather than that of a besotted fool.

Lucy closed her eyes, not wanting to ask the questions, much less seek the answers. She couldn't take the risk of knowing Khaled again, of opening her heart to him.

Of watching him walk away again.

So why, despite her insistent refusals, was she actually thinking of it, of Khaled, again?

Wanting.

Marriage.

It was absurd, unnecessary. Ridiculous. *Dangerous*.

Tempting.

That was the problem, Lucy realised despondently. No matter how hard she tried to guard her heart, Khaled stole round the barriers, toppled the fences. He came right in without even realising it and laid siege to her very soul.

And she couldn't let him. She couldn't let herself risk or feel love.

It was too hard when it all came crashing down. And she knew from hard, painful experience that it was just a matter of time until that happened.

By the time the sun peeked over the jagged mountain-tops, Lucy felt even more exhausted than when she'd gone to bed. Sam, however, in the manner of most three-year-olds, was fairly bouncing off the walls of their room, peppering Lucy with questions.

'When will we go swimming? Where's Khaled? What about the spiders?'

'I don't know, Sam,' Lucy replied wearily, yet still managing to summon a smile. 'I imagine we'll see Khaled at breakfast, and he can tell us about our day then.'

A female servant soon knocked on their door and led them to a terrace where there was a table set for breakfast, overlooking the gardens.

'Good morning.' Khaled strode towards them, smiling, and with a squeal Sam flung himself round Khaled's knees.

'Sam!' Lucy said reprovingly, but Khaled shook his head. He tousled Sam's hair and disengaged himself from the stranglehold on his legs with only the faintest grimace of discomfort.

'I'm happy to see you too, Sam. Are you hungry?'

Lucy looked round for Ahmed, and saw with a twinge of relief that he was not present.

'I thought we could relax today,' Khaled said as he led them to a table set with a wide variety of breakfast items, from English sausage to the more traditional Arabic flat-bread with a spicy topping of tomatoes and white beans. 'Recover from jet lag, swim and just enjoy the gardens.'

'Swim!' Sam shouted, and Lucy laid a steadying hand on his shoulder.

'He's just a little bit excited,' she said with a wry smile, and then felt one of those disconcerting lurches when Khaled smiled back, his golden gaze so very direct.

'I'm glad. And how are you this morning, Lucy? Did you sleep well?'

'Well enough.' Lucy kept her voice light as she accepted a cup of coffee from Khaled, made just the way she liked it, including the sugar. 'And you?'

'The same,' he said, and somehow she knew she hadn't fooled him. It gratified her—stupidly, perhaps—to think he hadn't slept either.

Had she kept him awake? Had memories of other nights, nights they'd had together, kept him awake, as they had her?

Had he had memories of them lying together, their limbs twined together among the sheets, sleepy and sated?

Why was she thinking like this, feeling like this?

Remembering at all?

Lucy took a hasty sip of coffee to divert her mind, nearly scalding her tongue, as well as diverting Khaled's knowing gaze.

After breakfast they all returned to their rooms to fetch swimming costumes. A few minutes after Lucy had changed into her modest one-piece and wrapped a sarong firmly around her waist, Khaled knocked on their door. Sam flung it open.

'Ready?' Khaled asked, smiling.

'Ready!'

He led them down to the pool, which was every bit as spectacular as the view from above had promised. It had been built into the mountainside to resemble a natural lagoon, complete with waterfalls, rock slides and a little bridge.

Equipped with armbands, Sam was in heaven. He plunged in up to his waist, and then turned to Khaled.

'Come in!'

'All right.' Khaled shrugged off his tee-shirt, and Lucy sucked in a breath.

She'd forgotten how beautiful he was.

Yet she hadn't, not really; she'd tried to, and failed. For just one glimpse of the hard, sculpted muscle of his chest, golden skin and fuzz of dark hair made her remember with a rush how that chest had felt against her body, how his hair had tickled her lips. How his skin was hot and taut and so surprisingly smooth.

Khaled wore only a pair of swimming trunks, and Lucy saw the thick support brace wrapped around his knee, covering his leg from mid-thigh to nearly mid-calf.

Lucy watched Sam and Khaled swim together, content for the moment to spend some time stretched out on a lounger. Sam hadn't had much experience with pools or swimming, but he caught on quickly, and within minutes he was launching himself at Khaled, who caught him before tossing him up into the air. Each time Sam landed with a splash and a giggle of glee, and bemusedly Lucy didn't know which sound was louder.

It tugged at her heart to see them together, looking so natural, so happy, so right. It made her regret the years they'd all lost, when Khaled hadn't been a part of Sam's life.

She'd convinced herself that Sam didn't need Khaled, that *she* didn't.

Now she wondered whether they both did. The thought terrified her.

Sam hurled himself into Khaled's arms yet again, and Lucy

smiled wryly. Khaled couldn't have created a better picture of familial bliss if he'd planned it. Maybe he had, she acknowledged, but he couldn't have contrived Sam's devotion to him. In fact, she wondered if Sam's easy acceptance had taken Khaled by surprise, had made him determined to suggest this outrageous marriage.

A loveless, sensible marriage.

Is that obvious as well?

Stop it, Lucy told herself crossly. *Stop thinking, wondering, hoping.*

A marriage between them would never work.

Why not? a voice whispered insistently, and Lucy forced herself to answer with a cool mental logic.

Because she couldn't live her life entirely in Biryal. Because she didn't love Khaled, and he didn't love her. Because getting married simply for the sake of a child wasn't a good enough reason.

Because Khaled would get tired of her. Again. He would leave. Again.

You're afraid.

She could almost hear Khaled saying the words, although the revelation had come from her own heart.

She was afraid of being hurt again, of loving Khaled and losing him one more time.

'Mummy, come in and play with us!' Sam held out his arms beseechingly, and with a smile Lucy rose from the lounger.

'All right.'

She could feel Khaled watching her as she slid off her flip-flops and sarong and self-consciously adjusted the straps of her swimming costume, as if she could somehow make it cover more of her body.

And why should it matter? He'd seen her already, all of her, had touched and kissed every part.

Of course, that had been before Sam. She carried a few more pounds now—not too many, but enough for her to notice.

She had several stretch-marks on her tummy that had faded to persistent silvery streaks. She looked different.

She found herself glancing at Khaled's damaged knee, now submerged in the pool, and thought, *We're both different*.

They both had battle scars, marks which showed that sometimes life was hard. It had changed them on the outside, as well as on the inside, and that, perhaps, wasn't a completely bad thing.

They spent another hour in the pool, laughing and chasing each other, and even as she played with Sam Lucy couldn't shake the feeling of awareness that prickled along her skin and warmed her body both inside and out. She was aware of Khaled, aware of his slick, bare, water-beaded skin so close to hers, aware of his golden eyes sweeping over her even when he wasn't looking at her.

She knew he was aware too, that he felt the tension and expectancy build with the latent force of a volcano; that he felt the same pressure that mounted inside her when his arm or thigh brushed against her in the water. When Sam did a particularly daring jump his laughing eyes met hers—and held them.

She couldn't look away. She didn't even want to.

She felt the need and the desire—building inside her, threatening to overflow—and something else, something warm and hopeful and good—and she didn't try to push it back down or pretend it wasn't there. She should have; that would have been the *sensible* thing to do. But for a moment she didn't feel sensible.

She felt wanted.

Wanting.

Finally Sam tired out, and Lucy towelled him off on her lap, loving the feel of his damp, sun-warmed little body.

Khaled slung a towel around his hips—had his navel always been so taut and flat?—and said, 'I'll have lunch brought to the terrace. And then, Sam, perhaps a rest before we see the spiders?'

It was a sign of how tired Sam was, as well as how much he'd come to listen to Khaled, that he only protested once, and even that was halfhearted.

They ate by the poolside and Lucy could see that Sam was already fading as he picked at the chicken nuggets—English food that Khaled must have arranged.

'I'll take him upstairs,' Lucy said, and Sam curled around her, his head on her shoulder, as Khaled led her back through the palace to the bedroom.

'I wonder if I'll ever get used to the size of this place,' Lucy said after she'd tucked Sam in his bed. Khaled was in the little shared sitting room, still clad in only his swimsuit and towel. 'I might need a map.'

'I hope you'll get used to it,' Khaled replied with a smile, but Lucy didn't miss the intensity in his eyes. Her breath hitched and her heart began to thud.

'Khaled…'

'Don't.' She stared in surprise, and he crossed the room to press a finger gently against her lips. 'Don't say no. Don't tell me all the reasons why this isn't going to work.' Lucy tried to speak, but her lips just brushed Khaled's finger, and her tummy tightened at the sensation.

'Just let's *be*, Lucy,' Khaled said, his voice a soft, lulling whisper. 'Do you remember how it was before—enjoying each other's company, enjoying each other?' She shook her head, not wanting to go there, even though it was already too late. Her mind, heart and body had all travelled down that dangerous road, remembering just how sweet it had been.

False; it had been false.

Yet could *this* be real?

She reached up and caught his hand with her own, pushing it away from her mouth.

'All right,' she found herself saying, surprised. She hadn't intended to say that at all. She'd meant to lay out her arguments, all those logical, sensible reasons she'd catalogued in her mind.

'Let's enjoy these few days,' she said, her voice firm and un-wavering. 'For Sam's sake.'

'And for our own?' Khaled's eyes burned into hers, yet Lucy heard a lilt of what sounded almost like uncertainty in his voice—uncertainty and hope. 'Just to see how it could be?' he added in a whisper.

'It can't,' she said, and she'd never sounded so uncertain, so desperate *not* to be right.

Khaled smiled, uncertainty replaced with satisfaction. Damn him. He knew his effect on her, knew how weak she was.

'A few days,' he agreed, and from his tone Lucy knew he thought that was all he'd need.

The next few days passed in a pleasant haze of sightseeing, swimming and enjoying the surprising treasures of Biryal. Khaled took them to see the pearl divers on the coast. The art of Biryal's ancient trade was now a tourist attraction, as pearls were now made synthetically in an oyster farm.

He showed Sam the spiders with their huge, yellow webs as promised. Lucy stayed well behind, even as Sam stared, fas-cinated, his hand clasped tightly with Khaled's.

He took them to a national museum in Lahji, and Lucy was impressed with the clean, wide streets; the ancient build-ings were cheek-by-jowl with modern skyscrapers. It was a small city, compact and well-maintained, and she could begin to see why Khaled was proud of his country, why he was dedicating his time, his life, to improving the condition of its people.

During these outings Lucy let her mind drift, enjoying the sun on her face, the breeze from the sea, the feeling that they were a family. A real one.

She didn't let herself think about how it couldn't last, what would happen when she returned to London, to her life. Khaled…what would he do?

What would he want, demand?

Her mind slipped away from such questions, and certainly from their possible answers.

Yet even in the pleasant passing of time she felt the latent need and memory deep in her belly, and also in her heart. She felt it lurch inside her every time Khaled looked at her, that knowing little smile quirking the corner of his mouth upwards, his eyes gleaming, making her ache.

Her mind slipped away from that too.

A week after they arrived, Khaled stretched out on the lounger next to hers as Sam splashed in the shallow part of the pool.

'There will be a magnificent sunset tonight,' he remarked casually, too casually, and Lucy waited, eyebrows raised.

'I thought we could take a picnic supper to the Dragon Grove.'

'Dragon Grove?' Lucy repeated, smiling. 'That sounds intriguing. I'm sure Sam will love it.'

'Alone.' Khaled's eyes sought hers and found them. Lucy swallowed.

'What about Sam?' she asked, her voice sounding rusty. Khaled shrugged.

'He is comfortable here now, is he not? I have hired a nurse to watch him. She is reliable, warm.'

'You didn't think to consult me?' Lucy asked, hearing the sharpness in her tone, feeling it, and so did Khaled. He reached out and brushed her cheek with his fingertips; Lucy flinched away.

'So prickly, Lucy. Does it matter?'

'I don't like you making decisions about Sam without me,' Lucy replied stiffly.

'I hired a babysitter for an evening.' Khaled shrugged. 'Do you want me to clear every decision I make with you, Lucy? Because, I am telling you now, I will not. Sam is my son—as much my son as he is yours. Remember that.'

Lucy half-rose from the lounger, her body tense and ready to fight. 'Are you threatening me?'

Khaled muttered an oath in Arabic, his eyes darkening dangerously. 'No, though you see threats everywhere, like spiders! I am telling you, Lucy, that you cannot threaten or manage me. I won't grovel for Sam's attention or access to his life. So don't try and make me.'

'I wasn't—'

'Weren't you? You are always trying to be in control, to make the decisions.'

'Of course I want to be in control,' Lucy snapped. 'I'm not going to sit here passively while you rearrange Sam's life to suit your own purposes!'

'Which are at cross with your own?' Khaled shook his head, and his voice turned soft. 'You see how easy this would be if we were married?'

'Hardly,' she replied, even though her heart bumped unevenly in her chest. 'Then you'd just expect me to do your bidding.'

Khaled laughed, one eyebrow arched. 'Oh? And wear a *hijab* as well? Who told you that?'

Lucy felt her cheeks flush. She was uncomfortably aware of the assumptions she'd made, and yet she felt in her gut that they were true. That they could be, anyway. 'No one did,' she muttered. 'I don't need to be told.'

'Because this is an Arab country? We are Westernised, you know. Civilised too.'

Lucy looked away. 'It doesn't matter.'

'It does,' Khaled said quietly, and she heard a note of sorrowful sincerity in his voice that resonated deeply within her. 'It does,' he repeated. 'Because you have so many of these assumptions, and I realise it is time to correct them, even if…' He paused, his gaze slipping from hers. 'Even if it is uncomfortable. The truth must be told and faced. I will do so tonight…when we are alone.'

The invitation had been replaced by a command. Lucy pursed her lips. She wasn't going to argue simply for the sake of it, and if Khaled meant what he said about correcting her assumptions then she wanted to listen.

She needed to hear the truth, whatever it was.

Sam was surprisingly amenable to being left with Hadiya, the nurse Khaled had hired. She was a young, smiling, round-cheeked woman and Lucy couldn't find a single thing wrong with her. Perversely, she had tried.

They left the palace in the late afternoon to give them enough time to reach the grove before the spectacular sunset Khaled had promised.

'What is this Dragon Grove?' Lucy asked as she climbed into the passenger seat of an open-topped Jeep.

'One of Biryal's treasures. I know it may look like a dusty, scrubby island to you, but the interior has many beautiful sights. One of them is this grove. The trees are native only to this island and one other.'

Intrigued, Lucy sat back and let the hot, dry breeze blow over her as Khaled started the Jeep and they began the precarious route down the mountain.

They didn't speak, but it was a surprisingly companionable silence. The heat made Lucy feel almost languorous, and the questions and worries that nibbled and niggled at her mind slipped away once more.

She would enjoy this evening she resolved. One evening, for pleasure. One evening without worrying, fighting, fearing. It was all too easy a decision to make.

Khaled turned off the main road that led to Lahji and entered a protected nature reserve, which was mostly rocky hills dotted with trees. Lucy knew this must be the grove he'd mentioned, for the trees were indeed unique. They had thick, knobbly trunks, their branches with bristly dark leaves thrust upwards, like a brush. It looked, Lucy thought, as if the trees were raising their arms to heaven.

'Dragon's Blood trees,' Khaled told her as he parked the Jeep. From the back he fetched a blanket and picnic basket. 'When their bark is cut, a thick, red resin comes out. It used to be called the blood of Cain and Abel. It is known to have healing properties.'

He reached for her hand to help her across the rough ground, and Lucy took it naturally. Khaled, she noticed, walked with that same stiff-legged gait, but he did not appear to be in pain.

He spread a blanket on a smoother stretch of ground positioned above the grove so they could watch the sun begin its descent towards the trees.

Lucy helped him spread the blanket out before they both sat down. Khaled rested his elbows on his knees, his thoughtful expression on the distant horizon. The sun was turning the colour of a blood orange, large and flaming.

Lucy watched him for a moment. The harsh profile had softened a bit in reflective silence, yet she thought she saw a certain determination in the set of his jaw.

'Shall we eat?' she asked, and Khaled turned to her with a distracted smile.

'Yes. I asked the palace cooks to pack a feast.'

As Khaled began to unpack the picnic basket, Lucy saw that there was indeed a feast: roast chicken seasoned with cumin, aubergine salad, pastries plump with dates and a bottle of chilled white wine.

'I thought countries such as yours forbade alcohol,' Lucy remarked, taking the glass Khaled poured her. She realised that wine had been served at most meals, although it hadn't really registered with her until now.

'I told you, we are Western now,' Khaled replied, smiling. He raised his glass in a toast. '*Saha.*'

'*Saha,*' Lucy repeated, and they both drank. 'What does that mean?'

'To good health. It is a traditional toast.'

They ate in companionable silence, although as it wore on Lucy felt her nerves start to fray. Before tonight there had always been the safety of Sam between them; Khaled hadn't tried to see her on her own after that first night. Evening meals had been chaperoned by Ahmed, and Lucy had retired to the safety of her suite, with Sam as her excuse. Khaled had let her go.

Now that they were finally alone, she realised how safe Sam's presence had made her feel. Her fingers felt thick and clumsy as she tried to manage a chicken drumstick or date pastry. The food was tasteless and dry in her mouth, and she could feel her heart rate kick up again, all in reaction to Khaled.

Had he always made her feel this way?

Of course he had. From the moment she'd first laid eyes on him strolling lazily across the rugby pitch, she'd been helpless. Hopeless. *Wanton*.

Cool, composed Lucy Banks had melted like warm butter in Khaled's hands under the heat of his carelessly given smile.

And he'd known. She'd always been able to tell that, had seen the amused flicker of awareness in his eyes, and still she hadn't cared. She couldn't change.

When Khaled had beckoned her, smiling with languorous confidence, she'd gone to him. Had been glad to.

And now it was happening again. Khaled's gaze had turned speculative and heavy-lidded over the rim of his glass, and Lucy felt herself begin to melt, her body betraying her as always. Desire took the place of reason, of pride. Of safety. Lucy forced her gaze away from Khaled.

The sun, she saw, was nearing the tops of the trees, sending out long, orange rays and flooding the sky with supernatural colour.

'You're right,' she said in an awkward attempt to fill the expectant silence, to keep the treacherous reactions of her own body at bay. 'The sunset is spectacular.'

'There are many beautiful things about Biryal.'

She glanced at him sharply. 'Is that a sales pitch?'

Khaled chuckled and stretched out on the blanket, his body long and lithe next to hers…close to hers. Lucy inched away; the temptation to sidle closer, to feel the long, hot length of his thigh against hers, was too great.

As much as she'd told herself she would enjoy this evening, she wasn't. She couldn't. Her nerves and fears were on high alert. She was so weak when it came to Khaled; he could have her so easily, and he knew it. Even now he knew it. And, if he did, what would be left of her happiness? Her self-respect? Her safety?

'Not really,' Khaled said after a moment. He reached one hand out to lazily brush a tendril of hair behind her ear. Lucy forced herself not to react. 'Your hair is always so silky,' he murmured. 'I've dreamed of touching it, of feeling it between my fingers like cool water.' There was a surprising ache of yearning in his voice that had Lucy shaking her head, sending more tendrils escaping to brush her cheeks. Khaled threaded his fingers through them, smiling.

'You haven't…?' she began, mesmerised by the feel of his hands in her hair, of his knuckles barely brushing her cheek-bone. She wanted more.

'Haven't I?' His fingers, tangled in her hair, drew her slowly, inexorably to him, as she'd been afraid they would. As she'd wanted him to.

He drew her towards him, and she went. She didn't resist, didn't even consider it. She couldn't, for she wanted the promise she saw in his eyes, and when his lips barely brushed hers she felt that promise fire her soul.

'Lucy…' he murmured against her mouth, like a supplication, a prayer.

'Oh, Khaled.' Her hands slid up of their own accord to caress the smooth skin on the back of his neck, his stubbly jaw, to rake through his hair. She wanted to feel him, every bit, had been *aching* for his touch. It had been so long. Too long.

Yet even as desire swamped her body her mind rebelled. *Not this. Not now, not again…*

Body and heart warred against each other and helplessly she shook her head. A tear she hadn't meant to shed escaped from beneath her closed lids and plopped on Khaled's thumb. He drew back in appalled surprise.

'You're crying.'

'No.' She shook her head again, laughing a little bit, embarrassed, for two more tears had streaked down her cheeks. Even now her body betrayed her.

'Why?' He looked so genuinely bewildered that she laughed again, a hiccup sound halfway to a sob.

'Because…I don't know…' She drew a breath, willing the tears to recede, and the desire too; she needed to find her composure once more and don it like armour.

'I didn't mean to make you sad.'

She glanced at him from the corner of her eye and saw him frown ruefully and run a hand through his hair, mussing it. The last wedge of sun glimmered on the horizon before it sank beneath the mountains and the night settled softly around them.

'I'm not sad,' Lucy said, and her voice came out firmly. She swallowed the last threat of tears and forced herself to look at Khaled directly. 'Just emotional, perhaps. There's been so much change recently, and the future is so uncertain.'

'It doesn't have to be.'

She shook her head, not wanting to start down that road. 'And I've admitted before,' she continued firmly, 'that I am helpless when it comes to you, like a moth to the candle flame.' Her mouth set in a grim line. 'It's not something I'm proud of.'

'You make it sound like weakness.'

'It is.'

Khaled was silent for a moment. 'Would it be,' he finally asked, 'if I hadn't left?'

Lucy drew back, startled. 'What do you mean?'

He shrugged. 'You've defined everything—me, yourself, our relationship—by the fact that I left without telling you.'

'Of course I have,' she snapped. 'How could I not?'

'Sometimes,' Khaled said quietly, his eyes intent on hers, 'I wish I hadn't left.'

The breath left Lucy's body, left her feeling dizzy and

airless. She drew another breath and let it out shakily. 'Do you really?' she asked, hearing both the doubt and the desire in her voice. He offered her a twisted smile.

'I told you I would correct some of these assumptions you have,' Khaled said. His voice was soft, yet even so it held a certain grim resolution. 'And one of them is about why I left— left England, left rugby—left you.'

Lucy's hands curled into claws, her fingernails biting into her palms. Her heart began a relentless drumming. 'All right,' she said evenly. 'So, tell me.'

Khaled's gaze slid from hers; it was the first time he'd been the one to look away. Lucy felt his emotional withdrawal like a physical thing, as if a coolness had stolen over her.

'You, of all people, know how I've had muscle strain in my knee,' Khaled began. He kept his voice even, unemotional, his gaze on the now-darkened horizon. Lucy didn't speak. Of course she knew; she'd iced and massaged his knee many times in the two years he'd played for England. The team physician had diagnosed stressed ligaments, and Lucy had agreed. An X-ray early on had shown nothing more serious. 'I always assumed it was simply repetitive-strain injury,' Khaled continued. 'It was the easiest thing to believe—'

'It was the diagnosis we gave,' Lucy interjected quietly. She felt a sudden stab of guilt. If she had misdiagnosed Khaled, if the team physician had…

Briefly he touched her hand with his own, then removed it. 'This is not your fault.'

Lucy said nothing, but the question 'What isn't my fault?' seemed stuck in her throat and hovered silently in the air between them.

'I didn't tell you all my symptoms,' Khaled explained, his voice heavy and quiet in the stillness of the evening air. 'I ignored them myself. The severity, at least.'

'What?'

'It doesn't matter now. It's all past.' He gave a sigh, raking his hand through his hair once more. 'In the end, that final injury offered an unarguable diagnosis.' He looked at her directly, bleakly honest. 'I didn't have a torn ligament, Lucy. I had loose fragments of my knee bone, of the patella.'

'*Osteochronditis dissecans*,' Lucy murmured. It must have begun after the X-ray, otherwise they would have picked it up. It was a rare condition, one she never would have thought of without more information, where the patella's cartilage began to fragment and float. It was, she knew, very painful. 'Still, it is treatable, with surgery—'

'I had the surgery,' Khaled interjected. 'After my last injury. And that was when they diagnosed sudden onset of severe osteoarthritis. The osteochronditis had gone too far to be controlled.'

'Hence the flare ups,' Lucy murmured, silently adding, *and the finished rugby career.*

'Yes.' Khaled fell silent, and Lucy felt a ripple of frustration. He acted as though he'd explained everything, and she most certainly felt he had not.

'I still don't understand, Khaled,' she said quietly, 'why such a diagnosis would make you leave me in the way you did.'

Khaled averted his gaze as he spoke. 'The doctor told me the arthritis would be degenerative, probably quickly so, because of my age and its severity. He gave me a year or two at most at my current mobility… Eventually I'd need a wheelchair.'

'But you're still walking,' Lucy objected.

'For now.' He turned, smiling wryly, although there was a deep bleakness in his eyes reflected from his soul. 'It's only a matter of time, Lucy. And of course you need to know that…if you marry me. At some point I will most likely lose the ability to walk.'

'At some point,' Lucy repeated. 'Have you had any X-rays since then?'

'Yes, and the consultant admitted the damage was much less than he'd anticipated. But I still have the condition. That cannot be changed.'

Lucy was silent, trying to make sense of what he was saying. 'You didn't think to tell me this when you learned of it? When I was asking for you?'

'I didn't want to burden you with it,' Khaled said, and a brusque note entered his voice. 'I've seen what happens when someone is saddled with the long-term care of a loved one. I know it's an impossible choice, and I didn't want you to have to make it.'

'But you should have let me,' Lucy insisted quietly. 'It was my right.'

'And I considered it my right to keep the information to myself,' Khaled returned, his voice sharpening.

Lucy shook her head, sorrow flooding through her. Her heart ached for Khaled four years ago—learning of such a devastating diagnosis—and for herself, longing to be with him. 'I wanted to be with you,' she said quietly. 'Then. I would have stood by you, Khaled.'

'I didn't want your pity.' Khaled jerked a shoulder. 'I still don't. I've learned to live with it, Lucy, but four years ago I couldn't stand the thought of everyone I knew treating me with kid gloves, damning me with their mercy. Of you being that way. And if I'd told you, there would be no way to prevent it.'

Lucy drew her knees up to her chest. 'I'm sorry you went through that,' she said quietly, choosing her words with care. 'And I can understand why you left, but…' She felt Khaled tense—felt herself tense, and forced herself to continue. She knew it had to be said. Confronted. 'If you really cared about me, Khaled, you would have been in touch. A letter, a phone call.' Her voice trembled and she strove to control it. *'Something.'*

'I thought about it,' Khaled told her, and from the low intensity of his voice she believed it. 'Many times. I wanted to.'

She shook her head. Even now the doubt was strong, the evidence overwhelming. 'Did you really?'

'Yes. But I didn't in the end, Lucy, because I didn't think it would ever work. For you. I didn't want to be a burden to you, or to anyone. I know what that's like.'

'Do you?' Lucy asked. 'How?'

'My mother was diagnosed with MS when I was little more than a baby. By the time I was five, she was bedridden. It was why there was never any more children. I saw how my father tried to care for her, how it poisoned their marriage.'

'Poisoned?' Lucy repeated, revulsion creeping into her voice.

'He began to resent her. He didn't want to, but I could tell. She could tell. He wanted a wife by his side, healthy and strong, giving him sons. And instead...' He shrugged, spreading his hands. 'My mother shrivelled and withered under his disappointment, and I couldn't stand the thought of being the same.'

Lucy was silent, her heart aching for the boy Khaled must have been, as well as the man he'd become. His mother's illness as well as his own injury had shaped him, hardened him.

Could there be an end to his bitterness? Could she provide it? 'And you thought I'd react the same way?' she asked in a low voice when the silence had stretched on too long. 'That I'd be...disappointed somehow?'

Khaled exhaled heavily. 'You wouldn't mean to be.'

'I wouldn't,' Lucy broke in. 'Full stop. But you never gave me that choice.'

'It was *my* choice,' Khaled returned, an edge creeping into his voice again. 'First and foremost.'

And that was at the heart of it, Lucy thought, too sad to feel resentful. Khaled made the choices for both of them—he had four years ago, and he was doing the same now. 'But what's changed, Khaled?' she asked. 'Your medical diagnosis hasn't, so why are you willing to risk marriage with me when you weren't before?'

'Because of Sam,' Khaled replied. 'And because I want to. I want you.' His face hardened with determination. 'I'm willing to risk it. I have to.'

Want, Lucy thought. Not *love*. Not even close. But what had she been expecting?

'I know...' He stopped, his expression hooded, distant, yet

with the shadow of vulnerability in his eyes. 'I wasn't—I'm still not—the man I once was. The man you fell in love with. I'll never be that man again.' This last statement was delivered with an achingly bleak honesty that made Lucy stare at him with speechless revelation, sorrow swamping her once more. They'd both changed. They were different people now, re-shaped by heartache and disappointed dreams. 'Although,' he continued, 'you say you weren't in love with me at all.'

There was an honesty in his eyes that reached right down to her soul, and she was compelled to be honest as well. 'Maybe I was,' she admitted in a raw whisper, and gently Khaled reached out to brush a tendril of hair away from her cheek.

'And now?' he asked, his voice just as soft as hers. Her heart began to beat so fiercely, she felt as if it would burst through her chest.

She wanted to tell him she loved him. She wanted to believe she loved him, this man who had shown her his weakness, who had given her his vulnerability. She wanted to trust in this moment. But as she stared at him speechlessly she knew she couldn't. In the end all this was was an evening, a moment in time, an orchestrated intimacy, and she had no idea if it was real.

If Khaled was real.

Even now her heart rebelled, her mind whispered, *you can't trust him, what if he leaves again? What if he decides what's best for you again?*

And then a far more alarming whisper: *what about Sam?*

Could she marry Khaled for Sam's sake, to give him the family neither of them had ever had? Could she keep herself from loving Khaled, from being hurt by him? And was that the kind of life she wanted for herself, for them all?

The other option was to trust him, give herself and her heart to him. Even now every instinct rebelled against that final, frightening step.

'Lucy?' Khaled stared at her, his jaw clenched tensely, re-alizing what her silence meant.

'I…I'm sorry.' She swallowed, feeling tears rise in her throat and crowd her eyes.

Khaled turned away, his gaze resolutely fastened on the horizon. 'Then we must have a marriage of convenience,' he said flatly. 'For Sam's sake. For your own too, perhaps. You would not enjoy living half a life with him, would you?'

'No…' A tear slipped coldly down her cheek and she dashed it away. She knew starkly that marriage to Khaled was best for Sam. Best for her, for, if she didn't marry Khaled, if she didn't keep involved in Sam's life as a royal in Biryal, she would slowly, inexorably lose him to a life he would come to love—a life she wouldn't even understand.

She might keep pace for a while, a few years, but what then? What about when Sam was older? When he didn't need his mummy to come along for hugs and hand holding? She'd be left alone in London, hanging on, desperate, *useless*. Unless she married Khaled and stayed fully, firmly in Sam's life.

After a long moment when both of them were lost in their own silent, separate miseries, she asked, 'Just how…convenient would this marriage be?'

'Not that convenient,' Khaled replied, glancing at her sharply. 'Surely you don't want to be celibate for the rest of your life—especially considering what has been between us?'

The rest of her life; that was what they were talking about. Lucy swallowed. 'No, I suppose not.'

'Good. Because I certainly do not. I have been celibate long enough.'

'How long?' she asked, genuinely curious, and he shot her a quick, sardonic smile.

'Long enough. There are not many opportunities in Biryal, even if I wished to take them. So.' He turned to face her, his voice brisk, his face half-shrouded in darkness, although she could still see that his eyes burned. 'Will you marry me?'

It was hardly how she'd imagined a proposal, a marriage, yet Lucy knew there was only one answer to give. Her heart twisting, breaking, she gave it through numb lips: 'Yes. Yes, I will.'

CHAPTER EIGHT

THE admission seemed to surprise both of them. Khaled stilled, his gaze intent on hers.

'Do you mean it?' he asked in a low voice, and Lucy swallowed, still blinking back tears. 'Yes, I do. For Sam's sake.'

Khaled pulled back, his expression closing, folding in on itself. 'Of course.'

Lucy looked away, feeling as if she'd disappointed Khaled, disappointed herself. Yet Khaled had never even told her he loved her! Perhaps he wanted her as an adoring limpet once more and that was all. Perhaps this would be a marriage of convenience for him, and happily so. Questions and doubts raced through her mind, making her almost dizzy with fear.

Something rustled in the trees behind them—a bird or a small animal—and the wind that blew over them had no last warmth from the setting sun. It was night, and it was cold.

'Well, then.' Khaled's eyes had darkened and he gave an impatient little shrug as he rose stiffly from the blanket. 'It is late. We should return to the palace.' His voice was cool, his face averted.

Lucy nodded, and they set about gathering the discarded plates and glasses, returning the food to the picnic basket and folding the blanket. Mindless tasks that kept both of them from facing what had just happened, or needing to talk about it.

What had she done?

It was a question borne of panic, of fear. For a moment Lucy considered telling Khaled that she wouldn't marry him, that she *couldn't*. Yet the words wouldn't come. They crowded thickly on her tongue, and she choked them back helplessly. For Sam's sake.

They walked back in silence through the darkness, the only sound the crunch of dirt under their feet, and the chattering of a bird high in a Dragon's Blood tree.

Wordlessly Khaled opened the passenger door of the Jeep, and Lucy slid inside.

It seemed as if all of Biryal was quiet and dark, was empty. Lahji's lights glimmered on the horizon, tiny and seemingly insignificant against the vast darkness of both island and ocean. Lucy tried to imagine spending her life here, but couldn't.

Khaled's fingers flexed on the steering wheel and his jaw was tight. Although he didn't speak, Lucy knew he was angry. Annoyed, at least. At her. She'd let him down, and the realisation made her feel angry right back. What right did he have to ask her if she loved him, when he'd never declared himself? He hadn't been that vulnerable after all, had he?

Back at the palace, Khaled dropped her off in the courtyard before returning the Jeep to its garage. Lucy knew he didn't need to perform the mundane task; there was an army of servants waiting to do his bidding.

He just wanted to be away from her, she supposed.

Or perhaps *he* regretted the marriage proposal, her acceptance?

The thought jolted her; it frightened her. It was the thought that her mind had been skittering away from for so long.

What if he walks away from me…again?

She might not have told him she loved him, but Lucy had a fearful feeling that her heart might break all the same.

Pushing the thought away, she returned to her room to dismiss the nurse and check on Sam, who was fast asleep. She prowled the suite of rooms restlessly, wondering if Khaled would come and find her, wondering if she wanted him to.

He didn't.

She dressed for bed, brushed her teeth and washed her face, yet sleep had never felt so far away. Questions tangled and cascaded through her anxious mind, questions and doubts. Fears.

After a moment of indecision where she hovered on the threshold of her bedroom, Lucy muttered under her breath and then stalked from her bedroom out into the corridor.

She was going to find Khaled.

It wasn't easy. Lucy had begun to familiarise herself with the palace, but its endless corridors still defeated her. Everything was eerily silent, lost in shadows. She felt like she might stumble upon Bluebeard's skeletal cache at any moment, as she'd joked when she'd first laid eyes on this place.

She didn't hear the bare feet padding softly behind her, so that when a hand closed around her elbow she nearly screamed. A breath of terrified sound escaped her and she whirled around, knocking the hand away.

A servant stood there, dressed in a plain cotton *thobe* and turban, holding his hands up in a gesture of apologetic self-defence.

'So sorry, mistress. I only wonder if I can help you.' The man smiled rather toothlessly, and Lucy's heart rate began to slow.

'You scared me. I'm sorry; I think I frightened you as well.' She smiled wryly. 'I'm looking for Prince Khaled.'

The servant gave a regretful little shake of his head. 'He has retired for the night.'

Just those innocuous words caused Lucy to picture a host of images: Khaled lying in bed covered in nothing but a sheet, slung low on his hips, as she'd seen him before, as she remembered him.

'Still,' she said firmly, pushing those images away, 'I'd like to see him.'

The servant looked both shocked and doubtful, and Lucy met his gaze directly. 'I have important business to discuss with him.'

After a moment the man lifted one shoulder in a little shrug, as if to say what is it to me what the foreign woman does? Then he turned around silently so Lucy had no choice but to follow.

He led her to the back of the palace, past her own bedroom, where she quickly checked to see that Sam still safely slept, to another suite of rooms. Khaled's.

He knocked softly on the door, shrugging again, and padded softly back down the hall. Lucy pushed the door open with her fingertips; warm, yellow lamplight spilled from inside onto the hall floor.

'Yes? Yusef?' Khaled's voice, low and sure, seemed to vibrate through Lucy's bones. Why was she so nervous? She opened the door further and stepped inside.

'Hello, Khaled.'

He looked up, his eyes widening in surprise, his mouth thinning in—disapproval? Displeasure? Lucy lifted her chin.

'Do you want something?' he asked in a voice made remote with politeness.

'Yes. I want to talk to you.'

He shrugged, leaning back against the sofa cushions where he sat, and Lucy's gaze took in what he'd been doing for the first time.

Dressed only in pyjama bottoms, his chest golden, taut and bare, he was playing chess. By himself. He held one piece, the rook, between long, brown fingers.

'You play chess?' Lucy exclaimed in surprise, and a wry smile flickered across Khaled's face.

'Is that what this is?' he gently mocked, holding up the piece of carved ebony. 'Do you play?'

'Not really.' Lucy quickly shook her head. She had painstakingly learned to play when she was eight, but she'd never actually played a proper game. She'd never had the chance. 'Are you very good?'

Khaled shrugged. 'How does one answer that?' Which Lucy surmised meant he was very good indeed.

'You're playing by yourself?' she remarked, moving further into the room, suffused as it was with both warmth and tension. She studied the board, and could see that Khaled had been moving the pieces on both sides.

He shrugged. 'It is a pastime.' His fingers tightened round the rook and he replaced it on the board. 'What do you want, Lucy?'

Her head was bent, her hair falling down in front of her face like a dark curtain. She pushed it back. 'I want to talk. I just agreed to marry you.'

'Did you?' he mocked and Lucy bit her lip.

'I'm scared, Khaled.' She hadn't meant to say that, or confess it. She didn't want Khaled to know her secrets, her weaknesses, even as she silently acknowledged that he'd given her his.

Khaled wasn't in the mood to be forgiving. He shrugged one powerful, bare shoulder. 'So decide, Lucy. You can't live on the knife edge of fear for too long—you lose your balance.'

And that was how she felt, as if she were about to topple over into an endless abyss of uncertainty. Swallowing, she perched on the edge of the sofa, as far away from Khaled as was possible.

'So, tell me what this marriage will be like.'

He shrugged again. 'Why don't you tell me?'

'I want to spend at least part of the time in London. Sam has family there—my mother especially. And I have my work—I won't give that up, not completely.'

'That's not exactly describing our marriage, Lucy,' Khaled said, his voice low yet threaded with dark amusement. 'You sound as if you're negotiating a business deal.'

'And isn't that what this is?' Lucy pressed, stung by Khaled's words. 'A business deal, for Sam's sake? I suppose many royals have such arrangements.'

'It would seem so.' Khaled had stretched his arms out along the back of the sofa, and Lucy was uncomfortably aware of the long, muscled length of his arm, his fingers scant inches from her own shoulder.

She felt awkward and formal, stiff and polite, and she couldn't shake it.

They were strangers, or nearly so; their affair had been nearly half a decade ago, and had lasted a mere two months. Could she even say she really knew this man?

Or that he knew her?

'So, tell me what you expect from this marriage,' Lucy pressed, and Khaled smiled.

'This arrangement?' he mocked. 'I expect you by my side, in my bed. For us to be a family. If more children come, then so be it. All the better. As for your little requests—' he shrugged '—I see no reason why we cannot spend at least part of the year in London. Sam needs to know all his family, and I think you would probably go mad on Biryal all year. Perhaps we all would.' His hard smile glimmered briefly in the dim lamplight. 'If work is so important to you, then by all means work. Part-time, anyway. You will have duties, obligations as Sam's mother, my wife…and princess.'

Lucy swallowed. Khaled sounded so cold, so unconcerned. There was no love on his side, she realised bleakly. Not even close.

'Thinking of backing out?' Khaled said softly, his voice too close to a sneer. 'Cold feet?'

'I won't back out,' Lucy replied. 'For Sam's sake.'

'Good.'

'I've come to realise,' she replied evenly, 'that what you said was true. Marriage is sensible.'

Khaled muttered something in Arabic that sounded like a curse. He rose from the sofa in one fluid movement, went over to a side table and poured himself a drink.

'Have you taken your—'

'Don't,' he said dangerously, turning round, 'treat me like an invalid. God knows that's the last thing I need from you now.'

'I was just asking,' Lucy said stiffly. She couldn't think of

Khaled as an invalid, not when he stood before her radiating power, beauty and strength. Anger, too. Yet she felt her insides start to yearn, melt, as they always did when he was near. She wanted to reach him, to clamber over this wall of awkward formality that her fear had built brick by unbearable brick, and yet she couldn't.

Khaled might not leave, she realised starkly; he might not walk away as he did before, but he could still hurt her. Could break her heart…if she gave him that power. If she let him in.

'Have you thought of a date?' she finally asked, her throat dry and scratchy. 'For the wedding?'

'No later than a fortnight from now.'

'A fortnight!' She stared at him in disbelief. 'But that's—'

'Soon?' Khaled finished, one eyebrow arched. 'Yes. The sooner the better.'

'That's impossible. I have to tell my mother, at least. This is my *wedding*, Khaled.'

'And mine also. I want no time for gossip, speculation, tabloid smears. You'll find that the things you want—what, a white dress? Some flowers?—can be arranged.' He tossed back his drink, his eyes glinting at her over the rim of the glass.

Lucy shook her head. She wanted more than pretty flowers or a white dress. She didn't care about the wedding; it was the marriage that mattered. And it had already started to sour.

'Maybe we shouldn't do this,' she said, half to herself. 'It might hurt Sam more to have parents who…' She trailed off, her courage failing her, but Khaled finished the thought easily and sardonically.

'Who don't love each other?'

So he didn't love her. The knowledge hurt, even though she knew it shouldn't. She shouldn't let it. 'Right.'

'The important thing is we both love Sam,' Khaled said. He spoke in that terribly pleasant voice that Lucy knew was a cover for far darker, more dangerous emotions. 'As long as we treat each other with kindness and courtesy, Sam won't be affected.'

'How can you be sure?' Lucy pressed, and impatience flitted through his eyes.

'I can't. But many children have parents who aren't madly in love with each other and manage, so I think Sam will too. Now.' He set down his glass, his hands on his hips, every inch the arrogant, autocratic prince. 'Tomorrow morning I will inform my father of our plans, and within a day it will be news all over the world. You can ring your mother beforehand, if you like, so she doesn't find out about it in the papers.'

'Fine.' Lucy pushed aside the dizzying sense of her life spiralling even further out of control. Khaled was right; she didn't have time to indulge her fears. It would be better for both of them if she didn't.

And yet she couldn't keep a sense of desolation from sweeping over her as she rose from the sofa. The future seemed unknowable, impossible. Unhappy.

'All right, then. I'd better go. I've left Sam for too long as it is.'

Khaled jerked his head in a nod of acceptance, but his eyes met and clashed with hers, burning her. She opened her mouth to say something—what? What could she say? What would bridge this chasm that had opened so unbearably between them?

What could heal their scars, calm their fears?

'Goodnight, Khaled,' she whispered, and slipped silently from the room.

Khaled's fingers clenched around his glass as he watched Lucy walk away.

Damn.

He had handled that wrong; he was handling everything wrong. He was losing her before he'd even had her, and he didn't know why. How.

Or perhaps he knew all too well. No matter what Lucy said she wanted, he knew one cold, hard truth: she'd loved the man he'd been four years ago. She didn't love him now, not the man he was, the man he would always be.

And there was nothing he could do about it.

Maybe we shouldn't do this.

He wouldn't allow her to back out. He didn't care if she was unhappy. He was that selfish, Khaled acknowledged as he gazed out over the darkened palace gardens, the surface of the swimming pool glinting in the moonlight. He wanted her that much, and now he wondered if it—he—would destroy them both.

Over the next few days Lucy had the sense of time speeding up, slipping by so fast she couldn't hold on to a single moment. Khaled told his father about their marriage, and with a jerky nod of acceptance—Lucy didn't dare hope it was approval—a host of plans that would change her life for ever had been set in motion.

She tried to avoid the newspapers and television—all eager to cover a breaking story of an unexpected royal marriage, and to an English woman!—but she couldn't avoid more personal confrontations. She needed to talk to her mother and to Sam.

The first conversation was the most difficult. Lucy's fingers curled slickly round the telephone receiver as she listened to the phone ring in her mother's house thousands of miles away.

They chatted for a few moments, and then Dana cleared her throat and asked, 'So when are you coming back from that god-forsaken place?'

Not a good beginning, Lucy thought wryly. 'Actually, Mum…' She took a breath. 'I'm staying for a while.' Dana was silent, and Lucy continued. 'The thing is, Khaled and I… We've decided the best thing for Sam is to—to marry.' More silence. Lucy closed her eyes and summoned her strength. She even managed a little laugh. 'Come on, say something, Mum.'

'I don't know what to say, Lucy.' Disapproval Lucy could have handled, but her mother sounded stunned. Shaken. Doubt swirled through her once more, putting everything into a hope-less fog.

'It's the sensible thing to do,' Lucy said. How she was tired of saying that. Thinking it.

'Really?' Dana's voice sharpened. 'Because it sounds incredibly foolish to me.'

'Mum—'

'Lucy, why? Why are you opening yourself up to that kind of pain again? Do you remember what happened? How Khaled treated you? How you felt? How can you—'

'It's different now,' Lucy interjected.

'Is it?' Dana sounded scornfully sceptical. 'How?'

Lucy closed her eyes, her knuckles white as she clutched the phone to her ear. 'It just is.'

'I don't know if I believe that, Lucy,' Dana said frankly. 'I've known men like Khaled, and I don't trust—'

'I'm not under any illusions about Khaled any more.' Lucy cut her off, unable to hear any more of her own fears parroted back to her. 'We're marrying for Sam's sake, to provide stability.'

'Is that really necessary? Plenty of children grow up in single-parent homes and they're fine. Look at you—'

'But Sam isn't me,' Lucy interrupted. 'He's the son of a prince, and one day he will be king.'

'So?' Dana sounded belligerent, and Lucy almost smiled. Her mother was always ready for a fight, ready to champion her cause, or the cause of single mothers in general: you didn't need a man. You were fine without one.

And Lucy had believed that and been strong without one, until she'd met Khaled and all her principles and opinions had toppled like flimsy cards. She'd been left with only wanting. Yearning. For him.

How weak did that make her? How pathetic? And it was happening again. Except, she told herself, this time she would be strong. She wouldn't need or want.

She wouldn't love.

'It's different, Mum,' she insisted quietly. 'And, besides,

Sam will be spending a good part of his life in Biryal. I'm not about to give him up to Khaled, to absent myself from such an enormous aspect of his life.'

'So you'll absent yourself from your own life instead?'

'My life *is* Sam,' Lucy said quietly. 'Surely you can understand that? I love my job, I love my house and my friends, but it's not my *life*.'

Dana was silent for a long moment. 'I just don't want you to be unhappy,' she finally said, and Lucy heard the sorrow in her voice. She felt it herself.

'I won't be.' *Please, God.* Please, now that she knew what she was getting into. Please let her be stronger than that.

Except, Lucy thought as she finally hung up the phone, she was unhappy. She wanted more from her marriage and her life than something sensible. She wanted the feeling of inexpressible hope, wonder and love that she'd experienced with Khaled before, even though it had been false.

She wanted to love Khaled, and sometimes she wondered if she could—if she could love this new Khaled, a man hardened and yet also humbled by his suffering, a man deeper and darker, and yet stronger too.

Or was that man even real? And would that man walk away, withdraw from their marriage, when he decided it was the best thing for both of them?

The conversation with Sam was far easier. She'd told Khaled she wanted to tell him alone, and with a little shrug, his mouth tightening, he'd agreed.

'But we will both talk to him,' he stipulated, 'about what it means to be a king.'

Lucy agreed; that was not a conversation she wanted to have today, or any time soon.

Now she perched on the edge of Sam's bed as he bounced up and down; he was eager to tear down to the swimming pool and begin another exciting, adventurous day.

'Sam, you've enjoyed it here, haven't you? With Khaled?'

He looked at her incredulously, as only a three-year-old can do, making Lucy feel rather silly. *'Yes!'*

'Good.' Lucy smiled, drawing a breath.

Sam interrupted impatiently, 'Can we go swimming now?'

'In a minute, darling.' She smoothed the hair back from his forehead, smiling a little sadly as he ducked his head away from her touch. He was growing up, growing away from her, even now. 'I want to tell you something. I think it will be good news.'

Something about her sombre tone made Sam turn to her, alert. He looked suspicious. 'What?'

'You know how we've been spending time with Khaled— and he's such a good friend to you? And…' she paused, sucking in air '…to me?' Sam nodded, still looking suspicious. 'Well…what would you think, Sam, if Khaled was your daddy? If you called him Daddy from now on?'

A look of incredulous delight passed over Sam's face like sunlight, and then suddenly he frowned. *'Is* he my daddy?'

How did three-year-olds know to ask such pressing, to-the-point questions? 'Yes.' She nodded. 'Yes, Sam, he is.'

She waited for a barrage of further questions: *why didn't you tell me before? Where has he been?* But perhaps such nuances were beyond him. It was unimportant now, anyway. A de-lighted smile brightened Sam's face and he hopped off the bed, ready to swim. 'Cool.'

And that was that, Lucy thought bemusedly as she walked with Sam down to the pool. He'd accepted Khaled—even living in Biryal—with insouciance and ease.

If only she could do the same.

Khaled was waiting for them by the pool, dressed in a formal *thobe* and *bisht*. He looked tense, and Lucy gave him a bemused smile.

'Sam's thrilled.'

'Is he?' Sam seemed to have forgotten their conversation, for he greeted Khaled as he always did before plunging into the pool. 'Hadiya will watch him now,' Khaled said, gazing at Sam as he splashed and played. 'There is a press conference we both need to attend.'

'A press conference?' Lucy repeated, feeling sick. Khaled's eyes narrowed.

'Yes. You should be used to them, from your days with the England team.' He made it sound as if those days were past— and perhaps they were. Lucy couldn't quite imagine returning to her old life, her old job; not now. Perhaps not ever.

'I know, but this is different—'

'Not really. Reporters ask questions, we answer them.'

'Do we?' Her voice sharpened. 'Honestly?'

'I don't suppose they need to know the details.' Khaled's voice was cool. 'It would certainly help Sam if we could play the loving couple.'

Play. Pretend. Because none of this was real.

Lucy nodded. 'Fine.'

The press conference was held on one of the wide terraces of the palace. Dressed in a cool linen sheath and low heels— both had been provided by a professional stylist—her hair swept up into an elegant chignon, Lucy faced the cameras and questions with a calm, smiling Khaled at her side.

As soon as they came onto the terrace, the cameras flashed and the questions came in an impossible cacophony of sound. Lucy couldn't distinguish one question from the other, and she blinked and squinted in the glare of the cameras' lights, but Khaled seemed entirely unfazed.

She merely heard words—*when, child, wedding, love*— while he answered questions.

He held up one hand to silence the journalists. 'The wedding will be here in Biryal, in a fortnight.'

Another battery of questions. Lucy blinked. Khaled smiled. 'Of course I love my wife. This marriage is a long time coming…for both of us.' His arm came round her waist, pulling her unresistingly to him. Her head fell back as she looked up at him, met his smiling gaze, sensed the hardness underneath. 'Isn't that right, darling?'

A smile stretched across her face. She felt sick with nerves, yet even so an answering flame sparked in her belly. 'Of course.' Khaled brushed her lips with his, the barest of kisses, but it caused the mob of journalists to cheer and howl with delight. Khaled moved away, and Lucy righted herself as best she could.

She didn't hear any more questions, barely felt conscious of herself. It was so surreal, so impossible that this was happening. This was her life. Would she ever get used to it?

Khaled took her hand and drew her back inside, dropping it as soon as the reporters and cameras were out of sight.

Lucy felt suddenly bereft, and miserably she answered his question: no, she wouldn't.

CHAPTER NINE

SUNLIGHT shimmered on a placid sea the morning of Lucy's wedding. She stood in front of the window, watching dawn break and bathe a pearly grey sky in a pale, luminescent pink.

She took a deep breath of the cool, fresh air and let it fill her lungs, buoy her heart.

Today was her wedding day. No matter how strained and artificial things had become between her and Khaled, no matter how convenient and sensible their marriage, today was real and she wanted to enjoy it. She wanted it to be beautiful.

Lucy turned to glance at her wedding dress, a simple silk sheath in ivory that she'd picked from a book of designs and had made by a seamstress on the island. Its nod to Arabic culture was a pattern of vines picked out in gold thread along the bodice, also giving the elegant gown an exotic feel. Her head she would leave bare, her hair down like a girl's.

A knock sounded, and her mother poked her head round the bedroom door. Dana Banks had arrived two days ago, and Lucy was grateful for her mother's strong, comforting presence. She'd kept silent about her concerns for this marriage in light of its pressing reality. Lucy hadn't invited anyone else to the wedding; really, there was no one else to invite. She'd thought briefly of Eric, who had been both her friend and Khaled's, but it seemed that relationship was over now.

So many things were changing, ending. But, she told herself, stroking the silk of her gown, some things were beginning too…for better or for worse.

'Did you sleep well?' Dana asked, and Lucy grimaced wryly.

'Not really. But Sam is still dead to the world—he has no idea what's going on, just that it's exciting.'

Dana gave a little smile. 'It's probably better that way.'

'Yes.' She and Khaled would spend one night at the palace, and then they were going on honeymoon. It was meant to be a surprise; Khaled had not told her the destination.

'You should eat,' Dana said. 'Keep up your strength. It's going to be a long day.'

And it was. The wedding was not taking place until late afternoon, yet the hours before the event were filled with activity—preparations, photographs, conversations with visiting dignitaries and royals. The wedding might have been planned in only a fortnight, but Khaled had still managed to bring together a dazzling array of guests eager for a show.

And that was what it felt like, Lucy thought—a spectacle. And she was at its dizzying centre.

All too soon it was time for the ceremony. Lucy stood in front of her mirror, dressed in the simple gown, liking the way it gently hugged her figure before swirling out around her ankles. Hadiya had taken Sam down to the formal reception room where the wedding was to take place, and Lucy was alone with Dana.

'Lucy…are you sure about this?' Dana asked softly. She laid a gentle hand on her daughter's shoulder. 'Because, you know, even now it's not too late.'

Lucy met her mother's concerned gaze in the mirror. She smiled and shook her head. It *was* too late. To back out now would shame Khaled and permanently damage their relationship. She couldn't let Sam suffer that, or Khaled, for that matter. *She* wouldn't walk away from *him*.

'Sam will get over whatever happens,' Dana insisted quietly. 'He's only three. He won't even remember.'

'No,' Lucy agreed. 'But there will be plenty of people who will remind him.'

'Khaled wouldn't be so spiteful.'

'Perhaps not, but there are others.' Certainly Ahmed, and any palace officials, other royals, dignitaries and diplomats. He would walk under a perpetual cloud of cruel speculation and gossip.

Dana sighed. 'I just don't like seeing you throw your life away, even for Sam.'

'I'm not.' Lucy took a breath and turned to face her mother. 'I'm thirty-one years old, Mum, and Khaled has been the only man in my life worth mentioning. I think—hope—I can have a future with him. A good one, a happy one.' Was happiness too much to ask for? she wondered. She'd already given up on love. Surely she could strive for contentment at least?

Yet the events of last two weeks did not bode well for such a future. Since the announcement of their engagement, Khaled had been distant, even cool, relating to her only through Sam. They had not even had a moment alone.

Lucy had told herself it was better that way; perhaps she and Khaled needed a little distance. Yet today she didn't want distance, she didn't want fear. She wanted hope. She wanted to believe.

She leaned over and kissed her mother's cheek. 'Don't worry about me, Mum. At least, not for today.'

Dana's arms closed around her. 'I'll try,' she whispered, and Lucy heard the trembling emotion in her mother's usually dry voice. She pressed her cheek against her mother's shoulder, breathing in the familiar scent of lavender soap.

'Thank you,' she murmured. 'For being here today, and every day.'

Dana gave Lucy's shoulder a squeeze and stepped away. Neither of them had ever been particularly adept at showing emotion; Tom Banks had taken care of that. Yet Lucy appreciated even these small gestures. They still meant so much.

A discreet knock sounded at the door, and Lucy knew it was time. She gave her mother a tremulous smile. 'Here we go.'

The palace corridors had never seemed so long or twisting. The only sound was the rustle of silk, and the thundering in her ears of her own beating heart. Her mouth felt dry, her hands cold and slick. Yet even amidst the tremendous nerves was a building sense of anticipation, of hope.

How she wanted to *hope*.

A liveried servant led her to the reception room where a hundred dignified guests waited in hushed expectation. Since Lucy's father was absent, she would be walking down the aisle alone for every endless step until she came to Khaled's side.

She could see him now, framed by the room's panelled doors, his profile to her—harsh austere, familiar.

'It is time.' The servant stepped away, and Dana went to find her seat with Sam. Lucy took a step forward into the room.

She felt the gaze of a hundred guests like a single eye trained on her, assessing this unknown English woman, now to be royal bride. Her legs trembled and her step wobbled. She looked up, and Khaled's gaze held hers.

He smiled.

It was a small gesture, perhaps it was meaningless, yet it didn't feel that way. It felt like sunlight, like a bond finally forged between them, drawing them together. Hope burst within her, blooming like a flower, twining its way around her heart and strengthening her soul. Lucy smiled back, and her steps firmed as she walked the rest of the way down the aisle to Khaled's side.

Silently he reached out his hand, his fingers twining with hers, drawing her closer as the service began.

Lucy didn't remember much of the service. They were essentially married twice, first in the Arabic tradition, and then in the Western one. She didn't have to say or even think much. She was conscious only of sensations: the fluid fabric of her gown against her hips; the strong, sure feeling of Khaled's hand in her own rather clammy one, the whir of a ceiling fan that sent intermittent puffs of warm, dusty air over her.

And then it was over. Khaled led her out of the hall, into another room, this one prepared for a feast. Crowds surrounded them, pressed kisses against her cheek, clapped Khaled on the shoulder. It was a blur, strange and just a little bit frightening, and Lucy was glad Khaled never left her. His hand never dropped hers. She needed his strength.

Platters of food and drink circulated, and people began to dance, both Western dances and traditional Arabic ones. The music was loud, the laughter raucous. Both Khaled and Lucy sat on the side, smiling and watching; by silent agreement, they'd chosen not to dance.

Lucy was content to sit there next to Khaled, to enjoy the flurry of activity and the peals of laughter, and feel his solid strength by her side. She greeted the guests who came to congratulate her, smiled, nodded and spoke words she couldn't remember. Somehow it all passed her by—the food and drink, the noise and music, the people and lights. She was conscious, so achingly conscious, of only one thing: Khaled.

And then it too was over. Khaled rose, drawing Lucy with him, and amidst a chorus of well-wishes—some bawdier than others—and more kisses and embraces, they left. Lucy kissed Sam, his silky hair brushing her cheek as he lay in Dana's arms, sleepy and satisfied. She met her mother's eyes over her son's head and they both smiled, needing no words.

Out in the corridor Lucy followed Khaled past the reception rooms and public galleries to a distant part of the palace, far from the noise and the people. They walked silently along the narrow corridors, up twisting flights of stairs, until in the highest tower he led her to a set of rooms that could only be described as the palace's honeymoon suite.

A wide four-poster bed dominated the bedroom, piled high with silk pillows in shades of umber and sienna. Candles flickered around the room, casting pools of light and shadow. The doors were thrown open to a terrace outside, and Lucy saw that the sun had set, leaving a violet sky spangled with stars.

She moved to the doors and let the night air blow over her, cool her flushed cheeks and calm her suddenly racing heart.

They were finally alone.

Behind her she heard Khaled move, and she tensed with both expectation and nervousness as he came towards her.

'Would you like a bath?' he asked after a moment. His voice was low, smooth, bland. She had no idea what he was thinking or feeling.

'Yes, all right,' Lucy agreed. She turned and saw Khaled gazing at her with dark, fathomless eyes. 'That sounds nice.' She didn't really want or need a bath, but it was a way to bridge the awkwardness of this moment, of this evening.

With a little smile she moved past Khaled to the door that led to a sumptuous bathroom suite.

'I'll be waiting,' he told her, and Lucy jerked her head in a nod.

Safe in the bathroom, she turned both taps on full blast and dumped half a pint of scented bath foam into the bath as she exhaled shakily.

Why was she so nervous? She was acting like a frightened virgin, and she wasn't that. She'd slept with Khaled before, for heaven's sake; she knew his body and he knew hers. She knew what he liked, how he buried his face in her neck, how he liked to kiss her.

'Help.' Lucy didn't realise she'd said the word aloud until it echoed through the marble-tiled bathroom. She held her hands up to her face and took two or three deep breaths. She needed to get a grip.

The bath was nearly full, so she turned the taps off and stripped, hanging her wedding gown on the back of the door. As she sank into the lavender-scented foam, she realised belatedly that she had nothing to wear other than her gown.

She had nothing.

Where were her clothes, her things? She felt vulnerable, as

if Khaled had stripped her of her belongings intentionally. Perhaps he had. She didn't know anything any more, didn't know how to go forward, how to act, how to feel.

Help.

She stayed in the bath until the water began to grow cold, knowing that to delay longer would be obvious and therefore make things more awkward. Insulting, even.

To her great relief she saw a thick terry-cloth robe hanging by the door, and she slipped into it gratefully. She brushed her hair and washed her face, making liberal use of the exotically scented body-lotion. And then there was nothing left for her to do but open the door and face Khaled.

Face her marriage.

Face her wedding night.

She took another deep breath, drawing the air deep into her lungs, and opened the door.

Khaled lay stretched on the bed, his coat and tie discarded, his shirt partially unbuttoned. He looked relaxed, rumpled and sexy, and just the sight of him made sweet need stab deep in her belly.

'Does your leg hurt?' Lucy asked, noticing that he had stretched it out, and then she tensed, waiting for Khaled to be annoyed.

He just smiled. 'No, I feel fine.' He shook his head. 'You're not a therapist tonight, Lucy.'

'I know.'

'You're my wife.' His smile widened and his heated gaze swept over her, from her damp hair to her bare feet.

'I don't know where my clothes are,' Lucy blurted, and Khaled arched an eyebrow.

'You won't need any tonight, I should think, but they're in the wardrobe if it makes you feel better.' He gestured to a large, teak wardrobe in the corner of the room.

'It does,' she admitted. She moved gingerly to sit on the edge of the bed, a good three feet from where Khaled lay.

'Why are you so nervous?' Khaled asked softly. 'I have to

admit, I have been looking forward to this for a very long time. Four years, to be precise.'

Lucy managed a smile. 'I don't know why,' she said. 'It's been a long time.'

'Too long.'

He reached out to grasp her hand and turn it over, then drew her slowly towards him so he could press a kiss in her palm. 'I've wanted this, Lucy. I've dreamed of it.'

This. Just what was 'this'? Lucy wondered numbly. Sex? It obviously wasn't love.

Khaled deepened the kiss on her palm. The feel of his lips on the sensitive skin sent shivers all the way through her, and she cupped his chin, enjoying the feel of his stubble against her hand, the warmth of his cheek on her fingers. Warm desire replaced cold fear.

'Kiss me, Lucy.' Although he spoke it as a command, Lucy heard the plea underneath and she leaned forward to brush his lips with her own.

She couldn't stop there, didn't want to. Her hand dropped from his face to tangle in his hair, pulling him closer even as his arms went around her and he brought her half onto his lap, her robe opening at the front so her breasts were pressed against his bare chest.

She'd forgotten how good it was, how right it felt to have his skin against hers, his lips on hers, his hands on her body, roaming free.

Yet perhaps she hadn't forgotten anything, Lucy thought hazily as Khaled rolled over so she was lying on the bed and he was poised on top of her. Perhaps this was new.

They weren't just learning each other's bodies once more, remembering how it had been.

They were discovering something new.

For they were different people, with different histories, new experiences—pain and joy, suffering and love. So much had happened, so much had changed them, in four years.

Khaled opened her robe and gazed at her naked body as Lucy's toes curled in self-consciousness. Smiling, he traced a silvery stretch-mark with one fingertip. 'Were you in very much pain for Sam's birth?' he asked softly.

Surprised, Lucy replied, 'For a bit. Then I had an epidural.'

'Good.' He bent his head to brush his lips against her belly, and Lucy stifled a moan of longing at the exquisite sensation of being touched so intimately. 'I don't like to think of you in pain.'

Lucy couldn't form a response; the sensations were too deep, too powerful. This felt far more intimate than any time they'd been together before. They were learning each other, finding new landmarks on the maps of their bodies.

And Lucy wanted a turn. She rolled over and let her hands drift down Khaled's taut chest and belly, fumbling with his belt buckle for a moment before she slipped his trousers down his legs. He kicked them off with an impatient groan, and then his boxers followed, along with Lucy's robe, and they were both gloriously naked.

Lucy let her hand trail along Khaled's thigh, and then lower, and lower still, to a new landmark—the twisted scar tissue of his damaged knee.

Khaled's breath hitched and he reached to still her hand. 'Don't...' he pleaded raggedly, but Lucy wouldn't stop.

She reached down to brush a kiss against the scar tissue and the swollen joint of his knee. She wanted to memorise this new landmark that had become so much a part of who he was. It had shaped and scarred him, and it was more than just these marks on his knee. There were deeper scars on his soul, in-visible ones of pain and bitterness, and Lucy wondered if she could help to heal him. If he would let her. 'Let me,' she said softly, half command, half plea, and Khaled gave a little shake of his head.

'Not this.'

'I married all of you,' she told him in a breath of a whisper, and she meant it. '*All* of you.' Lucy saw Khaled's eyes brighten with what could only be tears, and she felt her heart twist as she realised afresh what he'd experienced, how much he'd endured. They'd both suffered, and she wanted it to stop. She wanted a clean beginning, a healing one.

She bent her head and let her lips touch his knee again before trailing kisses upwards until, with a stifled moan, Khaled hauled her against him, their bodies now pressed length to length, and kissed her deeply.

Lucy returned the kiss, letting the tenderness flare into passion, letting her mind and body blur into sensation as pleasure blissfully took over and they were one once more.

Later, as the moon sifted silver patterns on the floor, she lay on the bed, Khaled's arm draped around her, sleepy and sated. She looked over at him; he'd fallen asleep, his lashes brushing his cheeks, thick, dark and impossibly long.

She smiled, for he looked so peaceful and yet so vulnerable. There was no hardness, no grimness in his eyes, in the taut muscle of his jaw. He was relaxed and rested. She wanted him to stay that way; she wished he could. Wished she could help him.

Could she? She couldn't restore his knee or his rugby career, but perhaps she could heal something much more important: his heart.

What business do you have with his heart? He doesn't love you. He might not even stay…

The inner voice of her secret fear was like an icy whisper that echoed around the room and in Lucy's heart.

Fear was so insidious. A few moments ago, lying in Khaled's arms, wrapped in the hazy afterglow of desire and love, she'd thought she'd banished it for ever. Yet now it crept back in with a sly, self-satisfied smile and crouched like a hungry cat in a corner of her heart.

How long was Khaled hers, if he really was hers at all? This was a sensible, convenient marriage; there was no love binding them together. Just lust…and Sam.

How long until he found another excuse to leave, just as her father had, just as all men seemed to?

Lucy closed her eyes. She wouldn't think of it; she wouldn't give the fear a foothold. And she wouldn't delude herself with silly daydreams of healing and love. Khaled wanted a marriage of convenience, and that was what they'd have. She'd guard her heart and keep herself from loving Khaled, from allowing him to hurt her.

She'd take what she was given and be happy, content with that, for God knew it was more than most people had.

She wouldn't live her life in fear. She would be strong.

She curled her body round Khaled's, drawing his warmth, wanting his comfort. There might not be love there, but neither was there fear. She clung to that truth as sleep slowly claimed her.

Lucy awoke to bright sunlight, and with Khaled gone from the bed. Her heart lurched with alarm and she bolted upright, searching the room as if she might find him crouching in a corner.

He wasn't there. She could tell, she could feel the emptiness. She drew her knees up against her chest, wrapping the sheet around her. She shouldn't feel this bereft; it was stupid and senseless.

Yet she couldn't keep it from swamping her soul anyway.

The door opened, and Khaled came in with a tray of coffee and rolls. He smiled. 'I didn't want a servant to disturb us.'

The relief that washed through her was just as alarming as the fear had been. Lucy smiled back. 'I'm starving.'

'So am I.' Khaled set the tray on the table next to the bed and began pouring coffee. 'Eat up. We leave for our honeymoon in an hour.'

'An hour! That's no time!'

'Your bags have been packed, and Sam is content with your mother. There is no reason to delay.'

Lucy accepted a cup of coffee and took a fortifying sip. 'Where are we going?'

Khaled's eyes glinted with humour. 'You'll find out soon enough.'

She didn't like surprises, Lucy reflected as they boarded the royal jet amidst another storm of paparazzi. She liked to be prepared, in control, even over little things.

Yet she knew Khaled was planning a nice surprise for her, and the gesture touched her. Even if she didn't like it.

It was the fear again, she knew. The agony of doubt, the pain of uncertainty. She'd trusted Khaled once—he was the only man she'd ever trusted. No one else had claimed her heart the way he had. She wasn't about it to give it to him again, yet, even so, she still felt nervous. Afraid.

Would the fear ever be banished? Could she ever trust Khaled, trust herself?

Glancing over at him, his head bent, lost in thought, she couldn't answer that question. Last night had been good. No, she admitted honestly, it had been wonderful. But a few moments in bed didn't change who they were, what they were capable of, how much they could give.

Did it?

How long until he leaves? Until he's tired of you?

The jet took off into the sky, leaving the island of Biryal far behind until there was nothing in every direction but glittering blue, endless ocean. And no answers.

It was late afternoon when the jet arrived at Dubai International Airport.

'Dubai?' Lucy questioned, for she'd never been there and didn't even know much about it.

'Wait and see,' Khaled assured her. 'You will be treated like a queen.'

A throng of paparazzi greeted them, and Khaled navigated

easily through the crowd, his hand clasped with Lucy's, ignoring most questions and fielding a few necessary ones.

'We are very happy. And, since this is our honeymoon, we'd like to be alone!' He spoke good-naturedly, and the journalists responded, allowing him an easy passage to the waiting Rolls Royce.

Lucy slipped into the luxurious leather seat and within minutes the car was pulling smoothly away. They left the airport and desert for the glittering lights of Dubai, a mass of needle-like skyscrapers straight down to the sea.

'Where are we staying?' Lucy asked.

'The best,' Khaled said simply. 'The Burj Al Arab.'

Lucy had never heard of it, but then there was no reason why she would have. This was Khaled's world, the sports star and the reigning prince who was used to luxurious hotels and servants leaping to do his bidding.

She'd let herself forget that the sunlit days in Biryal when it had just been her, Khaled and Sam, swimming and spending time among Biryal's far simpler pleasures.

Now the memories of Khaled as he was in London—fun loving, pleasure seeking, untrustworthy—came back full force as the Rolls swept up to the front of a huge skyscraper shaped like a billowing sail on its own artificial island right on the water.

Liveried attendants opened the car door and escorted them through the sumptuous atrium that soared a dizzying six hundred feet upwards, making Lucy feel faint and small. There was no need for Khaled to check in; everyone knew who he was. An attendant led them to a private elevator which went straight to the top of the towering building, and doors opened onto the most oppressively opulent suite Lucy had ever seen.

A gold and marble staircase, more impressive even than the one in the Biryali palace, led up to the suite itself. Lucy followed Khaled and the attendant, her footsteps clicking faintly on the carrara marble.

Upstairs the suite seemed to be an endless succession of rooms filled with gold leaf and marble, thick, tufted rugs and heavy mahogany furniture. Lucy glanced around, but she could see no end in sight; room after room stretched on, filled with furniture and paintings, every sign of wealth and luxury.

The attendant left, and Khaled turned to Lucy with a smile that looked just a little smug. 'Well?'

'It's amazing,' she said faintly.

His smile deepened. 'You're overwhelmed.'

'How could I not be?'

'Watch this.' They were in the bedroom, which was decorated in royal-blue and gold, with a magnificent, canopied four-poster bed. Khaled pushed a button and Lucy watched the bed rotate slowly on its dais.

'Wow,' she said lamely. Khaled turned to her.

'Is something wrong?'

Lucy shrugged and spread her hands out. How could she explain how this suite reminded her of their time in London? Of how overawed she'd been by Khaled, by his wealth and poise, his careless charm, his reckless ease? She'd never felt like his equal, and yet somehow in the last few weeks Sam had neutralised that feeling. With Sam, they were on an equal footing. But not here.

Here, in Khaled's world, she felt like a hanger-on, a beggar at the table waiting for the scraps of his attention.

His love.

She still wanted him to love her, Lucy realised with a jolt of panic. That was why she was so nervous, so afraid. She wanted, *needed*, Khaled's love, and she'd never have it.

'Lucy?' Khaled prompted with a frown, and she tried to smile, although her mind still spun.

'It's just so…much.'

'Is that a bad thing?'

'No, of course not.' This was her problem, Lucy knew. Her insecurity, her fear. She glanced around the room, taking in all the luxurious embellishments. 'It's wonderful, Khaled. Thank you.'

That evening Lucy dressed in one of the designer gowns that had been packed for her; she hadn't seen any of the clothes before, but they were all the right size. They took a simulated submarine ride to the hotel's underwater restaurant, Al Mahara.

They sat at a table right next to an enormous aquarium, watching fish swim lazily by; they dined on lobster salad and oysters washed down by a champagne that Lucy didn't want to know the price of.

A few people recognised Khaled, a mix of businessmen and society starlets, and Lucy watched as Khaled kissed their cheeks and chatted easily, smiling and laughing and talking about things Lucy could barely understand. This was his world. It always had been.

How could she have forgotten? Four years ago she'd been so dazzled, so grateful to be seen on his arm, but she was older now. She was wiser, too, and she didn't want to live like that.

Feel like that.

After what felt like an endless meal they returned to their suite. The bed had been turned down, the lights dimmed and a tray of fruit and Arabic sweets left by the terrace.

'Is something wrong?' Khaled asked, and Lucy heard a coolness in his voice.

She hesitated, not wanting a confrontation, not knowing how to explain how she felt. And what did it matter? There was no way to make it better.

'I'm just tired,' she said at last. 'It's been a crazy few weeks.'

'So it has.' Khaled came behind her, his hands resting heavily on her shoulders. 'But we can leave that all behind, Lucy, and relax for a few days. Enjoy being pampered, enjoy each other.' He dropped a kiss on the nape of her neck, making her shiver. His lips moved along her shoulder, his tongue touching her skin, and desire overcame doubt as she turned in his arms and gave herself to him.

At least here and now they were equals.

* * *

Lucy tried to relax over the next few days, and sometimes she even succeeded. Khaled was kind, considerate, yet there was no denying a slight distance in his demeanour, a sort of separateness that made Lucy both desperate and anxious.

She wanted more. She wanted all of him. But he was keeping himself apart, saving his passion for their marriage bed.

It was better this way, she told herself. This kind of distance was convenient, sensible, what they'd agreed. She hadn't agreed to more, hadn't bargained for more.

She was afraid of more.

And yet she craved it.

Still, she couldn't ignore the fact that he was in his element in the luxurious hotels and night-clubs, on the yacht, the beach, the high-end shops in Jumeirah, Dubai's shopping district.

In each place he ran into acquaintances, people like himself— rich, powerful, arrogant and self-assured—and each time Lucy shrank a little bit further into herself and her own fears.

This was the rugby star, the man who had used her and left her, the Khaled she'd fallen for, and she didn't want to again.

Yet at night those fears and doubts receded in the reality of their bodies. Then they were equals, lovers, exploring each other with freedom and joy, revelling in the marriage bed.

'You've been very quiet,' Khaled said on their last night in Dubai. They were getting ready to go out yet again, and Lucy gazed glumly at the rack of gowns that undoubtedly cost more than her year's salary.

'I'm tired,' she said, which had been her excuse all week. And she had reason enough to be tired; some nights she and Khaled had been still awake, loving each other, to see the dawn.

She glanced at him, saw him frown, and frustration bubbled within her. That chasm was opening between them again, despite the shared nights. The wall was coming up, and she didn't know what to do.

She wanted to bridge the gap, knock down the wall, run to Khaled, and tell him—what?

I love you.

No. She did not love him; she wouldn't. She couldn't. Yet the words still bubbled up inside her, from an endless spring of yearning. She couldn't love this man, this powerful, arrogant prince.

No, a voice whispered inside her. *You love the man who tickles your son, who shows you his scars, who wipes away your tears. You love that man.*

But which man was the real one? And could that man love her back?

Khaled crossed to her, put his hands on her shoulders and brushed a kiss against the top of her head. 'We don't have to go out tonight,' he said softly. 'We could stay in, order room-service. There's a private cinema, even, if you want to watch a film.'

Lucy hadn't even seen that part of the endless suite, yet the idea of staying in appealed to her almost unbearably. 'Could we?' she asked. 'I'd like that.'

'Of course.'

Within minutes Khaled had cancelled their dinner reservations and changed out of his evening suit into more casual clothes. He was looking through the suite's selection of DVDs when Lucy noticed the chess set by the sofa—an opulent set in gold and silver.

'How about we play chess?'

Khaled turned round, one eyebrow quirked. 'Are you sure?'

Lucy touched one of the pawns. 'Yes. I've never really played, but I learned how.'

'All right.' Smiling faintly, Khaled moved to the sofa. He glanced at Lucy, humour lurking in his golden eyes. 'I'm very good, you know.'

Lucy smiled back, suddenly feeling happy, light, comfortable, perhaps for the first time since she'd come to Dubai. 'Don't play easy on me,' she warned. 'I hate that.'

'Promise.' Khaled settled himself on one side of the chess-board, Lucy on the other. 'I'll thrash you, though, you know.'

'Bring it on.'

Of course, he did thrash her. But Lucy played surprisingly well, considering each move with so much care that when the game was finally over she said, 'Where did you learn to play?'

Khaled shrugged. 'Eton. I didn't discover rugby until my second-to-last year. Before that I was in the chess club.'

'Were you?' Laughter bubbled up; somehow she couldn't imagine it.

'Yes, I was,' Khaled replied, his lips twitching. 'Really.'

Lucy glanced down at the board. Checkmate. 'Do you miss it?' she asked quietly. 'Rugby?'

Khaled was silent for a long moment. 'Yes,' he finally said, his gaze on the board as well. 'I miss the thrill of the sport, but I've come to realise I miss something deeper than that too. I miss…' He let out a ragged breath. 'I miss what rugby made me.'

Lucy glanced up sharply. 'What did rugby make you?'

He shrugged. 'You saw.'

Yes, she'd seen, and it disappointed her somehow that Khaled missed that—the stardom, the popularity, the press, the life that had crushed her in the end. She didn't speak, and Khaled's mouth tightened, his eyes dark.

He gestured to the board, his voice purposefully light. 'You're really rather good. How come you never played?'

Lucy drew her knees up to her chest and rested her chin on top. 'I never had the opportunity.'

'Never?'

She hesitated and then, trying to keep her voice as light as his, continued, 'I learned as a child. My father was a terrific chess player. He was a bit of a layabout, but he used to play in the pub. I learned so I could play with him, but it never came to pass.'

Khaled held a knight in his hand, and he set it down carefully on the board. 'What happened?'

Another shrug; Lucy was surprised at how hard this was.

She'd made peace with her father a long time ago; time had healed the wound.

Hadn't it?

Yet now, avoiding Khaled's perceptive gaze, the chess pieces blurring in front of her, it didn't feel like time had healed anything at all. It felt fresh and raw and painful. She swallowed.

'He never came back.' She blinked back tears and looked up, composed once more. 'He was meant to pick me up one Saturday, spend the day with me. I'd learned chess by then, and was excited about showing him.' For a moment she remembered that day—standing by the front window just like Sam had, nose pressed against the glass, waiting, hopeful. Then the hope had slowly, irrevocably trickled away. She took a breath. 'He never came.'

Khaled frowned. 'Never?'

'Oh, he sent me a five-pound note in the post for my birthday a couple of times,' Lucy said. 'But after that, nothing. He just wasn't father material.'

Khaled tapped his fingers against the board. 'And that's why you thought I wasn't father material either.'

Lucy shrugged; the movement felt stiff and awkward. 'I explained this before,' she said, striving to keep her voice light but failing. 'My little bit of pop psychology, remember?'

'Yes. I remember.' Khaled's voice was dark. 'I just didn't realise he left you so…abruptly.'

Like you did. The words seemed to hover, unspoken, in the air. Lucy looked away.

'Well, thanks for the game of chess,' she said after a moment when the silence had gone on too long, had become awkward and tense and filled with unspoken thoughts. Accusations. She uncoiled herself from her seat and stood up.

Khaled looked up, otherwise unmoving. 'You're a good player.' He made no move to join her, instead looking away, gazing out of the window at the stretch of silvery ocean.

Lucy hesitated, wanting—what? She wanted Khaled's strength, his touch and caress to banish the memories the conversation had stirred up. Yet she couldn't quite make herself ask. It would feel like begging.

Sex, she realised despondently, was not the answer to everything. After another long moment, when Khaled did not move or take his gaze from the fathomless night outside, Lucy turned and went to bed.

Khaled toyed with the silver queen, gazing out at the twinkling lights in Dubai's harbour, each one so tiny, so insignificant, yet offering light. Hope.

He'd begun to feel the first, faint stirrings of hope this last week, with Lucy in his arms every night as he'd longed for these last four years. He'd begun to believe they could have a future together, a love.

That she would love him.

And he'd convinced himself that he could handle his condition, that Lucy would never see him debilitated, that it all could be managed. Controlled.

Yet some things couldn't be controlled, and finally Khaled understood the depth of Lucy's mistrust of him.

When he'd left all those years ago, he'd been thinking of himself, acting on his pride and his fear. He supposed he'd wrapped it up as self-sacrifice, told himself that it was better for Lucy, better for everyone if he left. That no one wanted a burden, and that was how he'd seen himself—a burden, a cripple, a man without the identity he'd clung to for so many years.

Yet now he acknowledged fully, for the first time, how his sudden departure had been essentially a selfish act, an act which had devastated Lucy. She'd told him often enough, but he'd pushed her objections aside because his reasons had made sense to him, and really it was easier to do so. He couldn't change the past.

And he still couldn't. He didn't think he could influence the future either.

Lucy didn't love him, didn't want to love him, and there was nothing he could say—nothing that hadn't already been said—that would change her mind.

He thought of telling her he loved her, but instinctively recoiled from the idea, the threat of rejection, of ruining what little they had. He shouldn't yearn for more, shouldn't expect it, because he didn't even deserve it.

He didn't deserve Lucy. And she deserved so much more than him.

Yet they were married now, and nothing could change that. He could give her space, time to heal, to stop being afraid, to trust.

If she ever would.

He couldn't, Khaled realised with a growing sense of desolation, give her more than that.

What little they had. Resolutely Khaled placed the queen back on the chessboard. What little they had would have to be enough.

CHAPTER TEN

LUCY was relieved to leave Dubai. Ever since their conversation the night before, a new awkwardness had risen up between her and Khaled. Funny, she thought without a trace of humour, how confidences shared could create such tension, such stiff formality. Weren't they supposed to bring you closer?

Yet as they took the royal jet back to Biryal she'd never been more aware of the yawning distance between her and Khaled.

He was as solicitous as ever, yet with that damning, cool remoteness that she despised. That made her afraid.

What are you thinking? What are you wanting?

Do you love me?

The questions crowded on her tongue and she bit them all back, staring mutely out of the window instead.

They sat in silence for most of the flight, the only sound the shuffle of Khaled's papers as he bent over his work.

By the time the plane touched down in Biryal, Lucy's already taut nerves were starting to fray. The sight of yet another crowd of clamouring journalists in front of the plane made her groan aloud. 'Is it always like this?'

'It will die down,' Khaled replied in an implacable tone. 'They are just curious because you are new and because…' he paused '…I have been out of the limelight for quite a while.'

'And your marriage has brought you back into it?'

'Yes.'

Lucy glanced at him, saw the careful, hard, expressionless mask he'd worn since last night, and suddenly asked, 'Khaled, will life ever be normal for us?' She couldn't elaborate or explain, couldn't tell him how wonderful 'normal' sounded right now. It encompassed a whole range of emotions: comfort, safety, love.

Love… That one was off-limits.

'I don't know,' Khaled replied after a moment, his voice bland to the point of coolness. 'I suppose it depends on what you consider normal.'

Back at the palace, Lucy and Khaled found Sam in his favourite haunt, the pool, with Dana. He ran out of the water, hurling himself at both of their legs.

'Sam, watch Khaled's suit.'

'I don't mind,' Khaled interjected as Sam pulled a mutinous face.

'I thought he was Daddy now.'

Lucy swallowed, her gaze sliding to Khaled, and she saw him swallow, his eyes bright with unshed tears. No matter what was or wasn't between them, there was something strong, right and good between Khaled and Sam. She smiled and tousled Sam's damp hair. 'You're right; I forgot. And I suppose Daddy doesn't mind if his suit gets a bit wet.' The word sounded funny and thick on her tongue, and came out awkward and uneasy.

Khaled glanced at her sharply, and Lucy felt despair curl around her heart once more. They related to Sam, through Sam, and that was all.

How could they have thought this kind of marriage was good for anyone?

It certainly didn't feel good to her.

They left for London three days later. They spent the night at Lucy's house, although after the Biryali palace—not to mention the royal suite in Dubai—it felt small. Too small.

Khaled made it feel small, Lucy realised. He was so big, so

present, so *much*—too much for the little rooms, her little bed. It was a double, but they couldn't lie in it without touching. And, now that this tension had sprung between them once more, Lucy wasn't sure that was a good idea.

Yet even so her body craved it, needed that physical reassurance, the comfort and thrill of his caress. Khaled, however, chose not to give it; as soon as the lights were off he rolled over onto his side, away from her. Lucy lay there, staring into the darkness, and wondered what he was thinking. She wanted to ask, yet was afraid too. Always afraid.

What would he say? she wondered bleakly. Would he admit this marriage was a mistake, that they should live separate lives? Would he lie and say he was thinking of nothing? Would he tell her brusquely it was none of her business? Or was he even asleep, completely unconcerned with her state of mind?

She had no idea, and it hurt. It hurt because she loved him. How had she hidden from it for so long? She'd denied it with every fibre of her being even as her heart had cried out to be heard.

She loved him, and she didn't want to. Didn't want to open herself up to the pain, the possibility of rejection. He wouldn't leave, perhaps, but he could cut her out of his life, his heart.

He could not love her back, and living with that day in and day out would be far worse than if he were never there at all.

The next few days were a struggle for normality. They moved to a luxury hotel in the centre of London for both security and comfort; Sam returned to nursery, and Lucy to work. She made arrangements to reduce her hours and eventually only work for a few months out of the year. Khaled busied himself with his own pursuits, promoting Biryal's tourist industry, acting as a diplomat and visiting dignitary.

Yet despite all these activities Lucy was ever conscious of the aching emptiness in the middle of their marriage, in her own heart.

Khaled remained remote, completely inaccessible, and she responded in the same way. They didn't talk or even chat, except for when Sam was present, because then, Lucy realised, they were a family. Alone they were simply two strangers sharing the same space, the same bed.

A week after their return to London, Lucy was invited to a party to celebrate one of the England team's recent victories.

'Bring Khaled,' Eric told her, his voice distant, as it had been since their return. 'I'm sure he'll enjoy his old stomping ground.'

Lucy smiled, feeling sick. Wouldn't he just? she thought. The trouble was, she wouldn't.

She mentioned it to Khaled that night, as they got ready for bed. 'There's a party tomorrow night, for the England team,' she said. 'We've been invited.'

Khaled stilled in the act of loosening his tie. 'Have we?' he said at last, his voice neutral. 'How nice.'

'Do you want to go?' Lucy asked, half-hoping he would say no. Khaled smiled; there was an edge to it.

'Why not? I'm hardly one to miss a party.'

'Right,' Lucy agreed. She watched as Khaled finished shrugging off his clothes, and then he climbed into bed, preparing for sleep. They hadn't made love since they'd returned to London, and tonight looked to be no different.

'Khaled…' she began, not knowing what she was going to say, but wanting to say something, change something.

'Yes, Lucy?' Khaled waited, coolly expectant, and Lucy opened her mouth to say—what? What could she say that would change this awful tension between them, would change who they were as people?

I love you.

Three simple, little words that she couldn't quite get off her tongue. Her heart raced, her adrenaline kicking in as if she were teetering on a precipice, preparing to jump.

And then, defeated, she took a step back, her heart slowing to a dull thud, her mouth dry and empty of words. She couldn't, couldn't risk it.

'Goodnight.'

Khaled's mouth curled in a sardonic smile that lacerated Lucy's soul. Had he known what she wanted to say? Was he mocking her?

'Goodnight,' he replied, and rolled over.

The party was exactly the kind of event Lucy dreaded. It was in the private room of an upscale nightclub, with pounding music, pulsing lights and free-flowing cocktails.

Dressed in an open-necked shirt and dark trousers, Khaled looked confident, sexy and slightly rumpled. He looked like the man she'd fallen so hard for, Lucy thought. She remembered when she'd seen him in a club just like this one, and he'd beckoned her over with one little finger, handing her the drink he'd already bought.

She'd gone home with him that night. She'd never done that before, had never even considered holding herself so lightly. So cheaply. Yet with Khaled she hadn't even considered another option.

She barely heard the buzz of chatter as they circulated among the guests—rugby players and their dates, the team's entourage and hangers-on. Lucy knew many of the people, had worked with them for years, but she still couldn't feel comfortable. Her gaze kept sliding to Khaled, watching as he smiled and laughed, chatted and flirted lightly. He was in his element.

She felt sick.

She accepted another glass of champagne, knowing she shouldn't, as Eric stole to her side.

'You don't look like you're having a good time,' he said quietly and Lucy froze, the champagne flute halfway to her lips.

'Why do you say that?'

'Because I know you, Lucy.' There was a thread of bemusement in Eric's voice. 'And I can tell.'

She shrugged. 'Then you know I never really was one for parties.'

'Khaled's enjoying himself.'

Lucy took a sip of champagne and let the bubbles fizz through her. 'Yes, he is,' she agreed, glad her voice sounded so unconcerned.

Eric, however, wasn't fooled. 'Why did you marry him, Lucy?' he asked. His gaze met hers, direct and sorrowful. 'After the way he hurt you…'

'Don't, Eric.' She couldn't take this, not now when she felt so raw, so fearful and uncertain. Eric, however, would not be deterred.

'You know what he said to me in the hospital—right before he left?'

'Don't.'

'I told him to see you, to speak to you. I said you'd been waiting, that you were worried…'

Lucy knew she should turn away. She shouldn't hear this. Shouldn't listen. Yet she remained, terribly transfixed.

'I said,' Eric continued, his voice hitching painfully, 'after all you meant to him you deserved more, and you know what he said?'

She meant to tell him to stop, but instead found herself whispering, 'What?'

'He said, "She's not that much to me". And you've married him, Lucy! You know a man like that could never love you!'

Lucy shook her head. She felt numb. *She's not that much to me*. Well, it was no more than she'd guessed. Than she'd feared, known. 'People change,' she whispered, and wanted to believe it. The trouble was, she didn't. Not inside, where it mattered. Where it hurt.

Eric glanced scornfully over at Khaled, who tossed back his drink with a loud laugh. There were three starlet types fawning all over him. 'Do they?' he asked quietly. 'Do they really?'

Lucy was quiet all the way home. Khaled glanced at her. 'Did you enjoy yourself?' he asked mildly, and Lucy clenched her jaw.

'No.'

Khaled's hands flexed on the steering wheel. 'I saw you with Eric,' he remarked blandly. 'He always was in love with you.'

Lucy squirmed inwardly, for she'd long suspected Eric of having feelings for her. 'He's never said as much,' she said after a moment as she stared out of the window.

Khaled was silent for so long that Lucy turned to look at him, and saw the sickly wash of street lights cast a yellow glow over his austere features. 'Sometimes you don't need to.'

He knows, Lucy thought. *He knows I love him; he's always known.* She closed her eyes, feeling sick.

It couldn't go on, she thought dourly two days later; this silence, this strangeness, this unbearable tension. The utter falseness of their marriage, of everything. It couldn't last. It would break—and what then? Would he leave?

Was that what was happening? Was some part of her testing him, seeing how much he would take before he left, before she forced him to admit this was a mistake?

Lucy didn't know; she felt like she didn't know anything any more. She was too exhausted and emotionally drained even to recognise her own feelings. She just wanted a release of this tension, an end to the awkwardness.

And then it came.

Sam was spending the night at her mother's, and Lucy came home in the early evening, dusk settling over the city as she rode the lift up to their penthouse suite. She felt bone-weary, aching in every muscle, and she dreaded another night of tension between her and Khaled, the awkwardness and discomfort, stiltedness and silence.

She opened the door to the suite—and she knew. She didn't need to check the emptied cupboards or dresser drawers to discover what she felt in every fibre of her being, in the empty echo in her soul.

Khaled was gone.

The suite was heavy with a deeper silence, a silence that

spoke of finality and loss. Lucy walked slowly through the rooms. Nothing had changed, yet still she knew. Still, she walked to the bedroom and opened a cupboard, registering the empty hangers, the missing clothes. There was no spill of change, no mobile or wallet on the bureau, no book or spectacles by the bed. Strange; all these little signs of his presence she'd taken for granted. Now the empty spaces mocked her, made the suite seem even more impersonal than it already had been.

Slowly, numbly, she walked to the bed and sat on the edge. Silence pulsed and thudded in her ears.

He'd left her. Again. Just as she'd known he would, just as she'd been waiting for.

Just as she'd driven him to.

Lucy bent her head, her hair falling forward, tears crowding thickly in her throat.

She hurt. She hurt so much, felt the misery and pain threaten to drown her in a tide of feeling, and she didn't want it.

After all this time, after all she'd already experienced, it was happening again—she was hurting again—and there was nothing she could do to stop it.

It wasn't fair, it wasn't right; she'd been trying to protect her heart, to keep this from happening.

And yet it had. She was still, would always be, the little girl with her nose pressed against the window, waiting, hoping…

A helpless cry emerged from her, an animal sound of pain, and her arms stole around her body. She rocked silently for a minute, shaking with the effort of holding back the tears.

They came anyway, or started to, until the realisation of her own powerlessness—and of Khaled's power over her—caused rage to replace the sorrow and hurt.

And then she heard the sound of a key turning in the door, and footsteps in the foyer.

Lucy rose from the bed, the anger and hurt propelling her across the room, her hands clenched into fists at her sides. She stopped in the doorway and stared in disbelief at a weary, rumpled Khaled. He dropped the keys on the hall table and looked up.

The rage took over.

'So, you decided to come back.' She shook with the force of the emotion coursing through her; her voice trembled. 'Did you forget something?' She glanced around the room, saw a discarded newspaper and picked it up. 'This, perhaps?' She threw it at him, and watched in satisfaction as it hit him hard in the chest.

Khaled caught the paper, clenching it in one fist. His eyebrows drew together in a frown. 'Lucy…?'

'Where are you going?' she demanded, hearing the furious screech of her voice and not caring. 'Running back to Biryal? Or somewhere else? God knows, it only took you a few weeks!' She felt the tears start and didn't bother blinking them back. 'I knew you'd leave me, Khaled. I told you I couldn't trust you, and I was right. Did playing happy families get old for you? Did we start to bore you?' Khaled's face was blank, wiped of all expression except for a coldness in his eyes that enraged her all the more. 'Did we?' she demanded, her voice breaking, and she could barely see him through the haze of tears.

'I suppose it seems *obvious* to you,' Khaled said coolly. He crossed the room, shrugging out of his jacket, his back to her, tense and powerful. 'As everything always does.'

'An empty cupboard and no note does seem rather obvious,' Lucy replied scornfully.

Khaled laughed, an abrupt, jagged sound. 'Judged and condemned.'

'How can I not?' Lucy demanded, her voice hitching. 'You're not even denying it!'

'Why should I?' Khaled turned around, anger and something else in his eyes—despair, Lucy realised with numbing surprise. It was in his voice too; she heard its broken edge, felt it. 'Perhaps I should,' he continued with a hard shrug, 'But I can't. I can't live my life justifying myself to you, Lucy. Proving to you what kind of man I am.'

'I don't *know* what kind of man you are!' Lucy's voice felt raw, as if it scraped her throat. She pressed her fists to her eyes and they came away wet.

'And that's the problem, isn't it? How can we live together, love together, when you don't trust me?'

'Love?' Lucy repeated, the word filled with disbelief, yet still edged with hope.

'Yes.' Khaled stood in front of her, his arms held loosely at his sides, his shoulders thrown back proudly. There was honesty on his face, bleak and true. 'I love you, Lucy. Don't you know that? I've always loved you. I hid from it, denied it, to protect myself. I told myself I was protecting you; I didn't want you to be saddled with a cripple—'

'You're not a cripple.'

'No, but I'd let my whole identity—my entire being—be defined by rugby. By my popularity and status.' His mouth twisted in sardonic self-acknowledgement. 'I had nothing before that, you see. When it was taken away, I felt I had nothing once again. *Was* nothing…and could be nothing to you.'

'Khaled…'

'I'm not the man you fell in love with four years ago,' Khaled told her starkly. 'I've changed. I suppose I was trying to show you I hadn't changed in Dubai, and at that wretched party, but the fact is I'm not the sports star or the playboy any more. I can't be that man.'

'I don't want you to be that man,' Lucy whispered. 'I never did.'

'Don't you?' Khaled smiled bleakly. 'You say you don't, perhaps, but you don't love me now, and you loved me then, even if you deny it. I know you did.'

He spoke so starkly, accepting the statement as truth, that Lucy felt sorrow and shame roil within her. 'I did love you then,' she admitted in a whisper. 'But…'

'You are afraid I'll let you down,' Khaled stated matter of

factly. 'You can't trust me. I see this, Lucy. I feel it every day, every time you look at me, speak to me. The only time I don't is when you touch me, and even then—'

'No, don't.' She blinked back more tears; she felt like a leaky tap. 'Don't, Khaled.'

'But it is the truth, is it not? I know what fear feels like, Lucy. I've been afraid too. When I was told of my diagnosis, I felt fear crawl straight inside me. I didn't know what kind of man I was, what kind of man I could be without rugby and all of its trappings. I didn't know if there would be anything left for you or anyone to love. There never was before.'

'You mean your father,' Lucy whispered, her heart aching, and Khaled shrugged.

'He had no use for me, it is true. He never has.' His eyes met hers, burning with intensity, with honesty. 'Then I was afraid of the future, of what it could hold for me—could there be anything good? Yet when you came back into my life I began to hope, and hope is dangerous. The more you feel it, the more you want it.'

'I know,' Lucy admitted, her voice raw.

'Yet, every time I began to hope, it was dashed again. You didn't love me, you were so determined to tell me—not the man I've become.'

'But that *is* the man I love,' Lucy cried. 'More than who you were before, Khaled. You are strong, and good, and honest—' Her voice cracked, and then broke. 'I was afraid you hadn't changed.'

Khaled laughed, a sound holding no humour, only sorrow. 'I'm afraid that I've changed too much, and you are afraid that I have not changed enough. So much fear.'

'There's no fear in love,' Lucy whispered and he smiled sadly.

'No. Perhaps not.'

'Khaled…' She took a breath, felt it fill her lungs. 'Where were you? Where were you going?'

'My father had another heart attack this afternoon. I was

telephoned and told it was serious. I left abruptly, but when they called me again they told me he was stable. So I returned. I have to fly out tomorrow.' He paused, and, although there was no condemnation in his voice or eyes, Lucy felt it. 'I left a message on your mobile.'

Which she hadn't checked. Her battery had died and she'd forgotten to charge it. If only…

Yet there was no 'if only'. This wasn't about a missed message, a simple misunderstanding. It was about trust.

She hadn't trusted him. She'd let her fear blind her, guide her. She'd refused to let go of the past, to give them a future. Lucy swallowed. 'I'm sorry.'

'So am I.'

He turned away, and Lucy's heart twisted. It broke. Wasn't it already broken? she wondered numbly. Hadn't it been shattered too many times before?

Hadn't both of them been through enough?

'Are you going to leave?' she whispered, and she saw him stiffen.

'I told you, I must fly out tomorrow. It is done.' So, in the end, he would still leave. She had made him leave, with her mistrust and her fear. It was ironic, Lucy thought. Ironic and terrible. When she finally had him, she would lose him, and this time she could only blame herself.

She watched him walk stiffly to the bedroom, and remembered how he'd trusted her with his weakness and secrets. After a second's hesitation she followed him, standing in the doorway while she watched him rummage through the few clothes he'd left. He was packing, she realised, taking everything away.

'Khaled, I don't want you to go.'

He shrugged impatiently. 'Lucy, my father is ill. I have a duty.'

She closed her eyes and summoned strength. Opening them, she admitted in a whisper, 'I mean from me. Don't leave me.'

He turned slowly to face her. 'Leave you?'

'I love you. I love the man you are now.' She was begging, she was desperate and weak, yet she didn't care. There was no fear in love. She'd lay herself bare for him; she'd strip her soul if that was what it took to keep him.

'Do you?' Khaled said, and she heard the disbelief in his voice. 'Do you love a man who would walk out on you even now, Lucy? Walk out on his son without a word?' His voice shook with a sudden, terrible emotion. 'Is *that* the man you love?'

Lucy shook her head slowly, not understanding. 'Khaled…'

'You judge me now without even realising it!' He shook his head, the movement one of both scorn and rage. Hurt. 'How can you love me and think I would do that—again? I've learned from my mistakes, Lucy. Have you?'

It took her a moment to understand. 'You mean you're not leaving?' she whispered.

'I'm going to see my father,' Khaled replied, 'And you're welcome to come with me. I'm not,' he added, his voice edged with irritation, '*leaving* you.'

'But—'

Khaled dropped the shirt he had bunched in one fist, shaking his head slowly. 'Lord, how I've hurt you. Even now…' He crossed the room to stand in front of her, his hands curling gently around her shoulders. 'Lucy, forgive me for leaving you before. Forgive me for causing you so much hurt, so much fear. Will you? Can you forgive me?'

Lucy blinked back tears, but they slipped down her cheeks anyway. 'Yes…' she whispered.

'I've kept my distance, tried to give you space to make a decision.' He paused, his twisted smile both tender and sad. 'To decide if you loved me.'

'But I do,' Lucy whispered, her throat clogged. 'That was the whole problem.'

'Is it?' Khaled questioned softly. 'Such a problem?'

Lucy shook her head. 'No, it isn't. It's…' She smiled through a shimmer of tears. 'My fear. I've been so afraid.'

'I know.'

'I didn't even realise how afraid I was until…until it was too late. Until I loved you, and I realised you had the power to hurt me again. That was what scared me most of all—the possibility.' She swallowed, sniffed. 'I don't want to be afraid.'

'Then don't. I'm not going to leave you, Lucy. I'm not your father. I'm not the man I was before.'

'I know that. I've realised that. But I was afraid to trust, to believe.'

'Believe.' His voice throbbed with sincerity. 'I'm not going to leave you or Sam. I love you both. You're my family, my life. I just need to know if you can believe me. Can trust me. Love the man I am now—a man who can't play rugby, who will be a king, who loves you.' He smiled crookedly, and his eyes glistened. 'Can you love that man…all of him?'

Lucy thought of her own words on their wedding night: *I married all of you.* 'Yes,' she said. 'I can.' She reached up to cup his face with her hands, and felt the rough stubble against her fingers. 'I *do.*' Her voice didn't tremble or waver; it came out strong and sure.

Finally she was cool, composed, in control. All the things she'd wanted to be, tried to be by hiding her fear, by pretending to be strong. Now, when she'd finally laid it bare, she felt strong. *She* was strong. She smiled. 'I love you, Khaled. So much.'

He turned his head and let his lips brush her fingers. 'Then there need be no more fear…for either of us.'

'No.' The realisation made her feel light, as if a shackling weight had suddenly turned to air, to nothing.

She was free. She was without fear.

She was in love.

Khaled gathered her into his arms and Lucy surrendered herself to the embrace, her cheek pressed against his shirt so she could feel the steady thudding of his heart.

Outside dusk settled into darkness and a peace stole softly around them. There were no words, no uncertainty.

Only love—pure, strong, sure.

Unafraid.

The Sheikh
Surgeon's Baby

MEREDITH WEBBER

Meredith Webber says of herself, "Some ten years ago, I read an article which suggested that Mills & Boon were looking for new medical authors. I had one of those 'I can do that' moments, and gave it a try. What began as a challenge has become an obsession—though I do temper the 'butt on seat' career of writing with dirty but healthy outdoor pursuits, fossicking through the Australian Outback in search of gold or opals. Having had some success in all of these endeavours, I now consider I've found the perfect lifestyle."

CHAPTER ONE

MELISSA peered out the window as the plane touched down. The late afternoon sun made mirrors of the sides of new, glass-fronted, high-rise towers so here and there square, earth coloured, flat-roofed dwellings were reflected in them, marrying old and new.

Zaheer! The country that had only been an exotic name to her was about to become a reality. Land of red desert sands and sweet oases, camels resting in the shade of stumpy date palms; land of desert warriors who'd once guarded travellers along the trade routes from west to east, some of their descendants still living a nomadic life.

'I would love to show you the desert,' Arun had said to her. They'd been lying in bed, watching the sun rise over the sea, knowing they were soon to part for ever, the magic they'd discovered together in the fortnight of the huge heart symposium in Hawaii already becoming a memory.

Now here she was, about to see the desert, though whether Arun would be the one showing it to her she didn't know. True, she'd be seeing him. After all, her best friend was about to marry his twin, but how would he treat her?

Politely, for sure—he was a very polite man.

Formally?

Probably, for this was his country and he had a certain position to uphold.

But the Arun she'd known had been a strong and generous lover, not a polite and formal sheikh.

The Arun she'd known...

She pressed her hand against the small bulge beneath the all-concealing caftan she was wearing. How he'd treat her wasn't really the issue—how he'd react was!

A feeling, so akin to panic her palms sweated, gripped her body.

She should have told him earlier.

But how, when she'd been so uncertain herself? When, even now, she was in a total muddle over the baby she was carrying. How ironic that she, the strong, efficient leader of a paediatric surgical team, a woman who could make split-second decisions that could mean life or death, should be reduced to a numb-brained blob of ectoplasm when she tried to sort out her thoughts about something as normal and natural as a pregnancy.

But she *should* have told him...

Arun stood inside the glass partition and watched the front door on the plane open, the stairs roll into place. In a couple of months the new airport would be operational and passengers would emerge into a tunnel, to be disgorged into the airport proper. But for now they had to clamber down the stairs.

He and Kam, his twin, on the rare occasions they'd returned from England for school holidays, had been met at the bottom of those stairs, the big cars lined up waiting for them to be whisked away to the family compound by their father's minions. Progress had stopped this practice but he *had* been allowed into the customs area the better to help the parents of the soon-to-be consort of the ruling sheikh, through the red tape of arrival in a foreign country.

All these thoughts flitted through his head as the stairs were secured. Were they a diversion—distracting him from thinking of the woman he was also meeting? The co-incidence wasn't all that strange. After all, Melissa, hearing he was from Zaheer, had approached him at the heart symposium they'd both attended four months ago. She'd been eager to learn something of the country where her best friend was working.

He'd been struck first by her smile—by the way it had lit up her face—and the red-gold hair that had sprung with such vibrant life around her head. Then somehow the magic of attraction had worked between them, two people who hadn't wanted commitment drawn into a brief but heated and very satisfying affair.

That Melissa's best friend was now about to marry Arun's brother was the coincidence.

Or was it fate?

His desert ancestors may have believed their lives had been governed by the capricious whims of fate, but he, a modern man of science, refused to go along with it. Although it was certainly strange to think he'd be meeting Melissa again.

Strange and exciting, his body suggested. But continu-ing what they'd both agreed would begin and end at the symposium would surely be impossible. She was here for

Jenny and Kam's wedding—her free time would be spent with her friend.

Or would it? Once he'd known she was coming, he had emailed her to ask if she'd mind doing some advisory work for him at the hospital. Perhaps fate did exist, he conceded. Just as he was about to set up a paediatric surgical ward at the hospital, an expert in paediatric surgery was arriving on his doorstep. Melissa would be able to tell him, from practical experience, what was needed in the way of equipment, how best the various services should be located, and what staffing levels he would require from the beginning.

Had he had an ulterior motive in asking this? Had he hoped she might prolong her stay? So they could renew their affair?

Surely not, when the non-hospital, non-work part of his mind should be focussed on the promise he'd made to Jenny and Kam—on finding a wife and beginning a family.

Melissa's reply had been brief and to the point—she would be happy to advise him. But she hadn't said how long she could remain in Zaheer, and he hadn't wanted to question Jenny about Melissa's plans in case he revealed their brief relationship had gone further than that of chance-met acquaintants.

The first passenger emerged from the plane, a woman, turning to speak to the older couple coming behind her. His body recognised her before his eyes did, stirring as it had stirred in heated dreams over the last four months.

The madly curling red-gold hair was covered by a blue shawl, but bits were escaping, springing with vibrant life around her face, and even from a distance he could see the wide smile that turned her regular, even unremarkable features into warm, irresistible beauty

Melissa!

He straightened his shoulders, tightened his gut, told his body to behave, and stepped forward, ready to greet the threesome as a bowing steward led them across the tarmac towards a private door into the customs area.

Excitement vied with apprehension as Mel came down the steps from the plane. Here she was, arriving in the country Arun had talked of with such deep passion she had smelt the dry desert air and seen images of oases, although they'd been in waterlocked Hawaii. Here she was, about to be reunited with her best friend, for the joyous occasion of Jenny's wedding.

Here she was, four months pregnant, and no one in the world other than herself knew…

Well, to be honest, her specialist knew…

She accompanied Jenny's parents across the tarmac, Jane Stapleton chattering, probably from nerves, about the first-class plane trip, the wonder of Jenny finally falling in love again—speculating about the man who'd healed her daughter's broken heart.

Mel could have told her something about the man— about his looks anyway—for Arun and Kam were identical twins. But the twins were obviously not identical in character, Kam about to commit to marriage, while Arun, by his own admission, had no intention of ever marrying again—or ever entering a long-term relationship.

'Two commitment-phobes,' Mel had teased when he'd told her this in Hawaii. 'The perfect match!'

How could a commitment-phobe commit to bringing up a baby? How would she, who knew nothing of motherhood, handle it? That was her biggest worry. Her constant worry!

One of many, to be honest. Childbirth was another, though she knew intellectually that was nonsense—something she had to get past—and how she'd juggle a baby and a job was a real concern.

Then there was the very real issue of single motherhood. Didn't a baby deserve two parents—if not as a baby, then certainly as a child, and for sure come the teenage years?

Arun had been adamant children weren't in his future.

Any more than they'd been in hers...

Oh, dear!

She saw movement beyond the glass in the terminal building and, pleased by the distraction, peered in that direction.

'It's Kam's brother, his twin—you've met him, haven't you? He's come to meet us because Kam's away.' Jane was positively bubbling with excitement. 'I didn't really expect the white robes, did you?'

Mel wasn't sure what she'd expected. Certainly not to feel her chest tighten and her heart rate zoom into dangerous arrhythmia. It must be because of the baby—it couldn't be the thought of seeing Arun.

Meeting him again...

Touching him...

Useless blob time again!

Numb brain!

She resisted the urge to slide her hand across her stomach as Jane and Bob Stapleton were bowed through a glass door into the terminal, the man in the snowy white robes—so regally erect, so noble looking, so like a desert-fantasy sheikh, Mel's knees felt weak—coming forward to introduce himself, shaking hands.

'Dr and Dr Stapleton, I am Arun Rahman al'Kawali.'

Mel stared at him—at the stranger in the white robe, barely aware of the Stapletons offering their first names and adding polite greetings.

'And, Melissa, we meet again.'

The pale green eyes she'd thought never to see again looked steadily into hers.

Would the baby have those pale, translucent-jade eyes?

'It is my great pleasure to welcome you to my country.'

He took her hand and clasped it for a moment, his warmth finding its way into her blood—heating it. Then he smiled and she knew he'd felt her reaction—not only felt it but had taken pleasure from it, seeing it as confirmation that the magic still worked between them.

And, no doubt, supposing their affair could be resumed…

Oh, dear!

Again she had to stop herself touching the barely there bulge, while her thoughts whirled uselessly through her head. I'm still attracted to him. I should have told him about the baby. What will he think—say?

Oh, dear!

'I hope while you are here I will be able to show you the beauty of the desert.'

He was watching her closely as he spoke, and Mel wondered how much of her confusion was obvious. But, whatever he read in her face, she could read nothing in his, and now he turned back to the Stapletons.

'When we met in Hawaii with water everywhere, Melissa told me of her love of the ocean. I tried to describe the desert as something similar, but I know it is too hard for those who have not seen it to understand the similarities.'

He sounded so casual, so silky smooth, so in control—but why wouldn't he? This was his country, he was the king—or half-king, sharing, Jen had said in an email, rule with his twin.

But it was the message implicit in the 'show you the desert' remark that was making Mel's anxiety levels spiral upwards—the message that now fate had brought them back together there was no reason for their affair *not* to resume.

To make matters worse, her body had not only received the message but had responded to it, getting hot and bothered and jittery right on cue.

Oh, dear!

She had to stop thinking like that. It was so negative, so weak, so utterly useless!

But what else could she think, with a brain like curdled blancmange?

For one mad instant she considered running back towards the plane. To escape to somewhere—anywhere—until she'd worked out once and for all just how to tackle the task that lay ahead.

But to run was cowardice and she'd never been a coward, so she stiffened her body and with it her resolve, and met his silky smoothness with her own.

'I would love to see the desert,' she responded, albeit a little late. 'And I'm sure Bob and Jane are looking forward to it, too.'

His gaze slid towards her and a small smile twisted his

lips. He nodded, as if to acknowledge her point, but she doubted he'd conceded it.

Not this man! Even as she'd met him in Hawaii, in Western clothes, another specialist among many, he'd exuded an aura of power, an otherness that set him apart. Quietly spoken, yet he'd been able to command attention, waiters falling over themselves to serve him before others were served, hotel staff happy to provide any service for him, people deferring to him purely because of his presence.

So, would he act as desert tour guide for all three of them?

Probably, because he was also scrupulously polite.

But would that be all Mel saw of the desert in his company?

She didn't think so.

Although she could refuse to go—refuse to accompany him anywhere. That way she'd be safe from the riot his presence was causing in her senses, the long robes he wore no barrier to attraction.

But how could they discuss the baby if she wasn't ever alone with him?

Oh, damn and blast…

'If you come this way,' he was saying, leading Bob Stapleton towards a waiting customs official. 'Your luggage will be checked here and we can go out to the car. It's parked at the side door so you can avoid the crowds.'

Crowds might have helped, Mel thought. I could have disappeared into them, never to be seen again.

Leaving Jenny short one bridesmaid?

Not possible.

So she just had to hide the surge of renewed attraction rattling her body and numbing her brain, hide a small matter of a pregnancy—thank heaven she'd dressed in deference to the country's traditions—until she had time to talk privately to him. In the meantime she would have to carry on as if Arun really was nothing more than a chance-met colleague at a medical conference.

If he could do it, so could she.

This resolve faltered as he ushered the Stapletons towards the customs official and slid close to her side.

'You are well? I cannot tell you how delighted I am that you are here in my country. There is so much I can show you, so much we can enjoy.'

The husky voice with its patent delight and suggestive undertones further weakened her resolve, but she refused to be seduced by husky voices or suggestive undertones— or by the pathetic behaviour of her body.

'You don't have to put yourself out for me,' she said. 'I know how busy you must be, with all the changes happening at the hospital. I know we'll be seeing each other from time to time, but—'

'Ah, you do not wish our affair to be resumed? Is that what you're telling me?'

No huskiness in his voice now, although a strand of steel ran through the words.

Mel tried for a really, really casual shrug and hoped she'd pulled it off.

'I'm not here long, so really there's no point.'

'Ah!' he said again, but this time there was more understanding in it. 'If that is how you feel, Melissa…'

If only he hadn't said her name. If only the word hadn't

brought back such memories. Arun whispering it, softly sibilant, as he caressed her body, or shouting it, triumphant, in the throes of love-making.

She could feel the coolness as he drew away from her, all his attention back on the Stapletons.

So what was this? Arun pondered as he watched the customs officer open the first suitcase. Oh, he got the literal meaning—their affair would not be resumed—but surely there was a subtext here, hidden from him the way her luscious, ripe, curvaceous body was hidden behind the soft folds of the all-concealing gown she wore.

Maybe she was embarrassed by the proximity of the Stapletons—unable to respond to him because of their presence.

But, no, she'd spoken plainly—there'd be no point...

He studied her as she opened her suitcase, noticing faint lines of strain in her pale face.

Tiredness from the flight or something else?

He wondered why he was considering it—why he was concerned she might be tired or stressed...

Because the memories of their time together had haunted his dreams for the last four months?

Or because he cared more for her as a person than he'd allowed himself to admit?

Impossible! It had been an enjoyable affair, nothing more.

A very enjoyable affair...

The customs official gave the bags a cursory examination and another official stamped the passports, then the porter wheeled the baggage towards the car, Arun escorting Bob Stapleton while behind him he could hear Melissa chatting quietly to Jane.

They settled into the big limousine, the three guests fitting comfortably in the back seat while Arun rode beside the driver in the front. He pointed out the landmarks in the city, naming the new hotels that had sprouted from the ground to accommodate first visiting oilmen and now the tourists who came to marvel at the desert and the facilities oil money could provide.

'Oh!'

Melissa's cry made him turn and he saw her pointing, wide-eyed with wonder, towards the west, where the sinking sun was reflecting the red of the desert into the sky, so it looked like a molten golden orb in a sea of red. Closer to them the rounded dome and tall spire of a citadel stood silhouetted blackly against the red glow, and through the visitor's eyes Arun saw again the daily magic of a desert sunset.

He spoke quietly to the driver, who turned off the main highway, taking them to a vantage point from which they could watch the final glories of the day.

'I can't believe the beauty of it,' Melissa whispered, as much to herself as to those accompanying her. 'I thought the sunsets over the river where I grew up were the most beautiful in the world. I never imagined a desert sunset could be like this.'

She turned from the view towards Arun.

'And you're right, it does remind me of the ocean.'

Wonder warmed her voice, and this, more than her physical presence, started Arun's body stirring again. They'd matched so well, enjoyed each other's company so much it had gone beyond sex in that brief interlude, although both of them had known from the start that had been all it was. He'd explained he had no intention of ever marrying again—had even spoken of Hussa, his wife, and the tragedy of that gentle and beautiful young woman's death—while Melissa had admitted to being married to her job, and to finding all the satisfaction she needed in her life in the work she did with very fragile infants.

So why was she upset that they'd met again? Why could they not be friends, if not lovers?

Inwardly, he laughed. As if that would be likely, with the fire that had flared between them. One touch, he was willing to bet, and it would flame again.

Just one touch...

'Jenny?'

Jane Stapleton's gentle reminder made him realise the nightly show was finished, the sky having changed from red to gold to pink and purple and now was a darkening blue. He spoke to the driver and they continued towards the family compound.

Shaken by the beauty she had witnessed, Mel sat quietly. How could she remain stiff and unyielding, impervious to all around her, when all around her was new and exciting, and so unexpectedly beautiful? But if she opened herself up to the experience, might not Arun slip in as well?

She stole a glance towards him. The pristine white scarf that covered his head was kept in place by two black twisted braids held together with a binding of gold thread. At the front, the pinpoint corners of the scarf fell to hide most of his face so all she saw, as he turned again towards the Stapletons, acting the perfect tourist guide, was his profile—the strong beak of a nose, the determined chin, and between them a glimpse of the lips she knew could fire her body to melting point.

In Western clothing, he'd been exotic, the most fantastic-looking man she'd ever seen, but in the robes—it was as if they spread an aura around him, a sense of command, of power, of...

Reined-in, hidden sexuality?

Don't think about him! Concentrate on the tour. The alley leading off that main street was the souk—the market—which accounted for the teeming crowds pushing down the narrow passageway.

'We will go there tomorrow,' he promised. 'During the day it is not so crowded and you will be more comfortable. And now here we are.'

They were approaching a corner where two high walls met, the area lit by bright lights both inside and outside the wall. They drove along one side until they came to a huge gate, hastily pulled open by two men who had been dozing by the wall.

Inside was another world, the courtyard they entered as bright as daylight, so the beautifully laid-out gardens and ornamental pools were clearly visible.

'You will wish to see your daughter immediately,' Arun said. 'She has been living in the women's house but has moved into the house she will share with Kam after her marriage, so all three of you can stay with her.'

'The women's house?' Melissa echoed, and Arun turned so she saw all of his face.

'It is custom,' he said. 'Strange to outsiders but it has worked this way for thousands of years, although, of course, in times gone by, they were tents, not houses.'

The bland explanation told Mel he'd got the message that what they'd shared was definitely in the past. He was as mentally removed from her as his body was behind the all-concealing gown.

So why did she feel a tremor of disappointment?

The car pulled up in front of one of the many large houses surrounding the courtyard. Long, shallow steps leading to a cloistered entrance where sandals were lined up outside marked the custom of the land.

Mel followed the Stapletons up the steps, but at the top, as she bent to remove her shoes, Arun touched her arm.

'Perhaps they would like some time alone, the family. If you wish, I will show you around the gardens.'

She studied him for a moment, knowing he'd probably read the situation correctly—Jen *would* like some time alone with her parents—but was wary of his offer.

He waved an arm towards the gardens.

'We will walk through here to the stables. As you see, there are plenty of people around so I am unlikely to— what is the expression?—jump on your bones?'

Another tremor sneaked through Mel's body, but this time it wasn't disappointment. Memories of the times he had 'jumped her bones' and she his brought a rush of warmth to her face, and she adjusted her shawl more closely around her face, hoping he hadn't noticed.

He took her silence for assent and led her back down the steps, then turned so they walked along a gravel path, neatly raked into intricate whorls and patterns, between perfectly manicured hedges that formed a border for the still ponds that ran down the centre of the courtyard.

The houses on either side were mirrored in them, so everywhere there were buildings, but above all a sense of calm and peace.

So calm, so peaceful, Mel was reluctant to ruin it with a declaration of her pregnancy. Although she'd have to tell him some time, and the sooner the better.

'You will explain?' Arun had touched her arm to guide her on to a side path leading between two of the sparkling pools, and now slowed his steps to ask the question.

Had he read her mind?

Did he know there was something she had to say?

Half her brain worried over this while the other half shrieked, Not here, not yet. You're tired and confused...

That half won!

'Explain?'

'This is awkward for you—the two of us meeting again? You are embarrassed?'

Could she lie—nod her head—let him believe embarrassment was the reason for her lack of response to him?

Of course she couldn't. Lies became too complicated.

'I'm not embarrassed,' she said, then realised she had no other explanation to offer for her behaviour. Not right now—not until she'd sorted it all out in her head.

Like that was going to happen!

'You have a new man in your life?' Arun persisted, no doubt seeking some valid reason for the fact that the magic which had brought them together was well and truly dead as far as she was concerned.

If only he knew how far *that* was from the truth! How skittery her skin was, and how her nerves were jumping like circus fleas.

'No,' she managed, offered what she hoped was an acceptable a smile. 'Commitment-phobe, remember?'

Arun nodded, but was obviously not satisfied.

'Your job? You had hoped to get a place on the team in Boston, had been interviewed and told you'd done well, yet you have flown here from Australia. You didn't get it? You are disappointed?'

This was getting worse. So bad, in fact, Mel had to smile—a proper smile this time—accompanied by a shake of her head, although she'd better not do that too often or she'd lose her scarf.

'Does there have to be a reason?' she asked, stopping by a still pool and lowering her body to sit on the edge of it so she could trail her hands in the water—cool her blood. 'Does your pride demand a valid excuse as to why a woman might not want to leap back into bed with you?'

The barb struck home, leaving Arun speechless—but only momentarily.

'I was not aware I'd offered you my bed,' he said, denying all the urges his body had been feeling since she'd stepped out the door of the plane. 'I was speaking more of friendship. But if your unwillingness to commit extends even to friendship, I am sorry for you.'

The light was good enough for him to see the colour leave her cheeks, and the blue eyes raised to his were stricken. She reached up and touched his arm, her wet fingers leaving damp marks on his robe.

'No, I'm the one who's sorry, Arun. It's just…'

The stricken look had been replaced by a plea. For understanding? How could he offer that when he had no idea what was going on?

How could he understand when the strong woman he remembered seemed—brittle? Vulnerable?

Surely not!

Then she smiled again, a weak effort, but it still had the effect of lighting up her face.

'Can I plead jet-lag for not being terribly coherent right now?'

She could, but he wouldn't believe her. This woman could think clearly—could even deliver a brilliant lecture at a high-level symposium—after a night of passion had prevented all consideration of sleep, so he doubted a trifle like jet-lag would faze her.

He settled beside her on the low balustrade, and leaned towards her, aware they were now completely alone in this side courtyard, aware he could kiss her.

'Is that all you want to plead?' he asked, remembering their love-making so vividly he could feel his body harden.

Another wavery smile.

'At the moment,' she said, 'but later, tomorrow, or after the wedding. Later we'll talk.'

'That's a promise?'

He'd leaned closer and she hadn't edged away, but her nod was distinctly nervous.

'Here in Zaheer we seal promises with a kiss,' he whispered.

He didn't give her time to protest, his head moving the couple of inches necessary for him capture her lips, to feel her mouth open to his demands, to taste her, to test the warm cavern of her mouth—to claim her with a kiss.

CHAPTER TWO

SURELY sheikhs shouldn't be doing this kind of thing in their own courtyard! That was Mel's first desperate thought.

Thank heavens they were both sitting so the bump kind of disappeared into her lap, was her second.

Then the heat Arun's kisses had generated from the beginning burnt through her and she gave in to sensation. Her breasts tingled, her bones turned to jelly, her insides to liquid, and she quivered with the need that only he had ever made her feel.

Damn it all, this was the last thing she wanted to happen, yet here she was responding to him like some sex-starved virgin. Well, maybe not a virgin, but certainly sex-starved...

She kissed him back, though she knew she shouldn't, revealing her need, admitting the power he had over her. Although the harsh sound of his indrawn breaths suggested she held equal power over him.

Shared passion! It had been so new to her four months ago—so new and so exciting, like exploring a different world.

If only...

Cool air brushed across her damp, kiss-sensitised lips

and she realised he'd moved away. Not only moved away but was standing up, looking down at her.

'So it isn't that the attraction's died,' he said quietly, and though his face was shadowed she knew his green eyes, pale and clear, would be studying her intently, trying to read beyond whatever stunned expression might be plastered across her face, to fathom what lay beneath.

To feelings...

Or was she imagining that? Would he even care about her feelings?

'No,' she said, answering his question, not her thoughts, for he was a sensitive man and *would* care about her feelings.

'Good,' he replied, then took her hand to help her to her feet. 'I'll take you to Jenny now. You are right. You will be busy. The excitement of the wedding has been building in the women's house all week, for all that Jenny says it's just a formality.'

He led her back to the large building where he'd left the Stapletons, introducing her to a young woman who met them at the door, telling Mel her luggage would already be in her room and Keira would show her where that was.

But Keira wasn't needed, for Jenny came bursting out of a side room into the huge vestibule.

'Mel! I thought Arun had whisked you away on the back of a camel, and was even now riding across the desert with his prisoner in true desert warrior style.'

Mel glanced at Arun before crossing the room to greet her friend. She could see the desert warrior in him today—and being carried off across the desert wasn't all that unappealing an idea...

Aaargh!

She *had* to get her head sorted!

'I'm a horse man, Jenny,' he was saying, but he smiled warmly as he spoke, as if Jenny was already someone special in his life.

'Mel rides,' Jenny told him. 'Mel, you should see the stable and the horses. They are beautiful. You'll love them. Arun rides most mornings, don't you, Arun?'

They had reached each other, and kissed cheeks, Mel careful not to get into a full hug, although her bump was hardly recognisable as pregnancy. Now Jen was standing with her arm around Mel's shoulders and matchmaking so obviously Mel knew she was blushing.

She looked from Arun's expressionless face to her friend's, glowing with happiness and excitement. 'I doubt I'll have time for riding for a few days at least,' Mel said, letting Arun off the hook, although he'd hardly rushed in and offered to take her riding. 'We've got a wedding to get ready for, remember?'

'If you wish to ride—' Arun began, and Mel had to laugh.

'You're far too late making that offer,' she teased, pleased the riding conversation had eased the tension she'd been feeling. 'And I understand, I really do. When I lived with my grandmother I rode a lot and, though cousins and friends often rode with me, there was never anything quite as good as riding on my own. Especially early in the morning, the dew still on the grass, and the world smelling fresh and new again. Just me and the horse and the countryside. I can understand your reluctance to have company.'

He smiled and she was sorry she'd relaxed her guard,

for the return tease in that smile crept through her already crumbling defences.

'With me it's the horse and the desert,' he said quietly. 'And a way to sort out the problems of the world when my brain is first awake and my senses alert to everything around me.'

His smile broadened as he added, 'Well, what I really think about are the problems of the hospital, and some of the problems of our country—not quite all the world.'

'But *your* world, the one that matters to you,' Mel reminded him, and was pleased to see she'd surprised him for he looked at her for a long moment before nodding agreement.

'I'll leave you now,' Arun said, and turned away. Not a moment too soon, he decided as he stopped outside the door to slip his feet into his sandals. It was all right to be physically attracted to Melissa Cartwright, and he'd enjoyed her sharp mind and probing intelligence as well as her body when they'd had their brief affair. But he didn't like the feeling that she might be in tune with his emotions or keying in to his thoughts. Such intimate closeness was the one thing he'd avoided since Hussa's death.

Jenny led Mel into a vast room, adorned with ancient tapestries, bright rugs, soft sofas and thick cushions. But the immediate impression was of colour—reds and golds, pinks and purples, unlikely mixes of geometric and floral designs, hidden corners behind drapes and screens. It was like something out of a fairy-tale, and Mel paused as her senses struggled to take it all in.

Bob and Jane Stapleton were sitting on a long leather

ottoman, studying something that looked like a map. In front of them a low table was laden with platters of fruit, nuts, cheeses, bread, and small cake-like delicacies.

'Come,' Jenny said. 'You need to eat and drink and I'm dying to tell you all my adventures. Then, when Mum and Dad have gone to bed, you can tell me all of yours.'

She paused and turned to study Mel, touching her hand to her face.

'You're well? Things are all right with you?'

Mel knew she was searching for disappointment—or perhaps some hint of a reason why Mel was not working in the hospital in Boston, in the job of her dreams. But the answer lay not in her face but in the shape of her body...

'We'll talk later,' Mel confirmed, although she knew she couldn't talk to Jenny—not properly—not until she'd told Arun.

But *how* could she tell him?

How could she explain why she hadn't told him earlier?

She followed Jenny across the room, hearing, and envying, the happiness in her friend's voice, although if anyone deserved happiness, it was Jenny.

Mel joined the Stapletons on the ottoman, took a damp scented napkin from a young girl standing behind her and wiped her hands, then picked up a plate and carefully chose a few of the exotic delicacies to try.

'I'm not really hungry,' she protested, when Jenny urged her to have more. 'They kept feeding us on the flight.'

'But you should drink something to keep up your fluid level. Try this juice, it's made from dates. You'll love it.'

Then, having urged food and drink onto her friend, she settled back to tell her tale.

'So I thought, loving him as I did, that marrying Kam just wasn't possible,' Jenny said, much later, coming to the end of the saga of her romance. 'He was the new ruler, he would need heirs and I didn't know…'

She pressed her hand to her stomach and all three of her listeners understood the gesture—remembering the pain and grief Jenny had suffered when she'd lost her husband and unborn son in a car accident. Worse still had been the news from the doctors who had pieced her back together again. They had doubted she would be able to have another child.

But Jen's face was still glowing—*and* she was marrying Kam—so obviously her possible inability to produce an heir no longer worried her.

'And *that* was when Arun made his offer,' she finished triumphantly, beaming at her listeners as if this was the most wonderful news she'd ever imparted to anyone.

Their blank stares must have told her something, for she laughed.

'Sorry. You don't understand. Kam had told me something of Arun's past, you see. Arun married when he was young—his wife was a beautiful young woman called Hussa. He was working in the city while she stayed, as was the custom in their father's time, in the women's house in the family compound in the country. She was young and very shy and when she had pains in her stomach she didn't like to tell anyone, and by the time someone realised she was sick her appendix had burst, peritonitis had set in, and she died before anyone could save her.'

'That's terrible, but it does still happen in this day and

age,' Jane said. 'Even back home, when people put the stomach pain down to something they ate, and the resulting infection resists drug therapy.'

Jenny nodded her agreement.

'Arun, naturally enough,' she continued, 'was devastated, and swore he'd never marry again. He's so like Kam and yet so different. Kam calls him a playboy, although I'm sure he's not that bad, but I could understand him not wanting to marry again.'

Mel, contrarily eager to hear more about Arun, had followed the story avidly, but surely it wasn't finished. She glanced at Jane and Bob, who looked equally puzzled.

'And Arun's offer?' Mel prompted, and Jen smiled again—smiled radiantly.

'He said not to worry, he'd marry and have children who could be heirs, and my reason for not wanting to marry Kam was swept away.'

'Oh, dear' was no longer strong enough. What Mel needed was a really bad expletive, but her grandmother had been extremely old-fashioned as far as even the mildest of swear words was concerned, and though Mel had heard plenty as a student, and still did in Theatre, she could rarely bring herself to use one.

Not even in her head!

But this was a disaster. She could hardly present Arun with her news when he was seeking a new wife, maybe already arranging to be married.

But he also wanted a child…

Their child?

Impossible!

Jen was still speaking and Mel tried to focus on what

she was saying. She'd learn what she could then later she could work out where to go next.

'You have to understand that things are done differently here,' Jenny explained. 'People still follow the traditions of hundreds of years ago, so a marriage of convenience, like Arun offered to organise for himself, is not unusual.'

'And has he done this? Organised it?' Mel hoped her voice sounded stronger than it felt as she croaked the question out past taut vocal cords. She also hoped the questions sounded natural, under the circumstances.

Apparently they did, for Jenny smiled.

'He hasn't said so, but knowing the way he and Kam work—think of something, get it done—I imagine he has it well in hand. In fact, I wouldn't have been surprised if he'd suggested a double wedding.'

'Oh, I'm sure he wouldn't want to take anything away from your big day,' Jane said, and Jenny laughed.

'Mum, it's not really a big day. Kam and I feel married already. This is just a ceremony for the family and an excuse for the local people to party. Although Kam's tried to explain things to me, and I understand a few words of the local language, the four of us will know nothing of what's going on.'

Jane looked doubtful but Bob was made of sterner stuff.

'As long as you're happy,' he said gruffly, 'and I can see you are, that's all that matters. Now, when do we meet this man of yours?'

Mel watched the colour rise in Jenny's cheeks and knew Bob had spoken the truth. Jenny was truly happy.

'Tomorrow night. We're having a big dinner. It's traditional the day before the wedding, although I shouldn't be attending it. But times are changing and I'll be there. Kam will be back from the refugee camp.' She turned to Mel. 'He took the new doctor up there a couple of days ago and was staying to see he'd settled in. You'll all meet him tomorrow.'

It became a signal for movement, the Stapletons deciding they were ready to retire and Jenny rising to see them to their room.

'You stay right there,' she said to Mel. 'We need to talk.'

But when Mel thought about what that talk would entail she shook her head. Better a small deceit than a larger one.

'I think our talk will have to wait, Jen,' she said. 'I'm bushed. Must be jet-lag.'

Jen's look was disbelieving but she didn't argue, leading all three of them back through the wide entrance, taking her parents to one room then showing Mel towards another further down a corridor.

'This small place is going to be your and Kam's house?' Mel teased. 'I should be dropping breadcrumbs so I can find my way back to the front door.'

'Keira will show you where to go. She will be your personal attendant while you're here, and will be sleeping in a little alcove off your room, so anything you want, just ask.'

'In English, or do I need a few words of Zaheer?'

Jenny smiled.

'Kam and Arun have made sure all the attendants—I know that's a strange word but they are more like family than servants, although they serve the family—have had good schooling, and that includes learning English. The twins have also paid tuition costs for any of the younger ones who want to go to university, whether here or overseas.'

As if to confirm Jenny's words, Keira was waiting in the room—far too large to be called a bedroom—set aside for Mel.

'I have unpacked for you,' she said, in clear, unaccented English. 'You would like a drink of something, tea perhaps, or milk, before you go to bed?'

'No, I'm fine,' Mel told her, following the young girl into a splendidly opulent bathroom, admiring its beauty, then assuring Keira she could manage to shower on her own.

Shower and shroud herself in her voluminous nightgown—she certainly didn't want word of her pregnancy spreading through the house before she'd told Arun.

Or Jenny!

She slipped into the big bed, feeling the softness of the sheets—surely not silk—wondering how Jen must feel, living in this house after her years in tents and mud huts in war-torn countries or refugee camps.

Not that luxury would change Jen…

But as hard as she tried to concentrate on Jenny and her future in this country, Mel's mind kept slipping back to Arun and to the new dilemma she now faced—his approaching marriage…

And as she listened to a distant clock chime three times, she decided. She would stop thinking about it, stop putting it off, just get up in the morning, go out to the stables where she knew he'd be, and tell him.

Let him decide what he wanted to do with the knowledge…

Arun was leading Saracen out of the stables when he saw her approaching, an anxious Keira by her side.

'Melissa?'

He paused, aware of many things. In the kind, pearly light of dawn she looked pale and tired, yet his body still responded to her.

Her usual confident stride was hesitant, and now, as she drew nearer, he read indecision in her face.

'You wish to ride?'

She shook her head, then nodded.

'I know you prefer to ride alone, but I thought…'

She stopped and looked around in a desperate fashion, as if seeking escape from the compound.

'I'd be happy to have you accompany me.' Good manners had saved him in many an awkward situation and this, with the confident Melissa looking positively haunted, could be classed as a very awkward one.

'I'm not really dressed for it. Didn't think to bring jeans or jodhpurs, thinking they might not be acceptable…'

Arun took in the loose trousers and tunic Melissa was wearing, not regular riding gear but surely unexceptional. He glanced towards Keira, wondering if something in her expression might shed some light on Melissa's uncertainty, but Keira's face was devoid of all expression, although doubtless she was wondering if all foreigners were as strange as this woman she was watching over.

'If you don't mind me riding with you, that might be best,' Melissa finally said, and Arun called back into the stable for one of the men to saddle Mershinga, a gentle mare his sisters often rode.

'It will be my pleasure,' Arun said, then he added to Keira, 'I will return Dr Cartwright to the house later.'

The young woman nodded and departed, Melissa turning to watch her move away before swinging back towards Arun.

'Maybe we shouldn't ride—maybe we could just go somewhere and talk,' she said, the words rushing out in a super-fast stream, as if she needed to get them said.

Saracen, perhaps picking up tension in the air, began to prance and Arun soothed him with a hand against his neck and a few quiet words.

Would that such a touch would soothe the visitor!

He handed Saracen's bridle to a young boy who was hovering nearby and stepped towards her.

'Melissa,' he said, coming close enough to see the evidence of a sleepless night in the blue-tinged shadows beneath her eyes, taking her hands gently in his. 'Come ride with me. Relax. Enjoy the desert. Later, if you wish, we will talk, but for now forget your cares and concerns and let the rhythm of a horse and the clean morning air of the desert work their magic.'

He touched his fingers to her chin and tipped her head so he could look into her eyes.

Then regretted it, for what he saw was anguish—an anguish so deep it touched his heart and made him want to hold her against his body, hold her safe in his arms, and promise her that everything would be all right.

Some promise, when he didn't know what ailed her—what was causing her such distress.

'Come!' he said instead, taking her hand and leading her to where another young man held the pale grey mare. 'This is Mershinga. She will carry you surely and safely.'

He held the horse's head while Melissa lifted herself

lightly into the saddle, then he adjusted the stirrups for her, being careful not to let his hand linger on her ankle—on any part of her—for, in spite of his knowledge of her troubled state, he still felt the attraction between them.

Surely and safely! Arun's words repeated themselves in Mel's head. Maybe Arun was right. Maybe she could just ride and enjoy the sensation of freedom being on a horse always brought her—the wind in her hair, the morning sun on her skin and the new experience of the desert. She could let the magic of a new day work on the tensions that had tormented her all night.

Then later—some other time—she'd talk to Arun…

He had mounted his horse, a bold, black stallion who frisked and gambolled as if reminding the rider who was the boss. But Arun held him under control, letting him prance a little but always reining him back in. You are not the boss, his strong but slender hands were signalling.

And as Mel watched the tussle between horse and rider, her own mount following sedately behind the pair, she did relax, her taut muscles loosening, her body adjusting the rhythm of the mare's gait, her lungs welcoming the crisp morning air.

They left the compound through a smaller gate than the one the car had entered the previous evening, and to Mel's delight were immediately in the desert.

'It's so close,' she marvelled, as Arun reined in his still fidgety mount and waited for her to come alongside. 'I thought we'd have to follow roads or paths to the outskirts of the city.'

Arun smiled at her.

'This *is* the outskirts of the city. From here the desert

stretches out towards those mountains, and in the other direction to an inland sea.'

He pointed to the mountains, indistinct behind a gauzy morning haze. They were like a metaphor for this place—veiled mountains, veiled women, curtains and screens—secrets.

'You wish to canter? You are confident enough on Mershinga?'

'Yes!'

Mel smiled as she replied, suddenly longing for a canter—for a gallop, in fact—to blow the cobwebs from her head. The secret wouldn't change for being kept a little longer.

They went slowly at first, no doubt because Arun wanted to see the level of her riding skills, but then he turned and raised his eyebrows at her.

'Faster?' he asked.

'Faster,' she agreed, loosening the reins and digging her heels into the mare's sides, taking off beside him, although the stallion soon outpaced her mount.

She caught up with him at what looked like a cairn of some kind, stones stacked on top of each other beside some squat palms.

'Is this an oasis?' she asked, not bothering to hide the disappointment she felt. Where was the water? Did three date palms count as lush forestation?

He laughed.

'A very small one, but none the less important if you were a traveller in the desert. Come, dismount and try the water. I can assure you that the most expensive bottled water in the world will not compare in purity or taste.'

He vaulted easily off his horse as he was speaking and

looped the reins over a post beside the cairn, then held the mare's head while Mel dismounted.

Leaving the mare untethered, her reins knotted loosely to they wouldn't trail on the ground, he led Mel towards a small well she hadn't noticed.

'This is a wadi—a place where one of the underground streams beneath the desert runs close enough to the surface for the palms to grow and for the people, in ancient times, to dig a well.'

He threw the wooden bucket that was sitting on top of the well wall down into the depths, then wound the handle to bring it back up, crystal-clear water splashing from it.

Cupping his hands, he dipped them into the water then offered them to Mel.

She drank, more out of politeness than thirst, then drank again for the water was as special as he had said.

'You're right, it's better than any water I've ever tasted.' Then she looked up into his face and laughed, surprising herself as her inner tension had been so great a laugh was the last thing she'd expected to issue from her lips. 'That sounds stupid, doesn't it? Water doesn't really have a taste.'

Arun grinned at her.

'No more stupid than me telling you it tasted better than any other water on earth,' he agreed, dipping his hands in again and drinking himself.

Mel watched him, the handsome man in jeans and sweatshirt, water running down his stubbly chin, staining the front of his shirt.

Her baby's father…

'I'm pregnant.'

The words came out before she could prevent them. So much for all the phrases she'd practised during the night, all the lead-in explanations and excuses!

She studied him, reading puzzlement in the face he raised towards her, then disbelief as it dawned on him why she should be blurting out such a thing—to him of all people.

'How pregnant?'

A crisp demand for clarification. Her stomach coiled in on itself at the coldness in his voice.

'Four months.'

'Impossible! I took precautions! Every—'

He stopped and she saw him frown as he thought back. Would he pick up on the memory she'd had when she'd discovered her pregnancy?

They'd opted out of a formal dinner, deciding instead to dine at a small, local, beachside restaurant someone had recommended, eating lobster on a deck beside the sea, wiping the butter from each other's chins with gentle fingers. Then walking back to the hotel along the beach— the secluded cove, the midnight swim, making love in the warm, enveloping water of the Pacific Ocean.

'And, presuming you're telling me now because it's my child, you're also telling me that for four months you've felt no need to tell me? Seen no reason to share this information?'

Arun paused, studying the woman in front of him, aware how pale and fragile she was looking, yet he was so angry—so enraged—he could no more stop himself from hurting her than he could turn back time four months.

'Would you have told me at all had not Jenny's wedding

brought you to Zaheer? Or, having seen the compound, are you after money?'

He saw her wince, although he could tell from the way she'd stiffened she'd tried desperately hard to stop the reaction, but he couldn't afford to feel sympathy for her, not when she'd kept such information to herself all this time.

Not when he was finding it difficult to process that same information—to work out how he felt and what it meant to him.

'Arun,' she began, moving so she could sit down on the stone seat at the cairn, her hands twisting in her lap. 'I know this is a shock—you have to believe it was just as great a shock to me. And, yes, I should have told you earlier.'

Blue eyes, dark with remorse and what seemed like a shadow of fear, looked pleadingly up into his.

'But I had no idea how to react myself,' she admitted quietly. 'I didn't know how to think, what to do.'

She paused, then added, 'I was terrified.'

So the shadow *was* fear, but why?

And surely terror was something of an overreaction!

She'd bowed her head, as if his scrutiny after such an admission was too much for her to bear.

But how could he not pursue it?

'Terrified?'

For a moment he thought his query would be ignored, but eventually she raised her head, and tried on a smile so pathetic it wrung his heart.

'Stupid, isn't it? I can operate on newborn babies without a twinge of fear.'

And now he understood—or thought he did—he sat down beside her and took her hand.

'You were frightened the baby might have something wrong with it? A congenital defect? That's not surprising, Melissa, considering your work.'

But she shook her head, and withdrew her hand from his, standing up, putting distance between them, pacing around the three trees she'd derided earlier.

'I was terrified about the pregnancy.'

She paused, as if startled by her own honesty, then rushed into qualifying statements, that to Arun's ears rang true yet not entirely true at the same time.

'What did I, brought up by a strict but fair and very proper grandmother, know about bringing up a child? Then there were the problems of single motherhood, not to mention juggling work and a baby. It all seemed to crash down on me until I couldn't think at all. So I didn't! I blotted it from my mind—pretended it wasn't happening, told no one, not even Jenny—thinking that once I'd calmed down I'd be able to break it down like any other task into doable-sized pieces and work out all the answers.'

She sighed then sat down again.

'That didn't happen. Even now, when I try to think about it, my mind goes blank—or turns to mush! I know this is a stupid reaction, Arun, and I'm only telling you because it might help you understand why I didn't contact you about the pregnancy earlier. Oh, I had all kinds of other excuses—I might lose the baby; you hadn't wanted a child, or any kind of commitment, so it didn't matter if you didn't know—but the truth is I tried to pretend to myself it wasn't happening, and if I didn't talk about it, the pretence was easier.'

He could feel her tension, the trembling in her body,

and knew what she said she felt was real—stripped bare of any pretence—although he sensed there was a lot more left unsaid.

And was it that—the fact she was holding something back—that stifled any sympathy for her? That fed his anger?

'If that was how you felt, why didn't you terminate the pregnancy?' The words were harsh, doing nothing to hide his anger or his simmering suspicion.

She swung towards him, disbelief in her face.

'Why didn't I what?' she demanded, steeling herself and meeting his anger with her own.

'Terminate the pregnancy,' he repeated, each word as cold and hard as a chip of ice.

'How could I when I *save* children's lives? That's my *life,* it's what I do! I'm not against abortion and I can understand, in a lot of circumstances, choosing to go that way, but me? How could I?'

She was so genuinely shocked he felt his anger drain away, leaving a huge void within his emotions. Understanding might have filled it, pity even, but he knew he couldn't afford either. Not until he'd thought this through.

Not until he'd actually accepted the fact that this woman was carrying his child...

'We should go back,' he said, standing up and moving towards his horse.

'That's all you have to say?'

He swung back to face her.

'You've just told me you still can't fully believe it after four months and you expect me to have some thoughts on this situation after five minutes?'

'This situation!' She echoed the words so faintly he knew he'd hurt her as badly as the slashing of a knife would have hurt her flesh. Then she straightened her shoulders, and tilted her chin—the strong woman he'd known back in control.

'No, of course not. That was stupid of me,' she said. 'We'll go back.'

She walked across to where Mershinga waited patiently, unknotted the reins and mounted the quiet mare, the grace of her movements telling Arun how at ease she was on horseback.

And was he thinking that so he didn't have to think about her shocking revelation?

Probably!

He mounted Saracen and eased the big stallion alongside the mare.

'Boston?'

The quick glance she shot his way told him she'd understood the question. In fact, she half smiled in response, her shoulders lifting in a dismissive shrug.

'I did have enough functioning brain cells to realise that was impossible. As soon as I knew, I contacted the team leader to tell him I couldn't take the job. Junior members of the team are on retrieval duty and could be called out at any time of the day or night, flying anywhere in the United States to collect a donor heart. Not exactly the ideal situation for a single mother.'

'You could have hired a nanny. Surely you'd have to do that anyway, if you intend to keep on working.'

Was he still thinking she was after money? Mel wondered as the cool, unemotional remark reverberated through her head.

She tried for cool and unemotional herself.

'I do intend to keep on working—somehow, some time. I have to work, not just for my own personal satisfaction but because I'm good at what I do—very good—and to me it would be criminal to not continue, considering all the time and effort other people have put in to get me to this standard. How I'll juggle things I'm not quite sure, but at least, now that I've turned down the Boston job, I have some time to consider options.'

'You're not working at the moment? Not at all?'

Mel breathed deeply, though she was barely aware of the desert air. It was more a relieved kind of deep breath. Talking work was so much easier than talking babies.

'I'd resigned, knowing I was going. Lately, I've been doing on-call work—filling in for colleagues taking leave—making up an extra pair of hands when a team is short. The hospital where I'd been working wants me back, but...'

How to explain that she couldn't commit to full-time work right now? How to explain her determination that the child she carried would have a loving, at-home mother, not a part-time carer or a nanny, at least for the first months of its life?

How to explain anything when thinking that far ahead brought on the insane, irrational terror, so strongly felt it verged on a panic attack?

CHAPTER THREE

ARUN tried not to glance towards her as they rode back to the compound, but his gaze drifted sideways, seeking a change of body shape beneath the loose tunic top Melissa wore.

Nothing!

Which was hardly surprising.

What was surprising was his need to see the shape—his need for confirmation—as if only by seeing a slight swell in her belly could he really believe this was true.

He was intelligent to know this was his mind's way of putting off the moment when it had to consider exactly what this pregnancy meant to him, and for his mind and emotions to adjust to the fact that this woman was carrying his child.

If he could hold onto his anger—justified, surely, by her failure to tell him—it might help, but the anger was already fading, giving way to a kind of free-floating confusion, a state of mind foreign to him in recent years.

And if he was confused, how must Melissa feel—the career-woman with the huge prize of a job in a top paediatric surgical team suddenly snatched away from her?

Although it needn't have been...

She *could* have terminated the pregnancy and no one would have been any the wiser...

The conjecture made him realise just how little he knew of her, having seen only the strong, confident, independent and undeniably sexy woman who'd won applause for her presentation at the symposium, and been spoken of as one of the up-and-coming paediatric surgeons on the world stage.

They'd reached the compound and he held Saracen back to allow the mare to enter first, watching the way Melissa sat the horse, seeing the straight back and the erect carriage of her head. She may have shown weakness when she'd told him of the baby, but he sensed she was once again in control of her emotions.

Well in control, judging from the way she dismounted then turned, looking up at him.

'I won't say anything to Jenny just yet,' she said. 'It's taken me eight weeks to get as far as I have in considering this, I can at least give you a couple of days to decide what, if anything, you want to do.'

'What, if anything, I want to do?' Arun said. His brain must be floating more freely than he'd realised for the words made no sense whatsoever.

'I'm quite prepared to raise the child myself,' Melissa added, and he wondered if she could see the confusion in his voice mirrored in his eyes, for she continued, speaking quietly, 'I know things have changed for you since we met, and that you've been making plans for marriage. I don't want to interfere with that in any way. There's no need for you to have any involvement with this child if that's the way you want it. I'm not asking for support, either physical or financial, Arun, I just knew you had to know.'

'Knew I had to know? Not have any involvement?'

New anger raised his voice, and the sound brought a couple of lads running from the stables.

'We'll talk later,' Melissa said. 'Somewhere private. When you're ready.'

But would he ever be ready? he wondered as he dismounted.

Of course he would. He just had to think it through.

And get to work—he was already late.

And organise the setting up of the new unit at the hospital while Melissa was still in Zaheer to advise him.

And get through the family celebrations this evening, then Kam's wedding tomorrow.

A piece of cake—wasn't that the saying?

Melissa was watching him, as if waiting for a reply, but he had no words for her—not right now.

'I'll go back to the house,' she said at last. 'Jenny will be wondering where I've got to.'

She had turned to go when a woman came running towards the stables, calling his name.

'Your sister, sir. They said come quickly. The baby—'

The baby? Coincidence or fate that babies were dominating the morning?

'Problems?' Melissa queried as he hesitated, trying to switch his thoughts from one baby to another. 'Is she pregnant?'

'Due next month,' Arun replied, his mind now firmly on his sister as he followed the messenger back towards the women's house.

Melissa strode beside him so he explained.

'I've been keeping a special eye on her. The foetal heartbeat has been strange. Probably more your field than mine. And, of course, in the way of sisters, she believes more of what her gynaecologist tells her than her brother. And, being a male, I've not been allowed to listen to it except through her voluminous gowns so I could be wrong.'

He was hurrying, but Melissa was keeping up with him, and part of him was glad, although he hoped with all his heart there was nothing wrong with Tia's baby—hoped that having Melissa present at the birth would prove nothing more than an unnecessary distraction.

But he wanted her there—he *knew* that!

Mel followed him back to a house beside the one she'd spent the night in—Jenny's house, although it was hard to think of it that way. This one seemed even larger, and as she slipped off her shoes she smiled to see such a variety of footwear lined up there, from tiny child-sized sandals to designer scuffs. Was this the women's house that so many people were inside?

She followed Arun in, awed by how palatial it was. Built from the same sandstone blocks as Jenny's, with most of the outer stones ornately carved into open fretwork so air and light came through, the rooms themselves were beautiful in their simplicity. But the rich rugs scattered on the floors, the satin and velvet cushions thrown around, the vibrant hangings on the walls depicting vivid hunting and battle scenes—they all contributed to an overall impression of exotic magnificence.

'Oh, Arun, the baby's coming, it's early and the doctor isn't here. What will we do?'

Arun put his arm around the small, agitated woman who'd approached him, her hands held pleadingly in front of her. He spoke to her, soothing words Mel didn't understand, then added in English, 'Have you called Jenny?'

'She's with Tia now. And Jenny's mother, who says she has delivered more babies than she can count and we are not to worry, but how can I not worry about my daughter's first baby?'

'Of course you're entitled to worry,' he said gently, then spoke again in his own language.

'And this is Melissa,' he added, switching to English. 'Jenny's friend and a baby doctor. Shall I take her in?'

'Melissa, I am Miriam, Arun's aunt. It is my daughter Tia who is having the baby.' The woman held out a small bejewelled hand and Mel shook it gently, fearing she might break such a delicate structure.

'It is bad this has happened to disrupt your first day in our country,' she continued, leading the way through the huge room then down a corridor to the right. 'But so many doctors here for my daughter must be a good thing, mustn't it? Although, of course, Kam is away and Mr Dr Stapleton has not been involved. But still four, if she allows Arun in, that is.'

Her chatter failed to hide her anxiety, and Mel understood the fear Miriam must be feeling for her daughter.

Understood it only too well. She steeled herself against her own misgivings, reminding herself of all the births she'd witnessed, the babies she'd delivered before specialising. So few women died in childbirth these days, her fear was laughable.

But laughter was a long way off…

Needing a distraction, a focus for her attention, she turned to Miriam.

'Are you hoping for a girl or a boy?' she asked. 'Or do you know?'

'We know it is a boy and this is a wonderful thing.' The awe in the words told Mel this was important, a fact reinforced when Miriam continued, taking Arun's hand and looking up into his face.

'Strange, isn't it, my Arun, that after all the years I tried to have a son and failed, and my other daughters have all had girls, yet Tia's first should be a boy.'

They entered a room large enough to be a village hall, filled, it seemed to Mel, with swathed and twittering women. One said something and they all turned, some drawing their veils close around their heads at the sight of Arun, while others wore Western apparel of jeans and T-shirts and greeted him with easy familiarity.

'I had a lot of girls,' Miriam said, slightly apologetically. 'Although, of course, not all of the women in here are my children.'

But Mel's eyes had already picked out Jen and her mother, both bent over a woman crouched in a corner of the room. Arun went directly to the corner to comfort his sister—or if her mother was his aunt maybe Mel had got the relationship wrong and the woman was his cousin. Whatever the relationship was, the young—very young— woman was obviously glad to see him, grasping his hand and bursting into tears.

'Stay with me,' she begged, her American-accented English suggesting she'd been sent to school in the US rather than England.

Mel slipped past the pair, virtually unnoticed, and touched Jenny on the shoulder.

'Is everything OK?' she asked.

Jen nodded but looked so grave Mel guessed things were far from good.

'Mel, I'm so glad you're here. The delivery is going all right—the head's crowned and she's ready to push—but I can't hear a foetal heartbeat. Your speciality may be paediatric surgery but at least you've got the paeds qualifications.'

Jane was kneeling beside the crouching woman, her hands ready to take the baby's head as soon as it was delivered, while Jen and Arun between them supported Tia as she strained to ease her baby into the world.

Melissa went to a table to one side of the action, where a jug of water and a basin had been provided for handwashing. She used a liquid soap and wondered if germs would be the least of this new baby's worries. If Jen couldn't hear a heartbeat…

She was tipping water into the basin to rinse her hands when Tia screamed, and although Mel knew this was natural—few women gave birth silently—her heart rate accelerated and fear for the young woman made her hands shake.

Fortunately for her state of mind, the baby arrived in the next instant. Her own pregnancy was forgotten as the little boy was delivered, shown to his mother then, with the umbilical cord cut, he was swaddled in a soft cloth and Jen carried him to a side table, leaving her mother to manage the final stage of birth but signalling with her head for Mel to come closer.

'He's breathing but he's not a very satisfactory pink,' Jenny murmured to Mel, 'and his heartbeat…'

Melissa took over the examination. Many years ago a woman doctor called Virginia Apgar had worked out a scoring system for newborns and her system was still in use today. One minute after birth the infant was checked for heart rate, respiratory effort, muscle tone, response to stimuli and colour and given a score of zero, one or two for each check. The numbers were then added together. At one minute the score could still be low, but if it was still low after five minutes, the baby needed serious support.

'I'll suction him to make sure his trachea is clear, but he needs oxygen. Was the birth to be here or at a hospital? Would there be oxygen available here?' Jen shrugged and Mel turned towards Arun, who had helped his sister to her bed and was presumably explaining that all babies had to be examined after birth.

He caught her glance and left Tia with Miriam, who had followed them into the room.

'He needs oxygen—is there any on hand?' Mel asked, and was dismayed when Arun shook his head.

'Then an ambulance asap,' she added. 'We need to get him to hospital. His breathing's laboured, his heart's tachycardic, his Apgar is appalling—two at a minute and from the colour of his hands and feet it's not going to be much better at five minutes.'

'I'll get someone to call.'

But Mel had stopped listening, instead bending over the tiny baby to blow air gently into his labouring lungs, her whole being focussed on this fragile child.

Was it instinct that made Tia realise something was

wrong? The woman gave a wailing cry, and struggled to get out of bed.

'I'll talk to her,' Jen said. 'You keep blowing.'

Mel didn't need this advice. The first boy baby in Miriam's family for two generations could die if she didn't keep blowing so as to maximise the oxygen his body was labouring to take in.

Arun returned as she rested two fingers on the baby's chest to check his heart again.

Arun! Childbirth! Babies!

She brushed the thoughts aside, compartmentalising her mind, *this* baby her focus now.

'What do you think?' Arun asked, handing her a stethoscope.

'I've no idea but his heartbeat's way too irregular and his breathing is so laboured he's tiring himself out and that's putting more pressure on his heart.'

She put the stethoscope to her ears and listened to the baby's chest, concentrating on the echoing sounds. The first heart sound seemed normal then she heard a recognisable click as a defective truncal valve opened, followed by a second loud and single heart sound.

'You can't diagnose on heart sounds but he definitely needs some scans and tests,' she said. 'Here, you're the cardiologist—you listen.' She handed the stethoscope to Arun.

'Not good, is it?' he said quietly. Then, removing the stethoscope, he gently palpated the tiny chest with one long, slender forefinger.

'Feel here—a systolic thrill.'

Arun reached for Melissa's hand to guide it into place,

touching her as naturally as he would have any colleague, but as she nodded, her face grave, he remembered she was there as a guest—a bridesmaid for a wedding the following day.

And pregnant as well.

How could he ask for her help?

How could he not, when Tia's baby needed the kind of help only she, right here and now, could give?

He recalled seeing her hands tremble as she'd washed them, and wondered what inner strength she must have to continue to work in her field.

She may have said it didn't worry her, but how could she not wonder if her own child was not properly formed in some way?

His child!

And standing there beside her, watching as she breathed life-giving air into his nephew's lungs, the anger he thought he had under control surged through him and he growled under his breath…

Growling wasn't getting him anywhere, so Arun tried a brisk shake of his head in an attempt to clear his brain, unable to believe these niggling thoughts had invaded it at a time like this. His mind seemed to have split into two parts, one concentrated on the baby, the other filled with questions about this woman who'd come so unexpectedly back into his life.

Terrified?

Surely that was an absurd word for her to have used.

He watched her bend over the baby, continuing to blow gently into his tiny lungs.

'I'll get him to the hospital,' he said, following the most important train of thought in his head. 'The ambulance will have to take Tia as well—there's no way she'll leave the baby,' he added as Jenny returned to the table to check on the newborn's welfare.

'You've paediatric specialists? A paediatric ICU? Surgical specialists?' Mel asked.

'Of course not,' Jenny snapped. 'The new hospital was built by greedy foreign specialists, both men and women, who wanted to make money more than they wanted to help the local population. Kam and Arun were helpless to change things before their father died, and even now progress is slow. With Tia pregnant they did start by getting some O and G staff and putting in a maternity ward and nursery. On the plus side, the hospital has first-class operating theatres, all the fancy machines you'll need to scan and image the little one, and if you have to use the ICU set-up for men and women recovering from facelifts and tummy tucks, well, at least it's got great monitors.'

Mel turned to Arun who nodded glumly.

'Our country has taken a strange route from the past to the present. In the past babies were born at home and lived or died. People got sick and they too lived or died. Gradually, as local people trained in medicine, clinics were established in the towns, where sick people could be seen by doctors and nursed if necessary. In the city there was a hospital of sorts. Then what is called progress happened and a new hospital was built, but by private investors who wanted to make money out of their investment.'

'You've a hospital that was built for the sole purpose of making money?'

Arun shrugged, but Mel felt his shame so deeply she wanted to reach out and touch his shoulder.

Far better not to touch…

'We are renovating the old hospital now, and changing things in the new one. You know I'm a cardiologist and Kam's a general surgeon,' he continued, 'and now we have physicians working there and a system of residents and registrars—but we cannot run before we walk.'

Perhaps hearing the pain in his voice as he explained, Jen took over.

'Apart from the work Kam and Arun and the new staff do, most of the surgical work is cosmetic. People come from everywhere, particularly India and Africa, to be operated on by some of the best surgeons in the world—'

'But little babies who need urgent surgery die?'

Mel broke into Jen's explanation and Arun sighed in the face of her anger.

'We fly them out to a country—a hospital—that can help them whenever we can. Kam and I have been doing that for years—using our own plane. It's not perfect, but it often saves a life.'

'Not this life,' Mel said, picking up the tiny baby and swaddling the blanket around him. 'This one needs help now. Is the ambulance here yet?'

'It should be here any minute.'

It was a statement, but Mel heard more in the words.

An unspoken plea?

She turned towards him.

'Will you travel with it?' he asked. 'Help me examine the baby? I don't like to ask it of you, a visitor to our country, but…'

Mel turned and looked into his face, so full of concern,

and something that looked like embarrassment, as if he'd hated having to ask this of her—or any visitor.

'Of course I'll come,' she assured him, and now read relief in his eyes.

Had he doubted she'd help?

And could she blame him? In spite of the time they'd spent together—in spite of the child she carried—what did they know of each other?

Her thoughts were interrupted as two women in dark gowns came into the room, pushing a collapsible ambulance stretcher between them. Arun lifted the new mother onto it, explaining to her in his own language, soothing her agitation. He accompanied the stretcher and the women attendants towards the outer door, Mel following close behind with the baby.

'You don't have to do this,' Arun said, as if uncertain she was going willingly.

'It's what I do best,' she said, and smiled at him, the smile promising that for as long as it took to get this baby stable, all other matters would be set aside.

Mel was aware of others following, but it wasn't until she climbed into the ambulance that she realised all the women who had been in the room expected to come as well. Fortunately Jenny was there to sort things out and it was she who helped the ambulance women close the doors against the thrusting, noisy crowd.

The young mother looked fearfully from Arun to the baby in Mel's arms. Arun leaned forward and put his arm around his sister, holding her close to his chest while he spoke words Mel didn't understand. But even without knowing their meaning, she could hear the understanding, support and love he was offering, along with the heart-breaking news that all was not well with her new son.

The woman responded more loudly, angry words of denial, Mel guessed, then she pushed away from Arun and lay back on the trolley, her back turned to the man who'd tried to comfort her.

'Women ambulance attendants?' Mel queried, mainly to break the awkward silence that had grown to fog-like proportions in the cabin of the vehicle, interrupted only by the soft crying of the new mother.

'You don't have them in Australia?'

'Of course we do, but I suppose because they're usually paired with men I don't notice them as different.'

Arun smiled and Mel saw again the devastating looks and charm that had swept her off her feet—and into bed—four months ago.

Felt it too, in a rising heat deep within her body…

How absurd to be feeling such…lust was surely the only name for it in an ambulance screaming through the streets of a foreign country, a tiny, fragile baby held in her arms.

'Here, many women are still not used to being in the company of men from outside their family. For them it is easier to be tended by women, even in emergencies. You will see in the hospital—in the general part of it, not the specialist centre—that we are bringing in more women doctors and all our nurses are also women, although more men are now seeing nursing as a possible career path.'

Arun's explanation was so clear—his mind so obviously focussed on medicine—she felt ashamed of her reaction to that smile.

The ambulance slowed and the doors opened, and Mel experienced the familiar rush of an ambulance arrival at a major hospital. It was the same all over the world, except that here, as Arun stepped out to take the baby while Mel alighted and Tia was wheeled out, men and women bowed their heads, some murmuring words of respect.

'They forget this when I'm on the ward,' he said to Mel as she reached out to take the baby from him. 'There I'm treated with as much or as little respect as I happen to earn that particular day.'

She had to smile, although her anxiety for the tiny scrap of humanity in her arms was growing. His lips and tiny fingernails were now a deep blue, and his little heart raced so hard she could feel it thudding against his ribs.

Arun must have seen the anxious glance.

'X-ray first, then what?' he asked, as he led the way through a pristine A and E department and along a passageway, following the trolley with Tia on it. 'An echo? Intubation?'

'We need oxygen to blow across his face first to make sure he's maximising his oxygen intake. Then fluoroscopy to look at his heart,' Mel suggested. 'You have all the machines—CT scanners, MRI's?'

'All mod cons,' Arun remarked and Mel heard a tinge of bitterness and wondered just how hard his job must be, attempting to change the hospital from one of private, and probably exclusive, specialisation to a place where all the people of his country could and would be treated.

A caring man! This facet of his character shouldn't surprise her, but it did, making her realise how little she really knew of him.

Mel glanced his way as he spoke to a woman hovering beside them, studying the strong features, hearing authority in his voice, although he spoke quietly. The woman disappeared, then returned, wheeling a crib. It had an oxygen bottle attached and Mel turned her full attention back to the infant, putting the tiny boy into the crib and adjusting the flow of oxygen so it blew across his face.

The woman moved to push the crib but Mel gently eased her aside.

'I'll take him,' she said, anxious to keep watch on him at all times.

They went up in a lift then out into a wide corridor, where Tia was wheeled into a large private room and transferred to the bed.

'Would she like to hold the baby while we organise things—or you organise things?' Mel suggested.

Arun took the baby's crib over close to the bed and spoke to Tia, who shook her head violently and let fly another barrage of words, these sounding harsh and guttural.

'She doesn't want to hold him because then she will love him and if he dies, if we kill him with what we are doing, she will be heart-broken.'

The stark statement made Mel pause and she looked up to see the sudden fear she was feeling mirrored in Arun's eyes.

'We *could* kill him,' she murmured helplessly. 'Babies do die in our attempts to save them.'

Arun nodded, then said, 'But if it was your baby, would you not at least try to save him?'

Mel's hand went automatically to her stomach, the protective gesture not lost on Arun.

'I don't know how you can continue to do this work,' he said quietly, and she shook her head, understanding that he thought her fear was for the baby when in reality it was far more selfish—a totally irrational fear for herself. Although that was wrong—it wasn't for herself but for the baby, in that he or she would be motherless if...

CHAPTER FOUR

MEL blocked it all from her mind.

'The tests—we need to start at once,' she reminded him. 'Where do we go?'

He nodded agreement and led her from the room, but the quick glance he'd shot her told her he knew she'd ignored his statement.

And that the conversation wasn't finished.

The radiology department was as up to date as Jenny had said it would be, and technicians, no doubt alerted by Arun, were on standby. Mel explained the views she'd need, and left the baby with the radiologist while she and Arun studied the pictures on the screen.

'His heart's enlarged,' Arun said, using his pen to outline it. 'But it's hard to see clearly. We need an echo?'

'Just a minute,' Mel said, watching the image change. 'See there.'

She took Arun's pen and pointed. 'It's blurry but it seems to me there's only one blood vessel coming out of the heart.'

'Truncus arteriosus?' Arun's voice was grave. 'We should fly him out.'

'To where? How far does he have to go to a specialist centre with a heart bypass machine? Because he'll need open-heart surgery, Arun, and need it soon—and I have concerns about flying so fragile a baby anywhere.'

'Can you be sure that's what it is?'

He wasn't doubting her, Mel knew, just reminding her there were more tests available.

'No, but we'll do an echo, that should tell us, and just to make sure, an MRI scan. They're all non-invasive and can be done quickly. I could do a cardiac catheterization, which would show the extent of the malformation, but I'd rather not put him through that if we don't have to.'

Arun spoke to the technician who wheeled an echocardiogram machine close to the crib and rubbed gel on the baby's chest. Once again Mel and Arun watched the monitor, although they would get all the results printed out and would be able to study and compare them later.

'See,' Mel said, again using the pen. 'One thick artery coming out of the heart and, here, a hole between the two ventricles.'

'We have a heart bypass machine.'

His voice was strained, as if the words had been forced out of him against his will.

And Mel understood why. He was a proud man, brought up in the ruling family of his country. To ask a favour of someone would be very, very hard.

And, she guessed, asking a favour of a woman would be even harder.

She turned her attention from the screen to his face, wiped clean of any emotion, although his eyes told of his stress.

'You want me to do it?'

'You're very good, I've heard enough of you to know that, seen DVDs of your work. And your ambition has always been to have your own paediatric surgical unit, to be the head of one with all the best equipment money can buy so babies from your regional hospital don't have to be sent to other places. If you are willing to do this for us, whether the baby lives or dies, I will guarantee you the equipment you need to achieve that ambition.'

Mel stared at him in disbelief.

'You're bribing me? You're bribing me to do an operation to save a baby's life?'

She wasn't sure if the radiologist and technician understood English, but she was so angry she didn't care.

'How could you think so little of me that you'd offer me money? It's a baby's life we're talking about here, not some pathetic tummy tuck!'

Arun held up his hands in surrender.

'It is asking too much of you—you're a visitor in our country, a guest. It is not your problem.'

He was losing ground with every word, but his pride and his upbringing made the situation impossible. He was a giver of favours, not one who asked for them, and this woman had already thrown him off balance once today.

Badly off balance…

He fought back the memory of her revelation and concentrated on what she was saying.

'Forget asking too much of me, and start thinking of how to get what we'll need. Two weeks after birth is the optimal time for a truncus arteriosus repair because if we leave it longer than that the increased pressure on the pulmonary arteries and other pulmonary vessels can cause irreversible damage. What we need to do is get him as strong and stable as we can in that time…'

'You can stay that long?'

He realised as soon as he'd asked the question that it had been stupid. Surely, given the circumstances of her pregnancy, she must have arranged to stay at least that long so they could discuss the future of their child. Or had she intended telling him then departing as soon as possible?

'I can stay.'

Her eyes defied him to question that statement but once again his mind seemed to have divided, one part concentrated on Tia's baby and the operation he would require, the other on the unbelievability of what was happening here. First the woman he'd thought never to see again reappearing in his life.

Carrying his child!

No, he couldn't afford to think about that right now.

But add the fact that she was the one person this baby needed to save his life, and here she was, right on hand to do the operation.

It *had* to be fate.

He followed the practical part of his mind, locking down the fate-flustered one in a distant corner.

'So what will you need?'

'*We* will need either a very small donated human artery with an intact valve for a homograft or a very small dacron artery with a manufactured valve.' She emphasised the 'we' just enough to let him know he was going to be taking equal responsibility for this operation. 'A donated human artery is best if you can get one small enough because it has the ability to develop normally so might reduce the need for further operations as he grows.'

'Kam and I, working with our own staff, have been cryo-preserving donated tissues for more than a year now. I'm sure we'd have what you need. And what about the patch for the hole between the left and right ventricles?'

'I should be able to use a piece of the pericardial sac, which will save any rejection problems, otherwise we can fix it with…'

She paused, and studied Arun's face, although he doubted she was seeing it, simply using it as a focus as she thought ahead.

'Sometimes we leave it open for a while in case the new artery causes high ventricular pressure but, no, I think we should close it if we can.'

'And for now?'

'Ah!'

Melissa looked down at the tiny baby in the crib. He would need to be as strong as possible before the operation, so optimal oxygen intake, some medication to help the heart work more efficiently and not over-strain, and adequate nutrition through high-calorie formula or breast-milk, possibly with supplemental feedings.

'Would Tia nurse him?' Mel quietly asked Arun, remembering how the young woman had reacted to being asked to hold the baby.

Arun looked from Mel to Tia then back to Mel.

'I doubt it, but I could ask.'

Mel shook her head.

'Let's not upset her any more, but maybe if we can

arrange to care for the baby here in her room, she might grow interested enough to want to hold him.'

Arun nodded, then *he* shook his head.

'You are one amazing woman,' he said, startling Mel because he sounded as if he really meant it and *that* made her feel all warm and fuzzy inside.

Dangerous stuff, warm and fuzzy!

'I'm not doing any more than anyone would,' she told him, hoping she sounded practical enough to hide her reaction. 'We can put in a nasogastric tube to feed him, which will save him using what little energy he has sucking either a breast or a bottle, and I need an IV line and an oximeter to keep an eye on the oxygenation of his blood and...'

She paused, wondering what else the fragile infant would need.

'And?' Arun prompted.

Mel shook her head.

'I want to keep things as minimally invasive as possible to give him every chance to get stronger. From a purely cardiac point of view, what do you think?'

'Let's get someone in to watch him so we can sit down somewhere quiet and work out a plan, looking at what we hope to achieve before the operation and what negatives might make it impossible to leave it for two weeks.'

He didn't wait for her answer but disappeared out the door, leaving Mel with the baby, and his mother, who lay with her face turned to the wall.

Having assured herself the baby was managing as well as could be expected, Mel crossed to sit beside the new mother.

'This is so hard for you—I can understand that—but

I'm nearly sure we can fix what's wrong with him. Had you chosen a name?'

Dark eyes opened and were soon awash with tears.

'I cannot give him the name,' Tia whispered. 'It is the name my husband chose, and if the baby dies he will want it for the next baby.'

'Oh, love,' Mel said, putting her arm around the young woman's shoulders, overwhelmed by the sadness in Tia's voice. 'This isn't your fault, you know. Babies are often born not quite right. No one is to blame.'

Seeing this comfort wasn't working, Mel tried another tack.

'Where *is* your husband? Are husbands not allowed to be present at the baby's birth in your culture? Is that why he's not here?'

The dark hair moved from side to side then Tia raised her head again.

'He's in America. He's studying. His father said he had to stay there—that he couldn't come home just to be with me for the baby's birth. I should have gone with him and been there and had the baby in an American hospital, but when I went to America before, I was so homesick I said I wouldn't go.'

Mel gave her a comforting pat.

'Where you had the baby wouldn't have made any difference,' she explained. 'This is something that happens when you are very newly pregnant, maybe eight weeks or so—the little heart just doesn't develop properly. But I have operated on babies as small as yours to fix their hearts, and they have been perfectly all right later.'

This time Tia turned right around and even hitched herself up on her pillows.

'You have? You can operate on tiny babies and fix their hearts?'

Hope crept cautiously into the words and flickered in the dark, tear-washed eyes.

'I have, and I can,' Mel told her, stroking Tia's long hair back from her face and smiling gently at the young woman.

'And you can fix my baby?'

Arun, returning to the room with one of his most trusted nurses, saw the improvement in his sister then heard the question and read Melissa's dilemma in her hesitation.

Would she lie?

He rather doubted it but for a moment he wished she would, just to keep Tia from diving back into the depths of misery.

'I cannot promise that, but more than ninety per cent of babies we operate on for this condition do survive. In fact, they not only survive, they thrive. It will take a little time, he'll need to be specially cared for before and after the operation, just for a few days, then another week in hospital. Later on, there are infections he might be susceptible to, and as he grows he might need another operation, but there's no reason he won't do well.'

Arun remained where he was, his arm held out to prevent Zaffra from entering the room. Melissa seemed to have worked some kind of miracle in getting Tia interested in the baby, and he didn't want to interrupt until he was sure the conversation was finished.

'I heard Arun say you must talk about what you have to do. Can I hold him—the baby—while you talk?'

Arun felt a grin as wide as the desert split his face and saw similar delight in the way Melissa hugged Tia.

'Of course you can. I'll put him in your arms then fix the oxygen so it blows across his face. That way most of what he breathes is pure oxygen, which will ease the workload on his heart.'

She crossed the room and gently wrapped the swaddling cloth around the infant then lifted him from his warmed mattress, carrying him across to his mother, who would warm him with her body.

'You take your time to look at him,' she told Tia. 'Later we'll put a feeding tube into his nose and he'll have to wear a nappy so we can work out how much fluid he's losing, but for now just hold him and marvel at the miracle a new baby is.'

Arun brought Zaffra forward and introduced her to both women then, while Melissa placed the oxygen tube from the wall unit so it would blow across the baby's face, Arun watched Tia's bemusement as she examined her little son.

'But he looks perfect,' she said, after checking all the limbs and digits were in place. 'Except his little feet are blue and his fingernails and lips.'

And Arun was pleased to see she was right. The baby had finally achieved some pinkness in the rest of his body so the oxygen was working.

'Later,' he told his sister, 'when Melissa and I have talked, I will sit down and explain what is wrong and how we fix it. I will draw you a picture so you understand and can show Sharif when he comes home.'

Tia nodded and, satisfied his sister was now as comforted as it was possible to be with a very sick baby on her hands, Arun touched Melissa on the shoulder and indicated they should leave.

'We won't be long,' she promised, turning back as she reached the door to reassure Tia once again.

Tia smiled as if confident Melissa meant exactly what she'd said.

'Working miracles with mothers now, are you?' he asked Melissa as he led the way down the corridor to his suite of rooms.

'It's hard for them,' was all the reply he got, and he turned back to see that, far from looking happy at what she'd achieved, Melissa looked…depressed?

Sad, anyway. Sad enough for him to want to put his arms around her, draw her close and hold her until the sadness went away.

Hold her?

Madness lay that way!

But sadness?

'Is it worse than you've been saying, the baby's heart?' It was a guess, and he knew it was the wrong one when she shook her head.

'No, it's the grief,' she said, studying his face as if hoping to see understanding there.

But how could she when he didn't understand what she meant?

'Grief?'

'Think about it, Arun,' she continued. 'A woman goes into labour, goes through childbirth, and though it's messy and painful at least there's joy at the end—a healthy baby to hold and cherish. For Tia, and mothers like her, where the outcome's not as good, she has to suffer the loss of that healthy baby she was expecting—she has to grieve for it. And while grieving, it is hard to accept the other baby— the one she did have—the one that's fragile and in need of care she has to rely on strangers to provide.'

He stared at her, then shook his head.

'I can't believe I've never thought of it that way,' he murmured, awed by the depth of her understanding and feeling something for this woman that went beyond renewed attraction.

This pregnant woman, he reminded himself as she let him off the hook with a smile.

'Your heart patients are usually a whole lot older and often victims of their own over-indulgence, so you see heart problems from a different perspective.'

He nodded acceptance of her excuse, but now his brain had thrown up the fact of her pregnancy once again and the knowledge that it was his baby she carried hit him like a shock from a faulty electrical connection.

His *baby*—she was carrying *his* baby!

OK, he could just about accept that, but how he felt about it—that was the problem. Would his thoughts become clearer as his mind reached full acceptance?

Would it have been easier to think about it if Tia's baby hadn't arrived so inopportunely?

What he did know was that this was hardly the time to be working out what he felt, let alone what he intended doing about it…

'So, a plan,' Melissa said, as Arun resumed their walk towards his office, finally opening a door and waving her into a large room, furnished with a wide desk littered with papers, and a leather-clad lounge suite set around a coffee-table.

A coffee-pot, cups and trays with a selection of cakes and fruit had been set out on the table.

'I thought you might need a snack,' he said, leading her towards one of the comfortable-looking chairs. 'It is terrible that we have whisked you from the stables to the hospital with no time for you to relax, to bathe and change, or even to eat something. So sit, eat, and then we'll talk. I had coffee sent up but if you'd prefer tea or a cold drink of some kind...'

Mel shook her head, although now she was away from the baby and had relaxed slightly, she realised she was starving.

'Coffee's fine, but with a lot of milk, if you have it,' she said, sliding into the big armchair and leaning forward to examine the enticing-looking pastries on display. 'And these are?'

'Various sweet treats, mostly flavoured with rose or orange syrup and honey, but also with nuts sprinkled between the layers of pastry. You will find similar pastries right across the Middle East, all the way through to Greece in Europe and Morocco in North Africa.'

Mel chose a pastry and bit into it, feeling the sweetness fill her mouth then honey dribble from her lips.

Arun came closer, a serviette in his hand, but rather than hand it to her he caught the tiny drop of honey on it, his fingers brushing the soft paper of the napkin across her lips at the same time. His body bent over her, his face close enough for her to see the stubble of beard and the shadow of tiredness beneath his eyes—lines of strain that had not been there when they'd met four months ago.

The time had not been kind to him and she felt a surge of sympathy. If health care in his country was as neglected as Jenny said, he must have enormous worries on his shoulders.

But he was also close enough for her to see, as he bent towards her, desire leaping in his eyes, a desire that was echoed in her body.

Her nipples peaked and her breasts swelled as anticipation tingled through her body.

Would he kiss her again?

Would she respond?

Wouldn't kissing Arun just make things more complicated?

Then, with his lips close enough to kiss if she straightened just a little, he moved away, leaving her feeling a sudden sense of loss.

Stupid! Irrational! How could she even think of kisses at a time like this?

'Arun?'

His name escaped in a sigh so soft Arun was sure she hadn't meant to say it but he responded anyway, bending over her again to brush the honey-tasting lips with his. To brush her name, 'Melissa', on them.

The chemistry that had worked between them from their first meeting flared back to life. Arun's hand slid around the back of her head, his fingers weaving into her hair, holding her captive.

Or was it *her* clasp on *his* head that held them together?

The kiss deepened, Arun feeling the power of it as desire shuddered through his body, tightening his muscles and heating his blood.

This was madness.

The baby…

They should stop…

She broke away from the kiss but not before he'd felt enough of her response to know the chemistry still worked for her as well. Now, leaning back in her chair, defiance shaded the desire he knew he'd read in her eyes.

'We have to talk about the baby,' she said. 'About Tia's baby.'

'And your baby? The one you say is mine? When will we talk of it?'

'The one I *say* is yours?'

Her disbelief was like another person in the room yet, now the words were out, he realised he did have doubts. With reason, for how could he be sure?

'How do I know you didn't take another lover immediately after me? Or have one before me, close enough that you can pass off the child you carry as mine?'

He spoke coldly, the words damning her, but surely he was right to be suspicious. Her reaction was immediate— the fire of anger in her eyes and fury in every line of her body as she rose to her feet and glared across the table at him.

'My love life is not, and never has been—apart from ten short days—any of your business, but I can assure you the baby is yours.' She spat the words at him, as angry as a mal-treated cat—her hands clenched, perhaps to stop her clawing him as well as mauling him with words. 'Now it's up to you. I will pretend you didn't say what you just said to me and we sit down and discuss the baby's problems—Tia's baby's problems—and together work out a treatment plan, or you call your pilot and get the plane ready to fly him out.'

She was right—Tia's baby was the issue. How could he have been so easily diverted?

Because he'd kissed her?

Tasted honey on her lips?

Felt the frantic beat of need in both their bodies?

Or because he was beginning to accept that what she'd said was true—that she carried his child? Added to which was the fact that, while in theory marrying and having a child was all very well, in reality the thought of fatherhood was very unsettling. What did he know about raising a child? Could he, who'd barely known his father, be a good father to a child?

He nodded stiffly, waited until she seated herself again, then sat opposite her, outwardly calm—he hoped—but inwardly churning with such a tumult of emotions he couldn't put names to them.

Mel watched him settle back in his chair. She took a deep breath, trying to calm her thudding heart, to settle the fear and hurt she felt inside.

But she hadn't got to where she was, a top paediatric heart surgeon, without being able to hide her emotions successfully. She hid them now and matched his earlier coldness with her own.

'So, shall we discuss this case?'

He hesitated long enough for her to realise few people gave him orders, but in the end he nodded.

And scowled at her.

Ignoring the scowl, she leant forward, opened the file and spread the prints on the table.

'You can see here the artery leaves the ventricles as one big trunk, and here, the hole in the ventricular wall. The problem is that too much blood is flowing through the pulmonary arteries where they branch here...' she pointed with a pen that had been beside the file on the table '...into the lungs, causing congestive heart failure. From the look of this there's a narrowing of the aortic arch as well, so the heart is having to work extra hard to get blood flowing around the rest of the body.'

'And the operation?'

She glanced up at the interruption, pleased he had switched his attention from personal matters, feeling her own inner agitation ease as they spoke professionally.

'I need to detach the pulmonary artery from the main artery and use a small piece of artery with valves intact to connect it the right ventricle, stitch it in place there, fix the hole between the ventricles and patch up the aorta where I've detached the pulmonary artery.'

'That's a huge operation for so young a child,' he said, frowning over the scans, following the lines she'd drawn with the pen. 'Saying it like that, you make it sound simple, but for an infant...'

He lifted his head to look at her, and Mel read the doubt in his eyes—doubt and pain.

'There's a ninety per cent success rate,' she said, to quell the doubt. The pain was something else. 'She means a lot to you, Tia?'

This time he looked surprised, then he offered Mel a twisted kind of smile, so sad it nearly broke her heart.

'Tia's mother, Miriam, was my father's favourite wife. She was also more a mother to Kam and me than our own mother was. Tia was an afterthought, the last child of my father, and Kam and I, when we came home from school in England, regarded her as our special pet—a living doll, I suppose, although boys are not meant to play with dolls.'

'Boys can play with anything they like,' Mel replied gently, hearing the pain and loneliness of the child he'd been behind the simple explanation. 'And this boy will, too, because we're going to fix his heart,' she added, to get them back on track. Feeling sorry for this man was a sure way to disaster. She was already doomed to feel attraction—but sympathy? Empathy?

Way too dangerous!

'For now we need to keep an eye on his oxygen saturation. Because of the hole in the ventricular wall, the oxygen-rich blood from his lungs is mixing with the oxygen-depleted blood from his body, which means the blood going into the aorta isn't as oxygen-rich as it should be.'

She glanced across at him and smiled.

'Teaching my grandmother to suck eggs, aren't I?' she said.

'Your grandmother to what?'

'It's an old expression—telling you things you already know.'

He returned her smile—with interest apparently because it made her forget all the reasons she didn't want to be attracted to Arun again.

Although, now he knew about the pregnancy...

Was she mad?

Of course they couldn't continue their affair. It would complicate matters far too much.

And, no doubt, start the dreams again—dreams where he held her in his arms, and brought such sensual joy to her body...

'I thought we were sensibly discussing the baby's case,'

he said quietly, and she looked across at him and saw a smirk that suggested he'd read her momentary distraction with ease.

'We are!' she protested, but it was a feeble effort. Somehow she had to shut away all memory of the past and concentrate on the present—now. 'I was saying how I needn't explain it all to you.'

'Ah, but you do, because although I know what is wrong and what must happen, hearing you explain will help me tell Tia.'

Mel understood and continued to run through the regimen the baby would need, with tube feedings for maximum nutrition, ACE inhibitors to dilate the blood vessels and make it easier for the heart to pump blood through the body, digoxin to strengthen the heart muscle, diuretics to help the kidneys remove excess fluid.

'So, we organise all of this now, and have nurses rostered on to keep an eye on him at all times,' Arun said. 'What about a doctor? Do you want a registrar to keep an eye on him? We could fly in a paediatric registrar.'

'You could? From where? Do you pluck them out of the air?'

She was teasing him, Arun knew, and for a moment he wondered if they could get back to where they'd been, not necessarily lovers again but two adults enjoying each other's company, talking and laughing easily, discussing every subject under the sun.

Except the future, which had been off limits, for they'd agreed that what they'd both wanted had been a brief affair. And if, in retrospect, it had seemed much more than that...

He forced his mind back to practicalities, at the same time registering that very soon the future would *have* to be discussed.

The baby's future—*his* baby's future…

'As I said, Kam and I have been working on changes at the hospital. The maternity ward came first, but paediatrics was to come next. We have been interviewing applicants for the positions available—a paediatrician and three paediatric registrars—and I am sure at least one of those we've short-listed could come immediately.'

'That would be great.' She sounded genuinely pleased so he wouldn't mention that money might have to change hands to achieve this as quickly as possible. Mention of money—or of what money could provide for her—had upset her earlier, despite his experience of women suggesting they were far more practical about gifts or payments for services than men were.

But this woman was unlike any woman he'd ever known—the dreams that had cursed his nights for the past four months had been enough to tell him that. And though, whenever he'd considered following up on their brief affair—maybe flying to Australia to see her—he'd ruthlessly dismissed the thought as a passing fancy, he'd known the attraction went deep.

Now she was here.

Carrying his child…

And about as friendly as a hungry barracuda!

'I will get moving on the medications first. You will fit the feeding tube? Should he be sedated for that?'

'A mild sedative.' She picked up a pen and turned over one of the printouts to write a list of what she'd need on the back of it, but as she pushed it across the table to him, their fingers touched. She drew her hand back as though she'd been burned and Arun knew she'd felt the searing awareness that had shot through his own blood at the touch.

'No,' she said, answering a question he hadn't asked. 'Later, when we have this baby stable, that's when we'll talk.'

He took the list and guided her back to Tia's room, leaving her there with the two women and the baby while he went to organise first the equipment and drugs and then another doctor so Melissa wouldn't have to spend all her time at the hospital.

Although he suspected she was conscientious enough to want to be here a lot of the time.

Which meant that, apart from the promised talk, he'd see precious little of her, as all her spare time would, naturally, be spent with Jenny, preparing for the wedding, doing girl things…

By the time he returned to Tia's room, it was filled with relatives. At least the hospital had been built with local customs in mind so the rooms were big enough for a mass of family to squeeze in, but to intubate a fragile baby with such chaos all around?

'I know I said it would be good for the baby to stay with Tia,' Melissa said, when he'd battled through the crowds to the side of the crib where she was fending off women who wanted to hold the newborn, 'but this is impossible, and he really needs to be monitored. An ICU room perhaps, but one somewhere not too far away so Tia can visit and sit with him, just her and maybe Miriam, not the whole family.'

'It will be hard to explain that to them,' Arun said, 'but, yes, you're right. We need to move him. Come.'

He handed the equipment he'd brought with him to Zaffra and pushed the crib from the room, calling back to Tia that he would come back and see her very soon.

CHAPTER FIVE

'Is it always like that in your hospital?' Mel asked, as she once again followed Arun along a wide corridor.

'The family thing?' he asked, glancing back over his shoulder and smiling at her. 'Pretty much. It's harder to handle at night when the lights are dimmed because family members tend to sleep on the floor of the hospital room and you can trip over them if you're not careful.'

They reached a double door, which Arun pushed open with one shoulder, and Mel followed him into a very modern ICU, the nurses at the central desk watching monitors, while other nurses could be seen through the windows that gave clear views into the patient rooms.

'This first room is empty and there's a procedure room beside it. We'll take him in there first to fit the feeding tube and a port for drugs, then hook him up to the monitors in the room.'

He led her into a small but well-equipped procedure room, then, to Mel's surprise, he swept off his shirt then stripped off his jeans.

'I should have changed earlier but there didn't seem to be time,' he said, no doubt reading surprise in her eyes.

But he'd read wrongly this time, for she was mesmerised not by him changing clothes but by the sight of his strongly muscled chest, his skin gleaming with good health, dark against the stark white underwear he wore.

Mesmerised by memories...

The desire she'd battled to keep at bay since first they'd met again erupted in her body, and it was only as he turned towards the sink to scrub that she remembered where she was, and what she was supposed to be doing.

She crossed the room to scrub beside him, then realised she, too, must smell of horse. He'd pulled a scrub suit from a cupboard by the sink—there'd be another one there. But though at times throughout her training she'd often shared a changing room with men, she was suddenly shy at the thought of disrobing in front of Arun.

Maybe he wouldn't look...

If she did it quickly...

Was she mad? There was a baby here in need of help— *that* was the issue, not her, or Arun, or modesty, or anything else.

She found a scrub suit, stripped off her loose tunic and trousers and pulled on the suit before joining him at the sink, using the foot pedal to get water, scrubbing her hands and arms, the motions automatic as she'd done it so often before.

'Have you been well in your pregnancy?' he asked, and Mel turned to stare at her companion. It seemed the most unlikely of questions, but she could read no hidden message on his face.

'Fighting fit,' she told him, rinsing off the soap and bumping the hot air dryer with her shoulder to set it going.

He was pulling on a glove from the dispenser on the

wall, taking two from the box next to it—mediums—and handing them to her.

'That's good,' he said, and once again Mel searched his face, certain this weird conversation must have a hidden agenda.

But all she saw was the strong-planed features that had first attracted her, the slightly hooked nose that had suggested arrogance though he'd never directed it at her, the unusual green eyes, pale and beautiful, and the lush lips whose magical powers had driven her body to distraction.

She crossed back to tend the baby, looking first at what Zaffra had laid out on the treatment table, taking the baby's chart to check his weight so she could calibrate the strength of the drugs she would give him, measuring him so she knew how long to make his feeding tube, thinking all the time of the problems that could arise and how to circumvent them if she could.

They worked well together, Arun decided as he held the sedated baby while Melissa inserted the feeding tube and taped it into place. She'd already slid a cannula into a vein on the back of one tiny hand and taped it into place, splinting the little arm so the access port couldn't be accidentally dislodged.

Now, as Zaffra settled him back on the warmed mattress of the crib, Melissa bent over the table, writing furiously, doing sums and checking them, working out dosages and feeding formulas, Arun guessed, although she was too absorbed in her work to explain.

So absorbed she probably didn't realise she was chewing slightly on her bottom lip as she worked.

He'd chewed gently on that lip, he remembered. It had

been late one night, and they'd attended lectures during the day but had skipped the formal dinner, going off instead to a little waterside restaurant he'd heard was good. They'd walked back along the beach towards the hotel, rounding an outcrop of rocks and coming to a smaller cove, so deserted, so enticing, they'd stripped off and swum.

That had been when he'd nibbled on her lip. Nibbled on it as he'd held her close, making love in the water…

Making love in the water!

Unprotected!

He'd half remembered earlier—an instance of stupidity—but hadn't placed it until now. Although it hadn't seemed like stupidity at the time.

Madness perhaps, but not stupidity.

And now?

So the baby *could* be his and she *hadn't* told him!

For four months she hadn't told him.

He couldn't think about it right now, not with Melissa standing there, looking at him as if expecting some reply.

Had she asked a question?

About the baby?

It had to be.

'He's left us for another planet,' Mel said to Zaffra. 'So maybe you can tell me what formula you have in the maternity ward for newborn babies.'

'There are many—come and see,' Zaffra suggested.

Mel glanced at Arun, who was looking slightly less thunderous than he had a little earlier, though still angry enough to bite if teased.

'Will you hook him up to the monitors while I check out the formulas?' she asked.

He frowned at her so fiercely she wondered if it had sounded like an order instead of a request, but in the end he nodded abruptly then leant over the crib, moving it towards the wall where the monitors stood.

Two hours later they had the baby hooked up to monitors, nurses rostered to be with him at all times, feeding and medication regimens in place, and the little boy as safe and stable as they could make him.

'Come, I will take you back to Jenny's house,' Arun said, as Mel leant over the crib for the hundredth time, checking and rechecking, worrying and wondering. Had she done all she could? Would he be all right? Should she—?

'I don't know if I should leave him,' she responded worriedly. 'Not for any length of time. Jenny spoke of a party tonight—I should go to that, she'd be disappointed if I didn't, but to leave him now, just like that...'

Arun frowned at her

'You're tired—probably jet-lagged. You need to rest for a short time at least or you'll be little use to the baby.'

And as he said it, exhaustion hit her like a bus, her limbs suddenly too heavy to move. But she had to find the strength to argue.

'You're right, but what if the baby needs me? If something goes wrong?'

The look on Arun's face softened.

'You would not trust a cardiologist to watch over him?' he teased, and it must have been the tiredness that made her feel warmed and cherished by his tone. But then the meaning of his words sank in.

'*You'll* stay?' She stared at him and imagined she saw a shadow cross his face.

'You sound surprised,' he said, the coolness back in his voice suggesting the shadow had been hurt—a suggestion made fact when he continued. 'Do you think I care less for my nephew and my sister's peace of mind than you, a stranger, would?'

Mel shook her head and reached out to touch his scrub-suit-clad arm.

'I'm sorry. You're right. I *am* tired, also desperately in need of a bath and change of clothes and even some food if that's possible. Do you have on-call rooms where I can rest? Is there somewhere I can grab a sandwich?'

A stream of words she didn't understand greeted her questions, but the angry shaking of Arun's head told her it was probably just as well she didn't understand.

'On-call rooms? Grab a sandwich? Do you think we treat our guests so poorly?'

Then his voice softened and he smiled and lifted his hand to touch her cheek.

'Although we have treated you poorly, have we not, Melissa? Rushing you to the house to help the baby, bringing you here and feeding you nothing more than a pastry.'

Arun looked at her, at the wild red-gold curls escaping the theatre cap she'd pulled on earlier, at the pale, pale skin and grey-blue shadows beneath her eyes.

'At least I can offer you something more comfortable than an on-call room. Kam and I have an apartment on the top floor that we share from time to time, although it's rare both of us are there together. It's a convenience, you understand. I'll take you there, show you around, and by the time you are bathed, there will be food.'

'That sounds great,' she said, although the words were

hesitant—the hesitation explained when she added, 'But won't that put you out? Wouldn't you want to use the apartment yourself?'

'I will stay near my sister and the baby,' he said, then couldn't help himself. 'So you will be perfectly safe.'

Bright colour rose beneath the pale skin.

'I'm sorry—I didn't mean it that way. I know you are an honourable man. It's…'

And he knew exactly what it was, because now, though both of them were tired and worried, the attraction that from the first had arced through the air between them was still alive and well, stirring, teasing, tantalising and tempting both of them.

He smiled, then leant forward and kissed her gently on the lips.

'There will be other times to finish that sentence. Other times for the talk you know we have to have, Melissa. But for now a bath, food and rest. Come.'

He led her along more corridors, then up in a lift, along another corridor and finally opened a door that led into a spacious living room, a wall of glass at the far side revealing the city spread out beneath them.

'Sit,' Arun commanded, and Mel was glad to obey. But he returned within minutes, held out his hand to help her to her feet, then led her to a bathroom where a rectangular tub was already half-filled with water. And floating on the top of the water, leaves—perhaps the source of the soft and subtle perfume that permeated the room.

'Towels, soap, lotions and a bathrobe.'

Arun waved his hand towards a white marble bench where these and more were laid out. Bottles of every shape, beautifully coloured, like precious jewels, lined another, smaller ledge of marble higher up.

'New toothbrush, hairbrush. Anything you can't find, just press the button by the bath—and, no, it won't be me who comes to tend you but our maid.' He shot Mel a grin that would have done the devil proud. 'Your chaperone.'

And tired though she was, she had to smile back.

'If she lives here in this apartment, I'm sure she's well trained to notice nothing.'

'Maybe,' he said, but his smile had faded.

But no sooner had he shut the door than the conversation was forgotten. Mel stripped off the scrub suit and her undies, thinking she'd throw the lot away. Then, realising she might need the undies when she dressed again later, she soaked them in the washbasin, squirting hair shampoo in with them to make suds.

Then she turned off the taps and climbed into the bath, feeling the warm water envelop her weary body, feeling the tiredness leach from her skin as she relaxed back, her head against a slightly cushioned end. A bottle of bath gel was near to hand and she soaped herself all over, then relaxed again, letting the water wash the soap away.

Relaxed...

She'd been far too long! Had she fallen asleep? Fool that he was! He should made sure Olara stayed with Melissa while she bathed. But he'd sent Olara out to buy some clothes for their guest and Arun had assured her he could look after Melissa.

Did that include checking if she'd drowned in the bath?

He'd knock.

No answer.

He slid the door open, saying her name, softly at first and then more loudly, but she didn't hear, not because, as his first heart-stopping thought had been, she'd drowned, but because she was so deeply asleep.

And so nakedly beautiful his heart stopped again, though only for a moment, before speeding up, thudding with desire—terrible in a man who had guaranteed her sleep.

But as his gaze slid across her body, the shame he should and did feel turned to fascination. For there, protruding in a gentle curve, was her pregnant bump.

Water…

The ocean swim…

His baby?

'Melissa?'

This time he said it louder, kneeling by the bath, his hand under her chin lest she startle and slip beneath the water.

'Wake up, sleepyhead. If you need to rest, you'll be far more comfortable in bed.'

She turned her head towards him, the blue eyes puzzled at first, then, recognising him, she smiled.

'Arun,' she said softly. 'You're in my dream again.'

But the words were barely out when she sat up, sloshing water over him, moving so quickly he grabbed her slippery wet shoulder to steady her in case she slipped and fell back.

'Wait! Take it slowly. You've been asleep. Here!'

He wrapped her in a bath-sheet so her nudity wouldn't panic or embarrass her, and steadied her as she climbed from the deep bath, then he dried her carefully, working so his hands stayed always on the towel, not her skin, not wanting to startle her again.

And once dry he let her keep the towel while he lifted a white robe from the bench and slipped it over her head, helping her ease her arms through the sleeves then pulling the towel from underneath it so she stood, fully clothed, but no less desirable because the white silk was no softer than her skin, and the flaming hair stood out around her head like a beacon, drawing him towards her.

'I have set out some food by your bed, and a Thermos of tea should you want it—cool drinks as well, fruit juices and yoghurt. I will show you.'

He turned away from that beckoning beacon and led her into the bedroom, showing her the tray on wheels that held the food and folding back the bedclothes for her.

'I was famished before but now all I want to do is sleep. It must be jet-lag,' she said, turning from her survey of the room to face him. 'You'll wake me in time to see the baby before I have to leave for the party?'

'I'll make sure you're woken up,' he promised.

'Thank you.'

She said the words shyly, but maybe he was imagining it, and it was only tiredness muting her usually strong voice.

But he answered her in kind.

'It is my pleasure,' he said gently. 'Sleep well, and from the bottom of my heart I thank you. You have done my family great service today, Melissa. It will never be forgotten.'

Mel heard the words and wanted to protest—to say she'd done nothing more than any other person with her training would have—but she felt that might trivialise what Arun had just said, and it had sounded so beautiful she didn't want to do that.

So she smiled and, still smiling, carried his thanks to bed, where she curled her hands around her small bulge, patted it and spoke to it, apologising for being so neglectful in their communication today.

But as she spoke the ease the bath had given her and the joy of Arun's words faded, leaving room for worry about what the future held.

For her and her small bulge…

She woke up to a soft voice saying her name—'Dr Miss'—it was close enough. Opening her eyes, she took in the young woman by the bed and slowly remembered the flight, the ride, the revelation—and then the newborn infant.

Jen, she'd barely spoken to Jenny. And where was Arun? How could she get back to the ICU to check the baby, then from the hospital to the compound where Jenny lived? Would she be in time for the party?

The young woman had disappeared. Had her job been to wake her up? Nothing more?

Too many questions that were impossible to answer so she lay for a while, thinking about fate, until hunger drove her from the bed. She washed and pulled on the satiny silk robe that matched the gown she wore, refusing to wonder why a bachelors' apartment would have such things at hand, then ventured forth.

The young woman was in the kitchen, looking anxiously at a bar laden with cut fruit and dishes of cold meat and cheese, small pancakes stacked on a silver platter and condiments in patterned jars and bottles.

'I do not know what you like to eat, but His Excellency said you would wake hungry and to feed you then show you the gowns.'

'I eat anything—but probably won't manage all of that,' Mel teased, hoping to take the anxiety from the soft, dark eyes.

She settled on a stool, picked up a pancake and wrapped some meat and cheese in it. The young woman offered her a jar.

'This is good, not too spicy.'

Mel dobbed a spoonful on her pancake, folded it over, and ate. Taste sensations she had never experienced before exploded in her mouth.

'It's delicious,' she said, and the young woman smiled and turned away, returning with a tall flask.

'It is tea,' she said. 'His Excellency said not coffee for you—not good for your baby.'

She smiled as she added the last phrase, saying, 'It is exciting, having a baby. So many babies, with my sister having one last week and Tia's and now you will have one. It is a sign the country will do well under the new sheikhs—a good omen.'

The woman was positively glowing with pleasure, and though Mel's main focus was on discovering all the various combinations of flavours of the food in front of her, a small part of it was wondering just how widespread the news of her pregnancy was. Jenny would be upset if she heard it secondhand and did this woman—had Arun mentioned her name?—know Arun was the father of her baby?

The pancake, her third, or maybe her fourth, lost its flavour and with a sigh she dropped it, half-finished, on her plate.

'I need to see the baby, but I have no clothes to put on. I'm sorry, I can't remember your name—'

'Olara,' the woman said, 'and there are gowns and underwear and other clothes for every day in the bedroom. His Excellency sent me to find things for you while you slept. You are going to the party—the wedding party tonight. He knew you would need something nice to wear. I will show you.'

The gowns were beautiful. Fine silk, decorated around the neck, on the sleeves and hem, with exquisite embroidery in gold and silver thread, they were so light it would be like wearing air.

Mel looked at them all, thinking choice would be impossible, finally settling on a dark blue, shot with purple. Purple was a little daring with red-gold hair, but tonight was special—Jenny's pre-wedding dinner—so daring should be OK.

Would she need a scarf?

She was wondering about this when she saw a row of hangers, each one holding a shawl to match a gown. Blue shot with purple on red-gold hair?

Olara hovered in the background—applauding her choice, producing a choice of new, still packaged, delicate underwear, showing Mel an array of make-up in a case as elaborate as a model's.

'I don't usually get dressed up like this,' Mel said, touching the soft silk of the knickers and the lacy confection that was a bra.

'But it is for the party,' the young woman told her. 'Everyone will be dressed up—I have a special dress as well.'

'You'll be going?'

Mel was sorry as soon as she'd said it, then hoped she didn't sound too surprised, but Olara seemed unbothered.

'Of course, we all go. We are the tribe, the family. You understand?'

'Not really, but I think it's wonderful that everyone can enjoy the party.'

She excused herself to shower, remembering as she towelled herself dry how gently Arun had dried her earlier— how circumspectly! Had she been less tired, she might have been disappointed that he hadn't touched her differently.

Oh, dear—what was she thinking?

In an attempt to block all thoughts of Arun—especially thoughts of him touching her—from her head, she dressed swiftly, pleased with the way the gown looked, even more pleased when Olara came back into the room and clapped her hands in delight, assuring Mel she looked very, very beautiful.

Searching through the make-up collection, she found a dusky mauve eye-shadow. Full war paint, she teased herself as she spread a skim of make-up on her face and added colour to her cheeks and eyes.

For Arun?

An enticement or a defence?

She couldn't answer either question, but as she pulled on the silver sandals Olara had produced, Mel decided it didn't matter. Tonight she was going to meet new people, learn new customs and have fun.

'You are beautiful!'

Arun was standing in the living room when she reached it, and his voice was so full of awe Mel knew he meant it. And suddenly she felt beautiful, although she knew, by and large, she was attractive at best, and that was mostly because of her colouring.

'Thank you,' she said, then to hide the delight his compliment had caused she added, 'You look pretty spiffy yourself!'

He was back in traditional dress, a white robe, although this one had rich and heavy gold decoration on the sleeves. The robes removed him from her—the remoteness she'd felt before—but at the same time they added another dimension to the attraction she felt towards him. She looked into his eyes, seeking the other Arun who was more familiar, and what she saw there made her mouth go dry.

Desire, so rampant she could feel it spreading from him through the air to touch her skin and through it to permeate deep into her body.

She *had* to resist, at least until they'd talked and sorted out the future of the baby—their baby.

Play it light.

She touched the gold.

'Special occasion robes?'

He smiled his agreement.

'Shall we go?'

He waved her towards the door and followed, and it wasn't until they were waiting for the lift that she remembered the other baby.

'Tia's baby—I must check him.'

She heard him sigh.

'I don't suppose my telling you I checked before I came up to collect you will make any difference.'

Mel shook her head, then remembered she was carrying her shawl over her arm. If she was going into the ICU she'd better put it on, although in such finery they were surely overdressed for hospital visits. She lifted it to put it on, but Arun took it from her, draping it over her head, then crossing the two ends loosely under her chin before throwing them back over her shoulders.

'To cover that hair seems a sin,' he said, 'although many here would tell you not covering it is a worse sin.'

How could he speak when just his closeness had dried her mouth again? How could he speak calmly when her body was so rattled by his proximity, and the intimacy of the action, she was surprised she was still upright?

Fortunately the lift arrived and they stepped inside then took the short journey down two floors to the ICU.

'How was he when you checked?' she asked, mainly to hide her reaction to his presence.

'Your charge is well. The monitors show his heart is not labouring too much, his kidneys are working without diuretics to help them, and Tia is badgering the nurses in an effort to get them to tell her more and more of what is happening and what the treatments mean. She has banished all the family except her mother, and has shifted into the ICU next to the baby.'

Arun smiled again.

'You worked a miracle in helping her accept the baby.'

'The miracle was the baby,' Mel said. 'Once she accepted that he might live, she was ready to fight both for him, and with him. She seems an intelligent young woman, so it will help her to know what is going on.'

Arun nodded, understanding and accepting what Melissa was telling him, but beneath the talk of the baby and Tia was his awareness of this woman.

The baby was indeed doing well, watched over by an exceedingly anxious-looking young woman, whose voice, when she spoke, suggested she was American. And if she was surprised to see a doctor in a flowing blue and purple robe and silver sandals entering the ICU room, she didn't show it, although Mel thought she read admiration in the younger woman's eyes.

But maybe that was for Arun...

'How do you do?' she said to Mel when Arun introduced her as Sarah Craig. 'I've read a paper of yours on the use of pericardial tissue for patches, and another on the pros and cons of not sealing the chest wound after open-heart surgery on very small children. Will you seal this one after the operation?'

Mel smiled at her, remembering the awe she'd felt—still felt—when she met people whose papers she'd admired.

Where had Arun magicked this woman from in the few hours while she had slept?

'You were working here in the hospital?' Mel asked Sarah, then turned to Arun for more information. 'You did have someone with paeds training already here?'

Sarah answered for him.

'I flew in an hour ago, and though I've been hoping to specialise in paediatrics, so far I've only got as far as

spending a lot of time in kids' wards. The al'Kawalis interviewed me for a job here last week, and I was waiting to
hear whether I'd been successful when Dr al'Kawali phoned
me earlier today.'

Mel turned to Arun.

'No wonder the story of genies coming out of old lamps
to grant wishes originated in this part of the world.'

He said nothing and though she wondered if money
rather than rubbing a cloth on a lamp had produced the
young doctor, Mel wasn't going to complain. She turned
back to Sarah.

'As far as closing the chest, I won't decide that until we
do the op,' she told her. 'In the meantime, it's our job to see
this little lad is as strong as we can get him before we do it.'

'I think you'll find he's doing well,' Sarah told her,
stepping back so Mel could examine the infant.

'That's his warrior blood,' she heard Arun's deep voice
say behind her, but she was doing her best to ignore the
owner of that deep voice so she didn't turn or falter in her
examination.

'You're weighing him, and measuring his fluid input
and output?' she asked, and Sarah handed her the chart.

'As I said, I've not long arrived, but the doctor who had
been here gave me this.'

'It looks fine.'

Mel spoke easily, happy and relaxed now she'd seen the
baby and knew he was doing as well as could be expected.
She'd watch his weight gain and, if possible, do the operation before two weeks.

'As long as the heart muscle is strong enough—echoes
should tell us.'

Sarah stared at her, a puzzled frown on her face, while behind her Arun was also looking a little bewildered— although she wasn't sure a face as strong as his could show such a feeble emotion.

'Sorry, thinking aloud—it's a bad habit. Usually there's just me and the baby and I'm telling him or her my thoughts. With a newborn, the heart muscle is weak and flabby, like a balloon full of water. I need that muscle firmer for a successful operation, that's why we have to feed him well and try to get him as strong as possible in as short a time as possible.'

She turned back to Arun, who was watching her with interest. Had he not expected her to be professional about this, considering her personal turmoil?

'Tia, is she about? Should I speak to her before we go?'

It was Sarah who answered.

'She's just gone to have a rest. She's not happy to be away from the baby for even the shortest time, but the other lady—is it her mother?—reminded her she needed her strength and took her off to eat then sleep.'

'I'll see her later, then,' Mel said, and turned to Arun. 'Shall we go?'

CHAPTER SIX

THEY walked out of the hospital through a wide entrance-way, decorated with so many lush plants it could have been a jungle.

'A jungle in a desert,' Mel murmured, noticing bright orchids flowering among the greenery.

'The magic of water,' Arun told her, 'and money, I suppose. Because the hospital was set up to attract wealthy clients, mostly from overseas, this foyer, their first view of the hospital, was designed to look as if they were entering a six-star hotel.'

'The familiarity of it making them relax,' Mel teased, but Arun wasn't smiling, and she guessed he was thinking of all that still needed to be done as far as medical services for his own people were concerned. 'Could you have done anything to change things before your father died?'

He sighed and shook his head.

'We did a little, here and there, encouraging doctors other than surgeons to come to work in our city, and we started on the modernisation of the old hospital, using our own money. No one in the government cared what we did there, but this was the place that had the equipment and the space to be a truly great hospital for our people as well as the foreigners.'

A long sleek black car had pulled up in front of them, and a porter from the hospital opened the back door.

Mel touched Arun's arm.

'Then you shouldn't have regrets—you shouldn't be looking back. You did what you could, and now you can do more. Holding onto the past adds to the burdens of the present, and you don't need that.'

He paused beside the open car door, turning to look at her—to study her—then he smiled, the kind of smile that made Mel's toes tingle and started a quivering hunger deep in her belly.

Had he felt a similar desire that he pressed a button, raising a darkened glass screen between the driver and the back seat?

But when he spoke she realised desire was the last thing on his mind.

'You must have some thoughts on your future with this baby,' he said, and Mel turned, hoping to see some glimpse of what he was feeling in his face.

No luck there—the word 'inscrutable' might have been coined for Arun's face right now. He had no need of veils or masks to hide his thoughts…

'I want the best possible upbringing for the baby,' she said, because, brain-boggled though she'd been, that was one thing she *had* decided. 'Maybe because I was brought up by a grandmother, I feel deeply that he or she should have two parents.'

Surely that would bring some twitch of emotion, some sign as to whether he was considering being part of the child's life. But, no—not so much as a shift in a facial muscle, so Mel, feeling increasingly trapped and desperate, continued with a rush of words.

'That's not to say you have to be one of those parents. I mean, you can if you want—if you decide you'd like to be involved—and we can work out some kind of custody arrangement, but if you don't want to, well, that's OK, too. We—I mean, the baby and I—won't be alone as I have a good friend at home, Charlie, who has offered to marry me and be a good role model for the baby. I've said no to marriage and we haven't agreed anything, but I can tell you now that he loves kids and he's very well adjusted so he wouldn't have any hang-ups about it not being his biological child and—'

'Enough!'

She flinched not only at the harsh order but a thunderous expression on the previously blank face.

'What *is* this nonsense you are spouting? Who is this Charlie you intend to give my child to? Who knew about my child before I did? How—?'

He stopped as if his indignation was choking him.

Mel thought she'd start by answering the easy part.

'Charlie's an old friend. He's a great guy and has always been there for me. And I didn't tell him—he was worried about me and worked out for himself that I was pregnant.'

'Stop!'

Arun held up his hand this time.

'Strange as it may seem, I am not the slightest bit interested in the behaviour of this Charlie, although now he's entered the picture, how can you be sure it's my child you carry, not his?'

'Charlie's?'

Was it a measure of her tension that for a moment the question made no sense?

'But I've never been to bed with Charlie,' she managed. 'Charlie's a friend.'

'A friend, who, presumably, you *will* go to bed with once you've decided to marry him.'

Could frost form on words in warm desert climates?

Definitely!

But the coldest of frosts couldn't cool Mel's growing anger.

'I told you that I said no to marriage,' she began, but she doubted Arun was listening, for he'd given an explosive snort and was holding his head in his hands, with little regard for the neat points of his scarf.

'Can you tell me,' he demanded, in strangled tones, 'how this conversation got from my baby to making a life with this obviously bloodless man called Charlie? Although, before we leave him, why, if he so adores you, has he not taken you to bed? Is the man dead below the waist?'

Stung by this insult to her second-best friend, Mel rushed in again.

'Of course he's not—he's had dozens of affairs. Just not with me, because it wouldn't have been fair of me to have an affair with him knowing I didn't want to marry him. Besides, I've never wanted to have an affair with him— he's not that kind of friend.'

But blurting that out only made her feel more confused and it obviously wasn't helping Arun for he was shaking his head in disbelief. He spoke into some kind of two-way radio and the driver slowed down slightly. Now Arun turned, put his hands on Mel's shoulders and peered intently into her face.

'You will listen to me,' he said, his voice deep and slightly raspy, as if it was only with difficulty he wasn't shouting at her. 'You will not marry Charlie. In fact, I do not ever want to hear his name again. It is bad enough that he knew of my child before I did, let alone that you would consider letting him take my place as the father. But there is one thing you got right in all that nonsense you have been spouting, and that's the fact that, ideally, a child should have two parents. You are one of those parents and I am the other, right?'

Where was this going?

Unable to guess, Mel did the only thing she could think of. She answered truthfully.

'Biologically speaking, yes,' she said, and saw the gold braid on Arun's gown catch the light from the bright lights outside the compound as he flung his arms into the air in sheer frustration.

'I am not talking about biological parents,' he growled. 'I had a biological father, thank you very much, and a lot of good he did me! My child will have a real father. Me!'

But how? Mel thought, although she thought it best not to say it. She'd upset him quite enough for one evening…

The building they stopped at, inside the compound, was yet another house, one Mel hadn't been inside before.

She glanced sideways at her companion, who'd been silent for the final minutes of the journey. What was he thinking? What did he mean about being a proper father to the baby?

The remote look on his face and his earlier anger suggested she'd be better off not asking.

Not right now…

'It's bigger than the others,' Mel said, as she got out and looked around, smelling the scent of lemon blossom on the warm night air.

'It was my father's house and though neither Kam nor I have any intention of moving into it, we will use it for functions and celebrations. Celebrations especially. It deserves some joy.'

He spoke calmly—tourist guide again—the anger gone. Or hidden?

But hearing something in his words, Mel sighed. Just as she'd steeled herself against this forceful, sometimes overbearing man, he said something like that—the house deserving joy—and she caught a glimpse of an unhappy little boy inside him and started to feel sorry for him. Not that he'd accept sympathy from her—not this proud descendant of desert princes.

She adjusted the shawl around her head, knowing full well her rebellious hair would escape anyway, and followed him up the steps. He held her arm as she slipped off her sandals, and the touch fired again all the longings she'd been feeling.

Would it hurt to revisit the affair—to enjoy the pleasure they'd shared once before?

Of course it would, her brain shrieked, but her brain wasn't having a lot of control over her body right now, and she had doubts, if it came to an argument, as to whether her brain would win. Although going to bed with Arun wasn't going to help sort out the baby problem…

'This is the stateroom where visiting dignitaries from overseas are usually entertained.'

Arun led her into a room that looked like something out of an opera set. Colourful tapestries draped the walls, a long table seemed to be set with gold plate, though, when Mel looked more closely, she realised the plates were white and merely edged with gold. As were the glasses, and the vases that held displays of brilliant flowers, their colours merging with the colours of the coverings on the chairs, the curtains, the tapestries and the bright silks of the women.

'I understand why you men wear white,' Mel whispered, as they stood just inside the door so she could take in the scene in front of her. 'With all the other colours, you stand out.'

Arun smiled at her, then led her forward towards one of the white-robed men. He saw them coming and stepped swiftly towards them.

'Brother,' he said, greeting Arun with a cheek-to-cheek embrace. Then he turned to Mel. 'And Melissa, best friend of my Jenny, who tells me you were put to work from the moment you got up this morning and that you are caring for our Tia's baby.'

He took Mel's hand and bent over it, then his fingers tightened on it as he looked into her eyes.

'The little boy? He is all right? Jenny said truncus arteriosus, but you can operate? Is that right? Can you spare us the time to do that?'

The green eyes, so like Arun's, looked worriedly into hers, but it was Arun who answered.

'Unhand the woman, Kam, and give her time to speak,

although when she does she'll brush away your concern and assure you she wants nothing better to do than to hang around in Zaheer long enough to operate on Tia's baby.'

Kam laughed.

'I can see why you and Jenny are friends, Melissa. You think the same way. I tried to persuade Jenny we should take a honeymoon—at least a week away. Somewhere quiet we could be together, but could I get her to agree? Not when there is so much work to be done here, she tells me. She is going to be a slave-driver, that woman. This I know already.'

'You're talking about me?'

Mel turned to see Jenny, looking radiant in a gown of palest cream decorated with rich red embroidery. Her eyes gleamed with happiness and her skin shone with health, but it was the look she gave her husband-to-be that assured Mel her friend was really doing the right thing. These two were so in love you could warm your hands on the glowing warmth of it that shone in the air around them.

Mel glanced towards Arun, and knew he saw it, too, because although he smiled, his eyes looked sad.

He was thinking of his own wife, Mel guessed. A beautiful young woman who'd died too young, he'd said, though he'd not mentioned much more than the bare bones of the story.

'Hey, it's a party. Don't look sad.'

Jenny's teasing remark startled her out of her thoughts and she let her friend draw her further into the room where the Stapletons were standing talking to Miriam and another woman Jen introduced as the twins' mother.

More and more people, sisters by the dozen, nieces by

the score, uncles, cousins, friends and family, everyone smiling but all the time checking out the strangers in their midst. But seeing Jen move among them, hearing her utter little phrases in their own tongue, Mel knew her friend would cope. In fact, this was probably the challenge Jen needed—not only marriage, but marriage that brought with it responsibilities she could handle—a marriage that would be a true partnership as she and Kam strove to bring their country into the twenty-first century.

But would the tasks in front of them make up for their lack of children? Would Jen's concern about not giving Kam an heir prove a tiny crack that could widen with time and spoil their bliss?

Don't even think about it, Mel's head warned, but it was hard not to when she was carrying a child who could be the heir Kam and Jen needed.

The thought made Mel shiver as, for the first time, she considered her baby in that way. Originally, coming here, her mission—apart from being Jenny's bridesmaid—had been to tell Arun about the baby. And, aware from the beginning of their relationship that he hadn't wanted children, she'd thought the telling would be the beginning and the end of it.

But now?

Suppose he was serious about being involved with the child?

Worse still, suppose he saw her pregnancy as an option that saved him from marrying—an option he'd certainly not have chosen had Jenny not had the problem she had.

In which case he'd want the child brought up here, not in Australia, and how could she fight for custody against a man with seemingly limitless financial resources?

Jane was chattering about all she'd seen that day—the souk, the desert, the winter palace—and Mel let the words wash over her, hoping they'd eventually chase away a new fear now nestling in her heart.

'You enjoyed it?'

They were in the limousine, returning to the hospital, when Arun asked the question.

'I did,' Mel said, telling him the truth, for the whole affair had been so mind-boggling she'd been able to set aside most of her anxiety about Arun's possible plans. 'The food, the conversation, everything—you certainly know how to throw a party.'

'Ah, but it's the people who make it happen,' Arun said. 'And family can be counted on to make things lively, can they not? They can fight and argue, yet remain friends. Kam and I, brought up mainly in schools overseas, have taken longer to learn this. But especially in the past, in the times when all the people roamed the desert, family had to come first to ensure survival. So it was always the most important thing, and though members of the family might squabble among themselves, in times of trouble they would stick together.'

Mel thought about his words—yes, there'd been arguments, some quite loud and fierce, at the dinner table, but there'd been laughter, too, and gentleness, a little girl sliding from her chair to walk around the long table and climb onto the knee of her white-robed father—the look of love in the man's eyes as he'd nestled the sleepy child on his lap wonderful to behold.

'I had a different kind of family to most,' Mel admitted.

'I was brought up by my grandmother, so my family was her, although in the holidays cousins came to stay.'

Arun touched her cheek, placing his hand against it so his palm curved under her chin.

'I could give you family,' he said, so quietly it took Mel a moment to process what he meant.

'You mean—'

'Marriage,' he said quietly.

Mel lifted her hand and rested it on top of Arun's.

'You can't mean that—you've barely had time to think about all the repercussions of the baby. You'd be rushing into it, it's impossible—'

'You would consider marrying Charlie to give the baby a father, so why not marry me?'

'Charlie's safe.'

The words were out before she could stop them and no amount of 'oh, dear-ing' could take them back.

Yet Arun said nothing, his face closed against her once more, although she doubted it was the last she'd hear of the subject.

The car took them swiftly through the quiet night streets but not so swiftly that Mel missed the sight of the full moon riding high in the sky. The silvery beauty of it made her forget her concerns, her whole being caught up in the magic of the night.

'Oh, look at it,' she said. 'Could we stop where we stopped to watch the sunset so I can see the desert in the moonlight?'

Was he getting soft that such an innocent appeal could make his heart hurt? Arun wondered. Especially when he was angry with her?

'Charlie's safe'—what did that mean? That he, Arun, was dangerous?

But he gave an order to the driver and the vehicle turned off the main road, pulling up minutes later on the top of what had once been one of the highest sand dunes in the area.

Only now it had been stabilised and housing stretched down one side, while on the other side was the desert— the red-brown sands that still sang in his blood.

Perhaps that's why Melissa's words had affected him.

The driver opened his door but Arun told him to stay where he was, he would help the lady out. But the lady had already moved, opening the door and standing up, holding the door for support as she slipped off her sandals.

'You should keep them on. It's a lookout—there could be glass or rubbish lying about,' he told her, but she shrugged his words away.

'No worse than the needles that can be found on beaches at home,' she said, 'but I still love to feel the sand between my toes. The moon's bright, I'll walk carefully.'

And so saying she began to pick her way down the dune, the sand sliding with her in places so she had to hold out her arms to keep her balance. In the dark gown she looked like a shadow on the earth, but as he followed, the light wind lifted her shawl and he saw the flaming hair.

She was beautiful and he wanted her, not entirely, if he was honest, because of the baby. He wanted her physically, but he wanted more than that. The challenge of her, the meeting of their minds—she'd laugh if he said that.

He looked up at the moon and sighed, for it must be that which was making him so fanciful, but then she turned to face him, the moon shining on her face.

'It is beautiful,' she whispered. 'So beautiful I want to celebrate—to dance and sing out loud and, believe me, that's not a good thing because I'm a dreadful singer. But it awes me, if you know what I mean, yet makes me feel so good.'

Her obvious delight in the world that meant so much to him filled him with a happiness he doubted he'd ever felt before. Very gently, he reached out and touched her, taking her face between the palms of his hands.

'I will show you all the desert,' he promised. 'By moonlight, and at sunset, and in the early dawn when it slowly wakens, pink and rosy like a woman, from a love-filled night.'

He leant forward and kissed her, long and deep, delving into her mouth, finding her tongue and tangling with it, drawing her breath into his lungs, sharing his with her, making promises with a kiss.

'If you will let me,' he added, moving so their bodies touched.

And through the layers of their clothing, through his robe and her gown, he felt her body respond, her nipples harden into tight nubs, even as his own desire became evident.

She kissed him back, leaning into him, her hands slipping beneath his scarf to hold his head to hers, then the kissing stopped and she slid her hand into his.

'Isn't this a bit public for a sheikh?' she whispered, the promise in the teasing words making his erection even harder.

It was too easy. They fell back into their special rhythm of love-making as if they'd never been parted. Mel felt her skin tighten in response to his touch, felt her body heat and soften for him. Felt the same heat in his skin, and in the bunching of his muscles as he lay beside her in the big bed—her big bed, not his—controlling his need until he had her almost begging to be taken.

'I have dreamt about this for four months,' he murmured into the sensitised hollow of her neck. 'I am not going to hurry.'

'Not until I beg?' she whispered, blurring the words against his short-cropped hair.

'I would never make you beg,' he promised, but as his fingers worked their magic she knew she might.

Soon…

Languor crept through her, so hot and heavy she felt as if she was melting into the bed, yet all her nerve endings were alert, thrilling to the lightest brush of his fingertips or the briefest touch of his lips.

'Arun!'

She found herself whispering his name, pressing the word against the tight tendon of his shoulder.

'Melissa,' he murmured back, scything his teeth across her nipple so the next time she said his name it was gasped, not whispered.

So much sensation, her fingers reading his desire, her lips teasing him, while all the time the pressure built within them both, until Mel wondered who would give in first.

She did, for all his touch was gentle it was expert, while he watched her as if in wonder of the pleasure he could bring her, making her feel so special she floated on a sea of bliss, shattered only when the climax came, zinging first down to her toes then shuddering through her body, too dramatic to hide, too exhilarating to want to hide it.

Only then did he slide inside her, and once again he

teased, so the pleasure built and built again until they could peak together, shattering with cries they couldn't control, then lying, spent, in each other's arms.

Mel felt his weight against her and revelled in it, holding him close, hearing the sharp, deep intakes of the air he needed to replenish what he'd lost. She revelled in that, too. She hadn't had many lovers but she knew enough to know she pleased him, and that added to her own pleasure.

Then he was talking, but as she stopped thinking about pleasure and concentrated on his husky murmurs, she realised he was speaking in his own language, and from the way his hand pressed against her protruding belly, he was talking to the baby, not to her.

Oh, dear!

'Don't do that!' she pleaded, and she must have sounded anguished for he lifted his head to look at her, his hand pushing her wild hair back from her face so he could see her better in the moonlight.

'Don't talk to my child?'

He sounded more puzzled than affronted and she lifted her hand to press it against his lips.

'No, I didn't mean that—well, I did, but not that way. Nothing's decided. I know you mentioned marriage, but that's not a solution, you must see that. Your brother's married someone from outside your culture, and if you're marrying for children—to provide an heir—then surely you should marry one of your own people. Wouldn't that make it easier for him—the heir—to take over later? Make it easier for him to rule?'

She sighed and rolled away from him.

'I'm probably not making sense but I was in a muddle about this before you mentioned marriage, so imagine how much worse that muddle is now.'

'Why?'

Why?

She peered at him, searching for a valid reason, aware of the excited beating of her heart—but that was just, she was certain, because they were so good together in bed.

'Because it's silly even thinking of it.'

'Is it?'

He slid up in the bed and propped his hand on his elbow so he could look down into her face.

'I have promised Jenny and Kam I will marry and have children. I was happy to arrange a marriage of convenience. I already had Miriam looking for a possible wife. Then here you are, pregnant with my child, willing to share your life with someone called Charlie of all things to give that child a father—so why would you not marry me?'

Mel tried desperately to think of a valid response but he touched his finger to her lips before she could frame a single word.

'You wish to keep working—you can do that here. We are setting up the paediatric surgical unit—it will be yours to order and staff as you wish. And while you work you can rest easy about the child. Children are brought up, to a large extent, in the women's house—going between there and their parents' houses as happily as the young kids play among a goat herd. You will have your child yet when you are working you will know he or she is in a secure and happy family environment—in an environment of love.'

Here was something she could refute.

'You weren't,' she reminded him. 'You were sent overseas to school at six.'

'Which is why,' he said, his voice cold, 'my child will not suffer in that way. Oh, I have doubts, too, Melissa. What kind of father will I, who never knew a father's love, make? I have real doubts, but that will not stop me doing the best I can.'

'Oh, Arun,' she said softly, and reached up to wrap her arms around his shoulders.

She sounded so genuinely unhappy for him Arun sat up, turned on a bedside light and looked at her properly. She was beautiful—flushed and rosy, her wild hair splayed across the pillow, her pale body with its nest of curls beneath the barely swollen belly the source of such delight...

But this reluctance to give in to marriage...

'You like me?'

It seemed a strange question to be asking after they'd made love so satisfactorily, but it seemed important to find out.

She nodded, opened her reddened lips to add words then closed them again, allowing him to continue.

'We're good together in bed?'

Another nod, this time with a slight smile that made him want to take her again—right now.

But he couldn't do that—not until a lot of things were sorted out.

'So why are you hesitant about marriage?'

Mel looked at him. Long and lean, but well muscled with the leanness because he could lift and hold her with ease, although she was no lightweight. Intelligent, caring—his love-making showed that—apparently wealthy, if what she'd seen at the party was any indication, great in bed, so why not marry him?

Because he didn't love her! How could he when he was still in love with the memory of his beautiful young wife? It would be like competing with a ghost...

The answer came so unexpectedly and was so pathetic Mel decided it must be wrong. She was thirty-five. Surely she wasn't still lost in a dream of finding the perfect love?

But it was the only answer she could find to explain why she was so hesitant.

'I can't explain,' she said, then she added, 'And now I have to sleep. I have to see Tia's baby in the morning, then it's Jenny's wedding in the afternoon. Are you staying or going?'

'Staying or going?' he repeated.

'In my bed.'

And as she said the words she wondered again why they'd ended up in her bedroom, not his, but this time the obvious answer came to her—his bed was the one he'd shared with his wife, the wife he'd loved.

With a sigh that hid the sudden surge of sadness in her heart, she turned over on her side, pulled the sheet up to her shoulder, tucked her hands beneath her head and prepared to go to sleep.

She felt the bed move and thought he was leaving but then his body curved around hers, warming her back, and his hand rested gently on her hip.

'Technically, this *is* my bed,' he whispered, nestling closer, reminding her of how good it had been, four months ago, to have him sleep beside her.

He should have gone back to his own room. He knew that. But he also knew he wanted, more than was wise, to sleep with her again. Just sleep. At least until the morning, when anything might happen, and probably would...

CHAPTER SEVEN

MAKING love in the morning, Mel decided as she stood in the large shower with Arun making soapy circles on her back, was probably one of the nicest things in the whole wide world. She had set aside her worries about the future and what it might hold, refusing to think about Arun's suggestions until she was on her own and could think clearly. So right now she was relaxed and at ease and ready to take on whatever the world had to offer her right here and now, although if he kept soaping there, taking on stuff might be a bit delayed.

'I have to get to work,' she scolded him, and he laughed, then turned her so she faced him.

'You do not have to go to work!' he told her sternly, although the words lost a little of their firmness with the hot water streaming all around them.

'But I do—there are things to organise if we're operating here, and the baby to see. I do wish he had a name—Oh!'

The thought was so shocking she forgot about playing with Arun in the shower and stepped out, winding one towel around her hair and drying herself on another.

'Do you think,' she asked, as Arun turned off the water and stepped out himself, 'that she doesn't want to give him the name they chose because she's still uncertain that he'll live? How awful if she's thinking that way. How unhappy she must be!'

Arun shook his head.

'Despite a plenitude of sisters, I have not and will not ever understand women. How could you be thinking of Tia's happiness or otherwise while we were in the shower?'

Mel smiled at his disbelief.

'Multi-tasking?' she responded, tucking one towel around her body then taking the one off her hair to rub at the wet tangled mess. 'It's a woman thing! See, I can dry my hair, wonder how long it will take to get the tangles out, plan out the day—I'll see Tia's baby first but later I'm going to need to work out exactly how we'll do the operation. And when do you work? See patients? You seemed to be looking after me most of yesterday.'

He stared at her for a little longer, then shook his head, wrapped a towel around his waist and left the bathroom, poking his head back in long enough to say, 'I'll tell Olara breakfast in ten minutes—does that suit your schedule?'

Mel's towel had slipped so she wadded it and threw it at him, then saw the desire leap again in his eyes and knew it was a mistake. But easing that desire would have to wait—there was so much to be done.

A young man was in the ICU room with the baby—a doctor from A and E, Arun explained, relieving Sarah until another paediatric registrar could be brought on staff. Arun took Tia to one side as Mel examined her small patient, smiling as she realised the little one was doing well.

'How can you tell? What do you look for?' Tia asked, and before Mel could explain, Arun took the chart and carefully pointed out to his sister the different measurements and what they meant, assuring her the baby was more than holding his own.

'See,' he said, gently, 'he has even gained some weight.'

Tia hugged him hard, then hugged Mel as well, before changing the subject to ask about the party. Had Mel enjoyed it? Had Jenny looked beautiful?

'It was great and Jenny looked gorgeous,' Mel assured her, happy that Tia was showing an interest in things other than the baby. They talked for a while, Zaffra, the nurse, returning to take over as the baby-watcher.

The young doctor from A and E remained near the door, hovering with some purpose, Mel suspected. Then Arun spoke to him and frowned at the young man's reply.

'What is it?' Mel asked.

'He was wondering if you could spare some time to go down to the A and E department,' Arun replied, although he still looked perplexed.

'If he and the other doctors sharing duty with Sarah are from there, they might want to know more about the baby's condition,' Mel suggested. 'I'm only too happy to go down, but someone will have to point the way. I've a feeling I could get lost in this place for ever if left on my own.'

'I shall be your guide,' Arun said, investing the words with a deeper meaning so Mel found herself not only shivering but thinking thoughts that should be far from her head in a hospital situation.

'Don't you have a job to go to?' she teased, hoping to hide her reaction.

'It will wait for me,' he said easily, then added, 'Though not for much longer. Come, the baby is being well cared for. We will go.'

Mel followed him, trying to take note of the corridors along which they passed, feeling she no longer knew which way was up and which down.

Feeling she no longer knew where she was in other ways as well. Was Arun serious about marriage?

She watched him as he paused to exchange words with a colleague.

Would it work?

As he'd said, marriages of convenience had worked in his country for centuries so he saw no reason for it not to work.

Yet he'd married Hussa for love…

'Now, this one takes us down,' he said, ushering her inside, and nodding to those already packed in the lift.

A polite man, but used to command.

If they did marry, then her biggest—and most irrational, she had to admit—fear would be allayed. Should something happen to her, her child would have Jenny to be a mother to him or her, and that was a far better option than leaving Charlie holding the baby…

It would, in fact, be the perfect solution.

'And down this corridor.'

He pushed open the double doors into the A and E department. And for a moment Mel could only stare, for the room in front of her was jam-packed with people, women, she now saw, women and children. Some babies in arms, some older children, but everywhere black-clad women, most of them with their faces masked or veiled, holding children.

A young man in a short white coat, stethoscope dangling from his pocket, rushed towards them, speaking not to her but to Arun.

'We didn't tell them,' he said helplessly. 'Somehow word just got around that there was a baby doctor in the city. They've come from everywhere, even desert people. There are *camels* parked outside.'

'Camels?' she said, the thought making her turn and smile at Arun, but he was staring at the crowd and shaking his head, a look of profound sadness on his face.

'What is it, Arun?' she demanded as the young man moved away to speak to a woman who was bringing her baby forward.

'It is shame, Melissa, that I did not know—we did not know, Kam and I—how very bad things are here. We thought we had time to fix the wrongs, but look at this. I must get help here quickly, must get onto the other paediatricians we have contracted to start shortly. The list is back in my office. Come, it is not your problem.'

'Not my problem? Women with sick children are not my problem? Of course they are. Now, where's that young man gone? He needs to get them organised. Do the nurses understand triage? I'll be more use to children with heart problems, so maybe if I see them first while the other doctors on duty do the initial examination of the others and pass on anything serious to me. Can we get Sarah Craig down here? As long as I'm in the hospital, she doesn't need to be with Tia's baby.'

Arun stared at her in disbelief.

'You *can't* do this!' he said.

She shook her head and smiled.

'That's where you're wrong. This is one thing I *can* do, and if I'm staying here for two weeks to operate on Tia's baby, I can work here for the next two weeks, maybe four because I can't leave straight after the op. That should give you and Kam time to set up your paeds ward and get it staffed, OK? Now, find me the young man, and a nurse who can translate for me, and let me get to work.'

It was Arun's turn to shake his head, but Mel knew there wasn't a moment to be wasted if she wanted to see even half of these women today and still get to Jenny's wedding.

'Shoo!' she said, and made a pushing motion with her hands.

He stared at her, his chin tilting upward as if to defy her order. Who, after all, was *she* to be giving orders to a sheikh? Then he smiled.

'I'm shooing,' he said quietly, but his eyes said something else. His eyes said, Thank you, though the gratitude was still tinged with shame.

And seeing that expression, knowing the beating his pride must be taking as he realised the extent to which his people had been neglected, her heart ached for him...

By lunchtime she had seven children lined up for radiological examinations but because the radiology staff had been hired for their skills with adults, not children, she wanted to be in the room with the children being scanned.

'I need to see for myself,' she explained to Arun, who had appeared from nowhere to insist she stop working to eat lunch. 'And I won't get them all done this afternoon because we have to get to the wedding. As well as that, some of the little ones might need to be sedated, so maybe in the morning, if I could have time in the radiology rooms and whatever staff are available, we can work through the day.'

He sighed and shook his head.

'I don't want you doing this,' he said, and she smiled at him.

'Liar! What you mean is that you feel bad that it is me doing it when I came over for a week of fun and celebration of Jenny's wedding. But, in fact, you're delighted to have someone who *can* do this.'

'And mortified to see the extent of the need,' he said quietly, the pain in his words so clear she could feel it. 'My father was ill for a long time before he died, but he kept control of what he could. He allowed the foreigners to spend their money where and how they wanted but he actively discouraged the local people from using any of these facilities. The wealthy families, of course, weren't swayed by this, and instead of going to Europe for their medical and dental treatment, they welcomed the new hospital and its attendant services, but we have always been a people who have shared whatever we've had, so this division between those who have the best and those who have nothing is very much against our traditional ways.'

Mel thought of the compound with huge houses encircling the inner courtyard and wondered about traditional ways, and Arun, perhaps guessing her thoughts, continued.

'People see our family—the houses we have—as

wealthy, but our compound is like a city, housing maybe three hundred people, many families, all living together. And if some work at one thing, preparing food and serving it, others, like Miriam, work at other things. She has made the loose trousers the children wear for as long as I can remember. Even my mother, who thought herself a princess and above work, made perfumes for everyone in the family, including those you might see as servants. It is our way.'

It is our way! Such simple words, but like the pain she'd heard earlier it pierced Mel's heart and for an instant she felt regret that he didn't love her, for it would be so very easy for her to love him...

Especially if they were married...

Satisfied that she had eaten well, Arun escorted Melissa first to the ICU where the baby continued to do well then back to A and E where still more women waited with their children.

'It's impossible!' he said. 'You'll never see them all. We'll have to leave by four to drive out for the wedding and you need to wash and dress. You should stop now.'

She checked her watch then smiled at him.

'Give me until three. I'll leave then. And this is worse than it looks. I've seen a lot of these children, their mothers are just waiting for follow-up appointments or medication. The staff here have been overwhelmed but they're doing a great job handling so many people at once—and the children, they are so good, waiting patiently with their mothers.'

'We are good at patience,' Arun told her, and knew by the flush that rose in her cheeks that she'd understood the double meaning in his words.

Would she marry him?

She hadn't said no, which gave him hope, but she certainly hadn't leapt at the idea.

And she was speaking in terms of staying four weeks, which wasn't a good sign.

Although surely a woman as intelligent as she was would see all the positives of such a union?

So why hadn't she said yes?

Was she fonder of this paragon Charlie than she admitted?

Anger fired and he knew he had to find a solution for it was unthinkable that another man should rear his child.

He set the subject aside, although he realised it must have been preying on his subconscious mind when, later, they settled into the car to take them back to the compound for the wedding.

Melissa was wearing a long gown in the palest blue, with darker blue flowers embroidered wildly all over it. A darker blue shawl hid her vibrant hair, making her eyes look bluer and her skin creamier. He wanted to tell her how beautiful she was, but saying it then asking her again about the marriage option might make the compliment sound hollow.

'Jenny's wedding,' he began, wondering how to approach the subject again, and surprised at his own unfamiliar hesitation. 'Has it made you think of my suggestion?'

Blue eyes studied him, and the smile he so enjoyed flitted momentarily across her lips.

'No,' she said, and smiled properly now. 'That's answering your question literally—Jenny's wedding has made no difference to my thinking but yes to what you're really asking. I have been giving your proposition some thought.'

Proposition?

'It was a proposal,' he said stiffly, angered that she seemed to be making a joke of a situation he found so difficult.

The smile disappeared.

'I would have thought a proposal had an element of love in it, Arun,' she said quietly, and once again he was struck by how little he understood the female half of the human race.

Which made him even more irritated.

'You were willing to accept Charlie without love—without even attraction, from what you tell me,' he snapped, then regretted opening his mouth for he'd sounded petty even to his own ears.

Once again she studied him, although now there was no hint of a smile.

'That was intended to be a safeguard for the baby. I have no family and Jenny, my best friend, at the time I decided on it, was committed to travelling to far-off places. I needed to know there was someone to take care of the baby if anything happened to me.'

'And you chose this Charlie, not the baby's father!'

Had she heard the anger simmering close to rage that she put her hand on his and said his name? All she said was 'Arun!' but it was enough to calm him slightly.

'I didn't know you'd be interested,' she added quietly. 'When we met you'd been adamant children weren't in your future. I had to make some contingency plans—just in case.'

He heard a quaver in her voice as she spoke and the uncertainty of it killed the remnants of his anger. Now it was his turn to study her, to remember something she'd said earlier—something about fear, about terror.

'Why don't you have a family?' he asked, but knew the question had come too late. The car had stopped and the crowds gathered in the compound were looking expectantly towards it.

Today there even more people around, all obviously in their best attire, although a lot of the women wore black gowns over their colourful dresses, the purples, blues and richest greens peeping shyly at the hemlines or the sleeves.

'This is the extended family, all of our people, come to celebrate with Kam and Jenny,' Arun explained, taking Mel's hand to lead her up the steps.

But when he was waylaid, someone touching his sleeve to attract his attention then talking to him urgently, she went on ahead, knowing there'd be someone somewhere to show her where she had to go.

Miriam rescued her, taking her arm and leading her to where Jenny was being prepared by a multitude of sisters.

'Look,' Jen said, holding up her hands to show a hennaed pattern on them.

'That's beautiful,' Mel told her, seeing the delicacy of the tracing of leaves and buds.

'We'd do it to you but it's too late,' Jen told her. 'You have to mix it to a paste and put it on thickly then hold it near heat to dry it so it leaves the stain on the skin. See Miriam's feet.'

Miriam lifted one foot to show the hennaed sole.

'I didn't do my feet because they're too ticklish to have someone painting them,' Jen explained.

Mel saw the happiness in her friend's face and heard

the delight in her voice and was so glad for her. That Jen, who'd suffered so much with the loss of her husband and unborn son, should find such joy again was a miracle, but while Mel was happy for her, she also felt a tiny twinge of not jealousy but regret that this joy had found Jen twice while somehow it had bypassed her completely.

She closed her eyes against the thought and found an image of Arun on the inside of her eyelids. Just his face, strong and clean-cut, the dark brows above his green eyes, the beautiful lips, moving, telling her they'd marry.

She blinked him away, although she knew in reality it would take more than a blink to get rid of him.

Especially now…

Then Jen was ready, her beautiful blue silk gown covered with a black one, her unbound golden hair covered with a black veil so she looked like a black parcel, wrapped ready for her husband to unwrap. The women escorted her out of the room into the big room where Jane and Bob Stapleton came forward to greet her with a kiss. Then everyone was shuffled into place, Mel beside Arun one step behind the bride and groom, and the ceremony began.

Had Kam explained what would be said to Jen before this started? Mel wondered, listening to the music of the words and understanding none of them, but what she did understand was a gasp from the crowd of people in the room, and she turned to Arun, eyebrows raised, hoping there was enough of a murmur going on behind them for him to explain.

Which he promptly did!

'He is saying there might be another wedding in the family

soon,' he said, his eyes daring her to argue, to make a scene in front of what must have been several hundred people.

'Yours?' Her whisper might have been quiet but it was definitely a demand.

'Of course,' he said.

Mel looked around desperately. On one side white-gowned men stood, most with prayer beads clicking through their fingers. On the other side the women, like bright butterflies, their black veils dispensed with because all the men present counted as family.

There was no help at hand but she wasn't going to give in just like that.

'I'm not marrying you!' she muttered at Arun, who turned with a smile and murmured,

'He didn't say who I was to marry.'

'Oh!'

She felt flat—deflated—although she'd known he had to marry. He'd promised Jen…

Then his smile broadened and somehow sneaked beneath Mel's guard, warming and exciting her at the same time.

'But I haven't given up on my first choice,' he told her. 'Have you not heard the legends? The stories of the desert sheikh who takes the woman of his desires and rides off with his bride across his saddle? Shall we ride in the morning?'

The question was as seductive as his touch had been the previous night, and Mel found her body trembling with re-membered desire.

How could he do this to her, with no more than words and glances? And how could they be having this conver-sation in the middle of Jen's wedding? All around them people were chanting now, rhythmic words Mel didn't understand, while Arun alternately joined in and spoke to her, tormenting her with his special magic, moving close enough for their bodies to be touching.

And how could she fight him when he had such an effect on all her senses?

No, not all her senses—surely she retained some common sense!

'I'm not the woman of your desires,' Mel said, edging away from him to evade his touch. 'And as for riding off across the desert, this is the twenty-first century in case you didn't know.'

'Oh, I know it,' he said, still smiling and still exciting her traitorous body. 'And I applaud what the new age has brought with it, but men and women still meet and are attracted. Can you deny that?'

'Attraction's not enough as the basis for a marriage,' Mel muttered at him.

'But attraction, combined with a baby on the way, surely is.'

Was that true?

Or was it a false presumption that would lead to certain disaster?

Mel looked around at the people gathered in the room, at the children, some standing quietly, others playing, also quietly, all of them happy and healthy, secure in this, to Mel, strange environment.

'Secure'—that was the killer word. What Arun was offering was security for her baby, security that went far beyond anything else Mel could put in place—security that eased the terror hidden in her heart.

She slid a glance towards Arun, ignored the shivers of desire, and studied his face.

Given his own childhood, she knew beyond a doubt he would provide the best possible life for this child, and his best would be a wondrous thing. But he would also give it the love that had been missing from his own life.

He might not be able to give Mel love, but the child, she knew without a doubt, would always know his or her father's love. That love tipped the scales.

She sighed.

'Yes, I'll ride with you in the morning,' she said, thinking to tell him then, where she'd first told him of the baby.

He seemed startled and she realised it had been a long time since he'd asked the question, but then he smiled and she knew he'd guessed her thoughts.

People began moving, Jenny was whisked away. Mel wondered whether she should follow, but Arun gripped her arm.

'Jenny will be dressed in the golden headdress and collar of the family now. It is very heavy but it is the bride's gift, so to speak, her financial future should things not work out between her and Kam. She has to wear it for a short time so everyone can marvel at it, then she and Kam will leave. Normally, they would go to the bride room and stay there for a week.'

The look that accompanied these last words made Mel's skin heat, but she hid her reaction as she was fascinated by this glimpse of a different culture.

'And then,' she asked, 'does she live with Kam or in the women's house?'

Arun smiled.

'Can you imagine your friend wanting to live separate to her husband? If you can, I assure you I can't imagine Kam wanting to spend any unavoidable time apart from Jenny. In the past, when men like my father had up to four wives, all the wives lived in the women's house, having specific nights they spent with their husband. Their husband was supposed to treat all of them equally, but that didn't always happen. Miriam was my father's favourite and she could have played up to that, but she is a fine woman and made sure the other wives were happy, or at least contented with their lot. But as well as wives, there are aunts and grandmothers and women who may not be related but are friends from long ago. Many women live there—it is the hub of the compound. Everything is organised from there, as far as family is concerned, and that way the men are free for business dealings.'

'It's very different,' Mel said, but she could understand how the tradition would have grown, the women crowded together for safety while their menfolk were away.

Then Jenny returned with such a weight of gold jewellery on her head and around her neck that she needed Kam's support to walk.

'Take a good look at it,' she said to Mel, 'because I'll give it ten minutes at the most then it's coming off. It's a wonder all the married women don't have tendonitis.'

Jenny paraded around the room, men and women nodding their approval, then she and Kam disappeared, to spend their first night as man and wife in a hotel in the city, and the partying began.

Mel was on a settee by the wall, listening to the Stapletons' latest account of their exploration of Zaheer, when Arun approached.

He excused himself to the Stapletons, put out his hand and drew Mel to her feet, his eyes studying her face.

'You are ready to leave?' he said, surprising her, for although she was feeling exhausted after a night of love-making and a hard day's work, she had doubted he would leave the party until it was finished.

'I am,' she admitted, 'but there's no need for you to leave as well. I'd like to go back to the hospital to check the baby before I go to bed, but all I need is a car and driver.'

'And another in the morning to bring you back so you can ride?' He smiled, not his seductive smile but the kind one that made her feel weak and woozy inside. 'I have just returned from the hospital. The baby is doing well. Your clothes are still in Jenny's house. You can spend the night there.'

Alone? she wondered, and was surprised by the spurt of disappointment she felt. But, of course, it would be alone. Arun would be unlikely to cause a scandal in this obviously close-knit community by spending the night with her.

So Mel did the only thing she could, she thanked him and allowed him to lead her out of the big building and across the courtyard towards Jenny and Kam's house.

'I can't believe it's only three days since I arrived and we walked through here,' she said, looking up to where the full moon rode high in the sky, visible in spite of the lights in the compound.

'Three days since I kissed you just here,' Arun whispered, drawing her into the side passage where they'd talked—and kissed.

But not like this. Not with heat and passion and an intensity that burned through Mel, made hotter and brighter and harder because tonight they wouldn't take their kisses to the logical conclusion...

CHAPTER EIGHT

MEL woke to the sound of Keira's gentle voice urging her to wake up. The spacious room was still dark, although the young woman had turned on the bathroom light so Mel could see the doorway and pick out various pieces of furniture as she slowly remembered where she was and why.

'You are riding?' Keira asked, and Mel nodded, then realised a tray, set with a teapot and cup and a plate of pastries, had been place on the bedside table. 'You might like something to eat before you go.'

Mel thanked her and poured a cup of tea, although now she was fully awake she remembered why she'd agreed to ride with Arun, and a feeling somewhere between excitement and apprehension churned in her stomach.

Setting down the tea, barely tasted, she left the bed and hurried into the bathroom, wanting to shower and get out to the stables—wanting to tell him before she lost her nerve!

He was waiting where he'd been last time, although this time there were two horses saddled.

'Haven't lost your nerve?' he said, echoing her thoughts so perfectly she could only stare at him.

How had he known she intended telling him this morning?

Or that her answer would be yes?

Although maybe she'd have been just as nervous over saying no.

'I have no idea what you're talking about,' she said, refusing to acknowledge his cleverness.

He smiled and held Mershinga while Mel mounted.

Would she read his doubt behind his smile? Arun wondered, thinking of the preparations he had made and wondering if they were all for naught.

But as he mounted Saracen he glanced towards the woman he hoped to soon make his wife and knew he hadn't guessed wrong, although she certainly didn't seem overwhelmingly happy about her decision to marry him.

In fact, she seemed very tense, her face pale, her lips set—more like someone going to the gallows than a woman contemplating marriage.

Which bothered him, although, thinking about it, if she was willing to go to this Charlie for security, surely what he, Arun, was offering, was more appealing.

They rode out of the compound and he heard her sigh and saw her stiffly held shoulders relax as she eased Mershinga to a halt and looked around.

And now he did know what she was thinking, for the look of wonder on her face told him as clearly as writing on a pad. He sat beside her, filled with joy that she could see and appreciate the beauty of the desert.

'You said rosy-tipped and I didn't take it in,' she breathed, whispering the words as if afraid noise might break the spell of early morning. 'But, look, the dunes are rosy, dark beneath and rosy-tipped, just as you said, the colour changing to gold while we watch.'

She eased her mount forward so the horse picked its way slowly across the sand, Arun falling in behind, content to watch her wide-eyed wonder at the spectacle.

They rode to the cairn where she'd told him of the baby, and there, as she was about to dismount, he joined her, stopping further movement with a hand on her arm.

'You have come here to answer me?' he asked.

She turned and looked at him, looking up as Mershinga was a full three hands shorter than his black stallion.

'I have,' Mel answered solemnly.

'You'll marry me,' Arun asked, a tightening in his gut suggesting he was really anxious about this.

'I will,' Mel said, and although he watched her as she spoke he could read no sign of joy in the declaration.

But joy would come in time, he decided, for this was a good thing in so many ways. Enough for now she had agreed and they could celebrate.

'Then come,' he said. 'We won't stop here this morning. We'll ride a little further.'

He led the way, guiding Saracen up the steep sand-stone slope behind the wadi, knowing Mershinga would follow. At the top the land levelled out and it was here he'd asked his people to set out the picnic. He pulled Saracen to one side of the track and waited until Mel reached the top, then enjoyed again the look of wonder in her eyes for from here she could see the desert spread in front of her, wave upon wave of dunes and cliffs, while behind her the city was bathed in the golden rays of the rising sun, the new buildings sparkling like jewels in the morning light.

'A tent?' Mel said, looking behind her now at the strange black shape.

'A picnic just for us, to celebrate our engagement,' Arun said, and the doubt that had been nagging at Mel ever since she'd made up her mind the previous night now returned—full strength.

'It's not really an engagement,' she protested. 'We're doing this for the baby—a marriage of convenience—you said so yourself.'

Arun had dismounted, tied the stallion's reins to a hitching post by the tent, and was now holding Mershinga's head, waiting for Mel to join him at ground level.

'Then we shall celebrate you agreeing to marry me,' he said, apparently unperturbed by her downgrading of their arrangement.

She slid off the horse, glancing uneasily towards the small tent, not sure whether to be disappointed or relieved when a white-clad attendant appeared in the doorway, unrolling a brightly coloured rug onto the sand in front of it.

'Come,' Arun said, taking her arm and leading her forward. 'For you today the best Zaheer can offer—breakfast in the dunes.'

He was so obviously proud of his country Mel weakened, turning to him with a teasing smile.

'The best? Better than the desert by moonlight?'

'It too is the best,' he said, so seriously she felt a little hitch in her heart and knew again how very easy it would be to love him...

They sat cross-legged on the carpet while the attendant prepared the special savoury pancakes Mel had eaten at the apartment. But these, cooked over a small brazier, were even more delicious, the yoghurt served with them thicker and creamier, the spice tastes more tantalising.

Or was it the company that made it all seem special?

She glanced sideways at Arun and caught him watching her.

'Your family,' he said quietly. 'You didn't answer me yesterday. An accident? Divorce?'

Mel shook her head.

'You will tell me?'

He phrased it as a question but she heard it as…not a demand so much as a need to know, and realised he deserved the truth.

'My mother died when I was born, my father opted not to have anything to do with a newborn baby who had, in his eyes, killed his wife. His family also turned away— supporting him, I think, rather than outright rejecting me. My mother's mother took me and raised me, and she died two years ago.'

Mel shrugged to show it no longer mattered and most of the time it didn't, but when Arun put his arm around her and drew her close she felt the loss again and had to swallow hard.

'You told me you were terrified, and I didn't understand. Yet you went ahead with this pregnancy?' he said, and she realised it wasn't her lack of family that had drawn his sympathy but his understanding of her stupid fears.

'It's such a rare occurrence these days it's hardly likely to happen twice in two generations,' she said, then added the bald truth. 'And it wasn't so much fear of dying that freaked me out, but leaving behind a child with no one to care for it.'

'Hence Charlie,' Arun murmured, more to himself than Melissa, as understanding of her situation not only dawned on him but caused him actual pain.

He moved slightly away on the pretext of passing her a plate of fruit.

So she *had* said yes to his proposal as the best option for her child.

And what was wrong with that?

Hadn't he couched his proposal as an offer of security for both her and the child?

Wasn't this what he wanted? A marriage of convenience?

He knew it was, knew the attraction was an added bonus, so why was he feeling perturbed?

Because it put him on the same level as this Charlie she spoke of—a bloodless wimp who would settle for marriage without the love of this strong, resourceful, beautiful and sexy woman.

She was talking of the children she wished to see again in A and E, of radiology appointments, but he couldn't get his mind around her conversation while his heart—no, it couldn't possibly be his heart, it had to be his pride—was suffering.

'I will arrange it,' he promised, although the promise he made to himself was very different.

He would change her thinking. He would woo and win her so she came to him in marriage wanting *him,* not a job or a safe haven for her child.

And that reminded him of her fear and he put his arm around her again, and held her as the sun's rays warmed the sands and the dawn slipped quietly into day.

'We should go,' Mel said, though having acceded to the marriage idea and with her hunger satisfied she felt pleasantly relaxed and could have sat on the carpet with Arun's arms around her for a very long time. 'I've got work to do and I'm sure you have as well.'

She edged away, standing up and shaking sand from her loose trousers, then, remembering it was less than twenty-four hours since Jenny's wedding, she turned to him.

'I don't want a big-deal wedding with all those people,' she said. 'You must have easier ways to get married here. A place where just the two of us can go?'

He smiled the lazy smile that started a quiver in her chest and said, 'You'll deny our people an excuse to party?'

'They've been partying all week for Jenny's wedding,' Mel reminded him. 'That's more than enough.'

Then something, maybe the quiver she'd felt earlier, prompted her to add, 'Our wedding's different anyway. It's a convenience, remember.'

Arun's face was raised to look at her, and the morning sun was shining on it, so she saw the shadow that passed across it, although usually his emotions were as carefully masked as the faces of the veiled women.

Did he not like being reminded that that's what it was?

Would he rather pretend it was a love match?

No, he was far too practical to think that way.

Wasn't he?

Mel pondered the question as they rode back to the compound where she showered hurriedly and dressed—again in loose trousers and tunic top, though thinking that she'd have to tell Jenny about the pregnancy and marriage fairly soon.

Before everyone knew…

The car was waiting at the door, Arun standing beside it.

Mel tried to read his expression but once again his face was wiped of all emotion.

Did the women wear masks and veils because they had less success at hiding their feelings than the men, although surely their eyes, the so-called windows of the soul, would give their emotions away?

'You are worried about the children?' Arun asked, as the driver steered the car through the compound gates.

Mel turned to him.

'Was I frowning?' she asked, and before he could reply she explained, 'I was thinking of masks and veils and whether as well as hiding beauty they hide emotion.'

Arun studied her for a moment, then smiled.

'Or perhaps conceal it so only the most persistent of lovers can penetrate the screen.'

Mel nodded slowly.

'So love is the key?' she said, her voice so quiet he barely heard the words.

And when he did make sense of them—literal sense— he wasn't sure he understood what she was saying.

Neither was he about to find out because she was speaking again, more loudly this time.

'How do I move around the hospital? Even when I know my way somewhere, like to the apartment or to A and E, how do I get access?'

Could she switch from talk of love to talk of work so swiftly?

Because that's all it was? Talk?

He didn't like the idea, but he, too, could make the switch.

'I will get you a key card that has your ID on it—it will get you wherever you want to go in the hospital and will also open the door to the apartment,' he said, then he muttered away in his own language for a moment, explaining as they arrived at the hospital that he must be as stupid as she was, so calmly accepting that she would continue working here.

'It is not your job,' he added, though he knew it was futile.

Out of the car now, she turned and smiled at him.

'Ah, but it will be—that's the whole point.'

'If you mean of our marriage, I am not marrying you to get a good paediatrician on staff. Kam and I had already interviewed someone who will make an excellent head of paediatrics. If you wish to work, then having you set up a paediatric surgical unit would be a bonus for our people.'

He knew he was speaking stiffly—hopefully not pompously—but her attitude to their marriage was grating on him. Not that he'd expected honeyed tones and melting glances, but they shared a strong attraction so surely a sense of—fondness? warmth?—wouldn't hurt!

Mel raised her eyebrows at him, aware he wasn't happy but unsure why. Did he want her to pretend it was a love match?

She shook her head in denial of her thoughts, knowing, the way she was beginning to think about him, that such a pretence would be dangerous for it would be too close to the real thing.

Thinking in terms of the convenience was much better, and remembering it was for security for her baby, not for the joy of being in Arun's company, was far, far safer for her mental well-being.

She followed him towards the main foyer, putting

thoughts of love and marriage out of her mind—screening them off—determined this time to notice where they were going so she could begin to find her own way around the hospital.

'Do you want to go up to the apartment?'

Expressionless face, voice devoid of emotion, yet still Mel shivered, thinking of what could happen should they go up to the apartment—remembering how good it would feel to be in his arms again.

'Best not,' she said, hoping her own face was as expressionless as his. 'Maybe the ICU then A and E. I've got a lot of those children I saw yesterday lined up for tests and scans, so I'll need to see them again, then there are all the others.'

They were walking towards the lift and she noticed the corridor that led to A and E.

'You spoke of clinics in different areas and I'm sure you mentioned hospitals, plural, when we spoke earlier, so why have these children not been seen somewhere else?'

She stood beside him while Arun pressed the button for the lift, a frown lowering his dark eyebrows.

'I wondered that myself, so I asked, and found they do not trust the other hospital—the old one which Kam and I have been trying to remodel bit by bit—because they say their children get sicker there than they are before they go in. And at the new one, this one, there have been no women doctors in the A and E department—I did not realise that—and a lot of the women who came yesterday are tribal women, not city women, and they did not want to talk with a man who wasn't a relative. There are baby clinics in the country, and here in the city, where women take their babies and a nurse will treat the child or give advice, but when the advice was to take the child to see a doctor, they held back.'

'Poor things,' Mel said, and Arun must have heard genuine empathy in her voice for he turned towards her.

'Poor things?'

He looked so worried she put a hand on his sleeve.

'To believe there is something wrong with your child and not be able to talk to someone about it.'

Arun nodded, but once again guilt was gnawing at him. That he hadn't known things were so bad—that he'd travelled the world to learn more in his specialty while at home facilities were so poor women were unable to get help for their sick children.

But it was useless feeling anger at the old man who, even ill, had clung to his power, refusing to allow his sons to fully modernise the old hospital or to nationalise the new hospital so free services could be provided to everyone.

'We will fix things,' he said, making the words a promise, knowing he would keep it.

They made their way to the ICU room where the baby was. Mel stopped at the door and stared around in disbelief. The pristine white room had been transformed into a fairyland, with toys, mobiles, posters and cards making it so vibrantly alive Mel had to blink a couple of times before she could take it all in.

'I can't believe it,' she said, turning to Arun who had obviously seen the decorations the previous evening when he'd come in.

'Just because the family cannot be here with Tia and the baby, it doesn't mean they can't send gifts.'

'Well, they've certainly done that,' Mel agreed, making her way to the crib where Sarah Craig was waiting to hand over the baby's chart.

The baby was doing far better than Mel had hoped, and she told Tia, adding, 'I'm sure it's all the attention you are giving him that is making him stronger every day.'

Tia beamed at her.

'My mother's attention too and soon his father's for my husband is coming back to be with me when the baby has the operation—is that not wonderful news?'

'The very best,' Mel agreed, giving Tia a hug.

Then she turned to Sarah.

'If you can get someone, a nurse would do, to relieve you, I could use your help again downstairs in A and E.'

'All but done,' Sarah told her. 'I've only been waiting for you to arrive. There's a nurse standing by to take over here. She's done a shift with the baby before so she knows what to watch for.' She glanced at Arun. 'If that's OK with Dr al'Kawali,' she added, smiling at him.

Mel wasn't sure if Sarah was checking with her nominal boss that this arrangement had his approval or pandering to him because he was such a handsome and sexy man.

And surely the squirmy feeling in Mel's stomach couldn't be jealousy…

Had she seen five hundred babies and small children? It certainly felt that way. As he had the previous day, at some stage Arun had appeared and drawn her off to a small sitting room, ordering her to sit, to eat, to drink some fruit juice or tea.

Sarah had worked in tandem with her through the morning, but had disappeared before Mel went to lunch, presumably to return to the ICU.

Or maybe she'd been off duty, working to a roster because she was actually employed by the hospital.

Though Mel doubted that would be the case. Most doctors she knew would keep working while there were still patients to be seen.

'Who's next?' Mel asked the young nurse who'd been helping her all day.

'No more,' the woman said. 'His Excellency says no more.'

'His Excellency?'

'The sheikh—Dr Rahman al'Kawali—he says no more. They must come back tomorrow or the next day. The women at the reception counter are even now making times for them to come. His Excellency says you must stop before you are exhausted.'

Dark eyes looked anxiously into Mel's.

'You will do this—stop—or he will be very angry.'

'Oh, will he, now?' Mel said, then realised she couldn't bring Arun's wrath down on this poor defenceless woman's head. 'And have you seen him very angry?'

The woman shook her head.

'But I have heard. It does not happen often, but when things are not as they should be—the floor soiled, or the staff careless—then he can be angry. Justly so, of course.'

Of course, Mel echoed silently, remembering how angry he had been when she'd told him about Charlie—coldly angry.

She closed her eyes for a moment, trying to blot out the

memory, and opened them to find not the nurse but Arun—the sometimes angry sheikh—standing in front of her.

'So, you are ready to go?'

'Back up to the apartment? Do you mind me staying there? It seems easiest, but if it's a nuisance or is breaking some rule for engaged couples or might offend someone—I'm sorry, I'm a bit muddled at the moment.'

He made an exasperated noise and seized her hand, dragging her out of A and E, back into the small room where she'd eaten lunch.

'You can't keep working like this,' he stormed. 'It's not right—and it's too much for you.'

Disconcerted by the grasp he still had on her hand, Mel tried to ease away.

'If you add "in your condition", I'll scream.'

To her surprise he smiled, and as the stern, rather forbidding face softened with the smile, all the reasons she shouldn't be so close—shouldn't be touching him—stirred to life again, firing every nerve in her body, so when he drew her closer, she didn't resist. In fact, far from it. She let her body slump against his, feeding on his strength.

'And will this draw such a fierce reaction?' he asked softly, his eyes holding hers as his lips moved closer, claiming her mouth with a hunger that burned like fever through her body.

'Arun, no…'

The protest died on her lips, for his hands were now smoothing across the loose fabric of her shirt, and her sensitive breasts were responding to the teasing touch, her nipples hardening to buds that sought more than teasing.

'The apartment…' she managed to murmur, and he

eased away, taking her elbow and guiding her out of the room. Mel was in such a daze, or haze perhaps, she once again forgot to take note of the corridors they walked along, or the turns they took.

Looking back, Mel could see that day set the pattern for the days to come, although most days they didn't ride, spending the dawn together in bed, wrapped in a tangle of arms and legs and the warm pleasure they took from each other's bodies.

Looking back, she could see she had already been falling for the man she was to marry, although instinct told her to hide it, not only from Arun but from Jenny and Kam. Sticking to the script of how convenient it was for them to marry, for the baby, and to make it easy for her to take on this wonderful new job, setting up a paediatric surgical unit in the hospital, secure in the knowledge the baby would be well looked after and lavished with love from the family.

But when she lay in his arms on the eve of her wedding day, she allowed herself to dream, just a little, of an Arun who loved her in return. She felt the warmth of his body curled around her back, his hands tucked against the bulge that was their baby.

So he slept every night, wrapping her not only in his arms but in security, and though she told herself this was a far greater gift than love, and one that would last for ever, sometimes she ached for love as well.

Greed, that's all that is, she reminded herself as Arun stirred, his hands moving across her belly, one higher, one lower, teasing her body to life, stirring it to excitement as he awoke wanting her.

'You are one most exciting, satisfying, generous and sexy lover,' he whispered in her ear, as he pulled her closer and she felt his hard erection slide between her legs and tease its way inside her. 'Have I told you that, Mrs al'Kawali to be?'

His hands caressed her breasts.

'Have I told you how I love to touch you, to feel your body tighten as you respond to me? Have I told you your skin is softer than the softest thistledown and finer than the most expensive silk? Have I told you how I love to touch you here?'

One hand slid lower. 'And here?' A thumb and finger tweaked her nipple. 'Until you catch your breath and tighten around me and say my name in such a husky whisper I can no longer restrain myself?'

Mel bit her lip as the pressure rose inside her, sweeping her up and up in a dizzying spiral of sensation until she peaked and splintered apart and breathed his name, as he'd predicted, then felt his release and heard him sigh, his arms tightening around her as if he'd never let her go.

But a wave of melancholy swept over her as Arun eased her hair aside to press a kiss to the nape of her neck, and though she could tell herself it didn't matter, she was beginning to wonder if it did.

If loving him would prove too much for her to hide.

And, should that happen, whether him knowing would embarrass him and affect the way he held her, touched her, made love to her?

And the ache that his love-making had chased away returned...

'I'll be away tonight,' he said, all business now as he

eased away from her, sitting up on the side of the bed and stretching, his toned muscles rippling beneath his satiny skin. 'I am flying out to the winter palace and won't be back until morning, but you can rest assured I will not be late for our wedding.'

He leaned across and kissed her cheek.

'And you, Madam Wife-to-be, are not to set one foot inside that hospital today. Go play with Jenny, shop, or drink coffee or do whatever women do on the day before their weddings. No work, understand?'

He tapped his finger on her nose as he gave the order, then, without waiting for a reply or a protest, rose, wrapped the white cloth he wore beneath his robes around his waist and left the bedroom, heading for his own room and the bathroom attached to it.

Mel watched him go, realising, as her melancholy deepened, that she'd never been inside that room—never been invited to see the room he considered his.

Was this room where they slept the equivalent of the women's house in the compound—a place where they could make love while his own room remained sacrosanct?

In which case, why?

She sighed.

There was only one possible reason.

Hussa!

Mel sat up, took a deep breath and tried a little positive thinking to throw off her gloom. Looking sensibly at the situation, if that *was* the case, then she, Mel, should be glad they used her bedroom, not his, for three in a bed, even when one was a ghost, was not a happy situation.

'This is a marriage of convenience,' she reminded herself, saying the words out loud to help her head remember, although it wasn't her head but her heart that needed help.

'Stupid heart,' she muttered, crossing to the bathroom and starting the shower running. 'Stupid, stupid heart.'

CHAPTER NINE

JENNY arrived as Mel was finishing her breakfast, full of plans for the day.

'I can't believe you've been here for ten days and haven't seen the city,' she announced, bubbling over not with her usual newly wed bliss but with the excitement of the proposed shopping expedition. 'Arun said we were to shop till we dropped and I was to buy you anything you wanted—a whole new wardrobe for your pregnancy and a dress for your wedding, and isn't it just the most amazing thing, the two of us falling in love with twins?'

'Marrying twins is amazing,' Mel said, 'but me marrying Arun is different—I told you that.'

Jenny smiled.

'And you can keep on telling me that,' Jenny responded, 'until you're blue in the face, but I only have to look at you when you're with Arun to realise you're in love.'

'Nonsense, that's lust, it's different,' Mel protested, because the love she held for Arun was a secret she wanted to keep hidden deep within her heart.

But to make Jen happy she shopped, allowing her friend to talk her into the most extravagant gown of golden silk for her wedding, although she stuck to practical outfits for the rest of her new wardrobe.

'I'll be working,' she reminded Jenny when they sat down for lunch in a café in the huge new shopping centre.

'Not all the time,' Jen reminded her, then she looked up and smiled as Miriam came in, having agreed to leave Tia for long enough to have lunch with the two women.

'I was telling Mel she won't be working all the time,' Jenny explained to Miriam, before turning back to Mel. 'You'll have days off to ride with Arun and explore the country. In fact, it's surprising Arun didn't take you out to the winter palace today. It's a fascinating place.'

'I suppose because he went to talk to Hussa,' Miriam said, sounding so matter-of-fact it took a moment for Mel to process the words.

But when she did she felt the hurt—as deep as a knife thrust in her chest.

'Hussa's dead, surely?' she blurted out, dismayed by the statement and the pain.

'Of course,' Miriam agreed, still totally unperturbed. 'But her mausoleum is there. He goes to talk to her, to explain about the baby and marrying you—so it would have been rude to take you with him.'

The pain expanded, filling Mel's chest, squeezing her lungs so she could barely breathe.

Jenny was looking at her anxiously, so Mel smiled as if she'd known all along that was why she hadn't accompanied Arun, and as if it didn't matter in the least to her that her husband-to-be still talked to his dead wife. But she must have been smiling too hard, for Jenny touched her arm.

'Are you all right?'

'No,' Mel managed. 'I don't feel well. It's been coming on all morning. Must be the excitement. Do you think you could call the driver and get him to take me back to the hospital? I'll go up to the apartment and rest. You and Miriam can stay here and have lunch.'

'As if!' Jenny said, signalling to a waitress and asking her to call their driver. 'I'm coming with you.'

'No, Jen!' Mel said, looking directly at her friend so Jenny could see she meant it. 'I just need to get home and lie down for a while. I promise you I'll be all right.' She tried a smile as she added. 'Trust me, I'm a doctor.'

'Well, it doesn't seem right,' Jenny grumbled as she took Mel's arm and walked with her out to the car. 'And Arun will be furious if he hears I've let you go home on your own when you're not feeling well.'

'Arun needn't know,' Mel told her. 'Now, go back to Miriam and make sure she understands that. I'm fine, just a little woozy. It's been a kind of hectic couple of weeks.'

'It has, that,' Jenny said, kissing Mel on the cheek as the driver opened the car door for her. 'You take care and, whether you like it or not, I'm going to be calling at the apartment just as soon as Miriam and I have finished lunch, and you'd better be resting or I *will* tell Arun.'

Relief that she was finally alone flooded through Mel as the car pulled into the traffic and began the journey to the hospital. Although now she was alone, she'd have to think.

Have to work out why Miriam's words had cut into her so deeply.

She'd known all along that Arun didn't love her, so why was she upset?

Because she'd hoped he'd grow to love her—maybe

had even convinced herself he was falling in love already—mistaken his natural kindness and courtesy for more than that...

The common sense part of her head was showing little mercy, but showed even less when it pursued the thoughts to their logical conclusion.

And now, it murmured to her, you know that won't happen, because no matter how he feels about you he still loves Hussa!

Oh, dear!

Back at the apartment she undressed and climbed into bed, curling herself up into a tight ball, hoping sleep might come so she didn't have to think, but sleep eluded her, which wasn't surprising, for how could she sleep when her mind kept replaying little videos of times she'd been with Arun?

Riding over the dunes, walking in the sand by moonlight, Arun soaping her back in the shower, Arun holding her as she shattered in a climax...

It was useless trying to sleep so she got up, had a shower and dressed, but what next? Arun could hardly class checking on Tia's baby as work so she left a message for Jenny with Olara and went down to the ICU, only to find Jenny and Miriam both there with Tia.

'He doesn't seem as well as he did yesterday,' Tia said, and Mel knew her instincts were probably right, although, just looking at the baby, she could see little change.

Mel checked the monitor. His pulse rate was slightly up, his blood oxygen slightly down, not enough to worry about in a healthy infant but in a baby so fragile...

She made a note for a slight change to the medication that was helping his heart and promised Tia she'd look in later. Assuring Jen she was all right now, it must just have been tiredness making her feel ill, she returned to the apartment and this time when she crawled into bed she did fall asleep, but only after she'd thought the situation through and decided what path to take.

Were her dreams bad that she frowned as she slept? Arun wondered as he stood beside the bed and watched the woman he was about to wed.

So beautiful, but did he really know her?

Not that it mattered. He told himself that repeatedly, reminding himself that no one really ever got to know another person completely. Yet it did bother him, just as her regular reminders that their marriage was a convenient arrangement bothered him.

She stirred and opened her eyes, smiling then frowning at him.

He took the fact that she smiled first as a good omen and sat down on the bed.

'You weren't coming back until tomorrow,' she said, pushing herself up on the bed until she was sitting with her back against the pillows. She frowned again. 'Did Jenny contact you?'

'No.' He answered truthfully because it was Miriam who had phoned to tell him Melissa wasn't well, and, given the frown, he guessed she'd given Jenny strict instructions to not mention her indisposition.

'Well, that's all right,' his bride-to-be announced, 'because it's good you are here. I've decided something and it's probably better I tell you today rather than tomorrow.'

This was not good, whatever it was. He knew for sure

he wasn't going to like whatever was coming. And the way Melissa took a deep breath before launching into what she had to say warned him it was as bad as news could be.

'I've decided not to marry you,' she said, her clear blue eyes steadfastly holding his. 'It won't change much. I'll live here or in the women's house and we can sleep together wherever and whenever you like and the baby will grow up in the compound with all the other kids so you will have the same paternal input into him. But we won't be married.'

The words were ringing in his head, so clear they were repeating themselves—*I've decided not to marry you*— over and over again. But they made no sense.

'You've—?'

'Decided not to marry you,' she said, as if maybe he hadn't heard the first time. 'But I can't see that it will make much difference to our lives, unless, of course, there's something really dreadful in your culture about us continuing to sleep together if we're not married, in which case that should stop, too.'

Mel ached as she said it, but she'd thought it through and decided a little pain now was better than being in pain for the rest of her life, and to marry Arun, loving him as she did, without him loving her back, would guarantee a lifetime of heartache and regret.

She watched him try to come to terms with her decision, today his thoughts not hidden from her. He was bewildered, as well he might be. So bewildered he hadn't asked the obvious question—why.

Not that she could tell him why.

Because you still love Hussa would sound lame.

She eased her legs off the bed.

'I've got to go to see the—'

The phone interrupted her. Arun lifted the receiver, and once again his face failed to hide his emotion, concern deepening to worry.

'That was Sarah Craig. The baby—'

Mel nodded, forcing everything else from her mind—all that mattered now was the baby. 'I saw him earlier,' she said. 'If he's still losing ground, I'll need to operate immediately. How quickly can you get a surgical team ready? Kam's agreed to assist. And Sarah. You'd lined up anaesthetists, perfusionists and someone who is experienced with the heart-lung machine for the op—do you think you can get them to come in tonight?'

Arun stared at her for a moment, unable to believe she'd switched from a declaration that she couldn't marry him to organising an operation in a split second.

He'd barely nodded when she continued.

'We'll need the best theatre nurses you can find—Kam will help you there—and most importantly the homograft and possibly a couple of tiny dacron ones as well in case the homograft doesn't fit. We need to move now, although we won't need the theatre team for a couple of hours. I want to be sure everything is in place before we start, and I'll want to talk to all the people who'll be in Theatre so they know what I'm doing.'

She didn't want to marry him? His mind swerved between that and business.

'I'll phone Kam then go down with you to the ICU to get the rest happening. He knows the surgical staff and can phone ahead with orders for what and who we'll need.

We'll get your team if we have to fly in staff from a neighbouring country.'

Satisfied that things were moving, and with her mind now fully focussed on what lay ahead, Mel went through to the bathroom to wash before heading for the ICU.

'If he is not thriving, is it safe to operate?'

Arun was putting down the phone and asked the question as she returned to the bedroom, her hands raised as she plaited her unruly hair into a thick pigtail.

'That's the one question I'd rather you hadn't asked,' Mel said, snapping a band on her hair and turning to him with a sigh. 'I suppose it will be up to Tia. I do wish her husband was here because she shouldn't have to decide this on her own.'

'He is here, or he should be. He was due to fly in this morning. Kam arranged for him to come home as soon as we knew the baby had problems, but getting flights and connections…'

He paused, then added, 'Why are you so concerned? Why do two people need to make the decision?'

Mel sighed again.

'You must know why,' she said, cross that he was forcing her to say it. 'If the baby's health is deteriorating, it means his heart isn't coping and so we have two choices. We do nothing more than keep him comfortable until he dies, or we operate, knowing he's very young and losing the battle already, so he might die anyway.'

Arun took her hand and squeezed her fingers.

'At least that way he gets a chance,' he reminded her, but Mel refused to be comforted.

'Not that great a one,' she said. 'Think of all the variables. Will he survive a switch to a heart-lung machine? Will he even survive the anaesthetic? Will his heart muscle be patent enough for me to stitch it after the operation, will whatever homografts you have in storage be the right size? We need more than a chance, we need a miracle.'

'Miracles happen,' Arun reminded her, pulling her closer to him and holding her against his body. She hadn't mentioned no physical contact, just that she wouldn't marry him. 'Jenny and Kam found each other and fell in love in a rebel stronghold, you're having the baby our country needs as an heir. I know it seems we've had our share of miracles, but shouldn't they come in threes?'

'I'd like to think so,' Mel said, but it was a grudging admission, mainly because being held in Arun's arms reminded her of all she was turning away from with her decision to not marry him. She pushed away.

'We've got to go,' she said, and left the room.

The little boy was struggling, his lips much bluer than they had been when Mel had seen him only hours earlier, his oxygen stats on their own low enough to be a concern. Mel examined him, an anxious Sarah hovering by her side.

'It happened so suddenly I thought at first the monitors must be playing up,' the anxious young doctor said.

'It can happen quickly,' Mel assured her. 'Don't blame yourself. Where's Tia?'

'In the visitors' room across the hall,' Sarah responded, nodding towards the small room families used as a refuge. 'Dr al'Kawali went in there to talk to her.'

Mel finished her examination, then made her way to the next room.

Tia sat on the couch with a young man in jeans and a polo shirt, looking so anxious he had to be the baby's father. Arun squatted in front of the pair, his hands holding a hand of each of them.

'I have told them the two options,' he said to Mel as she entered the room.

Mel felt relief, then wondered how much time the young parents would need to discuss these unhappy options.

'We want to go ahead with the operation,' Tia said, looking directly at Mel. 'That was what I had already decided, and when my husband was asked, he said the same. The baby deserves to have the chance of life and without the operation that is taken from him.'

'You understand he still might not live,' Mel pressed, because she had to hear for herself that they had considered that.

Both heads nodded, and the young man reached out to clasp his wife's hands.

'OK, we go ahead,' Mel told them. 'I'm going to take him now to Radiology for some scans while Arun collects the team of people we'll need for the operation and Kam organises the theatre and makes sure we have everything we need on hand.'

She looked at the two young people, so patently lost in their concern and grief, and stretched out her hands to them.

'It's going to be a long, hard wait for you two. Why don't you go somewhere private—maybe out to the compound—so you can comfort each other and perhaps even think of other things while the operation is going on?'

Tia looked at Mel and managed a weak smile.

'Private at the compound? I don't think so. No, we'll stay here in my room. We'll sit and talk and pray and know you're doing the best you can for our baby.'

She took her husband's hand and led him away. Arun turned to watch them go, a small, sad smile on his face.

'So my baby sister has grown up,' he said quietly, and Mel felt the weight of what she was about to undertake press down on her. So many people wanting this baby to live—so many people's happiness dependent on this operation…

She straightened up and took a deep breath. She could do this!

She went back to the baby's room

'Come on, kid,' she said to the little mite in the crib. 'Let's get you sorted.'

To Arun the most amazing thing was the noise in the room. He'd imagined operating theatres as places of deep quietness, but here, as he stood beside Kam, second assistant and general dogsbody, it was the noise that struck him.

He tried to think back to his student days when he'd done stints in Theatre, but although he remembered music playing in the background, and surgeons telling stupid jokes as they worked, he didn't remember the buzz of the Bovie as small blood vessels were sealed off or the blip of the heart monitor and the puffing noise of the ventilator.

He looked at the tiny baby on the table, his eyes taped closed, a ventilation tube in his trachea, a tube feeding into the radial artery at his wrist, a central line in the jugular vein in his neck and a fourth line, just in case, in his foot.

The anaesthetist was organising the necessary mix of gases into the stressed lungs and the drugs that were needed in the blood. Heparin, Arun knew, to thin the blood so it wouldn't clog up the heart-lung machine when the little one went on bypass. The anaesthetist had everything on hand, blood, saline, drugs, ready for any emergency. The perfusionist was taking blood all the time, checking the balance, while the monitor showed everyone in the room the baby's blood pressure, heart rate, oxygen saturation and temperature.

Melissa had used shears to cut the small chest open, and while he held it open with retractors Kam had fitted brackets to the sides of the sternum and turned a handle—more noise—to give Melissa a good opening to work in.

The heart-lung machine was ready, the baby's temperature was being reduced and they were approaching the moment when he would be connected to the machine.

'I'm cutting these small pieces of pericardium to use as a patch for the ventricular septum,' Melissa explained, using a stitch to secure two small squares of the pericardial tissue to an intercostal muscle. 'By stitching it there I'm not frantically looking for it when I need it. Now I use a stitch to keep the pericardium out of the way so we can get to the heart cleanly.'

Arun knew she was explaining this for the benefit of Sarah, who was in Theatre with them, but he couldn't help feeling proud that she was making the effort to explain while ninety-nine per cent of her mind must be concentrated on the difficult task.

'Now we put a cannula into the aorta, and it will send blood from the machine around the body while this cannula goes into the right atrium and we'll be sucking blood through it into the machine. Heart rate?'

'One-thirty,' someone answered.

'Temp?'

'Thirty.'

Arun shivered, thinking how cold the deep hypothermia must be, but it slowed the heart rate and made it easier to transfer the baby to the machine.

'Now we need to check the pulmonary artery. We come back from where it divides to right and left arteries to where it merges with the aorta—that's where we cut and put in the grafted artery. We'll fix that to the right ventricle…'

He was following it all, mainly because Melissa had called them all together earlier and drawn diagrams on a whiteboard, taking everyone who'd be involved through every stage of the operation. But how could she be so calm, operating on a baby—stitching together blood vessels so small one misplaced stitch could close them completely?

Yet she worked with a concentration that excluded all outside thoughts, quietly telling Kam what needed to be done, giving orders to the theatre staff to tie this, Bovie that, suction here, check the screen. And as he watched, and helped, he felt a sense of pride. This was *his* woman, doing this—*his* woman producing the miracle the baby needed.

Or was she?

She'd said she wouldn't marry him.

Why now?

What had happened to make her change her mind?

And why was it so hard to accept?

Painfully hard.

'OK, now we go. Pavulon to paralyse the heart muscle then we're going onto the machine—you all know what you need to do.'

Arun forgot everything but the baby on the table, and even the theatre noises seemed to abate as Melissa cut and stitched, fixing up the malformation that something as simple as a virus in Tia's early pregnancy might have caused.

He stood beside Kam, suctioning, passing instruments, tossing debris away, totally concentrated on the baby now, barely breathing, although he didn't realise that until Melissa said, 'OK, coming off bypass now,' and he had to take a gulp of air.

'This is the moment,' Kam whispered to him as Melissa reconnected the baby's vein and artery then massaged the heart to get it beating. Drugs were flowing into him to stimulate the heart, and those gathered in the room held their collective breaths and waited for the heart muscles to contract and lift the floppy, patched and stitched heart back to a working organ.

'There,' someone said, and they were right. The little heart was beating valiantly. Arun looked across at Melissa and behind the goggles she was wearing he saw the brightness of tears in her eyes. She must have sensed his regard for she looked at him and shook her head.

'That's the easy part,' she said lightly, although he could hear exhaustion in her voice and knew how much it had taken out of her. 'Now we have to put him back together again, then get him through the after-effects of the terrible trauma we've caused him. First off, Kam, could you check for bleeding on any of the joins we've made? And I want oxygen stats, BP and heart rate. No point sewing him up if there's still a problem somewhere.'

The results must have pleased her for within minutes she bent her head again, working swiftly and surely, putting, as she'd said, the little baby back together again.

'I'll stay with the anaesthetist and the baby,' Kam said to Arun when Melissa finally stepped back from the operating table. 'You take Melissa back to the apartment. She'll be exhausted—it's mental strain as much as the physical effort of concentration. Tell her I'll call if there's any change.'

Arun moved away—the theatre was noisy again, instruments clanging together, people talking, most in awed tones, as they cleared away the debris of a long operation. Melissa was at the far side of the room, stripping off her gloves, the fourth set she'd worn during the operation.

'Come, there's a room here where you can change in privacy, then I'll take you home and get some food and drink into you—you must be totally depleted.'

She had slid the goggles she'd been wearing to the top of her head, and now pulled them off.

'Home?' she echoed, a tired smile on her face.

'The apartment, you know I meant that—no talk, hidden agenda, not after what you've just done for us.'

She shook her head.

'Not for you, but for the baby. Not even for Tia and her husband, just for the baby.'

She pressed her hand against her stomach, and he wondered how often she worried whether the child she carried was OK. Working with babies with congenital conditions, she couldn't help but wonder…

'So, where's this private space?'

Her apron and outer gown had joined her mask, gloves and goggles in the bin and she stood there in the pale green scrub suit, looking so spent he wanted to lift her into his arms and carry her back to the apartment.

'This way. Your clothes are there, but if you don't want to change, you can come up to the apartment as you are and shower there.'

'I'll do that—just get out of the boots and into my sandals. Thanks.'

But as she was about to leave the theatre complex she turned back.

'The baby?'

'Kam will stay with him. He'll contact you immediately if there's any change or any cause for concern.'

She nodded and Arun realised just how tired she must be to not argue that he too should stay, or even she herself.

Mel let him take charge, leading her out of the warren of rooms around the theatre then up to the apartment, where with gentle hands he stripped off her clothes and helped her step into the shower, already running at a beautiful temperature, the water jets spraying from the wall just what she needed for her aching back.

Eventually, certain her skin had shrivelled to crêpe, she left the shower, to find Arun waiting once again, wrapping her in a big warm towel, then leading her to the bedroom where he sat her on the bed while he towel-dried her hair.

'Now, you're to eat—doctor's orders,' he said, and Mel looked around, saw daylight at the window and frowned.

'It's morning?'

Arun nodded.

'We went down to the baby's room at six last night and you've been working ever since,' he said. 'You were in Theatre five hours.'

'It didn't seem that long,' Mel managed, but as she spoke she felt a wave of tiredness bear down on her, all but engulfing her.

She sipped some tea and ate two pancakes, then shook her head.

'No more. I really, really need to sleep.'

But as she set her cup down she thought of the baby and looked up at Arun.

'You *will* wake me up if I'm needed?' she demanded. 'No nonsense about letting the poor little woman sleep?'

He smiled and in spite of her tiredness and her determination to stop loving him, her heart beat faster.

'Poor little woman indeed,' he teased. 'Woe betide any man who dared to use that description for you.'

Then he bent and kissed her on the lips.

'I will wake you up,' he promised. 'You can be sure of that, so sleep at peace, my beautiful one.'

She lay back on the pillows and he drew the sheet over her naked body, then touched her gently on the cheek and left the room.

'My beautiful one?' Mel murmured to herself, savouring the words, then she remembered back before the operation.

Remembered telling him they wouldn't marry...

Remembered he hadn't asked why...

She turned on her side, tucked her hands beneath her head and sighed, though for what she wasn't quite sure, and she was too darned tired to think about it now.

* * *

'His name is Shiar.'

Tia rose from beside the crib in the ICU room to greet Mel with this news as Mel, refreshed, fed and anxious to see her patient, entered at about midday.

'Oh, I'm so glad you've named him,' Mel told her, giving the young woman a quick hug.

'And you didn't meet Sharif, my husband—not properly,' Tia added, introducing Mel formally to the young man who bowed over her hand and rushed into a welter of thanks for all she had done for the baby.

'It is nothing,' she said, resting her hand on the sleeve of the white gown he now wore. 'And the little one, Shiar, is still far from well. We must wait and see.'

Both parents nodded, but Mel could read the hope in their shining eyes and prayed it would not be misplaced.

She checked Shiar, who was to be kept sedated for at least twenty-four hours, then said goodbye to the pair, but once outside the baby's room she leaned against the wall, uncertain what to do next.

It was to be her wedding day so the women who were still trickling into the A and E department with sick children had been told she wouldn't be available, although, having assured Arun she intended to keep working, she did have appointments lined up for the following day.

But today?

Perhaps she could ride. She'd go out to the compound—

'I was looking for you.'

Arun had pushed through the doors into the ICU without her noticing.

'Come!' he said, and took her hand. 'I want to take you somewhere.'

She tried to tug her hand away but his grip was too strong.

'I'm not going with you to get married,' she told him, and he smiled the kind of knowing smile that *always* made her heart flutter. Only today it made her angry as well and she tugged again at her trapped hand.

'Did I mention marriage?' he teased, releasing her hand but slipping his arm through hers so she would have to make a scene to escape his touch.

They reached the bank of lifts and to Mel's surprise he pushed the 'up' button rather than the 'down' one.

'We're going up? Are your rooms up? No, they're on the same floor as the ICU, aren't they? Why are we going up?'

'You'll see,' he said.

And Mel did, for the doors of the lift opened onto a flat roof and there, not forty feet in front of them, was a small green helicopter.

'I thought I'd show you my kingdom,' he said, leading her towards it. 'So you can see what you're missing out on by not marrying me.'

Mel frowned at him. Surely he couldn't think she would have been marrying him for riches or property or to be the sheikhess—no, that was wrong, Jenny was a sheikha. But her annoyance was more than outweighed by excitement that she would be seeing more of this beautiful desert country. With Arun…

He helped her into the helicopter then walked around and climbed in on the other side, taking the controls himself.

'There are parts of the land where you can't fly helicopters—out near the mountains where Jenny was, for instance—but most of the country is accessible this way and flying takes many hours off a journey.'

His long slender fingers worked easily at the controls and the little machine lifted into the air and took off, circling the city first, Arun pointing out the port where ships from all over the world docked to take on oil, and the swathes of green contrasting with the red-brown desert sands—golf courses and resorts—playgrounds of the wealthy. Then the city disappeared and beneath them lay the desert, dotted here and there with encampments of black tents or clusters of palms that indicated oases.

'This is the long wadi—there are oases all along it,' Arun explained as they banked over a small village, stone and earth brick houses clustered by the green patch of vegetation. 'And here we are—see below—the winter palace.'

The winter palace?

Where Hussa was buried?

Mel felt her chest grow tight and her breathing become shallow and irregular. Why was he bringing her here?

She turned towards him, wanting to ask, not about Hussa but about the reason for the visit, but he was concentrating on putting the little aircraft down on the ground, onto a white circle painted on a concrete pad just outside the walls of the rambling, red stone building he'd called the winter palace.

CHAPTER TEN

HE TURNED the engine off and climbed out, ducking beneath the slowing rotor blades to come around and open the door on her side.

'Come,' he said once more, the word peremptory but not an order. He took her hand to help her alight then led her towards the long shallow steps that rose towards the entrance of the huge, many-turreted building.

'In the old days, when this was first built, it was a fort as well as a home, so instead of many buildings, as we have in the city compound, all the functions are in one main palace, broken up into many…I suppose you would say apartments—for different families and different uses.'

Mel looked around. The red stone, much of it ornately carved, was old enough to be crumbling in places, but she could see the design of an ancient fort in it, for the windows were narrow slits, many of them inset with carved stonework. Huge wooden doors were folded back and they walked beneath an arch and into a courtyard, not landscaped, as the city courtyard was, but cobbled.

Around the courtyard was a cloister, and Mel glimpsed, here and there, robed figures flitting through the shadows.

'It was here the men prepared their mounts and armed themselves for raids,' Arun said. 'It was built for practicality, not beauty, but walk carefully—the cobbles are old and very rough in parts.'

He took her arm, drawing her across and to the left where they passed into the shadow of the cloister and shed their sandals before entering the building. Once inside she had to gasp for instead of the red stone all was cool white marble—the floor, the pillars, the walls, all the same white-grey, streaked here and there with black, and inlaid in the arches and above the windows with what looked like precious gems.

'You cannot show your wealth to the enemy,' Arun explained, leading from room to room, pointing out the tapestries and telling her the history of his family that was depicted in them, showing her the great hall where he and Kam would still hold audiences for their people, listening to grievances, trying to right wrongs.

Then up a winding staircase, into one of the turrets.

'We played here as children, Kam and I, although we were forbidden to do so,' he said, and she could imagine the twins racing each other up the stairs.

'Or perhaps because you were forbidden,' Mel said, knowing the lure of the forbidden to a child. 'But is the whole place deserted now?' she asked, thinking of the waste that all the rooms should be empty.

'Far from it,' he said, leading her out onto a small balcony that ran around the top of the turret. 'Look.'

He pointed down and she saw that he'd landed on the shortest side of the huge building and led her into only one part of it. Below them was another courtyard, thick with palms and fruit trees, where men raked paths, and women walked, and children played.

'When my father was alive, he wanted all the family to live here permanently and used whatever pressure he could, financial and emotional, to keep them here. I imagine it was part rebellion against his strictures that when he died most of them immediately moved to the city. But a couple of my sisters, some aunts and a few unrelated dependants still live out here all year round. Some prefer the old to the new.'

'It's very beautiful,' Mel said, seeing the stunted date palms from the top and yellow lemons bright against the glossy leaves of their trees.

'This part I have been showing you was my father's domain,' Arun continued. 'Kam hates it still, but it has always had a special place in my heart, in spite of the unhappiness the old man caused us. Knowing this, Kam has insisted it be mine and after me it will be my child's, because this is his or her history and heritage. I thought, in seeing it, you might understand why marriage is important to me.'

Mel could, but the word 'marriage' reminded Mel of Miriam's words in the shopping centre.

'You came here yesterday?' Mel began, unsure what to say next.

Arun looked puzzled for a moment, then frowned.

'Miriam told you? Yes, I did.'

He hesitated and Mel felt the chill of Hussa's ghost floating between them.

Then Arun took her hand and held it gently, as if it was something very precious.

'My first wife, Hussa, is buried here. I came to see her, Mel, to tell her all about you and about the happiness you've brought me, and as I sat there, I realised she would want me to be happy. It was an ending, Mel, so I could move on. So I could marry you—or so I thought.'

He was studying her face and although she could feel happiness singing in her blood, uncertainty held her mute.

Fortunately, Arun still retained the power of words. In a voice husky with an emotion she dared not guess at he said, 'But you should know, Melissa, that I won't force you to marry me any more...'

He paused and looked out over the buildings and beyond them to the desert, baking under the afternoon sun.

Then he turned and took her hands and looked at her.

'Any more,' he continued, 'than I can force you to love me.'

Mel frowned at him, the words not computing into anything intelligible in her head.

'Force me to love you?' she repeated. 'Why would you say that?'

A self-deprecating little smile pressed a line into his left cheek.

'Because love has been off limits? Because of your insistence that our marriage is a practical arrangement? Because it's so damn difficult for me to believe what I feel, let alone make a fool of myself by telling you?'

He turned away as if looking at her caused him pain, but Mel was catching up.

'Arun?'

He swung back to look at her, strain around his mouth now and uncertainty in his eyes.

'Make a fool of yourself,' she begged, smiling at him as she said it. 'Tell me.'

He sighed, then shook his head, the in-control sheikh suddenly lost.

'I love you,' he managed, then added, 'There, it's said!' And sighed again.

'That's all?' Mel teased, so happy she wanted to leap into the air and shout her joy to the world but holding it all under control because she wasn't finished with this man yet.

'Isn't it enough?' he grumbled, as if sure he'd made a total idiot of himself.

'Of course it's not,' Mel told him. 'Now you have to kiss me and tell me why you love me and whisper sweet nothings in my ear.'

'Sweet nothings?' he repeated, suspicion dawning in his eyes. 'You're happy about this? You're not annoyed?'

Mel smiled at him and put her arms around him, drawing close to his body.

'Why would I be annoyed when you've just made me the happiest woman in the world?' she murmured. 'When you've just told me the love I have for you is returned. When—'

'Love is returned? You love me, too?'

He pushed away so he could look into her face.

'If you love me, why did you say you wouldn't marry me?' he demanded, and Mel drew him close again, embarrassed by the intensity of her feelings and not wanting him looking at her as she confessed.

'I thought you didn't love me—couldn't see why you would—especially when you'd so loved Hussa. Then I thought loving you without you loving me back would be easier if we weren't married than if we were, so...'

Arun put his hands on her shoulders and eased her away, his face stern now.

'Let us back up a bit here,' he said, his voice stern as well. 'I know we never talked of love, but surely you must have had some inkling of how I felt? And as for Hussa, yes, Melissa, I did love her, but she is gone and you have come to fill all the empty places in my heart. You must understand that or you will make yourself miserable. It is you I love—my brave, strong, independent, argumentative and beautiful Melissa. You I love now and will love for ever.'

And finally he kissed her, so sweetly, so tenderly Mel wondered if her heart might burst apart with the love it held, although she knew full well hearts were very tough structures and hers would probably handle the strain.

EPILOGUE

Two women robed in blue sat on easy chairs beneath the lemon trees in the courtyard, warmed by the sun reflecting off the red stone building.

'Bliss?' Mel said, turning to pick up the baby girl who grizzled quietly in a woven basket by her side.

'Bliss!' Jenny echoed, lying back, her hands linked around her bulging stomach. 'Although it would be nicer if the men were here.'

'Your wish is their command, I'd say,' Mel said, turning her head the better to hear the rattling noise of the approaching helicopter.

It flew over them like a shiny green dragonfly, swooping low enough to make Mel shake her fist at the pilot.

'He knows not to do that in case it wakes the baby,' she told her friend.

'The baby's already awake,' Jenny reminded her, nodding to the chubby infant sucking greedily on Melissa's breast.

'But she might not have been,' Mel complained, although her heart wasn't in it. Her heart, in fact, was dancing with excitement, although Arun had only been gone a couple of days—down to the city to the opening of the now completed renovations of the old hospital.

'So, the lazy women of the harem are taking their ease.'

It was Kam who spoke as the two brothers entered the courtyard, so alike yet easily identifiable to their wives.

'It's not exactly ease when I'm having Braxton-Hicks's contractions all the time,' Jen told him, though she rose to go towards him, greeting him with a kiss and turning in his arms so they could walk together. 'To think of all I went through to have this baby—operation after operation—and now it's doing this to me.'

'Ah, but it will all be worth it when you hold him in your arms,' Mel said. 'I think I was as excited as you were when you finally fell pregnant and then to learn it was a boy. Zaheer may be developing quickly but I'm not sure they'd be ready for a female ruler.'

'Or that my sweet little Nooria would want the job,' Arun said, reaching Mel's side and kneeling by her, his eyes feasting on his daughter.

'Sweet *little* Nooria?' Mel responded. 'This child is going to be the size of an oil drum, the way she eats.'

'She is beautiful,' Arun whispered, running his hand over the downy head. 'As is her mother.'

He reached up to touch Mel's lips with his fingers.

'You are well?'

Mel nodded, the emotion she felt tightening her chest too much for her to be able to speak.

How could it be that love could grow so much? That what she had felt for Arun when they'd married, a couple of days later than they'd planned, could be but a shadow of the love that had grown between them in the year that had followed?

'Is all prepared for the party?' Arun asked, and Mel found her voice.

'That's why we had to rest—we haven't stopped. That sister of yours is a slave-driver.'

She eased the baby off her breast and Arun helped her stand, then he slipped his arm around her and the five of them made their way into the grand hall, not for an audience today but to celebrate the first birthday of a very special, and very healthy, little boy.

Shiar.

But as Kam and Jenny walked under the arch into the cloister, Mel paused, turning to look back at the courtyard, seeing the greens of the trees deepen as the sun sank lower in the sky then the flush of colour above the palace walls as the magical evening light show began.

Arun turned with her.

'You are happy, my love?' he asked quietly.

She moved closer to his side and rested her head on his shoulder.

'Happier than I ever thought a woman could be, Arun. And you?'

His arm tightened around her shoulder and he bent awkwardly around Nooria to kiss Mel on the lips.

'How could I not be when you have given me so great a gift—when you have given me your love?'

Don't miss Pink Tuesday
One day. 10 hours. 10 deals.

PINK TUESDAY
IS COMING!

10 hours...10 unmissable deals!

This Valentine's Day we will be bringing
you fantastic offers across a range of
our titles—each hour, on the hour!

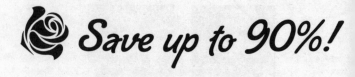

Save up to 90%!

Pink Tuesday starts
9am Tuesday 14th February

Find out how to grab a Pink Tuesday deal—
register online at **www.millsandboon.co.uk**

Visit us
Online

0212/PM/MB362

Negroponte, Nicholas P. "Products and Services for Computer Networks." *Scientific American*, September 1991.
What we can expect from pervasive ultrahigh bandwidth networks, by the director of the MIT Media Lab.

Nelson, Mark. "Bioregenerative Life Support for Space Habitation and Extended Planetary Missions." *Space Biosphere Ventures*, 1989.
Gets into the early attempts at self-sustaining space habitats.

Nelson, Mark, and Gerald Soffen, eds. *Biological Life Support Systems*. Synergetic Press, 1990.
The proceedings of a 1989 workshop on closed biological-based systems as human life support devices in space. Held at the site of Biosphere 2 and cosponsored by NASA. Technical but rich.

Nelson, Mark, and Tony L. Burgess, et al. "Using a closed ecological system to study Earth's biosphere: Initial results from Biosphere 2." *BioScience*, April 1993.
Description of the scientific experiment in Biosphere 2 written by Bio2 staff after the first year. Has excellent bibliography for this esoteric subject.

Nitecki, Matthew H., ed. *Evolutionary Progress*. University of Chicago Press, 1988.
Biologists don't know how to handle the idea of progress in evolution. Here leading evolutionists, philosophers, and historians of biology grapple with the controversial idea in these postmodern times, and come up ambivalent in the aggregate. A few of them find the notion "noxious, culturally embedded, untestable, nonoperational, intractable." Those who do acknowledge progress in evolution are uncomfortable. This is a good, revealing collection of papers.

O'Neill, R. V. *A Hierarchical Concept of Ecosystems*. Princeton University Press, 1986.
Treats the latest hot trend in ecology: a new perspective which considers communities as hierarchical structures with different dynamics for every level. Does a good job in setting out the questions that need to be answered.

Obenhuber, D. C., and C. E. Folsome. "Carbon recycling in materially closed ecological life support systems." *BioSystems*, 21; 1988.
Measurements of carbon pathways in closed ecospheres.

Odum, Eugene P. *Ecology and Our Endangered Life-Support Systems*. Sinauer Associates, 1989.

A quick introductory tour of the science of ecology by the guy who brought energy accounting to the field.

Olson, R. L., M. W. Oleson, and T. J. Slavin. "CELSS for Advanced Manned Mission." *HortScience*, 23(2); April 1988.
A paper from a symposium on "Extraterrestrial Crop Production." Good summary of NASA's closed system experiments.

Pagels, Heinz R. *The Dreams of Reason: The Computer and the Rise of the Sciences of Complexity*. Bantam, 1988.
A satisfyingly rich and perceptive scan on how the complexity of the computer makes visible the complexity of the world.

Parisi, Domenico, Stefano Nolfi, and Federico Cecconi. "Learning, Behavior, and Evolution." In *Proceedings of the First European Conference on Artificial Life*, The MIT Press, 1991.
Exploration of the role of learned behavior in accelerating evolution based on neural networks.

Pattee, Howard H. *Hierarchy Theory: The Challenge of Complex Systems*. George Braziller, 1973.
This is a book of all that was known about hierarchical systems 20 years ago, and it wasn't much. The authors ask some good questions which still have not been answered. In short, we still don't know much how hierarchies of control work.

Pauly, Philip J. *Controlling Life: Jacques Loeb & the Engineering Ideal in Biology*. University of California Press, 1987.
A scholarly biography of the guy who did most to make science think of biological organisms as mechanisms.

Pimm, Stuart L. "The complexity and stability of ecosystems." *Nature*, 307; 26 January 1984.
Tries to answer the question of how complexity and stability in ecosystems are related.

———. *The Balance of Nature?* University of Chicago Press, 1991.
Pimm treats food-webs as if they were cybernetic circuits, and out of both simulated and real food-webs has derived some of the freshest ecological news in a decade.

Pimm, Stuart L., John H. Lawton, and Joel E. Cohen. "Food web patterns and their consequences." *Nature*, 350; 25 April 1991.
An extremely informative review article on what is known about ecological food webs from a systems point of view.

Pines, David, ed. *Emerging Syntheses in Science*. Addison-Wesley, 1988.

An eclectic bunch of papers signaling the new science of complexity. The best papers in this anthology, derived from the founding workshop of the Santa Fe Institute, focus on the problems of complexity itself.

Porter, Eliot, and James Gleick. *Nature's Chaos*. Viking, 1990.

The exquisite color landscape photography of Eliot Porter is paired with the lyrical science prose of James Gleick. Both celebrate—in coffee table book format—the ordered complexities and complications of nature in its large and small details.

Poundstone, William. *Prisoner's Dilemma*. Doubleday, 1992.

Besides telling you more than you'll ever really want to know about the Prisoner's Dilemma game, this book also ties the game into the history of think tanks and the use of game theory in the arms race and the role of John von Neumann in both game theory and the cold war.

Powers, William T. *Living Control Systems*. The Control Systems Group, 1989.

A control engineer looks at the variety of control circuits in biological systems.

Prusinkiewicz, Przemyslaw, and Aristid Lindenmayer. *The Algorithmic Beauty of Plants*. Springer-Verlag, 1990.

Plants as numbers.

Pugh, Robert E. *Evaluation of Policy Simulation Models: A Conceptual Approach and Case Study*. Information Resources Press, 1977.

Evaluates world economic models such as Limits to Growth.

Raup, David M. *Extinction: Bad Genes or Bad Luck?* W. W. Norton, 1991.

The title is a very good question. This prominent paleontologist thinks it's a combination of bad genes and bad luck, but that "most species die out because they are unlucky." And thus he presents his evidence.

Reid, Robert G. B. *Evolutionary Theory: The Unfinished Synthesis*. Croom Helm, 1985.

This is the most interesting book on evolutionary theory I have come across. While other books can serve up more exhaustive critiques of neo-darwinism, none compare to this one in presenting a postdarwinian view. The author is not afraid to dip into nonbiological studies to shape his notion of evolution; yet he primarily dwells in biological fact. Most recommended.

Rheingold, Howard. *Tools for Thought*. Prentice Hall Books, 1985.

Subtitled: "The history and future of mind-expanding technology," this is a really hip and very informative chronicle of how computers became personal computers, of the visionary people behind that transformation, and of its social meaning and cultural consequences. I recommend it as the best history of computers to date.

Ricklefs, Robert E. *Ecology*. Chiron Press, 1979.
A textbook on ecology that is lucid, deep, and gracefully written and full of the author's personal insight, setting it apart from most rather antiseptic and formulaic ecology textbooks.

Ridley, Mark. *The Problems of Evolution*. Oxford University Press, 1985.
Here are the current bothersome problems in neodarwinian theory from within the perspective of neodarwinism.

Roberts, Peter C. *Modelling Large Systems*. Taylor & Francis, 1978.
Primarily on the difficulties of getting meaningful results via miniaturizing a large system.

Robinson, Herbert W., and Douglas E. Knight. *Cybernetics, Artificial Intelligence, and Ecology*. Spartan Books, 1972.
A few helpful ideas and a fair representation of cybernetic thinking.

Root, A. I., ed. *The ABC and XYZ of Bee Culture*. A. I. Root Company, 1962.
For over a hundred years a perennial encyclopedia of bee culture lore for first-time beekeepers. Remarkably timeless, last updated in 1962.

Rosenfield, Israel. *The Invention of Memory*. Basic Books, 1988.
A survey view of the brain as having a nonlocalized memory, and a long prologue to an exposition of Gerald Edelman's controversial idea of "Neural Darwinism," or the natural selection of thoughts in the brain.

Sagan, Dorion. *Biospheres: Metamorphosis of Planet Earth*. McGraw-Hill, 1990.
Speculations on the science of biospherics—human habitats as extensions of Gaia.

Salthe, Stanley N. *Evolving Hierarchical Systems: Their Structure and Representation*. Columbia University Press, 1985.
Can't say I completely understand this book, but it is very provocative in picturing evolution as working differentially at various levels.

Saunders, Peter T. "The complexity of organisms." In *Evolutionary Theory: Paths into the Future*, Pollard, J. W., ed. John Wiley and Sons, 1984.
Saunders sees complexity arising out of self-organization rather than from natural selection.

Schement, Jorge Reina, and Leah A. Lievrouw. *Competing Visions, Complete Realities: Social Aspects of the Information Society*. Ablex Publishing, 1987.

Thoughts on communication networks as social structure.

Schneider, Stephen, H. Penelope, and J. Boston, eds. *Scientists on Gaia*. The MIT Press, 1991.

Some of the papers in this compendium are more rigorous than others, but all strive to describe Gaia in scientific rather than poetical terms. I found the papers which worried about the definitions of Gaia to be the most productive.

Schrage, Michael. *Shared Minds: The New Technologies of Collaboration*. Random House, 1990.

In a network society the tools of collaboration become essential and wealth-generating. Schrage reports on current research into new network skills.

Schull, Jonathan. "Are species intelligent?" *Behavioral and Brain Sciences*, 13; 1, 1990.

Since the analogy between learning and evolution is at least as old as the idea of evolution itself, the author examines species as thinking structures. His idea is critiqued by cognitive scientists and evolutionists.

Schulmeyer, G. Gordon. *Zero Defect Software*. McGraw-Hill, 1990.

An introduction to the controversial zero defect concept. I take this book as one method to construct reliable complex systems.

Scientific American, eds. *Automatic Control*. Simon and Schuster, 1955.

Primarily for historical interest, this anthology of early *Scientific American* articles on cybernetic control talks about the impact of automatic systems on society at a time (late '40s) when the population of computers in the world was exactly one.

Simon, Herbert A. *The Sciences of the Artificial*. The MIT Press, 1969.

There's a lot of common sense about how to build complex systems packed into this small book. It also offers rare insight into the role and meanings of simulations.

————. *Models of My Life*. Basic Books, 1991.

A dull autobiography about the extraordinary life of the last renaissance man in the 20th century. In his spare time he helped invent the field of artificial intelligence.

Slater, Philip. "Democracy is Inevitable." *Harvard Business Review*, September/October 1990.

Best argument I'm aware of for this provocative thesis: "Democracy becomes a functional necessity whenever a social system is competing for survival under conditions of chronic change."

Smith, John Maynard. *Did Darwin Get it Right? Essays on Games, Sex and Evolution*. Chapman and Hall, 1989.

Deals with current controversies in evolutionary biology in an even-handed and intelligent way.

Smith, Reid G. *A Framework for Distributed Problem Solving*. UMI Research Press, 1981.

General computer science introduction to constructing programs that work in a distributed environment.

Sober, Elliott. *The Nature of Selection: Evolutionary Theory in Philosophical Focus*. The University of Chicago Press, 1984.

This is an incredibly profound book. It is a philosophical examination of evolutionary theory which begins with the frequent criticism that neodarwinism is rooted in a contradiction, that "survival of the fittest is a tautology." Sober illuminates this causality puzzle and then goes on to reveal evolution as a system of logic. His work should not be missed by anyone doing computational evolution.

Sonea, Sonrin, and Maurice Panisset. *A New Bacteriology*. Jones and Bartlett, 1983.

The "new" here is a view that sees bacteria as not primitive and not independent, but as a superorganism communicating genetic changes worldwide and rapidly.

Spencer, Herbert. *The Factors of Organic Evolution*. Williams and Nograte, 1887.

At the time of Darwin, the philosopher Herbert Spencer had an enormous impact in forming popular notions of the meaning of evolution. As laid out in this book, evolution is progressive, internally directed to improvement and perfection, among other things.

Stanley, Steven. "An Explanation for Cope's Rule." *Evolution*, 27; 1973.

One of the rare accepted trends in biological evolution—increasing size in animals—gets debunked.

————. *The New Evolutionary Timetable*. Basic Books, 1981.

Gingerly considers selection of units larger than individuals and addresses long-term directions in macroevolution, but does so without strong conclusions.

Steele, E. J. *Somatic Selection and Adaptive Evolution: On the Inheritance of Acquired Characters*. University of Chicago Press, 1979.

The controversial experiments of immunologist Ted Steele, who claims to demonstrate Lamarckian evolution in inbred strains of mice, is presented in the experimenter's own words. Steele's work has not been confirmed.

Stewart, Ian. *Does God Play Dice?* Basil Blackwell, 1989.

For technical insight on chaos and dynamical systems, a better book than Gleick's bestseller *Chaos*. Stewart doesn't have Gleick's narrative flair, but he does go deeper into the whys and hows, with numerous graphs, illustrations, and a bit of math.

Stewart, Thomas A. "Brainpower." *Fortune*, 3 June 1991.

Article about the role of knowledge in creating wealth for companies. I picked up the term "network economics" here.

Symonds, Neville. "A fitter theory of evolution?" *New Scientist*, 21 September 1991.

In lay science terms addresses results suggesting "Lamarckian" evolution in *E. coli* soups.

Tainter, Joseph A. *The Collapse of Complex Societies*. Cambridge University Press, 1988.

I disagree with the author's basic tenet that declining returns on increasing complexity causes collapse of stable civilizations, but his argument is worth reviewing.

Taylor, Gordon Rattray. *The Great Evolution Mystery*. Harper & Row, 1982.

Taylor treats evolution as an unsolved mystery and trots out both conventional Darwinian explanations and conventional doubts about those explanations. It is the most palatable and easy to digest anti-Darwinian book, although a real anti-Darwinist skeptic will need to proceed further via its good bibliography for the convincing details.

Thompson, D'Arcy. *On Growth and Form*. Cambridge University Press, 1917.

A classic reminder of the ubiquitous influence of form in life.

Thompson, John. *Interaction and Coevolution*. Wiley & Sons, 1982.

Solid compendium of the most current thinking, evidence, and analysis in coevolution.

Thompson, Mark. "Lining the Wild Bee." In *Fire Over Water*, Williams, Reese, ed. Tanam Press, 1986.

Story of the guy who put his head inside a wild bee swarm, and who writes about the meaning of bees and hives.

Thomson, Keith Stewart. *Morphogenesis and Evolution*. Oxford University Press, 1988.

A wonderfully refreshing and completely undogmatic view of evolution by a renegade group (the "heretics") at Yale. Thomson theorizes that internal constraints determine "themes" within evolution and "clusters" of species. Highly recommended.

Thorpe, Col. Jack. "73 Easting Distributed Simulation Briefing." Institute for Defense Analyses, 1991.
An executive summary of the Gulf War 73 Easting Simulation pitched to win support for further military simulations.

Tibbs, Hardin. *Industrial Ecology*. Arthur D. Little, 1991.
This white paper for an industrial consultant is an early sketch of what a full-bore industrial ecology would look like.

Todd, Stephen, and William Latham. *Evolutionary Art and Computers*. Academic Press, 1992.
In addition to gorgeous color plates of William Latham's evolutionarily generated art forms, this book doubles as a technical manual for the computer science and philosophy behind the images.

Toffler, Alvin. *PowerShift*. Bantam Books, 1990.
Futurist Toffler speculates pretty convincingly on expected trends in a networked economy and society.

Toffoli, Tommaso, and Norman Margolus. *Cellular Automata Machines: A New Environment for Modeling*. The MIT Press, 1987.
Tiny universes created by simple rules as a means to explore worldmaking. This is the most comprehensive text on the science of cellular automata.

Travis, John. "Electronic Ecosystem." *Science News*, 140; 10 August 1991.
Good introduction and background on Tom Ray's artificial evolutionary Tierra system.

Vernadsky, Vladimir. *The Biosphere*. Synergetic Press, 1986.
First published (and ignored) in 1926, this Russian monograph has only recently garnered attention in the West. It is a poetic-scientific foreshadowing of the Gaian notion—life and Earth as one organism.

Vernon, Jack A. *Inside the Black Room*. Clarkson N. Potter, Inc., 1963.
An early follow-up to Hebbs's original experiments in sensory deprivation at McGill University, Vernon did his at Princeton University during the late '50s in a soundproof room in the basement of the psychology building.

Vrba, Elisabeth S., and Niles Eldredge. "Individuals, hierarchies, and process: towards a more complete evolutionary theory." *Paleobiology*, 10; 2, 1984.

There is a hunch that large-scale pattern in evolution (macroevolution) derives from the hierarchical nature of nature. This paper makes a preliminary case for the argument.

Waddington, C. H. *The Strategy of the Genes*. George Allen & Unwin Ltd, 1957.

The book that gave theoretical biology respect. Waddington wrestles with the influence of the gene's agenda upon evolution and tackles the Baldwin effect.

Waddington, C. H., ed. *Towards a Theoretical Biology*. Aldine Publishing, 1968.

For a field that lacks more than one example, biology has always yearned for more theory. These proceedings stemmed from a series of memorable symposia that Waddington hosted to launch a more comprehensive systems-style look at biological organisms. The "Waddington conferences" have taken on legendary status in the postdarwinian community.

Wald, Matthew L. "The House That Does Its Own Chores." *The New York Times*, 6 December 1990.

Report on the opening of the first demonstration "smart" house in Atlanta.

Waldrop, M. Mitchell. *Complexity: The Emerging Science at the Edge of Order and Chaos*. Simon & Schuster, 1992.

A popular account of the Santa Fe Institute's approach to complex adaptive systems. Good stuff on economist Brian Arthur and biologist Stuart Kauffman. Waldrop's book is better than Roger Lewin's identically named *Complexity*, because he explains more and attempts to synthesize the ideas.

Warrick, Patricia S. *The Cybernetic Imagination in Science Fiction*. The MIT Press, 1980.

Science fiction has enlarged the thought space for imagining cybernetic possibilities, which science proper can later fill.

Weinberg, Gerald M. *An Introduction to General Systems Thinking*. John Wiley & Sons, 1975.

Helpful introduction course on "thinking whole."

Weinberg, Gerald M., and Daniela Weinberg. *General Principles of System Design*. Dorset House Publishing, 1979.

Perhaps the best book on modern cybernetics. Works well in a classroom because it includes cybernetic exercises.

Weiner, Jonathan. *The Next One Hundred Years*. Bantam Books, 1990.

A journalistic survey of our Earth as a closed system.

Weintraub, Pamela. "Natural Direction." *Omni*, October 1991.
Readable and fairly reliable report on Hall and Cairns's work on directed mutation in bacteria.

Weiser, Mark. "The Computer for the 21st Century." *Scientific American*, September 1991.
It may be a while, but I believe that someday this will be considered a seminal article staking out the role computers will play in our everyday lives.

Wesson, Robert. *Beyond Natural Selection*. MIT Press, 1991.
At times, a mere tedious cataloging of evidences and examples of nonadaptationist evolution. At rare moments, it gets to the "so what" of it all. I owe the late author a couple of key ideas.

Westbroek, Peter. *Life as a Geological Force*. W. W. Norton, 1991.
A geologist's personal recounting of evidence that life shapes rocks.

Wheeler, William Morton. *Emergent Evolution and the Development of Societies*. W. W. Norton & Company, 1928.
An early, slim volume—a paper really—on holism.

Whyte, Lancelot Law. *Internal Factors in Evolution*. George Braziller, 1965.
An informed and bold speculation on the internal selection within the genome. Readable and thought provoking.

Wiener, Norbert. *Cybernetics, or Control and Communication in the Animal and the Machine*. John Wiley, 1948.
The germ of all cybernetic texts. Except for the preface, it is unexpectedly technical and mathematical. But worth delving into.

Wilson, Edward O. *The Insect Societies*. Harvard University Press, 1971.
An indispensable book of fascination, great insight, and clear, lucid science. Required meditations for Net-mind.

Wright, Robert. *Three Scientists and Their Gods*. Times Books, 1988.
Wonderfully crafted profiles of three world-class thinkers on a quest for the unifying theory of information. Wright has much to say about whole systems and complexity. Highly recommended. On rereading this book after I finished mine, I realize that it is probably closest to my own in spirit and range.

Yoshida, Atsuya, and Jun Kakuta. "People Who Live in an On-line Virtual World." *IEEE International Workshop on Robot and Human Communication*, technical report 92TH0469-7; 1992.
A fairly intensive study of users of a virtual networked world—Fujitsu's Habitat system in Japan—and how they used it.

Zeltzer, David. "Autonomy, Interaction and Presence." *Presence: Tele-operators and Virtual Environments*, 1; 1, 1992.

Locating autonomy and control as one axis of three in a matrix of virtual reality. (The other two are degree of interaction and presence.)

Zorpette, Glenn. "Emulating the battlefield." *IEEE Spectrum*, September 1991.

From the engineers' own mouths, a report on the new and increasing role of simulations in warfare.

Zubek, John P., ed. *Sensory Deprivation: Fifteen years of research*. Meridth Corporation, 1969.

A compendium of survey articles reviewing the literature of sensory deprivation up to 1969, when this topic was fashionable. The effects of SD are about as elusive as those of hypnosis, and all the hopes for the field have evaporated as uneven data piled up.

Zurek, Wojciech H., ed. *Complexity, Entropy and the Physics of Information*. Addison-Wesley, 1990.

Some attempts to define complexity.

Cybernetics. Josiah Macy, Jr. Foundation, 1953.

Contains transcripts from one set of the Macy meetings. Including great dialogues of befuddlement as Ashby introduces his "homeostat machine."

Self-Organizing Systems. Pergamon Press, 1959.

The fascinating proceedings of a major conference with an all-star line up of principal cybernetic pioneers. After each paper is a revealing record of the panel discussions, where the true learning happens. Why don't other books do this?

Transactions of the 9th Conference on Cybernetics. Josiah Macy, Jr. Foundation, 1952.

Remarkable discussions that have hardly aged on the emergence of control in biological and mechanical systems.

INDEX